A WARTIME CHRISTMAS

Carol Rivers, whose family comes from the Isle of Dogs, East London, now lives in Dorset. Visit www.carolrivers.com and follow her on Facebook and Twitter @carol_rivers

Also by Carol Rivers

Lizzie of Langley Street
Bella of Bow Street
Lily of Love Lane
Eve of the Isle
East End Angel
In the Bleak Midwinter
East End Jubilee (*previously* Rose of Ruby Street)
A Sister's Shame
Cockney Orphan (*previously* Connie of Kettle Street)

A WARTIME CHRISTMAS

Carol Rivers

SIMON &
SCHUSTER

London · New York · Sydney · Toronto · New Delhi

A CBS COMPANY

First published in Great Britain by Simon & Schuster, 2013
A CBS company

5 7 9 10 8 6

Simon & Schuster UK Ltd
1st Floor
222 Gray's Inn Road
London WC1X 8HB

www.simonandschuster.co.uk

Simon & Schuster Australia
Sydney

Simon & Schuster India
New Delhi

A CIP catalogue record for this book is available from the British Library

Hardback ISBN: 978-0-85720-832-3
Paperback ISBN: 978-0-85720-833-0
Ebook ISBN: 978-0-85720-834-7

Typeset by Hewer Text UK Ltd, Edinburgh
Printed and bound in Great Britain by CPI Group (UK) Ltd, Croydon CR0 4YY

This book is dedicated to the memory of those people who were lost in the tragic Bethnal Green Tube disaster, Wednesday 3 March 1943.

And for Mavis Eugene and The Cliff.

Acknowledgements

My thanks go to everyone I have interviewed for this wartime story. Some, as very young children, had uniquely terrifying memories of the Blitz of London and subsequent V1 and V2 bombings. I consider myself fortunate to have been included in their reminiscences. Thanks also to Denise for sharing her insights into out-of-body and near-death experiences. And my gratitude goes to Conway, whose insight into espionage has been invaluable throughout the writing. Last but not least, publication of my books with my editors and 'The Team' at Simon & Schuster, is always a delight – as is working with Dorothy Lumley, my amazing agent.

Chapter One

May 1941
London's East End

Kay Lewis opened her sleepy grey eyes to the sights, sounds and smells of the world as she had known it for the past eight months of the London Blitz. Her immediate thought was that, unbelievably, she was still alive. After another night's intensive bombing over the Isle of Dogs – the heart of London's East End – the corrugated iron shelter was still in one piece over her!

Kay inhaled the damp and stale air and tried to breathe shallowly as she watched the glistening drops of condensation slide one after another down the rust-pitted walls. With a strong sense of relief, she could hear the wail of the all-clear fading. However, the relief didn't last long for, as always on waking, a sharp dart of longing went through her. Being parted from her two-and-a-half-year-old son throughout the bombing had been almost unbearable. Though she knew that she and her husband, Alan, had had no choice but to evacuate Alfie to her brother and sister-in-law's home in the country, it didn't stop the pain of separation. What she wouldn't give to have him here and in her arms! She could almost feel his chubby body pressed against her skin and smell the silky-soft fragrance of his thick, dark hair.

'Oh, Alfie, I miss you so much,' she croaked as she shifted carefully on the narrow top bunk. 'But I know you're safe and that's what counts.'

With a huge effort, Kay drew her mind back to the present. Had Alan survived the night safely? During the Blitz, and much to her surprise, he had left his council job where he had been working in the maintenance department and joined the Heavy Rescue Squad. Kay had never quite understood why. Perhaps it had something to do with that letter he'd received. It wasn't his call-up, which he'd been expecting, but from another section of the military. He'd dismissed it as just a lot of red tape and she hadn't pressed the point. Alan was a man who, once he had decided on a course of action, would rarely change his mind. Nevertheless, she worried. His night shift would be ending soon, but that was no guarantee he'd be home. If there was someone trapped and in danger then it was down to Alan and his team to rescue them.

Kay forced her arms and legs to move; every bone in her body ached. Her back creaked, her bottom was numb and her shoulders seized in a painful cramp as she ducked her head under the tunnel-shaped roof. During the night, her long, chestnut-coloured hair had escaped its pins and she pushed it back wearily from her face.

'Ouch!' Kay groaned as she landed hard on the floor. Even sleeping fully dressed in her coat together with two thick jumpers and a pair of Alan's combinations under her utility trousers, she was chilled to the bone. It was May, but it was still winter in the Anderson.

Kay shook the huddled form in the lower bunk. 'Vi, wake up. The all-clear's gone.'

At this, the elderly lady threw off her threadbare blanket and stared up at Kay. Her careworn face, framed by scraps of thin grey hair, squeezed into a gummy smile. 'Blimey, gel, are we still in the land of the living?'

'It seems we are.' Kay was as surprised as her friend to find they weren't buried under tons of rubble from the overnight raid. 'Are you all right?'

'Nothing a fag won't cure, love,' Vi croaked as Kay helped her to her feet. Then Vi took a scarf from under the pillow and wound it expertly into a turban, tying the ends in a knot on top of her head. 'Now me brains are safely in, where are me teeth?'

'Try your pocket,' Kay suggested with a grin.

'Oh yes, course.' Vi retrieved a pair of worn yellow dentures and snapped them into place. She gave a wide smile. 'How's that look?'

'Like you've got your teeth in,' Kay returned lightly as she handed Vi her battered old handbag. It was never far from Vi's reach and had stayed with her throughout the bombing.

'Ta, love, mustn't forget me life's savings. Not that there's much, but enough for a rainy day.'

Kay leaned her shoulder against the battered door of the shelter and pushed. The bright shaft of daylight momentarily blinded her and she took a crumpled hanky from her pocket to wipe her face. The corners of her mouth were filled with grit. Her skin felt as stiff as a washboard. If she hadn't been so exhausted, she would have laughed – or cried, she didn't know which. Throughout the Blitz she had felt she was living in a surreal world, constantly fighting her way through an endless stream of chaos and destruction. The basics of life had become luxuries: a comfortable bed to sleep in, fresh air to breathe and clear running water that was not restricted by damaged sewers.

'Is yer house still standing?' Vi demanded as they stepped out into the foggy, sulphur-smelling air that made Kay's eyes smart all over again.

Her heart thumped as an indistinct shape loomed out of the swirling mist. Her two-up two-down end-of-terrace house still seemed to be attached to the Tripps'. She thought briefly of the couple who had once lived there; Stan and Elsie Tripp had evacuated to Wales and the safety of their son's home. Kay missed them and often wondered if she'd ever see them again. They weren't the only ones who had evacuated either. Two thirds of the street's houses were either standing empty or too bomb-damaged to be occupied. Only a handful of neighbours were left. The long, winding street following the curves of the River Thames had been so vibrant before the war. Now the road was just a shadow of its former lively self.

'Our roof's still on and so is the chimney,' Kay answered Vi. 'But the back door's blown open. Goodness only knows what mess we'll find inside.'

'And yer windows?'

Kay smiled ruefully. 'Alan's idea to strengthen them with strips of wood over the tape seems to have paid off. I'll bet you're glad he did the same for your place too.'

'You can say that again,' Vi agreed quickly. 'I didn't want him to bother as he's never got a minute to spare, but there he was one morning, standing on his ladder and 'ammering away.'

'There's not much he wouldn't do for you, Vi,' Kay told her friend as they made their way towards the back door. Her husband had a soft spot for Vi and had done all her odd jobs during the Blitz. Vi returned his affection and had told them that Alan reminded her of her only son, Pete Junior, who had died from diphtheria at eighteen.

The two women were smiling as they entered Kay's kitchen but their smiles disappeared when they saw inside. Every surface was covered in a thick blanket of dust and dirt. 'Strike a light,' Vi breathed. 'What a mess!'

'Just look at this,' gasped Kay, pointing to the dresser. 'My best set of china's come off the shelves!' She stared in disbelief at the floor where the teapot and her best cups and saucers were all in pieces. 'Oh, Vi, that was a tea set from Mum an' all.'

'Bloody Hitler,' grumbled Vi when she saw the extent of the damage. 'He's got no respect for other people's property.'

At this, Kay found herself laughing – laughing so much her face seemed to crack under the layers of dirt.

'What's so funny?' Vi asked in a bewildered tone.

'You. Course Hitler's got no respect for our property. He's bombing it, ain't he?'

Vi patted her arm. 'It's as well you can see the funny side, gel.'

But Kay realized the laughter was more like hysteria and she was dangerously close to tears. When she looked inside the larder, she clapped her hands to her face. All the bottles, packets and even vegetables were covered in the same thick, grey grime. 'How did this happen?' she wailed. 'The larder door was shut.'

Vi bustled past her and lifted the wire gauze that protected the square wedge of Spam. 'Don't worry, ducks,' she said, shrugging. 'A quick wipe and Bob's your uncle.'

'I don't want to wipe me Spam, Vi. I want to eat it,' Kay moaned.

'Spam's got no taste anyway. You might as well be eating rubber.' Vi clattered the gauze back into place unsympathetically.

'It comes to something when you can't preserve even the little food you have,' Kay heard herself complaining. 'Anything tasty is on ration and there are queues as long as your arm for the decent bits.'

'I must admit,' Vi said with a sigh, 'I've not seen a nice chop since before the war or even a bit of pork cracklin'.'

'At least the tea is safe.' Kay nodded to the tin caddy beside the gas stove. 'Do you reckon the gas is on?'

'Shouldn't chance it yet,' Vi warned. 'Wait till the warden or the gas blokes come round. There was an explosion in Westferry Road last week, remember? The old girl turned on the gas tap and the mains was ruptured. The bang was so ferocious it sent her flying out the back door. Lucky she was deaf already and only had a few bruises to show for the fright.'

Kay felt exasperated as she looked round, gauging the work ahead of her. The clearing up after the nightly raids was not unexpected. But she had never encountered anything on this scale.

Vi inhaled a wheezy breath and gave Kay a quick glance. 'Good job your boy is safely away, love. Imagine him here in all this.'

Kay nodded dejectedly. 'Yes, but I miss him, Vi.'

'Course you do, flower.'

'I worry about how he's taken to being away from us,' Kay admitted as she thought of her brother Len and his wife Doris in Hertfordshire. The couple were well-meaning enough but had no children of their own. 'Doris doesn't have a clue about babies. Alfie was into everything and very mischievous when Len and Doris drove down to collect him last September. I hope they've been able to cope.'

'What does she say in her letters?'

'Not much.' Kay shrugged. 'Only that he's filling out, whatever that means.'

'Your sister-in-law seemed nice enough when I met her,' Vi recalled. 'And it was good of 'em to drive here to save you the bother of going on the bus.'

'Len likes to show off his car,' Kay pointed out. 'He's lucky enough to have a petrol allowance as he works in a specialized engineering department for the government.'

Vi moved towards the empty coal cupboard and yanked the door open. She unhooked a broom hanging from a nail on the back of it and began to sweep up the broken china. 'You go and check upstairs,' she called over her shoulder, 'whilst I chuck this lot in the dustbin.'

'I won't be a minute. Then we'll go over to your place.'

'Gawd knows what state me house is in, as I didn't have time to cover anything up,' Vi was saying as Kay left for the front room.

Kay was relieved to find that the fireguard and boarding that Alan had wedged into the fireplace had prevented the worst of the muck from spilling down the chimney. As she had covered the couch and dining table with old sheets, the room was a big improvement on the kitchen.

But upstairs was a different matter. A chunk of plaster had fallen from the ceiling to the landing, spreading a white coating over the banisters, stairs and the floor below. Carefully picking her way over the mess, she poked her head into her and Alan's bedroom where a layer of dust had covered the wardrobe and three-mirrored dressing table. Luckily she'd had time to cover their bed and Alfie's cot with sheets and the window remained intact thanks again to Alan's ingenious boarding. The only other bedroom was very small and so full of clutter she could hardly open the door. Alan had put newspaper over everything in here. Somewhere underneath were the bits and pieces they had collected together from the markets or had been given by their friends and neighbours, yet with the onset of war had been forced to lump into one room until such time as they could restore order to their home.

Kay came back to the present with a jolt. Someone was yelling in the street. She rushed downstairs, kicking up clouds of dust in her wake. The front door was open and she ran outside. In the distance was Vi's small figure just visible through the mist.

'Look at me house, Kay!' Vi screamed as Kay ran to her side. 'The devils have done it in!'

It was a moment or two before Kay took in the huge black crater on the wasteland next to Vi's house. It was strewn with debris, a mixture of tiles and rafters from Vi's roof. Despite all of Alan's careful precautions, every window had been blown out and the front door lay in the road. Glass and rubble were everywhere. A flicker of orange flame came from inside the dark passage.

'I've got to save me stuff!' cried Vi, lurching forward.

'You can't, Vi.' Kay grabbed her tightly. 'The rest of the roof could collapse.'

'It won't do that, will it?'

'I don't know. But you can't take the chance.'

As Vi choked back her sobs, Kay looked around for help. Where was everyone? The Home Guard, the firemen or the police and Rescue Squad were usually first on the scene. Suddenly she saw a lone figure appear out of the smoke. It was Harry Sway, the warden, pedalling his bike as fast he could go, his tin helmet askew on his head.

Chapter Two

Harry was panting as he dropped his bike on the ground and hurried over. 'Are you two all right?' He coughed, swivelling his helmet round to display the large letter W printed on its top. 'Sorry I couldn't get to you before, but half the city is on fire.' He glanced across at Vi's house and gave a groan. 'Oh, Christ, what a mess! Is anyone in there?'

'No, I ain't had a lodger since the Blitz started,' Vi informed him.

'Lucky you was with Kay,' Harry said with a sigh. 'Luckier even that the council didn't have room to put an Anderson in yer yard, Vi. You'd have not stood a chance with that blast.'

'But what about all me furniture, me books and photographs?' Vi whimpered.

'You know the ropes,' Harry told her. 'No one goes into a damaged building until after it's made safe.'

Just then there was an eerie creak and what was left of the roof disappeared. 'Step back, ladies, please,' ordered Harry as a plume of smoke curled up in the air.

'Oh, me poor house,' Vi sobbed, grabbing Harry's sleeve. 'When is help coming?'

'I told you, Vi,' said Harry gently, 'the CD and Home Guard has been hard at it all night. We're short of fire engines and ambulances as so many people need assistance.'

Kay looked along Slater Street towards Crane Street, beyond the empty and abandoned houses. Because of the bend in the road she couldn't see as far as her closest neighbour's house. Paul Butt and his father, Neville, still lived in one of the last surviving houses near the two Press sisters, who had also refused to evacuate. Their yards backed onto Crane Street which had also taken a pounding as the German fighters had aimed for the areas closest to the docks. Kay turned and her eyes searched in the other direction. There wasn't much to see there either. Their good friends Babs and Eddie Chapman, the Suttons, Tylers and Edwards' houses were all closer, but they too were lost in the mist.

'There's nothing we can do here, Vi,' Kay said as she threaded her hand around Vi's shoulders. 'Let's go back to my place.'

'Good idea,' said Harry, picking up his bike. 'I've got a flask in me bag, so at least I can give you a cuppa.'

'Is there any more damage to Slater Street?' Kay asked as they walked, not expecting the devastating reply she was about to receive.

Harry nodded. 'Number two was the worst.'

'The Suttons?'

Again Harry nodded. 'None of 'em made it I'm afraid.'

'What!' Kay stopped abruptly, wondering if she'd heard right.

'Howard and Madge, old Mrs Sutton, young Robert who is fifteen and Kevin who was ten . . .' Harry's voice tailed away.

'But weren't they in the Anderson?'

'The shelter was demolished too.'

'I can't believe it,' Kay gasped incredulously. 'I only saw Madge at the shops last week. And those lovely young boys . . .' She stopped, staring at the warden. 'Are you sure they weren't at a public shelter?'

'We're checking, but from what has been found, it looks like they was all there.'

Kay felt ill. She just couldn't take on board that a family of three generations had been wiped out in an eye blink.

'The Chapmans have lost their house too,' Harry informed her. 'But they're accounted for.'

'Thank goodness.' Kay breathed in relief. 'But I can't imagine how Babs is feeling right this moment.'

'I tell you, they were sensible to have gone to the public shelter and they won't regret having sent their two kids to stay with relatives in Essex. It was hard at the time, but just imagine if they'd all been at home. It doesn't bear thinking about.' Harry shook his head. 'The only casualty was the cat. I told 'em enough times to get rid of it. But they never took any notice.'

'What am I gonna do now?' Vi whimpered, her gaze vacant as she appeared not to have understood what the warden had told them. 'I've got nowhere to go, nothing!'

'Have you got your gas mask?' Harry asked ill-advisedly as he leaned his bike against the wall of Kay's house. 'You must keep it with you at all times.'

'Harry Sway, do you imagine a gas mask was the first thing I thought of when the bombs started dropping?' demanded Vi, suddenly rearing up. 'Would I have said to meself, Vi, don't worry about putting on yer warm coat and boots and three layers of clothing that will save you from dying of pneumonia in a rotten old tin shed. Instead go and find that flamin' contraption that neither you nor the rest of the population has ever had the need to wear!'

Harry stared down at his dirty boots. 'Sorry, gel. Didn't mean to upset you. But rules are rules.'

At this, Vi burst into tears. Kay led her into the kitchen where Harry pulled out one of the four wooden chairs tucked under the square table. After brushing the dust from the seat, he stepped back, allowing Kay to make Vi comfortable.

Kay's hands were trembling as she did so. She was feeling weak and shaken. The news of the Suttons' deaths had made her feel physically sick. It was the worst tragedy in the street so far.

'Harry, have you seen Alan?' asked Kay, as Vi blew her nose loudly while continuing to glare at Harry. 'Is he working in this sector?'

'Don't think he is,' Harry replied with a frown. 'His squad might have been sent up West to help out. Word came through to the ARP depot this morning that the House of Commons, Westminster Hall and St Paul's all bought it. What's worse, there's hundreds buried under the rubble all over the city. There's people still trapped as it's too dangerous to try to rescue 'em.'

Kay felt another wave of nausea. Alan was in the thick of it and though she prayed every night and morning that her husband would be safe, she knew there was always a chance he wouldn't come home.

'Don't worry, he'll be all right,' Harry said when he saw the effect his words had on her. 'There's no one savvier than your Alan. He knows when not to push his luck.'

Kay hoped so, although she wasn't as certain as Harry that Alan wouldn't risk his own life to save someone else's. He worked in dangerous situations helping the fire-fighting teams and demolition squads to rescue victims of the bombings. Knowing Alan as she did, she suspected it was his heart rather than his head that sometimes governed his judgement.

'Well, where's that cuppa you promised me?' Vi blinked back the tears and frowned at Harry's canvas bag. 'Gawd, I really fancy a smoke too. But I suppose striking a match is out of the question?'

'Fraid so, love,' Harry said. 'But I've got a sandwich if you'd like it.' He slipped the bag from his shoulder and opened the flap, removing his whistle, respirator and flask, together with a brown paper packet covered in greasy stains.

'I ain't hungry,' Vi said sourly. 'The Rosie will do.'

'You should have a tot of something stronger with it,' Harry suggested. 'Got any brandy, Kay?'

'We keep some for medicinal purposes.' Kay hurried to the front room to fetch the small bottle from the sideboard. Once back in the kitchen, she added a tot to Vi's tea.

'Go on, Vi,' urged Harry. 'Trust me, it will help.'

'It ain't bad,' Vi admitted after a sip or two.

'Don't worry about nothing,' Harry said cheerfully as he repacked his bag. 'We'll soon have you sorted. The council will see you go somewhere safe for the future.'

At this, Vi nearly dropped her mug as she stared up at the warden. 'What do you mean, "somewhere safe"?'

'Well, you can't stay here, love.'

'I've lived in Slater Street all me married life!'

'Yes, but you ain't got a—'

Kay was relieved when Harry stopped himself in time from repeating the obvious. Vi was in no mood to be told again that she had just lost her home.

'Well, can't stop.' Harry patted his pockets and took a step to the door. 'Gotta meet the rescue services in Crane Street now I've checked on you two. But I'll let you know when the gas is safe to use. Keep the flask, ladies, till I see you next.'

He didn't wait for Kay to reply but rushed out, leaving Vi staring after him. 'He wants to get rid of me!' she exclaimed.

'He was only trying to help.'

'Well, he didn't. He put the wind up me instead.'

'Drink your tea.' Gently, Kay drew the mug to Vi's lips. She knew Vi must be in a state of shock. She hadn't even registered the deaths of the Suttons or the Chapmans becoming homeless.

Vi downed two more cups of alcoholic tea before allowing Kay to take her to the front room. In a matter of minutes she had fallen asleep on the couch. Kay gently removed her boots and lifted her feet, her heart squeezing with pity as she saw the big holes in her thick socks. Covering her with a blanket, Kay drew the curtains and, closing the door softly, made her way back to the kitchen.

Standing quite still, her thoughts went to the Suttons. They had been a lovely young family. Madge Sutton had vowed she would never leave her East End home but had evacuated her two boys. But Robert and Kevin had taken it into their own hands to return. Just after Christmas, they had appeared on the doorstep, refusing to go away again. Tears filled Kay's eyes as she remembered the brave family.

'Snap out of it, Kay,' she told herself firmly, sliding the palms of her hands over her damp cheeks. 'Find yourself something to do.'

Rolling up her sleeves, she set to work washing every surface in the kitchen with cold water and Lifebuoy soap, leaving the air smelling pleasantly of disinfectant. She threw the pails of dirty water over the yard and swept the path clear of punctured sandbags. There were roof tiles and bricks scattered everywhere. Alan would be able to replace a few, but most were broken. At least the toilet in the yard was working. She could hear the clang of fire-engine bells in the distance. That meant the demolition and rescue squads were on their way to clear the roads and check the gas mains. She thought the noise would wake Vi and fully expected her to come bursting out of the front room, but she didn't. Kay guessed that Vi was exhausted both from the shock she'd received and their nights of broken sleep.

By the time Kay had restored order to the kitchen and upstairs landing, it was the afternoon. The last time she and Vi had eaten was in the shelter and too many hours ago to admit. She was tempted to take Vi a snack, but instead she let her sleep. Going to the larder, Kay did as Vi had suggested and wiped the Spam clean with a cloth. As much as she hated Spam, she carved two thin slices and lay them on a small wedge of bread taken from the safety of the bread bin. She found she was ravenous and didn't care about the taste. With the sandwich devoured, her spirits revived.

Feeling more like her old self, Kay took out a small, rust-pitted mirror from the kitchen drawer. All the other mirrors had been taken down. No one wanted seven years' back luck if they were cracked in a raid. To her horror, the woman who returned her stare was a complete stranger. The dust and ceiling plaster had formed her coppery-coloured waves into stiff, ugly spikes. Her skin looked like a mask. It was only the soft, light grey of her eyes that showed any sign of life. 'Kay, what's happened to you?' she gasped. 'You look a hundred and seven, not twenty-seven!'

She considered dragging in the tin bath and braving a scrub in cold water. But one of the civil defence workers or Harry might knock to tell them about the gas supply. No, she would have to make do. And since she didn't have to go to work at the armaments factory on Sunday, there was time to stand at the sink and wash.

When she felt clean again, she brushed as much dirt from her hair as she could then leaned over the sink and put her head under the cold-water tap. The remains of the Lifebuoy was not the best shampoo in the world but was better than nothing. When she looked in the mirror again, her skin was back to its normal healthy colour. Her high cheekbones had regained their prominence in her oval-shaped face. Shaking out her damp hair, its glossy thickness started to dry. Kay even considered changing her clothes but what would be the point? In a few hours' time she and Vi would return to the shelter for another cold and sleepless night.

Just then, Kay heard the front door open. She ran into the passage and very soon was buried in the arms of a tall, lean man with unruly black hair. As usual her husband was clad in his dirty overalls and his beautiful brown eyes looked tired under their heavy lids.

Alan Lewis lifted his wife's small chin with his dirty hands and kissed her hungrily.

Chapter Three

'Thank God you're safe,' Alan whispered, his lips pressed against her hair. 'I was worried about you.'

'It was a terrible night, Alan.'

'The worst,' he agreed. 'The city took a real pasting, with very few sectors left untouched.'

'Yes, Harry Sway told us.'

'Are you and Vi all right?'

'Vi's asleep in the front room whilst I've been cleaning round. The back door blew open and the dust got everywhere.' Kay pressed her face against his chest, inhaling the smells of the city. The London as it was now, in the raids and under pressure and in some parts razed to the ground. The fumes and dust and polluted gassy air, the mustiness of ancient buildings, the dampness of the slums and the river with its wet, mossy wharfs and timbers reeking of tar. There was oil too, and grease and the faint whiff of some ingredient that Alan had told her was contained in the dangerous explosives they dealt with. But most reassuringly of all, she could smell Alan himself. His sweat and his energy. His essence.

They walked slowly into the kitchen, arms linked. 'There's tiles off the roof,' he noted, 'and bricks dislodged from under the eaves. But they were loose already and will have to be mortared when I get the chance. We seem to have no broken windows at the front or back. I hope Vi's house has fared the same.'

Kay looked up at him. 'You didn't pass her place?'

'No. I came home through the Cut.'

'The waste ground was bombed and Vi's house took the impact.'

Alan closed his eyes for a second then opened them. 'But Vi was safe with you in the shelter, right?'

Kay nodded. 'But she's lost everything, Alan. Everything except her overnight bag and the few personal things she keeps in the Anderson.'

'Can't anything be done for the house?'

'Very little, I'd say.' Kay tried to keep her voice steady as she continued. 'And there's more. Babs and Eddie's house was destroyed, although they're both safe. Thank God Tim and Gill are in Essex. But the Suttons . . .' Kay's voice trembled. 'The family was at home when the bomb fell.'

'My God, not the boys too?' Alan gasped.

'The whole family.' She swallowed. 'I . . . I was only talking to Madge in the butcher's on Friday. She had enough coupons to buy sausages. They were Kevin's favourite and she hadn't been able to get them for ages so we queued for over an hour because there were still some left on the butcher's shelf. Madge wanted them for

Saturday's dinner. Oh, Alan, that would have been the last meal she cooked!'

'Come on, love.' Alan hugged her. 'Don't torture yourself.'

'I can't help it.'

'Close the door on your imagination,' Alan said sternly. 'It's the only way. You can't let your feelings get the better of you. This is a hard and sometimes unforgiving world we live in.'

Kay knew that Alan spoke from experience. He had seen terrible things during the Blitz and had to steel himself against the sight of death, maiming and gruesome injuries. He always kept the worst to himself. She knew he didn't want to frighten her. But all the same she didn't like to hear him speak so bitterly. In fact, it frightened her when he showed this side of his character – which wasn't often – and yet the closed look in his eyes and strained expression caused her to think that something in his past, the past that they rarely if ever discussed, still haunted him.

'I'd better go down the road and see if there's anything that needs to be done for the Suttons,' he said, shaking his head slightly as if to return himself to the present.

'But you've only just finished your shift,' Kay protested before she could consider her words. Then, realizing his meaning, she put her hands to her mouth. 'Oh, of course, you might have to help with the identification.' Kay knew that sometimes there was no family or even neighbours who could perform this awful procedure. Alan had to give what help he could to the teams who dealt with the remains.

'You won't be too long, will you?'

He drew his hand gently down her cheek. 'When I come back we'll discuss what's to be done for Vi.'

After he'd gone, Kay sat on a kitchen chair and looked around her. She had washed the dresser shelves and stood odd bits of china on them to replace the tea service. The puddle on the floor was gone and she had satisfied herself that there was no blast dust left to contaminate the food. But she couldn't help thinking that Slater Street had had more than its fair share of bad luck in recent times.

Just after Christmas, Amy Greenaway, a teacher who lived on her own at the top of the road close to the Butts and whose house had backed on to Crane Street, had died in a raid. She usually went to her church where the vicar had opened the cellars to provide shelter. But on this occasion she had been ill and in bed when the fatal bomb dropped. Then there was Florence and Herbert Shorter of number eighty-four. The elderly couple had survived damage to their house from a heavy explosive but both had perished from their injuries later. Now Vi's house and the Chapmans' were more notches on the Luftwaffe's belt. But no loss in the street compared to the tragedy of the Suttons.

Just then there was movement behind her. She glanced round to see Vi who had a look of complete confusion on her face. 'I can't take it all in,' Vi murmured hoarsely. 'Is it true my house was bombed?'

'I'm afraid so, Vi.'

'Did Harry say the Suttons were dead?'

'Yes.'

'I thought it was an 'orrible dream.'

'I wish it was,' whispered Kay sadly, 'and we could wake up to how it was before this rotten war started.'

'Anyone 'ome?' A loud voice came from the passage. Kay went to see who it was. The gas man stood there, his face black and greasy and, like Alan, his overalls were covered in grime.

'All safe to turn on now, missis,' he called. 'You can make that cuppa you've been gasping for.'

Kay thanked him for the welcome news. A cup of tea would go down very well at this moment. But when Kay turned back to Vi, she saw that the gas being restored was the very least of their problems. Vi looked utterly dejected. Her downcast face and blank, lifeless eyes told Kay just how much she was suffering.

That evening Vi helped Kay to peel the vegetables and cube the last of the carrots, potatoes and onions, and rolled out a pastry top to hide the unappetizing sight. A Woolton Pie was the government's own speciality recipe of carrots and leftovers hidden under pastry. The pie took its place in the oven and even more potatoes were crushed to death to mash with the last scrapings of marg.

When Alan came in, he held out his arms to Vi. 'Dunno what to say about your place, Vi. I just had a look. Don't think there's much I can do for you.'

'After all the time you spent on me windows an' all,' she whimpered as he hugged her.

'Any news on the Suttons?' Kay asked, knowing before Alan shook his head silently that there was none. Kay bit her lip and turned back to the sink. For a moment she couldn't see through the blur of tears. Then, trying to do as Alan had told her and turn off her imagination, she managed to compose herself. 'What about Babs and Eddie?'

'They've been taken to a hostel in Aldgate,' Alan told them. 'Till they get a billet.'

'Oh, poor Babs! She'll hate being away from her home.' Kay felt very sad for her friend. Babs loved her little house and kept it spick and span. But now, with it all gone, and gone in one day, Babs must feel desperate.

Vi sank down on a chair, wiping her hands on Kay's apron which was tied around her middle. 'Looks like it'll be me next, going on what Harry said. But who's gonna want a knackered old 'orse like me?'

'The Vi I know is a long way from being knackered,' Alan assured her.

'All my adult life has been spent in that house,' Vi murmured. 'Me and my Pete was happy there till he popped his clogs ten years ago. We raised our boy Pete Junior, Gawd rest his soul, in Slater Street. And all me lodgers have been decent sorts, providing me with an income that I wouldn't have got elsewhere.' Tears filled her eyes again. 'I s'pose I should feel grateful the bomb didn't take me with it. But to tell you the truth I'd rather it had been me than the Suttons. In fact, I'd have volunteered meself if I'd have known what was going to happen.'

'I don't want to hear talk like that,' Alan said firmly as he took a seat beside her. 'Don't know what you think, love,' he continued as Kay placed the hot pie in the middle of the table, 'but I reckon we could put Vi up in the spare room till something is worked out.'

'I was going to suggest the same,' Kay answered immediately. 'What do you say, Vi? Will you give it a go?'

'What!' Vi gave a snort of disgust as she sniffed back her tears. 'You and me might have kipped in your Anderson for eight months, Kay, but that's a long chalk from having an old duffer round yer feet all day.'

'I'd be glad of the help as I'm at work all day,' Kay replied, then grinned. 'After helping to churn out thousands of the army's ball-bearings, it's not top of me list to come home and get out the duster.'

'You know you don't have to stay at the factory, love,' Alan put in quietly. 'There's other sorts of war work you can do.'

'I know,' agreed Kay, 'but I don't want to start changing jobs when I've got a son to look after – least, when he comes home I will. And please God, that will be soon.'

Vi smiled sympathetically. 'I understand how you feel, love.'

'So,' continued Kay, eager not to have any opposition from Alan about bringing their boy back from the country, 'there's a put-u-up bed and a chest of drawers in the small bedroom under all the junk. It's about time we had a good clear-out. You won't be uncomfortable, I'm sure.'

But Vi shook her head firmly. 'You are such good kids and I love you to bits. But I can't impose.'

Kay raised her eyebrows and glanced swiftly at Alan. 'Well, if our home isn't good enough for you, Vi, so be it.'

'So it looks like evacuation,' Alan continued in the same regretful tone while keeping a straight face. 'Matter of fact I'll walk you down the Sally Army right after we've eaten.'

For a moment there was complete silence. But then Kay and Alan began to laugh and Vi pulled out her hanky to blow her nose loudly. 'I dunno what to say. I'm speechless.'

'That's a first, then,' said Alan, which brought another burst of laughter all round.

After their meal, Alan helped them to clear the small room, then grabbed a few hours of sleep.

'Are you sure about this, flower?' Vi asked as she sat down on the put-u-up that Kay had furnished with two thin pillows, a sheet and an eiderdown that was faded but still had good wear in it. 'I don't know how to thank you.'

'You'd do the same for me and Alan, I know, if the position was reversed.'

'No doubt about that.' Vi nodded vigorously. 'And this has got to be a business arrangement. I'll pay you a fair rent. I've got me savings in me bag and if I can't use 'em now, then I don't know when I will.'

Kay smiled as she folded a spare nightgown into the chest drawer along with a few other items of clothing that might come in useful. She didn't want to take any rent from Vi. But she knew how independent her friend was and decided not to argue the point. 'It was you and Babs who welcomed us when we first moved here,' Kay reminded Vi. 'You brought us mugs of tea and some of your bread pudding, remember? Little did I know then that I'd be working with Babs up at Hailing House to earn a few much-needed pennies in the months before I had Alfie.'

'Course,' nodded Vi reflectively. 'Babs got you that cleaning job, didn't she? And a nice little earner it was for you too. The pair of you had a right old time swanning around with yer dusters.'

Kay laughed at the memory. She had enjoyed working with Babs at the island's charitable institution in the months before Alfie was born. The housework had been light and very enjoyable. Hailing House was one of Kay's favourite old buildings; maintained by the aristocratic Hailing family, it still had a faded elegance about it. But the many rooms, all in use for the benefit of the island's residents, needed quite a lot of attention. In fact, Kay had loved to clean the needlework rooms and kitchens. Here the women were encouraged to learn how to make their own garments and provide their families with economical but healthy diets. There were always scraps of material left over and Kay had been given permission to take them home and make use of them. And being pregnant, she'd quickly developed a liking for the cook's homemade scones.

'We felt sorry for you struggling with all yer stuff the day you moved in,' Vi was saying, returning Kay to the moment. 'I can never understand why your mum and dad gave you the cold shoulder for marrying Alan. You was dead upset about that.'

'Yes, I was and still am,' Kay admitted. 'Mum and Dad and Len never really took to Alan.' She sighed. 'Alan's different, I know that. He's got his opinions, which can sound a bit, well, arrogant. Sometimes he even puts the wind up me with some of the things he comes out with.' Kay hesitated. 'It's like . . . well, as though it's another Alan talking.'

Vi scowled at this. 'What do you mean, love?'

Kay raised her shoulders in a half-hearted shrug. 'I don't know how to explain, Vi. Most of the time I can read him like a book. But then, well, just occasionally, it's as if he's got something buried – yes, that's it. Something pushed right down inside him that he won't let out.'

'In that case, whatever it is, is better left buried, Kay. Like us all, there's things we don't want aired and sores that don't need scratching, as my old mum used to say.'

Kay grinned. 'Your old mum certainly had a way with words. But yes, it's true. Alan thinks things out real deeply. He won't go along with the crowd. Did you know before he met me, Alan fought in the civil war in Spain?'

'Yes, now you mention it, I think Alan did say once.'

'British people frowned on all that. The freedom fighters, as they were called, were often labelled as radicals or idealists or even worse, as cranks. That's what Mum and Dad didn't like. Alan just don't conform to what they think is normal.'

Vi lifted her shoulder with a puzzled shrug. 'Well, I can't speak for the rest of the nation and I certainly don't know nothing about politics. But I do know Alan. He's salt of the earth, a real genuine bloke who's stuck up for his country and works hard to keep the East End safe.' She took in an indignant breath. 'Now, far be it from me to say, but your mum and dad upped sticks and left Poplar as soon as war was announced in 1939. Even though they was East Enders born and bred and brought you and your brother up here, neither of 'em considered staying put when the chips were down. No matter that the East Enders that was left had nothing but brooms and rakes to stick up Jerry's arse if he landed. But we didn't budge. And it's blokes like Alan we've got to thank for getting us through.'

'To be fair, Mum was terrified at even of the mention of bombs,' Kay recalled, reluctant to add to Vi's outrage by saying that she too had been shocked when Lil and Bob had boarded one of the first evacuation buses out of Poplar to the safety of the countryside. 'And with Mum's widowed sister, Aunty Pops, living in Berkshire, it seemed the sensible thing to go and live with her.'

'If you say so, gel.' Vi's small eyes glittered mischievously. 'But as far as being out in the wilds goes, with all them lonely fields and mooing cows – well, it'd drive me bonkers.'

Kay was inclined to agree. 'Fancy not having a market on your doorstep,' she pondered. 'Or the river and the boats. Or the cinemas and cafes and—' Kay paused as a siren began to wail.

Vi looked out of the window and up at the sky. 'I reckon we'll back in the bunks tonight.'

Kay nodded resignedly for she too guessed it was to be another long haul in the Anderson.

Much to her surprise, the following morning Kay woke up in her own bed. The daylight crept in through a chink in the blackout curtains and spilled over her clothes which had been thrown haphazardly over the chair.

Pulling on her jumper and trousers, the events of last night began to return. The warnings and all-clears had been going on and off to no pattern. The noise of aircraft had been distant and it had been impossible to tell if it was the enemy or the British fighters above. She and Vi, unable to sleep and more than curious, had left the shelter in the early hours.

Kay hurried to the landing where she found Vi already dressed. 'Vi, what's going on?' Kay said.

'The Luftwaffe must've overlooked us,' Vi replied, rubbing her eyes with her knuckles. 'Either that or I slept so heavy I never heard a thing.'

Just then the front door opened and they both leaned over the banister as Alan called out and rushed up the stairs. Before either of them could speak, a big grin spread over Alan's dirty face. 'They reckon there's going to be a lull on London,' he told them. 'And not before time too.'

'Are you sure?' said Kay.

'The radio and newspapers say it's a possibility that as a result of German military strategy, Hitler's now going for his grand plan. That is, to invade and defeat the Soviet Union.'

'Do you think it's true?' asked Kay. 'Or is it a trick?'

'Could be,' said Alan with a shrug. 'On the other hand, the Luftwaffe met their match on Saturday night. The figures are coming in that despite the bright moonlight giving their bombers the advantage, it acted for our boys as well. We heard this morning that the RAF shot down at least thirty of their planes, not counting the ack-ack's totals. I reckon Hitler has given up on London for the time being.'

'Yes, and some other poor sods will be targeted,' said Vi bitterly.

'A man's still got to eat,' said Alan, patting his stomach and grinning. 'Any offers?'

Soon the smell of cooking was in the air as Vi bustled around the kitchen making breakfast. 'In all honesty, the city couldn't have taken much more,' Alan confided as he sat with Kay at the kitchen table. 'Half of our squad were sent up as reinforcements to St Paul's. The district around it looks like a wasteland. The rest of us went to

Stepney where there are still people trapped under the rubble since Saturday. All the hospitals are under pressure. Some of them, like St Thomas's, have been damaged but are still taking casualties. There's warehouses, blocks of flats and factories all burning.' He scratched the dark stubble on his jaws and blinked hard. 'Piccadilly, Soho, Holborn, Paddington and over the water to the Elephant, Bermondsey and Greenwich, you name it.' He held his hands out. 'Them blasted Junkers and Heinkels didn't leave much untouched. There's tangled pieces of metal, lumps of masonry and rubble scattered as far as the eye can see . . .'

As Vi served up slightly burned squares of fried bread and hefty helpings of porridge, Kay felt heart-sick for the Londoners who had lost their homes and their loved ones. And perhaps even hope for a future. But most of all – and selfishly – she hoped she would never have to see her own home under piles of rubble. They had escaped so far, but with the way things had been going, she had to accept their lives were balanced on a knife's edge.

Chapter Four

Kay and Vi were listening to the wireless early one evening towards the end of May. 'The British nation has taken its revenge,' the commentator announced proudly. 'When Britain's most distinguished battle cruiser HMS Hood was sunk in the Denmark Strait with the loss of all but three of her crew, the Royal Navy set out to hunt down the aggressor, Germany's newest and fastest battleship, Bismarck. Their mission was a success. A few hours ago the Bismarck was despatched to the bottom of the Atlantic, with the recovery of over one hundred survivors, by British warships.'

'My Pete might have been one of those sailors if he'd lived,' Vi said as they waited for Alan to come home. 'Or even your Alan. Just think how we would feel now, if they'd served on the Hood. The pride of Britain's naval fleet an' all.'

'Like the Bismarck,' agreed Kay. 'Now all of those lives have been lost. You can only feel for the wives, mothers and sisters of those men too.'

'Makes you wonder what war is about,' Vi said with a nod as she took a dish of corned beef and mash from the oven. 'One life for another. It don't make sense.'

Alan walked in, kissing them on their cheeks before sticking his dusty head under the cold-water tap. When he'd washed his hands and dried his face, he took his place at the table.

'You look all in, love,' Vi said softly.

'Yes, I've had better days.' Alan sighed as he waited for Kay to pour their drinks.

'Did you hear about the Bismarck?' Kay asked.

'It was all over the wireless,' Vi added, watching Alan stare at his dinner.

'The German navy had their card marked when they sunk the Hood.' Alan poked at his potatoes without much enthusiasm. 'It was inevitable our fleet would take their revenge.'

'What's the matter?' Vi asked. 'Ain't you hungry?'

'Don't think we should talk about it before dinner.'

'Do you mean the sinkings?' asked Kay.

'No.' Alan looked up at them.

Kay put down the spoon she held in her hand. 'You'd better tell us, Alan, whatever it is.'

He twisted uncomfortably on the chair. 'I've just spoken to the undertakers and arrangements have been made for the Suttons' funeral. They were considering, well . . .' He raised his dark eyes to each of them. '. . . having only two or three caskets.'

'What!' exclaimed Kay. 'They can't do that.'

'You mean the tight swines won't spend their readies on five coffins?' Vi demanded, slapping the dish on the draining board.

'It's not that, Vi. The undertakers ain't responsible for paying out for the dead. If they was, they'd be out of business by now.'

'But how are they proposing to fit five—' Kay stopped as the words lodged in her throat. She looked into Alan's eyes as he answered quietly.

'Space isn't the problem, Kay.'

Kay took a breath.

'The bomb was a high explosive,' Alan said simply. 'Not much survives from that kind of impact.'

It took some time before Kay composed herself and by the time she had, Vi had turned her back and was attending to the pudding. Kay knew that Vi was also hiding the sorrow she felt.

'Anyway,' said Alan, 'I took it upon meself to say that if they could muster up five boxes – and we agreed they couldn't be of the best material and no metal on either, just plain and simple – I'd have a whip round at work and in the street, come up with enough to cover costs.'

'I'm sure everyone would want to contribute,' said Kay.

'What about the Suttons' family?' asked Vi, turning round and clearing her throat. 'Anyone shown up?'

'One relative has been traced. A distant cousin who lives up north and doesn't think he can attend.'

'Who's gonna pay for the funeral, son?'

'The funeral directors have arranged for the service to take place in a chapel of rest just off the Commercial Road. There's no charge as it's run by volunteers. But it's in doubt as to whether they'll have their own graves.'

'You mean they won't go in East London Cemetery but in a common grave somewhere?' Kay asked in dismay.

'Might be the case.'

The thought of not having a place to be buried made Kay's appetite vanish completely. She knew what it was like to lose someone you loved and to be able to go to a special place to remember them. Each year she still visited her late first husband's grave at the East London Cemetery. Alan sometimes came with her. They left a small bunch of flowers in front of the headstone. Norman Williams, her childhood sweetheart, had died in a road accident just before Christmas in 1933. They had shared barely two years of marriage before his death. At twenty years of age she had found herself a widow. It had been a long time before she'd recovered from the shock and it was important to her to have somewhere to go to remember him. Even though the Suttons appeared not to have any close relatives, she was sure their friends and neighbours would want a place to visit.

'The undertakers have asked me to be a pall-bearer,' continued Alan. 'Jenny Edwards' husband Tom, Bert Tyler and Paul Butt, all from Slater Street, have volunteered to help out. But I'm afraid it'll all be done on the cheap.'

'You did yer best, lad,' said Vi, shaking her head.

'Yes,' agreed Kay, 'the other alternative would have been too hard to bear.'

Vi served up the rice pudding though no one was swift to eat it. Kay knew they were all trying to deal with yet another unpleasant shock. After the dishes were cleared away, Kay decided to try to lighten the atmosphere.

'I wonder if Stan and Elsie will ever come back to Slater Street,' she said, referring to their immediate neighbours. 'Perhaps, like Mum and Dad, they like living where they are. Wales is supposed to be beautiful. And they are with their son.'

'Leaving yer gaff seems criminal to me,' said Vi, her tone still gloomy. 'Their place has got three bedrooms an' all. If I was them, I'd be back like a shot and get a nice lodger.' Her narrow shoulders drooped. 'That is, if I had me house back.'

Kay glanced at Alan, who seemed to have run out of steam and left the table to go out to the yard. Kay felt sorry for Vi; her friend had taken a chance by staying in London during the Blitz, whereas the Tripps next door, like Kay's parents, had left immediately the prime minister had announced Britain was at war. It seemed unfair that Vi's bravery had ended in loss, while the Tripps' house stood undamaged and unwanted.

'Never mind,' said Kay resolutely. 'We've got each other, Vi. And that counts for a lot.'

Vi's doleful expression suddenly faded. In its place a gummy smile appeared. 'And don't think I'll ever forget that, ducks,' she said. 'And I give you full permission to clout me round the head if ever I sound as if I do!'

Later, Kay joined Alan in the yard. They sat on the Cut wall in the warm evening sunshine, listening to the sounds of the gulls as they swooped over the rooftops, hoping for a last meal either from the dirty water that lapped against the dock walls or from some dustbin that had lost its lid.

Kay knew it had been a very rough day for her husband. Their group of friends and neighbours was dwindling and their closest friends Babs and Eddie no longer had a home. The Blitz had seen to that. Though Alan smiled, she saw the lines of worry growing deeper around his eyes and his dark features were shadowed.

'I feel so powerless, Kay,' Alan confided to her. 'We've had to stand by and watch people suffering. Good people, like Vi who loves this island and would never want to leave it. Now, God help them, the Suttons are gone. Babs and Eddie have lost all they've worked for. People we knew when we moved here in thirty-eight have been scattered far and wide. Even worse, some have gone for ever.'

'Alan, you've done all you can,' she told him. 'You can't fight the enemy single-handed.'

'That's just it,' he muttered. 'It's the invisible powers who think they know best in this war. Just like they did twenty years ago. What kind of world is this, to repeat the same mistakes and take millions more lives? Our blokes are fighting out there, making the supreme sacrifice sometimes and leaving their wives and kids at the mercy of fate. And all in the name of democracy!'

'Alan, please don't speak so bitterly.' Kay shuddered as his face shadowed and his eyes deadened in the way that made her feel she didn't know her husband at all.

He squeezed her hand, suddenly blinking and relaxing the muscles around his jaw. 'I don't mean to upset you, love.'

'You've not had a good night's sleep for a long while now,' Kay said, trying to ignore the fear that filled her when Alan seemed to slip away from her into this other world. Each time he withdrew from her, and it was becoming more regular now, she felt it had something to do with his past. A past she knew very little about. Alan was a south Londoner who had lost his mother in the 'flu epidemic at the age of thirteen. He'd told her his father had been a drunkard and waster and had spent more time in the care of His Majesty's Service than at home with his three young sons. In Kay's eyes it was to Alan's credit that he had run away to sea and made a life for himself. If only he would open up to her more. But Alan was a proud man and rarely allowed his emotions to show.

'Our shifts might change soon,' he told her with another rather forced smile. 'Word is that with the ease in the bombing, the squad might not be needed at nights.'

'Oh Alan, that means we can actually sleep together at the same time!'

He drew her into his arms and kissed her. 'Well, starting from tonight, we'd better do something about that.'

'You're not going out again?' she whispered delightedly.

'No.' He gazed into her eyes. 'So what have you got to say for yourself now, Mrs Lewis?'

'Only that I love you. Oh yes – and I ain't made the bed yet.'

They both laughed. 'No need now,' Alan told her with a wink. 'Let's say goodnight to Vi and grab an early one.'

Kay giggled. She knew Vi would see the funny side of this, no matter how tired they pretended to be!

Making love with Alan had always made Kay feel she was the luckiest woman in the world. He was a tender and generous lover, yet when passion overwhelmed him, he took her to the height of her own intense desire. He fulfilled every part of her. It never mattered what had happened during the day, whether the hours had been filled with fear or joy or frustration or exhaustion, he breathed new life into her. With Alan, she felt uninhibited, a far cry from her stifled self that had never been freed in her first marriage to Norman. Sadly their marriage hadn't been perfect; she had very quickly realized her mistake, yet hadn't been able to acknowledge it even to herself until she had met Alan four years later.

Kay sighed in contentment. Every time she and Alan made love, she felt something new and rich came from their coupling. And it was no different tonight as she lay in Alan's arms. They had reached that moment together, but with a trembling intensity that had shaken them both.

Alan lay beside her, their bodies damp with sweat and their hearts not yet slowed to a regular beat.

'My God, Kay,' he whispered against her ear, 'do you feel the same? I can barely catch my breath.'

She nodded at their unspoken joy, the knowledge between two people that almost couldn't be put into words. 'I can feel your heart racing,' she murmured.

'No wonder. You're a beautiful woman, Kay.'

She placed his hand to her own bare breast and he cupped it lovingly as his kisses travelled over her neck and lightly traced a path to where his hand paused.

Kay closed her eyes, her body arching in response. 'You'd better stop there for a minute,' she breathed, pushing her fingers through the thickness of his hair, 'or else me heart's likely to explode.'

She felt his chuckle of delight as he lifted her against him, content to hold her to the shape of his lean, strong body. 'We wouldn't want that now, would we?'

She snuggled against him, staring into his darkened face as they lay side by side on the pillows. 'Do you reckon Vi heard us?'

'Didn't think I made that much noise.'

'No, but I did.' Kay laughed softly as she traced a finger over his cheek. 'You know, I could get used to lazy evenings like this. I've missed our trips to the pictures and a quick drink at the pub.'

His breath came against her face. 'And that's not all,' he muttered huskily. 'If we go on like this we might give our Alfie some company.'

Kay gave a soft sigh. 'Oh, Alan, don't joke about babies.'

'I'm not. It's got to happen one day, love.'

'But why hasn't it happened already?'

He brushed the damp hair from her face and kissed her mouth. 'It's no wonder it's not happened, what with everything that's gone on. Me being on nights, you and Vi having to kip in the dug-out, the continual bombings and being dog-tired when we do get together.' He held her closer. 'I'm aiming for a football team, you know that.'

'You're a bit hopeful,' Kay couldn't help but complain, 'when we've not even got Alfie with us. Nor likely to have if the bombing starts again.'

Alan gave a soft sigh. 'I know. I know. But a man can dream.' He paused. 'Not heard from Len and Doris lately, have you?'

'No, not since that last letter saying Alfie was all right. You know Doris. She don't bother with any chat, just gives the plain facts.'

They lay for a few moments in silence, the peace and tranquillity of the moment disturbed. But it wasn't long before Alan heaved himself up and, stroking her thigh, he rested above her, muttering words of love in her ear. As his fingers teased her trembling skin, their problems once again vanished as if into thin air. Kay let herself be renewed in their lovemaking and for a short, wonderful while, the only thing that mattered was each other.

* * *

Kay had the day off from work to attend the funeral. She didn't have a black coat, but neither did Vi who hadn't been able to find anything suitable in the Salvation Army hand-out or at the market. So they both wore dark colours with armbands made from blackout material.

Kay and Vi caught the bus to the chapel, but Alan was already there at the door greeting the mourners as they arrived. The chapel was tiny and bare, no more than a large room with chairs lined up in rows. Alan had told Kay the building was often used for victims of the bombings who had no living relatives or funds to meet the funeral expenses.

'Jenny and Tom Edwards are here,' whispered Vi as they walked towards the five cheap-looking caskets lined to one side. 'And Alice and Bert Tyler from number fifty-four. Next to them is Paul Butt and his dad, Neville. It seems like years since we've seen 'em all.'

Kay nodded at the familiar faces that all turned their way and smiled. Their friends and neighbours from Slater Street suddenly looked older, greyer, as though the dust that had fallen on them during the Blitz was now indelible. Hazel and Thelma Press, two spinster sisters who lived at the top of the street, were folding a Union Jack flag across the first of the cheap wooden caskets.

'As the coffins looked a bit bare, we thought Howard would like the tribute,' whispered Thelma, pushing her spectacles up her thin nose as Kay drew close. 'He fought in the first conflict, you know.'

'Yes, Madge was very proud of her husband.' Kay thought again of the conversations she used to have with Madge Sutton. Rarely did Madge ever complain, even though Howard's job in the docks didn't provide much of a wage. She had worked in the ironmongers, preparing the bundles of firewood soaked in paraffin. Kay had seen Madge's fingers red raw in winter from the cold and the chaffing of the wood. Kay thought of this as she placed a small bunch of violets from the market on top of the boys' caskets next to the other tributes.

After they had taken their places, there were loud whispers at the back of the chapel. Everyone turned to see who it was. Kay recognized the two latecomers as Babs and Eddie Chapman. Eddie, usually a robust-looking man with light brown hair in his late thirties, looked thinner and somehow smaller. Babs was well turned-out with her fair hair cut short under a small black hat. But she looked tired as she took the seat next to Kay. 'Oh Babs, I can't say how sorry we are about your house,' Kay murmured as she hugged her friend and saw Eddie give a brief nod.

'It was everything we had in the world, Kay.'

'I know. I can't imagine what losing your home must feel like.'

'But we're alive,' said Babs with a shaky resilience. 'The Suttons weren't so lucky.'

'None of us can believe it still. It's like we're waiting for them to walk in here and tell us they're all right.'

Babs nodded slowly. 'We both had young families and were always in each other's places . . .' She stopped, unable to say more, sitting back to slide her hand in her pocket in search of a handkerchief. 'You think – well, you think to yourself, why was it them and not us?'

Kay gently touched her friend's arm. 'No one knows the answer to that, Babs. Fate, destiny, a higher power – who can say? But I'm just thankful I still have you all in one piece.'

Babs nodded, trying to smile with her eyes. Kay knew that whatever she said couldn't dismiss the horror that had brought them here today. Both Eddie and Babs had been spared, and their children Tim and Gill had been safely evacuated to Essex at the time the bomb had fallen on their house. Kay knew it was a blessing they would be fully grateful for as time passed.

Just then a man in a grey suit hurriedly walked in through a side door and stood in front of them. He gave the Suttons' names and ages, then said they would be sadly missed by their friends and neighbours. After handing them each a hymn book, they all sang 'Abide With Me'.

Then Alan, Tom Edwards, Bert Tyler, Paul Butt and Eddie Chapman, together with the undertaker, lifted the wooden boxes one by one and carried them outside to a waiting van. Kay had to stop her mind from thinking of what was in them. But at least each had their own small space to rest in.

Everyone remained seated in the chapel, as if hoping for something to happen which would restore everything to normal again.

Babs blew her nose. 'We just have to get on with it and do our best,' she sniffed. 'We're all lucky to be sitting here after that terrible night.'

A sentiment with which Kay knew everyone agreed.

Kay hadn't intended to host a wake, but as they stood outside the chapel she looked around at the small group of mourners and knew that she couldn't let the day end like this. She asked the assembled back to the house for tea and Alan told her he would join them after he'd reported back to his unit's headquarters in Poplar. Paul Butt and his dad had come in Paul's car and they offered Hazel and Thelma Press a ride in the back seat. The others joined Kay at the bus stop.

'Me and Eddie can't stay long as we have to get back to the hostel at Aldgate,' Babs said.

'How are the kids?' Kay asked as the bus came along and they climbed aboard.

'I miss them, but I was glad they were away when me and Eddie saw our house. Honest, Kay, it was the biggest shock of my life. And of course our cat, Fluffy, was killed. The kids will be really upset over that.'

'What are you going to do now?'

'Dunno.'

'Do you think you'll evacuate?'

'We'll have to,' replied Babs, glancing across at her husband who had taken a seat next to Bert Tyler. 'Though even after what happened to our house and the Suttons, I can't imagine living anywhere else.' She gave a shudder, hunching her shoulders. 'Me and Eddie have always lived in or around the East End. We moved to Slater Street just after Gill was born. Eddie's job in the docks' offices has been a godsend, what with so many blokes being unemployed. But most of all, I don't want to leave my best friend.' She smiled tearfully at Kay.

'But you might get a nice place somewhere else. Eddie could even find a better job,' interrupted Jenny Edwards, who leaned forward from the seat behind. Kay smiled at Jenny who, in her mid-forties, had a permanently worried expression on her pale face.

'Yes, there's always a chance, Jenny,' said Babs. 'And when you're issued with a billet, you have to accept it, even if it's miles away from London. The kids don't even like being in Essex. They can't wait to come home. If Eddie could find us somewhere to live round here, even if it was run down, I'd grab it.'

'But what about the kids if the raids start again?' asked Kay.

'They'd have to go back to Essex.' Babs frowned. 'And you, Kay? Would you bring Alfie home if you could?'

Without hesitation, Kay nodded. Then she added cautiously, 'But I'm not sure Alan would agree with me.'

'Men don't run on emotion like women,' Babs agreed. 'They're too level-headed.'

As if her thoughts had conjured up Alan himself, Kay caught sight of a tall figure as she looked from the bus window. Alan's black hair and upright bearing were unmistakeable. He stood outside a pub called the Pig and

Whistle, talking to a man who was carrying a newspaper.

She lifted her hand slightly as if to wave but then, with her eyes intent on the two figures, she let it drop back to her knee. Alan – her Alan – was in a place he shouldn't be, or at least a place he had no reason to visit, not if he was returning to the post as he'd told her. She stared at her husband, briefly obscured by passers-by, and the man, who had his back to her and was urging Alan forward inside the pub.

Kay took a deep breath, a slight sweat breaking over her brow as she watched them disappear from sight into the interior of the Pig and Whistle. She felt she had seen a vision, her mind wrestling with the inconsistencies of the facts she had been given by Alan and what she had just seen with her own eyes. She felt the blood draining from her face, but tried to pull herself together. There must be an explanation, though at this moment she couldn't think of one. Alan wasn't a drinker, certainly not at this time of the day, though he might very occasionally make an evening visit to the pub with a mate. But she thought she knew all of his friends; the men he worked with, the wardens at his post, their friends and neighbours in and around Slater Street. The appearance of this well-dressed stranger just didn't make any sense. More than that, she felt as if Alan had lied to her. The bus moved on and the pub was soon out of sight. Kay thought again about what Alan had told her. She was certain he had said he was going to the post. So why had he gone to the Pig and Whistle instead?

'All right, flower?' Vi called to her. 'You look as white as a sheet. Nothing wrong is there?'

Kay jumped and smiled quickly. 'No, I'm fine.' She wanted to tell Vi what she'd just seen, but somehow she couldn't. Knowing Vi, she'd wave the incident aside, saying Alan would tell her why he'd changed his mind in good time, so what was she getting in a state about? But Vi didn't know just how strangely Alan had been behaving lately. Or at least, to Vi, Alan was Alan and could do no wrong.

This last thought made Kay feel guilty. She should feel the same way too. Yet she had this unpleasant feeling inside her, desperate for a rational explanation yet unable to think of one. Kay was still troubled by these thoughts as the bus drew to a halt at Slater Street.

Vi had sliced the bread-and-butter pudding that she had made yesterday into tiny pieces and Paul Butt had hurried back from his house with a loaf and a small wedge of cheese. With this and an onion, Kay had managed to prepare a few decent sandwiches.

'Lovely spread, Kay, considering you wasn't expecting us,' said Alice Tyler, who was a tea lady at the local brewery and had provided the tea leaves. She sat beside Jenny and their husbands Tom and Bert stood by the fireside as if warming their backsides though it was a summer's day and no fire was lit.

'We couldn't let the day end on a sad note,' Kay said as she offered round the last of the sticky bread-and-butter pudding. 'Madge and Howard deserve to be remembered as the happy family they were. I don't want my last thought to be of them in those boxes. It's good to be able to remember them as friends and neighbours.' She wanted to say that they also deserved to have their own space in the graveyard, but as no one had mentioned that, she didn't.

'Where did Alan disappear to?' asked Hazel Press as she and Thelma stood together with their teacups balanced daintily on their saucers.

'He had to report to his post,' Kay told them though she was even more worried about Alan now as it was several hours since she had since him outside the Pig and Whistle.

Just then, Vi brought in a fresh pot of tea. 'Who's for a top-up?' she called and there was a 'yes please' from almost everyone. Kay thought that if it wasn't for the reason they had all gathered, this would be the first happy get-together in the street since before September last year and she deeply regretted that her husband wasn't there to share it.

'Alan busy is he?' a voice asked over her shoulder.

Kay turned to find Paul Butt beside her. He was not as tall as Alan, Kay decided, but certainly a good six foot and she had to crane her neck to look up at him. He had very penetrating blue eyes and had combed his fair hair back in a neat short back and sides. Like his father Neville, who sat talking to Jenny Edwards, he wore a dark suit and black tie as a mark of respect. 'Alan had to report in to work,' Kay said quickly. 'Thanks for the cheese, Paul. I hope you didn't leave yourself short.'

'Not at all. The cheese was given to me by a girl from the yard canteen. We're sort of seeing one another.'

'Like that, is it.' Kay grinned.

'Rose and me started going out last year before the Blitz,' he explained. 'But I don't know if anything will come of it. Who knows where any of us will be by the time this war is over.' He shook his head slowly and for the first time looked away. 'What upset me was the weight of those coffins, which meant what was in them was . . .' He cleared his throat. 'Just don't seem right a whole family is gone in a matter of seconds.'

Kay nodded. 'Yes, I think we all feel the same, Paul.'

Kay found herself wondering why a compassionate and warm-hearted man like Paul had never married. He had a nice way with him and couldn't be badly off as he'd always been in work at the steelyard. Vi had told her that Paul had had several serious relationships but he'd never settled down. He was close to his father and had been since Mrs Butt had died when Paul was fifteen.

'Thanks to Alan arranging the funeral, the Suttons had a decent send-off,' Paul said quietly, then glanced at the door and smiled. 'Here he is, an' all, the man himself.'

'Sorry I'm late, love.' Alan kissed Kay on the cheek. 'Call of duty I'm afraid, an emergency at work.'

'Dunno what we'd do without you rescue boys,' shouted Eddie, a comment with which everyone loudly agreed. Alan made conversation and Kay went out to the kitchen, taking with her the dirty crocks to pile on the draining board. She knew what Alan had told her wasn't true.

A few minutes later he was beside her. 'How's my girl?' he asked softly.

She looked up at him. 'Have you really been to the post?'

He frowned. 'Course I have.'

Just at that moment Babs and Eddie walked into the kitchen. 'We've got to go now,' Babs said. 'But thanks for the lovely spread. I wish I'd been able to bring something meself.'

Kay hugged her friend. 'Don't worry about that. When will we see you next?'

Babs looked tearful. Eddie slipped his arm round her as she got out her hanky again. 'Don't know,' Eddie said. 'I'm still working in the docks, but that will change when we're evacuated. I'll have to start all over again.'

'Eddie, have you thought about trying private landlords instead of the council?' Alan suggested. 'Some might be willing to let out their places again.'

'No, I never thought about that,' admitted Eddie with a frown.

'Oh, could we try, Eddie? Before they send us away.' Babs looked up at her husband with hope in her eyes. 'Even if we had to pay more rent, I could give up me cleaning and get a better-paid job. There's lots of factory work going. Then we could bring the kids back.'

'You and the kids are what's important to me, Babs,' Eddie told her sharply. 'If we brought the kids home, I wouldn't want you working all hours on an assembly line. You've been through enough already and deserve time with the kids. But it's true, if we stayed here, I could keep me job and maybe put in a few extra hours.'

'I'll ask around for you,' Alan volunteered. 'Drop into the post when you've time.'

'I'll take you up on that, mate.' Eddie shook Alan's hand hard. Kay thought there were tears in Eddie's eyes as they left.

'There might be a chance,' Alan said as he raked his fingers through his hair. 'I can see Babs ain't coping too well.'

Kay nodded. 'She belongs here. The island may not look much right now, but it means the world to Babs.'

'I'll put out some feelers,' Alan said. 'See what I can turn up.'

Once again, Kay's heart filled with love for her husband who never failed to help anyone in trouble. Since they'd come to the island just after they'd married in 1938, they had been happy living on the small horseshoe of land that stuck out into the great River Thames, known as the Isle of Dogs. It was all docklands and factories and small, winding roads crammed with smoke-blackened houses but Kay loved it. The community was close-knit and as everyone was hard-up and in the same boat, they looked out for one another. She and Babs had become the best of friends over the years and Kay wouldn't want to live anywhere else. She knew Babs felt the same. 'Alan,' she began hesitantly, 'I saw you from the bus this morning. You were standing with a man outside the Pig and Whistle when you'd told me you were going back to the post.'

He sighed. 'Oh, I've been rumbled, have I?'

'What does that mean?'

'There's no harm in me saying now, I suppose. After you'd gone, that relative of the Suttons turned up. He claimed to be Madge's brother.'

'I didn't know she had one.'

'Neither did I. He said he'd only just found out about their deaths. He sounded genuinely choked, so I offered to buy him a drink at the nearest pub which happened to be the Pig and Whistle.'

'Why didn't you tell everyone when you came in?'

'Because he turned out to be a scrounger. All he was after was money. Wanted to know what Madge left him. Even threatened to come round and pester his late sister's friends and neighbours.'

'Alan, that's awful! The Suttons had no money.'

'I warned him if I ever caught sight of him in Slater Street, I'd call the law. But I can tell you, I felt like knocking his block off.' Before she could speak he drew her to him. 'Sorry, love, that I made you worry.' His hands were strong and comforting and she knew she loved him so much.

'I should have known there was a reason.'

'I felt so angry,' Alan admitted. 'Madge and Howard never had two pennies to rub together. And what they did have went on their boys.'

Kay nodded. 'Alan, I missed Alfie so much today.'

'Me too.'

'Let's bring him home.'

'But there's always the risk of more bombing.'

'I know. But we could wait for ever.'

He thought for a moment. 'Tell you what. In June, if everything is as quiet as it is now, we'll go to Hertfordshire and get him.'

'Do you mean that?' Kay kissed him hungrily, her world put to right again. That was all she wanted to hear.

Alan lay awake for a long time.

Kay was curled in his arms and breathing softly. He loved hearing her little sighs and his hands brought her gently against him. In her sleep she gave a contented murmur, wrapping herself into the warmth of his body.

'I love you, Kay Lewis, more than you could ever imagine,' Alan whispered as he buried his face into her hair and felt its luxurious softness. She was all woman: beautiful, bright, funny. And when it came to their antics beneath the sheets, she never held back. He smiled as he thought of their lovemaking; never once had they quarrelled and come to bed unable to resolve their differences. They had always been physically needy and even when he was exhausted, hardly able to undress without a moan and a groan, her touch on him felt electric. No other woman had ever made him feel this way.

Alan quickly shut his mind to the past. He couldn't allow himself to think of his mistakes. And by God, they seemed limitless. When he'd met Kay, he'd been full of good intentions, deciding he'd tell her everything the moment he had the chance. But that moment never came. Or, perhaps it had and he'd deliberately ignored it. By the time Kay was pregnant and they had to get married, he'd lost his bottle. It was enough being on the wrong side of Kay's family without having to pile all his emotional baggage onto his new wife. At least, that was what he'd told himself then. But was he really just a coward and too dishonest to acknowledge it?

Like today when he'd had to stretch the truth about the Pig and Whistle. It had been the perfect opportunity to open up, yet he'd replaced hard reality with a better version of the truth. *His* version. And all in the name, he assured himself, of keeping Kay happy. Like Eddie had said today about Babs, Alan thought too: the women had suffered enough. First the bloody Blitz, then Alfie being taken from her and Kay working all hours on the factory line, then coming home to freezing cold and terrifying nights in the Anderson without him.

Alan moved his body slightly away from his wife's as the sweat rolled over him. The sweat of a guilty man. He looked up at the ceiling, as black as tar above them. The blackout felt just like his insides sometimes. As though he was finding his way in a darkened world that never shed any light into the corners full of booby traps. And his biggest fear was that one day, inevitably, one of those perishers would explode right in his face.

'Alan?' Kay's voice was full of sleepy confusion as she reached out for the touch of his skin.

'I'm here, love.'

She nestled against him and he drew his fingers through her hair, kissing her forehead. Her hand tightened on his stomach, her fingertips finding the lines of his ribs and slipping down further. Thank God, he thought, for his carnal self and the immediate desire that sparked in the pit of his belly.

Bringing her against him in a sudden rush of need he knew that for a while, once again, he could lose himself in their passion.

Chapter Five

Kay decided to write to Len and Doris again. It was June and the bombing hadn't resumed; at least it had only in short bursts and not over the island. She told Len and Doris that they hoped to fetch Alfie soon and would write closer to the time. Just putting her hopes on paper made her feel better, though she was disappointed not to receive an answer from Doris. Then, towards the end of the month, Alan came home to tell Kay that his night shifts had officially stopped.

'I'll be able to catch up on some jobs around the place,' he explained one evening as they all sat in the front room that was now, thanks to Vi's housekeeping, spotlessly clean.

'Are they going to put the lid on the Rescue Squad?' Vi asked in concern.

Alan shook his head. 'No, though there's not much rescuing to be done now. We're shifting the debris mostly and erecting warnings on the unstable buildings. The kids are the problem. They seem to want to risk life and limb by mucking about on the most dangerous sites.'

'Is there a chance of the night raids starting up again?' Kay asked.

Alan thought for a while before he spoke. 'Difficult question to answer, that. Everyone's watching and waiting to see what will happen next. Doubtless there will be more attacks but the Germans are busy with Russia. They're already at Minsk.'

'Where's Minsk?' asked Vi.

'Minsk is a Russian stronghold near Moscow. There's fierce fighting and tank battles near Kiev too. That's in the Ukraine. Churchill has promised some help to the Red Army as he knows if the Germans defeat the Russians, there'll be no stopping them.'

Kay felt a moment's panic. What if the Germans were triumphant and returned in full force to Britain? More than ever she wanted to hold her son safely in her arms. 'Alan, I can't wait any longer for Alfie,' she said, knitting her fingers together. 'There's always going to be a threat. I've just got to have him home.'

To Kay's surprise, Alan smiled and began to nod his head. 'I'm due a couple of days off next month. How does that suit you?'

Kay jumped to her feet. 'Next month – July! Do you mean it?'

'Course I do.'

Kay clapped her hands together. 'I can't wait to tell Len and Doris.'

'Better to wait until we know the exact details,' Alan replied with his usual caution.

Kay sat beside Vi. 'I can't believe it, Vi. Alfie really is coming home.'

'And you'll want the spare room I'm in,' Vi said in a quiet voice, trying to raise a smile.

'No, Vi, his cot will do for now,' said Alan reasonably. 'We don't have no plans to turn you out.'

'So cheer up and stop worrying,' said Kay, not wanting to upset her friend. 'You're part of the furniture now.'

'I don't want to wear out me welcome.'

'I'll let you know when you do.' Alan winked at Kay. 'In fact I'll write you a letter of dismissal.'

Vi grinned under her knotted scarf. 'You cheeky so-an'-so, you would an' all.'

Alan tapped his hand slowly on the arm of the chair, one eyebrow shooting up. 'And there's some more good news too.'

'What?' Vi and Kay said together as they sat on the edge of their seats.

'There are already evacuees wanting to return to the island.'

'Anyone we know?' asked Kay breathlessly.

'Eddie Chapman dropped in at the post a few days after the funeral. I gave him the address that Stan Tripp from next door gave to me before they evacuated in September. I suggested Eddie should write to Stan and Elsie to see if they had plans to return. Eddie wrote and got a reply. The Tripps have decided to stay in Wales.'

Kay gasped. 'For ever?'

'Looks like it.'

'Do you mean Eddie and Babs can try for their house?'

'That's the idea,' Alan said. 'With Stan's permission, Eddie's taken the letter to the rent office. There's a lot of red tape to wade through as Stan will be asked to surrender his rent book. And of course, there's the matter of all the Tripps' furniture.'

Kay had tears in her eyes. She would miss Stan and Elsie, but it would be wonderful to have someone living next door again, especially if it was the Chapmans.

On a sunny Saturday in early July, Kay was waiting in the queue outside the grocer's on Ebondale Street. She felt cool and comfortable in a blue-and-white sleeveless summer dress and, having decided against a rather old and lifeless straw sun hat, had pinned her hair up with a tortoiseshell clip. She took pleasure in her appearance now, after the long days and nights of the Blitz. It was also a relief to be free of the unflattering hairnet the women had to wear at the factory.

The sun played down on her bare arms and legs and was encouraging the freckles over the bridge of her nose. Jenny Edwards had joined her in the queue and the conversation turned to the hardships that the Russian people were experiencing as they defended their country. In the middle of what she was saying, Jenny narrowed her eyes into the distance. 'Isn't this Paul Butt coming towards us? That must be his latest girlfriend.'

Kay glanced along the road and nodded. 'She's very pretty, isn't she?'

'I should say so.' Jenny nudged her arm. 'Looks like they've seen us.'

'Hello Kay, Jenny.' Paul stopped and looked a little embarrassed.

Kay smiled. 'Are you joining us?'

'Don't think so.' He looked at the long queue. 'Unless it's for a bargain.'

'I wish it was,' replied Jenny. 'I'm after some bacon as our daughter Emily, who is eighteen tomorrow, said she'd like a nice rasher to celebrate. But I don't suppose there'll be any left by the time we get there. In the end it will be Spam I expect.' She paused, adding with a glance at the dark-haired woman, 'That was a nice piece of cheese you brought for the Suttons' send-off, Paul. It did us a treat.'

Kay could see Jenny was angling for an introduction to Paul's lady friend, but instead he made small talk about the weather.

'Well, mustn't keep you,' he ended after a while. 'The queue's moving up and you don't want to lose your place.'

After they'd left, Jenny frowned, shaking her head curiously.

'Can't understand how Paul never got himself hitched,' Jenny speculated. 'Good looking feller like him should have been married off years ago.'

'Perhaps he's happy to stay a bachelor.'

'Yes, an eligible one at that. Mid-thirties, with a good job making steel for our warships. A car, even in these depressed times. It's unlikely he'll be called up and he's got a very nice house. Old Neville wouldn't be any bother to keep. The more you think about it, Paul would make quite a catch for any girl.' Jenny brought her attention back to Kay. 'As much as we're all trying to do our part for the war effort, I'm relieved my Tom is too old to be called up. Don't know what I'd do without him.'

Kay walked home thinking the same about Alan. It was lovely having him all to herself lately. And those dark moods of his didn't seem to come quite so often. His work still took up a lot of his time but the jobs at home were gradually getting done. She wasn't surprised when she arrived home to find him at the top of a ladder. She smiled, gazing up to shield her eyes from the sun with her hand. Her husband's naturally olive skin was tanned and weather-beaten, giving him a rakish appearance. His black hair crawled over his collar and his forearms were tanned and muscular. She felt a strong physical tug of attraction. Just as strong as when she had first met him in 1937. Before joining the local authority, he had been employed briefly at the factory where she worked. No more than a couple of words had been exchanged between them. But she had known at once that Alan Lewis would be someone very special in her life.

'Did you get what you wanted at the grocer's?' he called, mopping the sweat from his brow with his forearm.

'Yes, Jenny bought her bacon for Emily's birthday. I decided to stop by the fishmonger's after. With veg and mash you won't notice the fish is invisible.'

He chuckled, tossing back the heavy lock of black hair that flopped across his face. 'I've one more brick to replace and then I'll be down.'

Kay went inside the house to prepare for supper. She loved her life in Slater Street, despite the bombs, dust, mess and often nerve-wracking situations. She had everything she wanted in a husband and an adorable son who had made their marriage complete. During the Blitz the loss of friends and neighbours had been very hard to bear and Jenny had reminded her this morning that the threat of another bombing campaign still hung over their heads. Kay accepted that the war wasn't over by any means. But she could no longer bear to be parted from Alfie. The moment she held her baby in her arms again, she knew her happiness would be complete.

Kay and Alan boarded the coach to Hertfordshire on a sunny day, three weeks later. Kay was beside herself with excitement. Alan had arranged the day-return tickets and seats at the front of the special service coach that left London for Hemel Hempstead. She and Alan had never travelled to her brother's home before. In fact Kay had only ever travelled short distances out of London. Len and Doris had lived in Little Gadelsby, Hertfordshire, since they married in September 1934. Her brother preferred to drive to London to visit them instead; each year he seemed to have a bigger and better car to show off. For this reason Kay had bought him a leather-bound book with an illustration of a Rolls-Royce on the front. For Doris she had found a set of Irish linen chair-back covers. She wanted them to know how much she had appreciated their help with Alfie.

Alan reached for Kay's hand as they made themselves comfortable on the seats. 'You look beautiful, love. With those pink cheeks you're my true English rose.'

'An English rose from the East End?' Kay teased.

'You're knocking my socks off, Kay Lewis, I don't mind admitting.'

'Only your socks?'

They laughed together, but she was pleased Alan had noticed the effort she'd made with her appearance. Though the pencil-slim green skirt and fitted jacket were bought at the market before the war, the outfit hid the weight loss she'd suffered over the duration of the bombing. Despite losing a little of her curves, she'd bought high heels from the market to give her more height and, hopefully, elegance. Though the shoes had had a previous owner, they were in very good condition and needed no coupons. The effect was meant to give her a more sophisticated appearance. She wanted to impress Doris and Len, but to hear Alan compliment her was the icing on her cake.

Not that Alan hadn't dolled himself up either, she thought admiringly. He wore his smart dark suit and clean white shirt and looked quite the gentleman. She knew he was nervous too, despite his calm exterior. Even though he and Len had not seen eye to eye over the years, she was certain this meeting was going to be cordial.

Kay returned her gaze to the window and the ghostly sights of London's bombed buildings as the coach swept them out of the city. Like Vi and the Chapmans' houses, there were rows upon rows of black, broken and tumbled dwellings and as many mountains of bricks, timbers and debris to replace them. 'Oh, Alan, what has this war done to us?' she sighed. 'Will London ever be the same again?'

'No, it won't, love, but something good will come of the conflict when the reconstruction begins.'

'But when will that be? The war's not even over yet.'

'It will be, one day, you can count on that. And Britain will still be a democracy.' Alan turned to smile at her, the expression in his eyes sincere and loving. He filled her with hope and expectation of a future. And that was what mattered to Kay.

Chapter Six

'How much longer to go?' Kay asked. The swaying green trees and long lines of hedgerows seemed to be endless.

'A few more stops before we reach Hemel Hempstead,' Alan told her, a grin on his face. 'How would you like to live out this way?'

'It'd be all right for a week,' Kay decided quickly. 'Then I'd want to get back to the island and a bit of life.'

Alan pointed to a quaint-looking little teashop. 'Our Alfie would enjoy them homemade scones and jam they've got displayed there.'

'Jam!' Kay exclaimed longingly. 'What a luxury! It doesn't look like a war's been going on here. Look, there's a sign saying fresh eggs and dairy butter.'

'That's country living for you.'

'I wonder if Doris has fed Alfie on homemade food,' Kay mused. 'Somehow she don't strike me as the type to cook a lot.'

Alan laughed, his eyes twinkling. 'What type is she?'

'She's one of them smart, intelligent types who knows things like their times tables inside out.'

'But Doris comes from Hertfordshire. Wasn't that why your brother moved there? To be near her parents who were farmers.'

Kay frowned. 'Yes, I suppose so. Me and Doris never talked much as she's a quiet type and not very forthcoming. Mum said Doris would have liked a family but it never happened.'

As they passed country inns with signs outside that advertised homegrown produce, Kay realized how little she knew about the more intimate side of her brother and sister-in-law's marriage. Len had been best mates with Norman and they'd shared a passion for cars, buses, trams, anything equipped with an engine and wheels. But since Len and Doris had moved to Hertfordshire, she'd only met them during their occasional visits to London. Living so far away, and with their history, perhaps it was only to be expected that Len and Alan had been unable to find any common ground.

'I didn't realize the countryside could look as nice as this,' Kay found herself admitting as she gazed from the window. 'When me and Len were young, Mum sent us away on the Country Holiday Fund. It always seemed to rain the week we went. Len loved it. Him and his mates enjoyed the smelly old barns full of mud and poo that the cows trod everywhere. But I was bored stiff.'

Alan wagged his finger. 'The rain is what makes the crops grow and is important to the farmers. All that muck and mud you hated is part and parcel of our survival, in town and in the country.'

She turned to Alan and made a face. 'Clever clogs.'

Alan squeezed her hand. 'Perhaps one day when the war is over we could come back for a holiday. Stay in one of those pubs we saw along the way.'

'I wouldn't mind that. We could visit Len and Doris instead of them having to drive all the way to us.'

Alan nodded thoughtfully. 'Me and Len might have had our differences but I know him and Doris have Alfie's best at heart.' He arched a wry eyebrow. 'Do you remember the look on your family's faces when we told them we were married?'

Kay rolled her eyes. 'Mum never let me forget.'

'She wasn't best pleased either when we told them you was pregnant and she worked out the dates.'

'But we proved them wrong in the end,' Kay whispered happily. 'You didn't turn out to be a fifth-columnist or revolutionary. Instead you gave them a grandson and nephew that me and Norman didn't—' Kay stopped abruptly. 'Oh, that's tactless of me, Alan. I only meant I'm so proud of Alfie being ours.'

Alan gave her a long, steady stare. 'I'm sure you and Norman, if he'd lived longer, would have had that family you and your parents always wanted.'

'Alan, it's us and Alfie who counts. You know that, don't you?'

'Yes,' Alan said with a smile. 'And I couldn't be prouder.'

Kay settled back in her seat. Sometimes she blurted out her thoughts without due care and consideration. She knew that Alan's few memories of his hard-working and long-suffering mother were some of his saddest. She had tried hard to make ends meet for her three young sons while her husband had been away in prison. But she had been taken early from her family. Alan had never known the love of his wayward father. He'd run away to sea at an age when most young boys were only just beginning to form their character. Kay knew that Alan wanted Alfie's life to be far different to his own. And she was determined she would always be by Alan's side to make it so.

'They're big cows.' Kay pointed to two large hairy brown heads sticking up above the five-bar gate.

'They're bulls,' Alan told her as they walked down the country lane. 'See their horns? I wouldn't want to annoy one of them.'

'I hope Doris don't let our Alfie near a bull!' Kay steered Alan to the far side of the winding path. 'It's a bit dangerous letting them loose like that.'

Alan laughed. 'The farmer keeps a good eye on them.'

Kay had to admit that everything she had seen so far had surprised her. There hadn't been one spot of rain and no mud at all. They'd enjoyed a very nice snack of tea and the luxury of apple cake at the coach station. The tiny shops had been stuffed full of things you couldn't get in the East End, like homemade marmalade, apple damson jam and hand-knitted woollen garments spun from the local sheep's wool. And there was even things like herb tea that people made from plants grown in their own back gardens. And what back gardens they were! Kay couldn't believe her eyes when she'd seen bowers of roses over doors and vines that crept right up to the chimneys and over the other side of the cottages, just like in picture books or magazines. Willow trees, identified by Alan, had waved their long branches over little ponds with tiny ducks floating on the calm surface.

Kay was mesmerized! She couldn't wait to tell Vi all she had seen, as they had both supposed that outside of London, there wasn't much to see or do. The truth was that people who lived in the country seemed very busy; they worked in the fields along with the Land Army girls who Alan said would probably be billeted on the local farms. There were dogs and cats too – pets weren't allowed on the island. During the bombing the government had told everyone to either put down their animals or remove them to safety. Briefly she thought about Babs Chapman's cat, Fluffy, who was killed on the last raid. She hoped the children wouldn't be too upset.

'*Albion*,' Alan said as he squinted through the hedges at the hidden gardens and looked for name-plates on the cottages. 'It's got to be down here somewhere.'

Kay was on tenterhooks. 'I can hardly speak I'm so excited.'

'I wonder if he's grown much.'

'He was a real mischief when he went away.' Kay suppressed the lump in her throat. She felt she had missed a vital part of his growing-up. 'This past ten months have seemed endless. I can't believe he'll be three in November.'

'This must be it,' Alan said, pointing to a large hedge in the form of an arch. The sign beneath it was an engraved brass plaque. 'See, this says *Albion*.'

As usual Kay had been so wrapped up in her thoughts that when she looked up the narrow path that Alan indicated, at first she didn't recognize the child standing beside a woman who was on all fours, attending to the weeds. The boy, like the woman, was wearing blue dungarees and had big eyes that seemed to fill his round face. His dark hair peeped out in wisps from under a blue wide-brimmed hat.

'My God,' Alan breathed beside her. 'Is that our Alfie?'

Kay was too overwhelmed to reply as she stared at her son, magically transformed from a baby into a sturdy toddler since she had last held him in her arms ten months ago before Len and Doris had taken him away.

Chapter Seven

All Kay's emotions were in turmoil as Doris caught sight of them and climbed to her feet. Kay watched breathlessly as Alfie held up his arms to Doris who lifted him with practised ease onto her hip. As Alan pushed open the garden gate, Alfie's plump hands went tightly around Doris's neck.

'Alfie?' Kay called, but Alfie turned away and buried his face in Doris's blonde hair.

Alan slipped his hand to Kay's waist, drawing her back a little. 'Don't rush him, Kay. We caught him by surprise.'

Kay realized that she had to be patient though her disappointment was bitter.

'Hello,' Alan said to Doris, who looked at them with a frown.

'So you've come,' Doris replied, her hand going protectively to Alfie's back.

'Yes, of course.' Kay had to restrain every muscle in her body from darting forward to Alfie. 'We wouldn't have let you down.'

'Your letter only arrived this morning,' Doris said hurriedly. She stepped aside from the fork and trowel that she had been using to dig in the rich brown earth.

'I'm sorry about that,' Kay apologized, her eyes fixed on Alfie. 'Alan only found out about his days off last week.'

Doris transferred Alfie to her other hip and nodded to the door. 'Well, now you're here, you'd best come in.'

Kay was shocked to find this rather plump, rosy-cheeked woman wearing dungarees and a grubby green gardener's apron with earth-covered fingers in place of the somewhat thin and pale sister-in-law who she remembered as her brother's wife. In ten months, Doris had blossomed. Obviously caring for Alfie had suited her. But what hurt Kay the most was Alfie's reaction. He seemed to have forgotten them.

'This is lovely,' Alan said as they entered the cool interior of the cottage. Kay tried to catch Alfie's attention but he continued to bury his face in Doris's shoulder. Despite Kay's urgent wish that he should look up and into her eyes he refused to do so. Alan squeezed her arm, as if to say he had guessed the thoughts running through her mind.

Tearing her eyes away from her son, Kay glanced out of the pretty lattice window at the rear of the sitting room. From here she had full view of the lush, flower-filled garden radiating with bright sunshine. A neatly cut lawn folded its way around a child's swing which was looped around the branches of an apple tree. There was also a large stuffed dog on wheels that had seen better days and was leaking horsehair. But the rope attached to it meant that someone was able to tow the rider along as they sat on the dog's back. The thought gave Kay a cutting pain across her heart. Her little boy must have spent many hours with that dog on sunny days. Either Doris or Len or perhaps both had towed him around the garden, laughing and playing with him.

Doris indicated two very large elderly chairs covered in flowered material and big, squashy cushions that spilled over the arms. While failing to catch Alfie's eye, Kay had time to look around. The cottage was homely, but not expensively furnished. The furniture was obviously well cared for and the same black oak beams that crossed the ceiling also surrounded the wide brick hearth. A round china jug stood on its mantel and was filled with fresh flowers. There were brass ornaments hanging on the beams – horseshoes and tiny bells – and a big copper kettle stood next to the grate. The walls were a creamy colour that looked a bit like lumpy ice cream and had old mirrors and pictures of farm scenes and landscapes hanging on them.

'Len's at work, but he'll be home soon,' Doris told them as she sat on the big settee with Alfie. 'He's not seen your letter as the postman was late. It's going to be a surprise for him to find you here.'

'I wrote in June to prepare you,' Kay reminded her sister-in-law. 'But we never heard back.'

Doris lifted her head sharply. 'We thought you were certain to reconsider as the war isn't over.' Doris slid off Alfie's hat and slipped her hand through his rich, dark hair, stroking it into place. Once again, Alfie refused to look in

Kay's direction. 'He's wary with strangers,' Doris said, then corrected herself quickly by adding, 'I mean I know you're not strangers, but he hasn't seen you for a while.'

Kay didn't need to be reminded of that. Every hour, every day of every month away from her son was engraved in her mind. She leaned forward, a trembling smile on her face. 'Alfie?' she whispered. 'It's Mummy and Daddy. We've come to take you home.'

At this, the little boy clung harder to Doris. 'You should have given us more time,' Doris berated, brushing her short hair from her eyes. 'We would have told Alfie you were coming and showed him your picture so that he understands.' She nodded to a shelf beside the settee. 'Look, Alfie, this is your mum and dad. Like in the photograph up there.'

They all gazed at the picture. It had been taken on the day when the council had kitted out Alan for his work with the Heavy Rescue Squad. He wore his new uniform of dark overalls and a tin helmet. Kay had been dressed in a smart utility suit with her hair coiled around her head. With arms linked, they smiled into the lens of the camera held by one of Alan's friends from work.

Alfie stared at the photograph. Doris lowered him to the floor and lifted the wooden-framed photograph from its shelf to place in Alfie's small hands. 'Alfie, give your mummy and daddy a hug.'

Kay sat nervously on the edge of the chair. Slowly she opened her arms. It would break her heart if he refused to do as Doris said.

'Go along, silly,' urged Doris as she gave him a gentle nudge. 'You're not really that shy.'

Kay kept her arms wide and her eyes hopeful, trying to find that place within her that would reach out and unconsciously reclaim him. This was her son, her beautiful boy, and she ached to hold him. Uncertainly, he came towards her. 'Yes, it's me, Mummy,' Kay said. 'Mummy from the photograph.' She reached her hand towards Alan. 'And this is Daddy.'

Kay guessed Alan was smiling but she felt his reluctance to move and frighten Alfie. She also knew Alan must be as upset as she was that Alfie had forgotten them.

The seconds seemed to stretch into long minutes before Alfie took another hesitant step towards them. Kay drank in his beauty: his softly tanned skin, chubby face and arms, the sturdiness of his legs under the blue dungarees, his little brown toes peeping out from the straps of the sandals. She wanted to burst into tears. All the pain of separation threatened to overwhelm her. The war had done this, as it had done to so many families. The day Doris and Len had come to collect him at the beginning of the Blitz still haunted her. The terror of the bombs had been nothing to the agony she had felt as she saw them taking Alfie away. He had been crying for her and Alan had to hold her in his arms as she'd fought to rush out to Len's car and stop them. Second only to Norman's death, it had been the worst day of her life. That night in the Anderson, she had cried continually.

Even Vi reminding her that the East End was no place for a child hadn't helped. Nothing had mattered then. She hadn't even cared about a bomb dropping on the house. Without Alfie, her life had seemed over.

'Alfie?' Kay fought back the threatening tears. 'Do you remember this?' She pushed her hand down into the shopping bag that Alan had carried all the way from London. She found what she was looking for. An old remnant of blanket from the cot she hadn't been able to part with. She had embroidered his name on the edge of the thin wool.

Kay pressed the blanket to her face and smiled. Alfie gazed at it with the same deep brown eyes as Alan. Cautiously, he took the blanket. Kay was certain that now he would walk into her arms. But instead, he returned to Doris.

'He's tired,' Doris told them as he curled in her lap. 'It's time for his nap.'

Alan reached forward for Kay's hand. Through the tears that she was struggling to control, Kay told herself she must be patient. At least the blanket had meant something to Alfie.

Over an hour later, Len arrived home. Kay saw how surprised he was to see her and Alan sitting in the front room. 'Good lord,' he muttered, his jaw dropping. 'What are you two doing here?'

Kay went to greet him, kissing his cheek. He was not very much taller than her and had thick auburn hair like her own, though there were now flecks of grey at his temples. He had grown a small moustache that made him look much older than his thirty-one years.

Alan stood up and took Len's hand. 'Good to see you, Len.'

'This is a surprise,' said Len sharply. Then, looking at Doris, he demanded, 'Where's Alfie?'

Doris was quick to explain that he was napping upstairs. Then she showed him Kay's letter. 'This arrived after you left,' she said. 'Kay wrote to us at the beginning of the week but the post must have been delayed.'

'You want to take Alfie?' he asked in a startled voice after reading it.

'That's the plan,' Alan replied. 'I'm sorry it's such short notice.'

'But come on, man, the war's not over,' Len protested. 'The Luftwaffe could be back any minute. And the docks will always be a prime target.'

Just then, Doris signalled to Kay. 'You'd better come upstairs with me.'

Kay would rather have talked to her brother, but she could see Doris ascending the stairs. She glanced at Alan, who had sat down again. Len had gone over to join him. He was clearly upset. She hoped that Alan would be able to calm troubled waters and explain satisfactorily their reason for wanting to take their son home.

Doris led her upstairs along a thickly carpeted landing and into a large room filled with soft toys and a small bed in which Alfie lay asleep. Beside it was a yellow painted chair and desk. The window above was open letting in the scents of the farms and the fields and the lace curtain moved slightly with the summer breeze.

Kay tore her eyes away from the coloured drawings pinned above the desk as Doris sat on the bed and drew back the cover. Kay remembered how, as a baby, Alfie had always been slow to wake. So she squeezed into the yellow chair and waited. On the floor were several pairs of lace-up shoes and open-toed sandals.

'Your Uncle Len has just come home,' Doris told Alfie, as he struggled to sit up. 'Shall Nanty take you downstairs?' Doris glanced across at Kay. 'He calls me Nanty. It's his version of Aunty Doris.'

'Does he say anything else?' Kay asked, as Alfie rubbed his eyes.

'Oh yes,' Doris said and nodded. 'He's quite a chatterbox. Though you have to listen carefully as he has his own language.'

To Kay's surprise, Alfie still had the blanket that she had given him in his hands. After a long yawn, he smiled. The first smile Kay had witnessed.

'Oh, Alfie, you have your teeth!' Kay gasped.

'Not all of them,' warned Doris. 'Just the front ones. He's teething quite badly.'

Once again Kay had the feeling she had missed so much about his growing-up. She swallowed, returning his smile. 'Can I help you to put on your sandals?' she asked.

'He likes doing that himself,' Doris said abruptly.

Kay watched Alfie climb out of bed and slip down to the floor. He wore just his cotton top and a pair of underpants. 'He's dry then, Doris?' Kay asked.

'Yes, no mishaps at all.'

'Nanty says you're very clever at this,' Kay encouraged as he pulled on his sandals.

Kay thought how very much like Alan he was. He had broad shoulders for a young child, and long legs. His hair grew in exactly the same way as Alan's, without a parting and flopping over his forehead.

'It took him some time to master the buckles,' Doris said. 'But he persevered. He's a very bright boy.'

Kay could only gaze in wonder at her son. 'How clever,' she murmured, admiring his strong legs, uncluttered by clothes, browned by the sunshine. He had lost none of his baby charm though. Rather, he had grown in proportion. Eventually, despite Doris's previous warning, she couldn't resist bending down to help him. She felt a tingling sensation all along her spine as her fingers touched his soft skin for the first time.

'Yes,' agreed Doris. 'And confident, He's come on leaps and bounds living here. I just can't understand why you should want to take him right now.'

'Doris, I know how upset you must be.' Kay was genuinely concerned for Doris, who was obviously under strain. 'I can see this must be very difficult for you.'

'You saw how upset Len was.'

'Yes, and I'm sorry about that too.'

Doris's tight face softened as she looked at Alfie. 'He's become a big part of our lives.'

'Then tell me how he's been, what he's done, all the things that have happened,' Kay urged as Alfie began to play with his toys. Suddenly it seemed important to get to know Doris better and understand the relationship she had shared with Alfie. Doris had acted as a replacement mother and it could not be easy for her to part from Alfie. 'I'd like to know as you didn't write very often.'

'I haven't had the time,' Doris said dismissively. 'What more can I say other than he's kept very well and been a good boy.'

'Is that all?' Kay persisted.

Doris turned on her, the resentment clear in her face. 'What do you want me to say, Kay? That he's missed you – pined for you? That he's led a miserable life without you? Well, he hasn't. In fact, he's been very happy here at the cottage. He missed you at first, but then he began to enjoy himself in the freedom of the garden and with all his toys. At night we read to him and in the mornings he always enjoys time with Len before he goes to work. I've spent every day with him, every hour really. Watching him. Playing with him.' Doris looked into Kay's eyes and suddenly Kay saw all her own feelings reflected in them. It was then she guessed that Doris had begun to think of Alfie as her own son.

'I don't know how to thank you,' Kay murmured, feeling this was inadequate. 'And I understand it must be a wrench to see him go, but—'

'How can you think of taking him?' Doris interrupted.

Kay got up to comfort her but she pushed Kay aside. 'How can you be so selfish? The war is still on. What if the East End is caught up in another Blitz? What if something happens to Alfie?'

'It won't,' said Kay, sympathetic to Doris but also annoyed that her sister-in-law hadn't given her any credit for considering these issues. 'Doris, me and Alan intend to make sure he's safe. Believe me, being without him hasn't been easy and we waited a good two months after the Blitz ended before coming to this decision.'

'Well, it's the wrong decision,' burst out Doris, wiping her flushed cheeks with the palms of her hands. 'You're putting his life at risk when he can be perfectly happy and safe here.'

Kay nodded slowly but she decided it was time to voice her own strong feelings. 'As I've said, you and Len have been very kind and Alan and me are grateful for all you've done. But it's also clear you've grown fond of Alfie. Perhaps it's not before time that we're taking him home.'

'What a selfish way to think!' Doris jumped to her feet, her face flushed with anger.

'Nanty!' Alfie ran to Doris. She picked him up and hugged him, the tears wet on her cheeks.

Kay felt her heart twist as she saw Alfie's concern. She knew then that, despite all Doris's insistence about the East End being unsafe for Alfie to return to, this was not the true reason for her wanting to keep Alfie. Her motives were far more complex and Kay knew that there would be no easy way of resolving them.

Chapter Eight

Alan was trying to control his temper. The insults and accusations thrown at him – of being irresponsible and selfish added to the old chestnut that had stuck in Len's craw ever since Alan had had the gall to marry his sister: the insinuation that Alan had almost wrecked the ties that bound a close family – had come thick and fast.

'Agreed,' Alan apologized again, trying to resolve the situation. 'I should have sent you a telegram the minute I found out the dates of my days off and given you both time to adjust.'

'Adjust!' Len repeated with a gasp. 'Do you realize what you're doing? How in heaven's name can you be certain the docks won't be targeted again? And they will, you know. It's just a matter of time before Hitler finishes with Russia and sets his cap at us again.' He pointed a finger in Alan's face. 'It's irresponsible behaviour, that's what it is. And don't go spouting any of your daft political notions at me. I had enough of those when you married my sister.'

'Len, be reasonable,' Alan said, ignoring the insult and telling himself that Len's reaction to their sudden appearance was understandable. Nevertheless he didn't like the way Len kept throwing up their past differences. Differences that should be long forgotten by now. 'This isn't about my beliefs, or yours come to that. It's about Alfie coming back to his family.'

Len pulled down his jacket with a sharp tug and stuck out his chin. 'You have no idea about families or what makes them tick,' he accused rudely. 'Otherwise you wouldn't have upset ours like you did. Mum and Dad still haven't recovered from finding out that Kay, a respectable young widow right up until the time she met you, was in the family way. It caused them a great deal of embarrassment.'

Alan looked at his brother-in-law and guessed that he was never going to be best buddies with this man, or indeed with Lil and Bob Briggs. But in the scale of things, that wasn't what mattered to him. What was paramount was Kay and Alfie's happiness. 'Look Len,' he began carefully, 'I didn't intend to upset you or Kay's parents. I fell in love with your sister and yes, we did get a bit carried away before we were married—'

'Carried away?' Len repeated in a hoarse whisper. 'My sister's unfortunate predicament was the talk of the neighbourhood.'

Alan paused before he replied, attempting to keep the mounting anger from his tone. 'Len, you weren't even in the neighbourhood in thirty-eight. You'd moved to Hertfordshire by then.'

Len did another jerk with his jacket. 'I'm speaking on behalf of my parents,' he crowed pompously.

'They spoke well enough for themselves,' Alan responded quietly. 'Bob has never been one to reserve judgement in my case and Lil always made it plain that I'll never come up to the standard of their first son-in-law.' Alan took in a careful breath. 'They're entitled to their opinion, as are you, but I feel that to continue this conversation is just going round in circles. It was because me and Kay fell in love and wanted to make a future together that Alfie came about. Yes, the wedding was a bit late, but in the long run it didn't make no difference.'

'There wasn't even an invite to this so-called wedding!' Len persisted. 'We were all very upset.'

'I'm sorry about that, but marrying by licence was what Kay wanted. Her dad wouldn't give us his blessing, you know that.'

'He believed Kay was on the rebound,' Len argued. 'And so did I.'

'Norman had been gone well over three years when I met Kay,' answered Alan patiently. 'Enough time for a woman of twenty-four to know her own mind.'

'You don't understand how hard Norman's death hit her,' Len insisted. 'She gave in her perfectly good job with prospects and went to work in a factory. Well, I mean to say, what was that all about? And when Mum and Dad tried to get her to see sense, she'd just say something daft, like she wanted to make new friends.' Len gave a stifled cough. 'Now, if that's not being on the rebound I don't know what is.'

Alan just couldn't button his lip any longer. 'What was wrong in changing her job? It was Kay's way of making a fresh start. She was bored in the office and did something to change her life. There was no question of her being on the rebound. Now, can we stop bickering about the past and talk reasonably?'

For a moment Len looked as though he was about to round angrily on him, but then a cry from Alfie drifted down from upstairs. Alan glanced round and stood at the same time as Len, but before he did so he caught the look of genuine concern in his brother-in-law's eyes. That look hit home to Alan and he immediately forgot about their differences, feeling as bad for Doris and Len as he did for himself and Kay.

Alan stepped beside Len and lightly placed his hand on his arm. 'Look, Len, I really am sorry – for everything. I should have given more consideration to yours and Doris's feelings, but Kay's my priority and she just ain't herself without Alfie. Try to imagine how it's been for her. He wasn't even two when she had to part from him. Then night after night in the Blitz she was down the dug-out, never knowing what disaster she'd find in the morning, or even if she'd see me walking through the door again. Losing her friends and neighbours and having this big empty space inside her that no one, including me, could fill. Honest, Len, I'm not making excuses, but your sister's had a real rough time of it.'

To Alan's surprise, Len stared at him, his eyes very wide and his eyelids flickering lightly, as though for the first time he had cooled down enough to absorb what Alan was saying. Then, very slowly, he seemed to crumble, his stiff shoulders sagging as he slumped down into the armchair. Pushing his hand wearily over his forehead, he sighed, lifting his chest hard and high under his shirt, so that Alan had an even greater sense of compassion for the man.

'Doris and I knew Alfie would only be with us temporarily,' Len breathed in a raspy voice full of emotion. 'You just don't imagine it to be so painful when the time comes to . . .' He looked up at Alan. 'We got too fond of him, I suppose. Always being about the place. At nights up there in his cot, just like he was—' He stopped abruptly and Alan saw him blink fast, disguising the moisture in his eyes.

Alan moved to take the seat beside him, giving it a few moments before he spoke. 'Look, it's none of my business, Len, and I ain't especially good with words as you know. I seem to have hit all the wrong notes today and I don't intend to add fuel to the fire. But it's plain you and Doris make damn fine parents. I'm sure it'll happen one day – kiddies, I mean. But until then, would you consider, well, adopting?'

Alan feared he had gone too far as Len's face tightened and again his body tensed. But to Alan's surprise, he gave a sharp cough and cleared his throat, making an effort to speak.

'I'd consider it, yes,' Len muttered, his shoulders braced. 'But it's a big step to take. And Doris isn't – she's not—' Len looked down at the floor over his folded hands. 'I've tried to talk to Doris about it, but she's always held out hope for – for one of our own. You see it's like admitting defeat if you go along another path.' He glanced swiftly at Alan. 'Anyway, not the thing to discuss here – and yes, you made your point about Kay. We'll just have to get over this the best we can.' Len swiftly resumed his former detached self, patting his knees and standing up.

Just then there were noises on the stairs. Kay appeared, carrying a small case. Doris followed with Alfie in her arms and Alan and Len took a step towards them.

'I suppose we'd better be on our way,' Kay murmured, looking to Alan as though she'd had all the life drained out of her. 'Don't want to hold you both up . . .' Her voice tailed off into a whisper.

'We've nothing on as it happens,' Len answered stiffly. 'Let's all have something to eat, shall we? I'm sure we can rustle up some cold cuts and potatoes. None of us can do very well on empty stomachs, including the lad here.' He stood beside Doris and ruffled Alfie's hair.

'That'd be really welcome,' Alan agreed, glancing at Kay, relieved to see the light come back into her eyes. Curbing his desire to take both his wife and son in his arms and run with them while he had the chance, he looked at Doris and ventured, 'That is, if it's all right with you, Doris?'

Alan raised his eyebrows hopefully and Doris tucked in her chin and silently nodded. Alan was relieved when he saw her hand the child over to Kay and, with a glance at Len, make her way out to the kitchen.

Chapter Nine

'I never, ever want a day like this again,' Kay sighed as they sat on the coach returning to Poplar. She looked down at Alfie who had finally fallen asleep in her arms. Her fingers couldn't resist threading lightly through his hair. But even this action reminded her of Doris's affection and the heartbreak her sister-in-law must be experiencing. 'I felt as if I was stealing Alfie away from her.'

Alan put a comforting hand on her knee. 'Doris must have known he'd have to come back to us in the end. Strikes me, the situation could've been far worse if we'd left Alfie there any longer.'

Kay nodded her agreement. She had never wanted Alfie to go in the first place. But the Blitz had started and there seemed no other choice at the time.

'At least the jellies made a good impression.' Alan smiled. 'Although sweets are rationed we keep a few at the post for the kids. Didn't think a couple would be missed for Alfie.'

'My clever husband.' Kay had never been more relieved than when Alan took a small packet from his pocket after they had taken their seats on the coach. He had pretended to chew a jelly and made silly faces, as though his teeth were stuck together. Alfie had begun to laugh. And as he enjoyed the sweets himself, they were able to distract his attention from the miserable parting in Hertfordshire. 'If only Doris had replied to my first letter. If she'd said how she felt, we could have stayed in Little Gadelsby for a few days. At the pub perhaps. Or they could have come down to us and we'd have put them up. But we had no idea just how attached they'd become to Alfie, or he to them.'

'How could any of us have known that the Blitz would last eight months?' Alan questioned, shaking his head. 'None of us anticipated the length of the bombing. It's been rough on everyone.'

'Poor Doris,' Kay whispered again, bending to kiss the top of Alfie's head. 'It's clear she's desperate to have a baby.'

'Never say never, love,' Alan replied quietly. 'They're still young and active. As a matter of fact, I had a word with Len about that today. First time we've ever really talked man to man.'

'You did?' Kay asked in surprise.

Alan nodded. 'We were both getting pretty heated, so I just tried to make him aware of how you – we – felt without our boy with us. Not easy when me dander was up, I'll admit. However, the ice was broke a bit and I chanced asking if they'd considered adopting a kid. Len admitted they had, or at least, he had.'

'But Doris don't like the idea?'

'Still hoping for one of their own, I think.'

'And Alfie must have fitted the bill,' Kay murmured. 'Being her nephew, it was almost like her having her own boy.'

'That's about it, I should think.'

Kay looked down at Alfie's pale, sleeping face. 'Ah well, at least we managed to eat a meal with them before leaving, but if I'm honest I felt so uncomfortable, every mouthful tasted like rubber. And that's no slight on Doris. She fed us good wholesome food and eventually made a little conversation but I kept looking at her and seeing the sadness in her eyes.'

'Tell you what, when I get back to work, I'll telephone Len from the post. They've got a telephone at the cottage, and I've also got Len's works number. Took it when Alfie first went to stay with them – in case of emergencies. I'll ask him and Doris to come and visit as soon as possible.'

'Do you think they will?'

'Dunno. But I'll make the offer anyway.'

Kay had had this very same idea as she and Doris had sat upstairs in Alfie's bedroom. But bearing in mind Doris's affection for her nephew, Kay guessed it would be as difficult for Doris to visit Alfie and part from him again as it was for Kay on the day that Alfie had been taken away from her.

Late that evening, Vi opened the front door to welcome them. 'Oh, Alfie, just look at you, son. How you've grown!' she exclaimed. 'Give old Vi a kiss like you used to.' She bent forward but Alfie once again turned away, pressing his face into Alan's shoulder.

Alan raised his eyebrows as he stepped past the door. 'Don't take it personal, Vi. He's been away a long time and didn't recognize us, either.'

Vi flipped her hand. 'The poor lamb, course it'll take him a few days to get his bearings. Now come along and I'll make you all a bite to eat.'

'I ain't got much of an appetite,' Alan admitted as they trooped into the front room and sat down.

'Me neither,' agreed Kay with a tired smile. 'But a cuppa would be nice.'

'What about the boy? We can try him with a little broth I made specially this morning.'

But Alfie refused to eat and willingly curled up in his cot after Kay had given him a quick top and tail. Doris said he was dry at night and needed no nappy. Kay loved washing his smooth plump skin and talking to him as if he understood all she was saying. After wrapping his teddy in his blanket and placing it beside him, she kissed him goodnight, though his eyes were already closed and his thumb tucked in his mouth.

But during the night he woke with a cry and Alan sprang out of bed, leaving Kay to turn on the light and hurry round to the cot.

'What's the matter, old soldier?' Alan cradled Alfie in his arms.

'Want Nanty,' Alfie sniffed as he rubbed his red cheeks.

'Nanty is his name for Doris,' Kay said with a sinking heart as she stroked Alfie's damp hair.

'You've been on holiday with your Aunty Doris and Uncle Len in Hertfordshire,' Alan explained gently. 'And now you're back home in London with Mummy and Daddy. Tomorrow we're going to have a lot of fun together.'

But Alfie only asked for Doris again. Kay had to turn away to hide her disappointment. She was upset for her son, for Doris and Len, and for herself and Alan.

Alan pressed her shoulder. 'Come on, love, this is the worst part, getting him used to how things were. It won't be long before he starts remembering us. Go back to bed and I'll see he settles.'

Reluctantly Kay did as Alan suggested. In bed, she listened to her husband's soft voice as he paced the room with Alfie in his arms. 'We'll go down to the river tomorrow,' he whispered, rocking Alfie as if he was a baby again. 'It was your favourite place before you went to your aunt and uncle's. Remember?'

Kay finally drifted into sleep and with Alan's arms around her she managed to sleep lightly, putting the cares of the day behind her.

The following morning Alfie woke with very red and swollen cheeks. He had a runny nose and refused to eat his porridge. 'He's still not hungry,' Kay fretted as Alfie pursed his lips. 'He's missing Doris. He keeps asking for Nanty.'

'More like he's teething,' Vi decided. 'We should get him one of them teething dummies.'

'Doris told me she didn't approve of those.'

'Well, you're his mum, Kay, it's up to you to decide what's best.' Vi pointed to the enamel mug that had contained Alfie's orange juice. 'Just look how he's chewing on that rim.'

Kay nodded distractedly. 'He hasn't said Mummy or Daddy yet. But he's asked for Nanty a dozen times.'

'I'm sure he asked for you when he was with Doris.'

Kay remembered what Doris had told her. 'Doris said he forgot us in a very short time.'

'Well, she would say that, wouldn't she? Your sister-in-law wasn't going to let you off the hook for spoiling her day.'

Kay sighed and craned her neck to look through the kitchen window. 'What's Alan doing out there?'

'He's been clearing the rubble to make a space for Alfie to play in. Why don't you take the boy out there with him?'

'I hope there's no nails or sharp broken bits.'

Vi gave her a gentle push. 'This is the East End, Kay. Not Hertfordshire. The sooner the lad gets used to his home the better.'

But Kay refused to lower Alfie to the ground as she joined Alan. 'He's wearing his sandals,' she said, pushing a broken tile with the tip of her shoe. 'He might cut his toes.'

Alan swept it away quickly. 'Does he need that frilly thing on his head?' he asked as he stroked his forearm across his sweating forehead.

Kay had dressed Alfie as Doris had done, in his dungarees and blue floppy hat that Doris had packed in his case along with other clothes she had bought him. 'The hat stops him from being sunburned.'

'Not much chance of burning sun round here,' Alan answered shortly. 'Not until this evening when the sun comes round the back of the houses.'

Kay frowned at the long shadows cast from the lines of terraced houses, dock walls, factories and warehouses that were all huddled together on the island. It wasn't like Len and Doris's big green garden where the sun seemed to fill every space, even floating down between the branches of the apple tree and dappling the grass beneath.

'Come along, son. Down on your feet. Daddy will see you come to no harm.' Alan held out his hand. 'Let's have a bit of fun in the Anderson, shall we?'

'You can't take him in there,' Kay objected. 'It's cold and damp.'

'He spent the two first weeks of the Blitz in the dugout, before he was carted off to Hertfordshire,' Alan reminded her as she reluctantly lowered Alfie to the ground. 'This was his home, Kay. And besides, he might remember something.'

Kay felt very anxious. She didn't feel as confident with Alfie as Alan did. In fact Doris's voice still rang in her ears. Kay felt she might do something wrong at any moment. 'I hope he don't remember the noise of the bombs,' she mumbled as she watched Alan take Alfie's hand and lead him towards the shelter. 'He might be frightened again.'

But as soon as they had disappeared into the Anderson, Kay heard Alan's low laugh and when he called to her to follow them inside, Kay was surprised at what she saw.

'He remembers the bunk beds,' Alan told her.

Alfie was, for once, grinning. He sat on the top bunk, dribble running down his chin.

'I fixed the ladder up again,' said Alan, looking pleased with himself.

'Is it safe?' Kay asked worriedly.

'As houses,' Alan assured her, as he swung Alfie to the floor again. 'Anyway, it's just a bit of fun.'

Kay smiled, but soon she went outside. It was clear that she was out of practice at being a mother. She saw danger lurking everywhere. Alfie seemed so precious and so vulnerable now. Was it the bombing that had changed her?

'Did you have a good time, Alfie?' Kay asked when Alan and Alfie appeared some time later. She drew him into her arms and wiped his chin with her hanky. 'Shall we get your pram out from under the stairs. You used to love our walks to the park.' She looked up at Alan. 'He might remember the places we took him.'

'Good idea.'

That afternoon, Kay pushed the pram into the yard. 'Do you remember this, Alfie?' She was disappointed when he gave her one of his long, frowning looks.

Alan poked her in the ribs. 'Let's sit him in it.'

Kay watched Alfie wriggle reluctantly into what had once seemed a large space. 'He's outgrown it,' she complained.

'It'll do for now,' said Alan, looking a little alarmed himself as he pushed the big hood as far back as it would go.

Vi came out to see them off. 'Let the lad have a good look round his old haunts,' she called. 'He's bound to remember us taking him under the arches and the railway line. Then there's the park and the swings. He used to love the sand pit, don't forget.'

Kay hadn't forgotten anything. All her memories of Alfie were carefully preserved in her head; her own invisible scrapbook that she'd turned the pages of a dozen times a day in Alfie's absence.

They set off through the gate and into the Cut, following the lane into Crane Street. When they got to the park, Alan lifted him out of the pram and set him on his feet. For a while Alfie was happy to play in the small patch of sand and help Alan and Kay build castles. Then Alan pushed the pram all the way back to the top of East Ferry Road at a snail's pace as Alfie insisted on walking beside him.

'Do you want to sit on Daddy's shoulders?' Kay asked as she bent to brush a few grains of sand from his chin.

But Alfie just shook his head.

'It's easy to say "Mummy",' Kay said, undefeated, as Alan waited for them. 'Or "Daddy".' She mouthed the two words, hoping Alfie would copy her, but all to no avail as her son remained stubbornly silent.

By the time they arrived home, the smell of mutton-and-onion stew was wafting from the back door. 'Well?' asked Vi expectantly, wiping her hands on her apron.

Alan raised his hands in the air. 'Not a word out of him.'

Kay merely shook her head. It was as if the ten months of living in Hertfordshire with Doris and Len had wiped the island clear from his mind.

The day before Alan was to return to work, he and Alfie brought home a punctured football they found at the park. 'One of these days you'll be scolding your lad, telling him to mind the window and play in the street,' Vi chuckled as she and Kay prepared the dinner, every now and then glancing through the window to see how the game was going.

'No, I won't do that,' Kay insisted as she ran a cloth around a wet dish. 'Alfie can bring all his friends round to play. Although . . .' Kay paused, her thoughts racing back to the lovely garden in Little Gadelsby. 'Our yard isn't up to much at the moment. There's still bricks and timbers piled up over there by the gate. And the soot and dust – well, we ain't ever going to get rid of that. But eventually the war's got to end and we can live decently . . .' Once again her voice trailed off along with her thoughts.

'What's up, flower?' Vi asked, crooking an eyebrow. 'Not worried about the boy, are you?'

'No,' Kay shrugged. 'Well, not really.'

'He's doin' marvellous considering what he's been through.'

Kay felt reluctant to express her thoughts – *if* she could express them. Her conversation with Doris had been going round in her head. Some of the things her sister-in-law had said had made an impression. 'I was wrong about life in the country,' Kay admitted. 'It wasn't all muddy and rainy and cold like I remembered. When Len and Doris took Alfie I thought he'd be going to somewhere he'd dislike as much as I did. Mum used to pack me off with the Country Holiday Fund and I soon got homesick. But that didn't seem to happen to Alfie.'

'He was just a wee baby, Kay.'

'And I thought Doris would be house-proud. But she wasn't. The cottage was really lovely and cosy, not fussy.'

'Well, ain't that a good thing?' asked Vi, pausing as she washed a dish. 'It means your sister-in-law got her priorities right.'

'Yes, but have I?'

'Come again?' Vi frowned.

'It's just that – well, I've always thought that me and Alan had a nice home – and we have. Don't get me wrong. I'm not ungrateful – I love me life here on the island.' Kay gazed down at the cup she was drying, the one that replaced her nice tea set that had broken. The cup had a hairline fracture and the flowers had faded, a far cry from the delicate china Kay had seen arranged on

Doris's dresser. 'But Alfie had everything he wanted in those ten months: nice new clothes and quality shoes and a big and beautiful garden to play in . . .' Kay knew she was stumbling over her words. What did she mean? What was she trying to explain? 'You should have seen their garden, Vi. It was beautiful. Len had made Alfie a swing under the apple tree. There was a dog on wheels that Alfie sat on, with a rope tied to it, so Doris or Len could pull it over the grass.' She trapped her bottom lip with her teeth. 'Real green grass it was, all shiny and thick with flowers round it.' Pensively, Kay ran her finger round the rim of the cup. 'I saw how happy Alfie was. And I never expected that.'

'Your boy will be just as happy here once he's found his feet,' Vi answered, wringing out the wet cloth.

'He ain't happy at the moment.'

'Course he's happy.'

'Then why doesn't he say something?'

'He will. Be patient.' Vi pointed to the yard. 'He might not have a swing or a dog on wheels, but he's got the Anderson.'

'That's just it.' Kay stared resentfully at the shabby tin shelter. 'The Anderson is a reminder of the bombing. How the war took people's lives away. And there's our Alfie, thinking a bomb shelter is a toy . . .'

'He don't know the difference, love.'

'No, but I do.'

Vi leaned forward. 'It's been a difficult time for you, Kay. Don't go thinking too deep.'

'Doris spent every day with Alfie,' Kay continued relentlessly. 'But I have to leave him and go to work tomorrow.'

Vi lifted her shoulders. 'I'll take good care of him. You know that.'

'It's just that Doris and Len – well, they've got everything – *everything*! The war hasn't affected them. It's as if it's passed them by and they live in this enchanted world of their own. But me and Alan and you, we've lost our friends and neighbours and you've lost your house. There's nothing to eat and we're all beginning to look like Woolton Pies—'

'Listen,' Vi broke in sternly, taking the cloth from Kay's hands and folding it over the handle on the stove, 'what's happened is not the war, but you've seen how the other half live. War or no war, there are the haves and the have nots. Always has been, always will be. But remember, you might not have a cottage in the country but you've something far more precious in Alfie than money can buy. Your brother don't have no son and heir, does he? I'll bet he'd trade his nice house and lovely garden, if he and Doris could have a kiddie.'

Kay knew Vi was talking sense. But Kay still found it hard to square things up; yet again her emotions were all over the place. Alongside the feeling of relief at having Alfie home, she was tormented by these silly notions going around inside her head all day. Was she depriving Alfie of something he should have, simply because she and Alan had made their home on the island and wanted it to be their future? Before going to Hertfordshire she had been quite content to stay at the factory and knew that, if she was to speak to her employers, they would allow her to continue part-time to look after Alfie rather than lose her. Everyone wanted to do their best in wartime and she was no exception. She and Alan had planned their future on the Isle of Dogs, had loved it from the first moment they'd moved there in 1938. So why should she be feeling so unsettled after one short visit to her brother and sister-in-law's?

Kay was certain Vi was right in that Len and Doris wanted children desperately. They had a lovely home, a pretty garden and none of the worries that city dwelling presented, including that of having been the focus for Germany's Luftwaffe. But they sadly lacked a family.

'So, what's all this about?' she murmured to herself. 'Is the truth that you've saddled yourself with a touch of the old green eye, Kay Lewis?'

It was not a happy admission to make, she realized, as she set about peeling the spuds. But then, she was only human and at times, she reminded herself, a flawed one. A few minutes later she had the potatoes on the stove and was humming to herself, thinking of how Alfie's room would eventually look when she had everything in place.

Chapter Ten

On the last Sunday of August, while Alan and Vi were trying to persuade Alfie to eat his breakfast, Kay was upstairs attempting to restore order to their wardrobe. One half had been given over to Alfie's clothes and shoes and toys. Kay was busy trying to squeeze everything into a small space, when there was a knock on the front door. She hurried downstairs, expecting to see Jenny Edwards who sometimes called by on her way back from church.

'Babs! Eddie! What are you doing here?'

Eddie hugged her. 'It's good to see you, Kay.'

'Come in, come in.'

'We thought we'd announce our good news,' Babs said, stepping in. She opened her bag. 'Eddie collected this on Friday.'

Kay stared at the key in Babs's hand. 'What's that?'

'Can't you guess?' Babs breathed, her eyes bright with excitement. 'It's the key for next door, Stan and Elsie's place, soon to be ours.'

Kay clapped her hands to her mouth.

'Yes,' chuckled Eddie. 'We move in tomorrow.'

'I can't believe it.' Kay threw her arms around Babs. 'You're not kidding, are you?'

'Not about something like this,' Eddie confirmed, a big grin on his face.

'Do Gill and Tim know?'

'They're coming back from Essex next week.' Babs was hardly able to contain herself.

Just then Alan and Vi appeared with Alfie. Once the good news had been shared there were embraces and handshakes all round. Kay lifted Alfie, who was determinedly wearing his solemn expression, into her arms.

'Alfie, how you've grown!' exclaimed Babs. 'You were just a baby when we saw you last.'

'What's up, young feller, don't you remember me?' Eddie asked kindly.

'Oh, leave the boy alone,' said Babs, slapping Eddie's hand away. 'With your ugly mug peering down at him, Eddie, no wonder he's frightened.'

Everyone laughed, but Kay had to hide her disappointment. Alfie had known the couple well before going to Hertfordshire. Was he deliberately pretending not to recognize them?

'We're going to have a quick gander at our new house,' said Eddie proudly. 'Stan and Elsie said we're welcome to use the furniture they left. And the Sally Army has turned up a couple of beds for the kids.'

'We've a few bits you might like,' said Kay, thinking of the items that had come from the small room when Vi had moved in. 'Alan's put them under the bunks in the Anderson.'

'I've a Rosie on the brew,' Vi said. 'We'll bring a pot and some cups in, if you like, 'cos the gas most likely isn't on next door.'

'Ta, Vi.' Eddie glanced at Alan. 'You know, mate, if it wasn't for you pulling a few strings we might be hundreds of miles away by now.'

Alan smiled ruefully. 'You might wish I hadn't, Eddie, if this lull doesn't last.'

'We'll take our chances,' Eddie replied as the two men exchanged glances.

Kay watched her friends walk away, happy to know they would soon be neighbours again.

'Come on, Alfie,' said Vi, crooking her finger, 'let's finish yer breakfast, lad.'

'Alan, what did Eddie mean about you pulling a few strings?' Kay asked when they were alone.

'Oh, it wasn't nothing.'

'Eddie seemed to think it was.'

'I just added my guarantee to Eddie's application for the house. Said they wouldn't get a more reliable tenant than Eddie Chapman.' Alan gave a dismissive shrug. 'Sometimes it helps if you've someone in your corner.'

'I didn't know I had such an important husband,' Kay teased, though she was surprised that Alan hadn't told her about the good deed he'd done.

'It might all have come to nothing.' Alan caught hold of her hands. 'In a way I hoped it might, as it's a big decision for a bloke to make to set up home in docklands at a time like this. Len had a point about us taking a chance with Alfie. The docks are always vulnerable. It wouldn't do for any of us to ignore the truth.'

'I thought it was Russia that Hitler has targeted,' Kay complained with a frown.

'He has,' agreed Alan patiently, 'but the whole world is up in arms. I heard Churchill is sending some of our Hurricanes and Spitfires to defend Leningrad. The crack Russian pilots are going to give it all they have. But if Russia collapses then it's curtains for their allies. This conflict is balanced on a knife's edge. And Eddie and Babs moving in next door don't mean that life is all rosy again.' Then slowly a wry smile formed on his lips and he planted a kiss on her nose. 'Chin up, lovely. Don't let me spoil your day.'

Kay understood her husband's gentle rebuke and the gravity of what he was saying. But for her, having her old friends move in next door meant more to her than Alan could possibly imagine. She accepted the world was at war, but she preferred not to think of that just now. 'Did you phone Len?' she asked, changing the subject.

'I telephoned his works, but he was in a meeting. I left a message for him to return my call.'

As Alan took her in his strong arms, she felt the love spread through her. He was doing his best to make amends with her brother and she loved him for that. As Alan had pointed out, the Luftwaffe might very well return to pursue their nightly raids. But meanwhile Kay was determined she wasn't about to let the war win.

Not in her house, anyway.

The following Saturday afternoon Kay took Alfie round to visit Babs and the children.

'Say hello to Aunty Kay and Alfie.' Gently, Babs pushed her two children forward. 'Gill, Tim, have you lost your voices? You remember Aunty Kay, don't you?'

Kay smiled at the slender little eight-year-old girl with plaits hanging over her shoulders. Like her mother, she had fair hair and blue eyes and pale skin dotted with freckles. Tim, who was two years younger, was the mirror image of his father. He had light brown hair cut into a straight fringe across his forehead and, like his sister, a sprinkling of freckles across his nose.

'Hello, Aunty Kay.' Gill gave a shy smile, elbowing her brother.

'Hello,' said Tim, giving a rather sullen look.

'You two have really grown,' said Kay.

Babs grinned. 'Tim's still getting over the effects of evacuation. He hasn't forgiven us yet, for sending him away and bringing him back to a house that isn't home.'

'Never mind,' said Kay, 'you'll soon get used to living here, Tim.'

'All me mates are gone,' Tim frowned. 'And we ain't got Fluffy no more.'

'No one's allowed pets, love,' Babs told him gently. 'Everyone is in the same boat. At least we're back on the island. And that was what you wanted when you was in Essex.'

'I want me old house, not this one.'

Babs rolled her eyes. 'Goodness gracious, Tim. Cheer up!'

Kay studied the two children who she recalled as carefree, outgoing youngsters before the Blitz. Tim was a typical boy, always getting into scrapes. Gill was a caring older sister, constantly bossing him around. Before the war, the children had had the freedom to do what they liked in the streets; every family knew their neighbours and there was always someone to keep an eye on their antics. But the kids had smiles on their dirty faces and a look of mischief in their eyes.

It wasn't long before Kay and Babs were seated at the kitchen table, talking about old times. Tim sloped off into the yard and Gill soon followed her brother. Alfie stood at the door, watching them with interest.

'Who would have thought we'd still be living in this street, closer now than ever before?' Babs reflected.

'The Blitz might have taken away your house,' Kay said, 'but it also gave you another one – right next door.'

'And the kids have a bedroom each here,' Babs pointed out enthusiastically. 'Once I can persuade Eddie to do a little painting and brighten this place up . . .' She shrugged and rolled her eyes. 'But you know what Eddie's like indoors. A bit hopeless when it comes to repairs.'

'Alan will always help.'

'Can't go calling on Alan every five minutes, can we? No, Eddie's just going to have to get cracking with a paintbrush.'

'Have the children seen the old house?' Kay asked softly.

'You mean what's left of it,' sighed Babs. 'I took them down last night. They'd have to see it sooner or later. What use is there in trying to hide what is now a pile of rubbish? I told Tim, we ain't never going back to number twenty-seven and there's no use moping about it.' She lowered her head, speaking in whispered tones. 'We passed the Suttons' place too. Tim and Kevin always knocked around together. And Gill had a bit of a crush on Robert, who was a very good-looking teenager.'

'Oh dear,' Kay said heavily. 'How did they take it?'

'Tim cried in the night. I went in and he said he hated it here and wanted his old house back. He said he'd never forgive us for sending him away.' Babs sniffed. 'I told him we had no choice but to evacuate them and we were all lucky to have escaped the bomb. But Tim finds it hard to accept that. Almost that if we'd been here together as a family, the Germans wouldn't have done it.'

'Babs, he's only young. Give him a day or two to come round.'

Babs nodded. 'I'm hoping that once school starts they'll be happier in a routine.'

As Babs was talking, Kay saw Alfie step outside into the yard. With his thumb tucked in his mouth, he watched Gill drawing lines on the hard ground with a piece of chalk.

'He's a little darling,' said Babs, 'but I can see, like Gill and Tim, he's been through a rough time without you.'

Kay shook her head. 'Quite the opposite. Alfie loved Little Gadelsby and country life. He still misses Doris, my sister-in-law.' Kay felt the tears smart and guiltily blinked them back.

'It was a shock to Alfie when he was taken away from you,' reasoned Babs. 'I'll bet he was just the same when he first lived with Doris. Always asking for his mum.'

'That's what makes me feel guilty. I've put him through such a lot.'

Babs smiled. 'Well, you've got him back now, love.'

'He's not called me "Mummy" yet. Or said "Daddy". And God knows, we've tried hard enough to persuade him.'

'He will in good time, Kay. In under a year, he's been through major changes. Resisting you is like a protest. He's been parted from you, had to adjust to Doris, now he's back with the person he loves most in the world, his mum. Wouldn't you kick up a bit of stink if you was him?'

Kay thought about this. 'Put that way, yes,' she agreed.

'Same's happened to Gill and Tim, but they was old enough to understand they'd always got me and Eddie to come home to in the end.'

Kay nodded slowly, taking a hanky from her sleeve and quickly wiping away a stray tear. 'I know I'm being daft.' She looked up at her friend. 'I'm ashamed of meself. Especially for feeling jealous of Doris.'

'I'd be the same.'

'But Doris done her best for him. And he thought the world of her.'

Babs grinned wryly. 'Almost makes it worse, doesn't it?'

Kay smiled, feeling better now that she had shared her feelings with Babs. 'I've been thinking about phoning Doris. I'd like us to patch things up – properly like.'

'Have they got a telephone?'

'Yes, there's one in the cottage and there's a telephone box outside the factory that I could use.'

'Good idea.'

'Do you think so?'

'Why not? Doris might appreciate a chat.' Babs rolled her eyes towards the yard, her attention shifting elsewhere. 'What do you suppose those three are up to?'

Kay followed Babs's stare. The overgrown Anderson, which had never been used by the Tripps and had suffered the same assaults of debris and rubble as every other shelter during the Blitz, was now being unearthed by Tim. He kicked away the broken bricks and pulled up the clumps of long weeds, while Gill reached for Alfie's hand, both an attentive audience. It wasn't long before Tim had broken open the door and the three children disappeared inside. Soon all that could be heard was the echoing of laughter from the depths of the metal shelter.

'Now, remind me, what was it we were worried about?' Babs continued, her eyes wide.

'Search me!' Kay said, and it wasn't long before Kay and Babs were joining in the laughter too.

'Alfie was all smiles this evening,' whispered Alan late that night, as they undressed for bed. 'Sorry to pip you to the post, but he forgot himself and called me Daddy at long last.'

'Don't worry, I got a "Mummy" too.'

'Really?'

'It was in Babs's house, after playing with Gill and Tim all afternoon, enjoying himself in the shelter.'

Alan breathed a long sigh of relief. 'P'raps it was just other kids' company he needed.'

'I hope so.'

Kay went to the cot where her husband stood gazing down on their sleeping son. 'All me and Babs could hear was laughter. I dunno how many spiders Tim hooked out from the Anderson but the three of them never stopped laughing the whole time.'

'That's what I like to hear.'

'Oh, Alan, I'm so glad we're a family again and with our friends living right next door.'

Alan cupped her face between his hands. 'Now you'll have company if I'm not here.'

Kay took a breath. 'What do you mean?'

'If I'm called-up, you'll have friends close by.'

'But you're needed here on the home front!'

'All British men between eighteen and fifty are now wanted for war service unless in a reserved job. And though I was exempt during the Blitz, rescues ain't an everyday occurrence now. The situation is changing fast.'

Kay breathed out a long sigh. It was no use arguing the point with Alan. They both knew that if his papers arrived he would have to do as he was told.

'Chin, up, love, it's not happened yet.'

'Please God, it never will.'

'Come on, let's get into bed.' He ran his hands over her shoulders. 'You're too beautiful to stand out here in the cold.'

'I'm not cold. Not with you beside me.'

A few moments later they were in each other's arms and whispering words of love, their bodies entwined. Kay always felt safe when Alan was beside her and didn't want to think of the future without him. Perhaps if she didn't worry about it, the worst wouldn't happen.

'You're not concentrating,' Alan chuckled, and brought her against him so passionately she almost let out a cry. 'That's better,' he murmured as he loosened the straps of her petticoat and tugged it roughly down from her breasts. 'Don't think of anything else except us,' he told her with kisses that burned her skin and aroused her so instantly that all worried thoughts flew away – far away – as his fingers found the special places on her body and left her breathless.

As much as Kay tried not to cry out, and at the risk of disturbing Alfie, she gave up on her fight, listening to her own wild moans with a mixture of surprise and delight until at last they both took equal pleasure in the same, rich and satisfying moments.

Later, much later, Kay found herself listening to Alan's soft breathing as he fell asleep. Her own last dreamy thoughts, a blessed result of the passion they had just spent, eased her earlier worries. Now her mind was filled with more positive things. Within the next few days she was going to muster enough courage to ring Doris. The worst that could happen was that Doris gave her short shrift. The best was that they might actually talk reasonably together again.

As her eyes began to close she wondered if Vi would agree to moving downstairs. Then Alfie could have the small room. He was growing quickly now and needed his own space. Kay blushed as she remembered the noises she had made during their lovemaking. It was a wonder they hadn't woken him! Or, come to that, poor Vi!

Chapter Eleven

Kay had arrived at work before eight o'clock that morning in order to ask her supervisor for permission to leave her shift early. Mr Marsh had been very good to her since Alfie had come home. Kay was grateful to him for agreeing to allow her to shorten or change her shifts to fit in with her new responsibilities, namely a young child to care for. Now, as Kay stood at the assembly line with the noise of the grinding, clanking and hissing machines around her making it almost impossible to converse, she was thinking about what she would say to Doris, when a tap came on her shoulder.

'It's our break soon,' Iris Fellows shouted, removing the goggles from her forehead. Kay did the same, slipping the clumsy protective gear onto her forehead, squinting at her colleague through the dust that was kicked up from the forging bench and the woman working there, dressed as she was in overalls, steel toe-capped boots and heavy duty gloves. Sizing the metal of the empty bomb cases with a blowtorch was a filthy and smelly job.

Kay nodded her agreement and, with practised dexterity, made a minor adjustment to the shell case in front of her on the bench. She was glad to be positioned here today – she had time to think. The work was not as demanding as the next stage of forming the shell. The machine she operated was easy to use, a noisy but efficient smoother to the rough metal. Then she would place the article back on the conveyor belt for the last stages of hand polishing and coating; it was a task that she performed almost automatically now.

Kay glanced across to the older man on the other side of the busy factory who would replace her for ten minutes while she sat outside in the fresh air with Iris. When she caught his eye and gave him the thumbs up, he nodded and finished screwing the end of the shell he was working on, ready to be loaded into their metal containers.

Two minutes later, after the break bell had rung, Kay was gasping in the air she so desperately craved and the noise of the docks outside was heaven in comparison to the ear-deafening chorus of the armaments factory. Plonking herself down on the wall beside Iris, who was already pouring their tea from a thermos, she lifted her face to the sunshine.

Inside her overalls Kay was sweating profusely, and her feet stuck to the inside of her heavy boots. If someone had told her, before starting at Drovers, that she would actually be enjoying this kind of work, she would have laughed in their face. But somehow it was fulfilling. The factory which had once been an engineering business now had a more important purpose; the production of ammunition for Britain was imperative and everyone under Drovers' roof put their backs into it.

'Here you are, gel, get that down you,' Iris chuckled as she passed a battered enamel mug full of steaming tea to Kay.

'Thanks, Iris, my mouth is as dry as a bone.' Kay took a tentative sip. The hot liquid was refreshing as it tingled on her tongue. She lifted her fingers to wipe the moisture from her lips, forgetting how dirty they would be.

'You should see your face,' said Iris with a laugh. At forty-five, Iris was a fiery redhead with sandy eyebrows and twinkling brown eyes. Kay laughed too. For Iris's face was also marked by the goggles, streaked with dirt and dust and, like Kay's dark hair, Iris's mop of waves was hidden by a camouflage green turban.

'You should see yours,' giggled Kay. 'I wouldn't like to bump into you on a dark night, come to that, in the day either.'

'Cheeky mare!' Iris threw back her tea and licked her lips, driving the dirt around her mouth into little clumps. They both laughed again and Kay took another gulp of the weak but welcome tea.

'Have you heard from the council yet? Do you know where you're going?' Kay asked, knowing her unmarried friend who supported her elderly parents had put in for evacuation. Iris had told Kay she'd had enough of the bombing and the munitions work. She couldn't wait to move to the seaside.

'Yes, we got a letter yesterday. Said they have possible billets in Oxfordshire and Somerset. I went down to the council immediately and said we wanted Somerset as it's by the sea. Well, some of it is, I think.' Iris grinned. 'I can get meself a bathing suit at last. I even threatened me old mum with taking her to the beach and making her swim.' Iris laughed loudly. 'But course, you can't get on a bloody beach these days for the barbed wire dumped over it.'

'You just wanted to scare your poor old mum,' Kay said disapprovingly but with a smile. 'Little things please little minds, so they say.'

'You've got to have a laugh somehow,' agreed Iris, a woman who Kay liked a lot and would miss when she went. Iris was the only worker at Drovers she'd really connected with since she started work there after Alfie was evacuated. Most of the other women were younger than Kay, all single and fancy free. But Iris was the bread-winner in her family and a home bird. 'What about you, love?' asked Iris suddenly. 'You gonna stay here on the island? Wasn't you tempted to move when you went to your brother's in the nice, peaceful country a while ago?'

Kay sipped the last of her tea and thought again about Doris and Len's cottage. She couldn't deny she'd been impressed, and she'd found herself unsettled afterwards. But in all honesty, now Babs was close, she had no hankering to move. 'Not likely,' Kay said. 'The island is home to us, come hell or high water.'

'I hope we ain't facing either of those,' answered Iris dryly. 'We had enough hell in the Blitz and the last thing the island can do with is a flood! Now, I suppose we'd better get back or old Marshy will have our guts for garters.'

'He's been very good to me,' Kay said as they stood up and shook their baggy overalls free of the grime. 'He let me cut down my hours and change them around – providing I could find someone else to step in for me. Like you!' Kay glanced at her friend gratefully.

'Don't mention it, cocker. With our move coming up I need the overtime.' Iris grinned showing a front row of teeth that were minus two. Kay always thought the gaps added to her colourful character.

Ten minutes later they were hard at work again. But Kay's mind was busy turning over behind her goggles as she worked with the heavy metal casings of the bombs. Talking to Doris on the telephone was not going to be easy. Doris might even not answer. She could have friends with her, which would make it hard for her to speak. But Kay was undaunted. She needed to resolve what had happened between them.

Kay stood in the public telephone box close to the factory, her freshly scrubbed fingers shaking slightly as she slipped the pennies into the metal box. She wasn't certain if it was the rushed wash and brush-up and change into her outdoor clothing before leaving the factory that had made her anxious or simply making the decision to phone Doris. It was early afternoon and Doris might be in the garden or out. Her brother would be at work, no doubt. The cottage might be entirely empty . . .

Kay had almost convinced herself this was the case when a voice spoke. Kay pressed button A in front of her. As she rarely used a public telephone, she held the handset tightly against her ear, afraid she might miss something. But when the button had been depressed, a voice came clearly down the line.

'It's me, Doris – it's Kay.'

There was a pause before the reply came. Doris's first sharp words were, 'Is everything all right?'

'Yes, it is, Doris. But I wanted to speak to you.'

'It's not Alfie, is it?' Doris's voice held a tone that said how much she must still care about Alfie.

'He's fine, Doris – but – well, he's missed you. And I – I wanted you to know that. He asked for Nanty quite a bit at first.'

Again there was a pause. Doris's voice was softer this time. 'Did he? Well, I missed him, Kay.'

'That's why I'm phoning, Doris. Alan's tried to get hold of Len but hasn't managed it. So I thought I'd just say . . .' Suddenly there was the annoying sound of the clicking pips, meaning that Kay's time was running out. Luckily she had brought along a handful of pennies and hurriedly pushed them in the slot.

'Have you got enough money, Kay?' Doris seemed concerned.

'Yes, enough for me to say what I need to. It's been on my mind, the way we parted. We didn't give you enough time to adjust – you were quite right. It was a rotten thing to do and bothered me and Alan a lot.'

A little sound came from the telephone and Kay thought it might just be a smothered sob. But soon Doris was speaking again. 'It wasn't just you and Alan, Kay. It was us, as well. We got too fond of Alfie. He's such a lovely little boy. You must be very proud of him.'

'Doris, you did so much for him. He still wears the clothes and shoes you bought.'

'I'm glad it's . . .' Doris paused. 'I'm relieved too that we're speaking, Kay. There's something I must tell you. Len and me have talked about adopting a child. I wasn't for it until we had Alfie, but now I've had that experience—'

Again the pipping sound went in her ear and Kay thrust the last of her pennies into the metal slot. 'Doris?'

'I'm here.'

'That's wonderful news!' Kay exclaimed.

'As I said, at the moment Len and me are just talking it over. We've made no final decision.'

'Doris, me and Alan would love you to come and see us.'

'I'm not ready for that,' Doris said after a short pause. 'Perhaps one day in the future, when . . . when our plans are firmer, and seeing Alfie again won't be so . . . so much of a wrench to the system.'

Kay swallowed hard. 'Yes, I do understand. Doris, thank you again for looking after our boy and I do hope one day Alfie will have a cousin.'

'Your money will run out soon.'

'I'll write,' promised Kay.

'Don't hold out hope for a letter back,' said Doris lightly. 'You know what I'm like.'

They both laughed and the pips began to sound. Abruptly they were cut off and Kay stood with the phone in her hand. Replacing it carefully, she expelled a long breath. She had finally spoken to Doris and they had parted in a friendly fashion.

Kay felt lighter as she walked home. The rift had been partly mended – perhaps not entirely. But then, after all this time she felt that she'd come to know Doris a lot better and at least Alfie's stay in Little Gadelsby had achieved something wonderful. She couldn't wait to tell Alan the news.

That night, when Alfie had gone to bed, Kay told Alan and Vi all that had transpired during the telephone call.

'I'm glad things are patched up,' Alan said quietly as the three of them sat in the front room enjoying a cup of cocoa.

'Perhaps not completely,' Kay replied, 'but it's a step in the right direction.'

'When this war is over, we should try to see more of them,' said Alan.

'The best news of all was that Doris said she and Len are talking about adopting,' said Kay eagerly.

'Do you think Doris is ready for it?' asked Alan.

'She said it was having Alfie that made the difference.'

'Adopting ain't easy,' Vi put in, pulling her cardigan around her shoulders. 'At least, before the war it wasn't. I knew a woman once in Poplar who waited five years for the little girl she wanted.'

'I'm sure it will be different now. The war has changed a lot of things,' remarked Alan. 'More orphans now than there's ever been.'

'Yes,' agreed Vi, 'but most people want babies, not kids that have had rotten lives and are unruly when they get them.'

Kay smiled. 'I'm sure Doris and Len wouldn't mind what child they had. She did mention babies of course, but if there was a child like Alfie—' Kay stopped, glancing at her husband. 'I just mean, a little boy perhaps, about the same age.'

Alan smiled at her. 'Our Alfie is one in a million.'

'I know.'

Later that night when Kay was snuggled up to Alan in bed, she thought about their earlier conversation. What if she couldn't have another baby and Alfie was their only child – would she consider adopting another little boy or girl? The thought had never crossed her mind before. Her first reaction was to think that relating intimately to someone else's child would be very difficult, perhaps impossible. Love wasn't manufactured. It came up from inside you without being bidden. The love she and Alan had for Alfie was immense – unending. It was difficult to imagine giving that same degree of affection to any other child.

Kay sighed lightly as she drifted into sleep. She admired Doris and Len very much. Although adopting wasn't for someone like herself, she was certain that it was the perfect solution for her brother and sister-in-law.

It was a mild September morning when Kay and Babs made their way to the temporary primary school in Quarry Street. Kay watched Alfie walking proudly in his new shoes as he tried to keep up with Gill and Tim who were wearing their navy-blue school raincoats and satchels.

'Thanks, love, for walking with us this morning,' Babs said to Kay as the children ran ahead. 'It's nice to have company on the kids' first day at school.'

'Alfie was up at the crack of dawn,' Kay said with a smile. 'He don't much care for the coat I've dressed him in – the one that Doris gave him. But as it fits nicely now, I persuaded him to wear it and told him this was from his Aunty Nanty.'

'Does he remember her?'

'Yes, I think so. He smiled when I said her name.'

'I'm glad you feel better now you've phoned her.'

'Yes, I do.' Kay chuckled. 'Just look at Alfie, trying to keep in step with Tim! He don't know what school is, but remembered that Gill and Tim told him they were going. I only hope he don't kick up a stink when he has to come home again.'

Babs laughed too. 'To be honest, I'm a bit nervous for the kids. Eddie and me spoke to the teachers last week.

We were told the school is going to practise air-raid precautions and the use of the children's gas masks before settling down to lessons. I hope it don't upset them.'

'I think it's a sensible idea.'

'Eddie don't! He thinks it's a waste of time. Gas attacks never happened in thirty-nine and he don't think they ever will. Still, the teachers, who are mostly retired and have been called in to staff the temporary schools, are very nice. Mr Barnet, the head teacher, told us that when the warning goes, not to rush up to the school to get the kids. Instead, they've prepared the underground cellar as a shelter. There's so many false alarms these days we'd be up and down like yo-yos. Still, everyone remembers what happened to Cubitt Town School in September 1940.'

Kay recalled the day vividly. She had passed the pile of still-steaming masonry, iron girders and wooden timbers melted together in the dust after the school had been bombed. Cubitt Town School had been used as an ARP station in 1940. The night it was hit there were a good many volunteers having a rest before being called out again. 'Thank goodness the children had been evacuated,' said Kay, 'but it was a tragedy nonetheless.'

Just then Tim, who was walking just in front, turned round. 'The Germans ain't gonna bomb our new school, are they?' he asked.

'Course not,' replied Babs quickly. 'And you shouldn't be earwigging grown-ups' conversations.'

'Wasn't.'

'Mr Barnet is taking air-raid drill with you this morning,' said Babs, pushing him on. 'He'll tell you everything you need to know.'

'Is 'e gonna give us guns?'

Babs reached forward and tugged Tim's ear. 'You cheeky little devil!'

Laughing, Tim ran off to join Gill and Alfie.

'Ignorance is bliss where kids are concerned,' said Babs pensively as they followed. 'As for us adults – well, we've seen and heard too much to have any peace of mind.'

'Not having doubts about staying on the island, are you, Babs?'

'No. Course not.'

Kay glanced at her friend. Babs had been through so much; it was only natural for her to be anxious even though she put on a brave face.

When they arrived at the old cinema, the set of imposing art deco front doors that had once welcomed an audience were now thrown open to schoolchildren and their parents.

'There ain't much of a playground,' complained Tim, wrinkling his nose at the few yards of concrete in front of the cinema. Workmen had long ago removed the metal railings and it looked very bare.

'No, but there's a big hall inside where they used to show all the films,' Babs told him.

'Can we watch 'em?'

'If you're a good boy, perhaps you can,' Babs said. 'Now say goodbye to Aunty Kay and Alfie. We've got to go in and find out what classrooms you've got. Bye, Kay, see you later.'

'Bye Babs, bye kids.'

'Is Tim goin' to school?' Alfie asked when they'd gone.

'Yes, love. But he'll be home later.'

Alfie watched until the school doors closed. Kay bent down and looked into his sad face. 'You can go too when you're four and a bit.'

Alfie frowned. 'I'm f'ree.'

'Three in November, yes.' She took his hand. 'Shall we go to the market?'

Alfie smiled and nodded. Kay knew the market was fast becoming his favourite place; although there were no longer any toffee apples to purchase at Lenny's tea-stall, there were always a few sweets.

The costermongers shouted the loudest as they arranged their vegetables carefully to attract the customers' attention. As always, the second-hand clothes stall was surrounded by women, pulling hems and tugging collars; there were still plenty of bargains to be found requiring no coupons that were issued by the government in wartime when clothing was scarce.

Kay was tempted to join the throng; Alfie needed new dungarees. His old ones were almost worn out and too short in the legs. He'd grown a lot since coming back from Doris's. All the clothes she'd bought him were too small now. The brown coat with its chocolate-coloured corduroy collar that Alfie was still wearing might with luck see the winter out. But Alfie pulled her over to Lenny's tea-stall.

'Sorry, folks, we've run out of sweets,' said Lenny when he recognized them. 'Tell you what though, what about these?'

Lenny searched in his apron pocket. 'Me missis makes 'em,' he said, handing something that looked like fudge to Kay. He lowered his voice. 'Don't let on to the kiddy but they're made of veg. Here you are, take these. The nipper can have 'em for free.'

'Are you sure?' Kay took the small packet.

'I got plenty back here.'

Kay gave the fudge to Alfie. It was gone in a flash.

'You wanna try making 'em,' Lenny said. 'The trouble and strife mixes carrot and sugar, and sometimes apple with a bit of cereal to—'

Kay was almost knocked over as a woman pushed by.

'Watch where yer goin', love,' called Lenny. 'Yer nearly knocked this lass flyin'.'

Kay looked round, expecting an apology. But the woman had disappeared into the crowd. There was only a man standing by the lamppost, a newspaper tucked under his arm.

'Some people ain't got no manners,' grumbled Lenny and gave Kay a wink as he turned to serve another customer.

Kay looked round again. Something had come into her mind. Was the man with the newspaper the same man that she had seen outside the Pig and Whistle with Alan? It looked like him – she hadn't really seen his face, but his height and dress were the same. But if that was really the case and this was the man from the pub, a person who knew Alan, it might mean he was watching her. But what were his motives? A cold shudder went over her. Kay couldn't believe it was true. It just wasn't possible!

When Kay and Alfie arrived home, Vi was dusting the sideboard. 'Did you see your mates off to school?' she asked Alfie, pushing the duster into her pocket.

Alfie gave a big yawn.

'Time for your nap,' guessed Vi, holding out her hand. 'Would you like to sleep up on Vi-Vi's bed?'

Alfie nodded and Kay watched them walk, hand in hand, up the stairs. Lately Alfie had taken to sleeping in the day on Vi's bed. It was clear to one and all that he had finally outgrown his cot.

Kay strolled to the open back door, her mind still on the stranger. Perhaps her nerves were on edge and she really had imagined it all. A smile crossed her lips as she saw that Vi had propped the door in position with the mop and pail. A soft September breeze trickled in. The smell of coal fires was everywhere. People were getting ready for cold weather. The last two winters of war had been very cold. Kay shivered at the thought of more icy nights spent in the Anderson. Nights like those she had shared with Vi as the bombs dropped close and they'd never known if they would see morning again. They had been through a lot together.

'He was out like a light,' Vi told Kay as she returned to the kitchen. 'Kay, he needs a bed now.'

'Yes, I know.'

Vi folded her arms decisively. 'I've decided to find meself another gaff.'

Kay gasped. 'You can't leave!'

'Why not? It's about time I did.'

'You're part of the family.'

'Bless yer for saying so. But the lad comes first. I'll try to find a room within walking distance of Slater Street. Then I'll still be able to look after the nipper.' Vi looked away, her eyes misty. 'I went over to me old house this morning. I had this silly idea in me brain that one day . . . that there might be a chance that . . .' Vi shook her head as if in answer to herself. 'Not with the best will in the world could anyone put it back into shape again. They'll bulldoze the lot. Probably build flats on it when the war's over.'

Kay hadn't realized that Vi had still held fast to the hope that she might move back to her old house again. It was a hope that must have kept her going since the night it was bombed. Kay knew her friend was just beginning to accept reality and it was a real shock. 'Let's sit in the yard and have a chat,' Kay suggested softly.

Kay put on the kettle. She gazed through the kitchen window to where Vi was making herself comfortable on the wall. A few bricks were missing and Alan hadn't replaced them. The space was just enough to seat two bottoms. As the whistle blew on the kettle, Kay decided this was the moment to convince Vi of her latest plan.

'There's not much colour in the tea,' Kay apologized as she joined Vi.

'It's wet and warm, love. Ta. Now what is it you want to talk about? I ain't gonna change me mind, no matter what you say. It's time for me to move on.'

Kay paused before she spoke. She wanted to get this just right. 'What would you say to moving downstairs, Vi?'

'What?'

'Your put-u-up will store behind the couch in the day. Alan will bring down the wardrobe. It'll go nicely by the window. And with a bit of manoeuvring, we can squeeze in a chest of drawers.'

After a few seconds, Vi made a face. 'Does Alan know about this?'

'Yes, course.'

'Kay, ducks, it's acceptable for families to make do and mend,' Vi argued. 'But I ain't family.'

'You're as good as.'

'No,' said Vi emphatically. 'I'll only be in the way.'

Arriving at this stalemate, the conversation lapsed. Around them the noises from the busy river filled the air: the hoots and toots and clanking from the cranes, the screech of the gulls and the strong scents that blew in with the breeze.

Kay thought of her first husband, Norman. What path would her life have taken if Norman hadn't gone to work that day and been knocked down by a bus? Would she still be here, sitting on a wall in the September sunshine with her friends and neighbours close by, and Vi who was now part of her family.

'Vi, please say you'll stay.'

'Well, if you twist me arm,' agreed Vi with a chuckle.

Kay clapped her hands. 'Let's go inside and plan it all out.' She jumped to her feet, worried her friend might change her mind.

But Vi grabbed her wrist. 'Give me a minute, love, there was something I had to ask you and it skipped me mind till now.'

'What's that?'

'A bloke called round this morning. Bit shifty he looked, said he was a scrap dealer and on his way through the Cut, clocked Alan's bits and pieces piled by the wall. He wanted to know if he could have them. I told him to buzz off; we don't want no hawkers or pedlars round here.'

Kay sat down on the wall again, immediately alarmed. 'What was he wearing?'

'Rough sort, he was.'

'Oh. That doesn't sound like him.'

'Who?'

'Do you remember the day of the Suttons' funeral? Well, the missing relative of the Suttons' turned up after the service. He told Alan he was Madge's brother. As he seemed upset, Alan took him to the Pig and Whistle and bought him a drink. I caught sight of them both from the bus. Alan, that is, and the man.'

'What did he want?'

'Alan said he was on the scrounge and only after any money that Madge might have left.'

'The cheapskate!' Vi exclaimed. 'He didn't even turn up for the funeral.'

'Today, I thought I saw him at the market.'

'What makes you think that?'

'He was staring at us.' Kay paused, frowning. 'And he was holding a newspaper. Like the man at the pub.'

'Lots of blokes have newspapers,' Vi said dismissively. 'Anyway, I'm certain Alan would have sent him off with a flea in his ear.'

Kay smiled. 'Yes, Alan did.'

'Forget him, love,' Vi reasoned sensibly. 'Reckon we're all a bit jittery these days what with the government telling us to watch out for spies and the like.'

Kay smiled. Vi was right. As Alan would warn her, her imagination was working overtime!

Chapter Twelve

Two weeks later on a cold October evening, Kay was hurrying home from the factory, her thoughts on the strange man who had appeared so mysteriously in her life. She kept on thinking about him, who he was, who he could be. And she was so occupied with her thoughts that when a tall figure stepped into her path, she almost let out a scream.

'Alan!' she gasped. 'You gave me a fright!'

'Sorry, love.'

'What are you doing here? You're supposed to be at work.'

He nodded, sliding an arm around her waist. 'I left early. Thought we might walk down to the river.'

'Is something wrong?' she asked as they began walking together, trying to compose herself again.

'Nothing unexpected.'

'Are Alfie and Vi all right?'

'Yes, course,' he said with a shrug. 'Come on, let's enjoy a stroll.'

Kay guessed something upsetting must have happened at work. This morning it had been a happy and cheerful

Alan who had kissed her goodbye. But tonight he seemed very preoccupied.

After a brisk walk they reached Island Gardens. The entrance to the foot tunnel leading under the river to Greenwich was busy with people making their way home to the south bank. Alan led her to the fence that divided the gardens from the river; this was their special place where it had been their practice to share their troubles or talk about something exciting. It was on this spot that she had told Alan she was expecting Alfie. And where, a few days later, Alan had asked her to marry him. This was where they brought Alfie, to the sparkling river and historic sights on the southern bank beyond. If the day was fine, it was possible to see the Old Royal Observatory peeping from Greenwich Park, dwarfed by the huge barrage balloons floating above, and the famous Naval College, framed by its green blush of trees. As twilight approached, the white glint of the Queen's House slowly faded as did the stirring sight of the tall, workhorse chimneys of London's great power station.

'No other way to break the news, Kay, but I've had my call-up.'

'Oh, Alan, no!' she gasped, 'not already.' Tears sprang to her eyes and he pulled her close.

'I'm so sorry, love.'

They sat on the bench in the dusk, both shivering with the cold. Like her, he wore his winter coat, but tonight the cold seemed to be inside them.

'In a way, it's a relief,' he said. 'I can make plans for the future now.'

'What do you mean?'

'If the raids start again, I want you to go to your brother's.'

'Oh, Alan, how could I, without you?'

'It wouldn't be for ever. And we do have Alfie to consider.'

Kay knew he was right but she sunk her head dispiritedly. 'I'd give it some thought,' she murmured, 'but only if it was really necessary.'

'That's my girl. I know you'll do what's best when the time comes.'

Kay folded her fingers tightly over his. 'When do you leave?'

'The day after tomorrow.'

Kay gave another gasp. 'So soon?'

'The army are sending me on recruitment training. Somewhere in Barnet.'

'Barnet?'

'It's not that far as the crow flies.'

'Write immediately, won't you?'

'Yes, but I don't suppose I'll be able to say much. Not with the censors reading our letters.'

'I don't care about the censors. I care about you.'

He lifted her chin. 'Service pay isn't very good. So I'll leave twenty pounds to pay the bills.'

'Alan, where did you get twenty pounds from?'

'I put the money by for a rainy day.'

Kay stared into her husband's dark gaze and felt, for the first time, a little lost. 'How did you manage that?' she asked. 'There's things I'm finding out about you, Alan Lewis, that still surprise me. I'm beginning to wonder who I'm married to.'

'It's me, the man who adores you,' he assured her, placing her hand on his heart. 'This is what matters, the love I have inside for you. A love that will never die.' He gazed at her intently, squeezing her fingers tightly as he bent to kiss her, stroking the side of her face and murmuring words of love against her ear. When they caught their breath, she buried her face in his shoulder, inhaling the chill of winter on his coat, an unwanted reminder of the long, lonely days and nights that would lie ahead.

'Dear Doris and Len,' Alan began to write as he sat at the kitchen table in the early hours of the next morning. He was no letter writer and had always struggled with the reports he had to make at the post. But he had a plan in mind now and was determined to set out his thoughts as plainly as he could make them.

Alan stared at the slightly crumpled sheets of lined paper in front of him. He'd stuffed the papers into his breast pocket together with a couple of envelopes when he'd borrowed them from the post supplies. At the interview with the SOE coordinator this morning, he had been given proof that Kay and Alfie would be taken care of in the event of his death.

Then, when he'd arrived home, he'd found a minute to talk to Vi alone. She promised to keep safe the things he'd given her. Vi was a trooper. She'd asked no questions and for this he would be eternally grateful. Tomorrow, he'd pack. Before leaving early the following morning, he intended to make the most of his time with his family. He wanted his boy to remember him. And God alone knew there had been little enough time already.

Now, it was up to him to put things one hundred per cent right with Len. His brother-in-law was an honourable man and loved his sister. But it would be tough for Kay, even if she was well provided for. She would need her family's support. He had to get Len on side, should the unthinkable happen.

Alan got up and stood in the passage. There were no sounds from the house; all was quiet. After satisfying himself both Kay and Vi were asleep he returned to the kitchen table and sat down to write. But the pen wasn't easy to control; his fingers were as nervous as his thoughts. He was wondering how many other men wrote letters of this calibre. But, as he knew that the odds were against him – were against any conscripted man who was involved with special army operations – he had very little alternative. Added to his unease was his fear of perishing without being able to tell Kay the whole truth – his truth – and not the way others saw it.

He started again.

If you're reading this, Len and Doris, chances are we won't be meeting again. I should like you and Doris to know how grateful I am for what you did for Alfie in the evacuation. It was my mistake that I decided to bring Alfie back to the East End. You were right, Len, and I was wrong. Hitler is not finished with us by any means. In my permanent absence I should like you to help Kay take care of our boy. There are funds put aside for him that will go to Kay in the event of my death. But I should appreciate you giving her all the help you can. She will need your strength and guidance. Lil and Bob's too. I'm hoping you'll find it in your heart to continue to give Alfie all the consideration and love that you and Doris have shown him in the past —

Alan took the second paper, stared at its emptiness and knew he could never write all the things he wanted to say to his wife. Things she would discover. Be told. What was he to say to her, in words that wouldn't seem shallow, empty and false? Should circumstances reveal him to be not the person she knew and trusted, he wanted her to know that his love was genuine and would last for all time.

My darling Kay and Alfie, after all that has happened, I can't expect you to understand or forgive. But you must trust that our marriage is real and perfect. I could not have wished for a better second chance. It was you and Alfie that gave me an honest life. Before that, there was nothing! Nothing that ever needed to be told. But I suspect, if you are reading this, some of it already has. There may be many things said against me, but please trust me, although it might appear I have lived two lives, the day I met you was the day I felt reborn. Our life together is the one and only true record of the man who will love you for all eternity. So chin up, lovely, and God bless you both.

It was several hours later that Alan slipped into bed beside Kay. She didn't wake and feeling her warmth and familiarity, he committed to memory this last night beside her. A memory he would draw strength from in the testing times to come.

Chapter Thirteen

Kay was trying to nail the broken fence back into place one bitterly cold morning in October when Babs came out of the house. She looked strained, pulling her coat round her shoulders to hurry up to Kay, her words coming out in a tumble.

'It's arrived,' Babs whispered, her breath curling up in the air. 'Eddie's call-up.'

Kay looked at her friend sympathetically. 'Oh, Babs, I'm sorry.'

'We knew it had to be. But the kids—' She stopped, biting down on her lip.

'When's he got to go?'

'Monday. We've all day today and tomorrow, Sunday.'

Kay placed the hammer she was trying to wield down on the frosty earth. She leaned forward and took her friend's shoulders. 'I know how you feel, but bear up. We're both going to manage somehow.'

'I hope so. What are you trying to do?'

'Mend this bit of fence. It's fallen down again.'

'I'll get Eddie to give you a hand.'

'No,' said Kay quickly. 'Just tell him to pop in and say goodbye.'

Babs nodded. She had tears in her eyes but held them back as, without saying more, she turned to go back indoors.

The next day Eddie visited and it was a sad moment as he hugged Kay. 'Look after her and the kids for me, Kay.'

'I will.'

'You ain't made a very good job of that fence,' he joked. 'I'll put a nail in it before I go.'

They both laughed as they knew the fence would still be as it was throughout the rest of the winter. Kay saw he was fighting back his emotion and when he'd said farewell to Vi and Alfie, she called out of the front door after him to say that it wasn't goodbye, just *au revoir*.

'You bet ya!' he yelled from the street and gave her a wink.

Kay knew that Babs would be sad and lonely for a while, but in a very short time she'd be back on her feet. With their men gone, they were the sole providers and would have to make sure their families were safe. It was this thought that kept Kay focused and the heartbreak of separation at bay.

The winter was setting in with icy November mornings and cutting winds, forcing Kay to burn some of the old wood that was stacked at the side of the outside wall. She knew Alan was keeping it for repairs to the house, but some of it was needed now and it helped to eke out the coal.

Money was so scarce in December that Kay and Babs decided to pool their resources for a special family day on Christmas Eve. Between them they planned to ask a few neighbours to drop in and share the festive cheer.

'My place has got more room,' Babs offered. 'And the kids will have space to perform their little concert.'

Kay nodded approvingly. 'We'd only need one fire as well. I'll get the kids to bring over some of Alan's wood.'

'That'd be lovely.'

'Me and Vi will cook up a few bits in the morning and bring them round for the afternoon.' Kay frowned. 'But what we gonna do about a tipple?'

'There's a few of Eddie's ales left in the sideboard,' Babs remembered. 'If we're careful we can share them out.'

With everything settled, Kay and Babs put the word out that there was going to be an open house at Babs's on Christmas Eve afternoon.

When the big day arrived, there was a loud knock on Kay's door. Expecting it to be one of their neighbours arriving early to help out with carrying things to Babs's house, Kay rushed to open it.

'Surprise, surprise!' exclaimed the smart, formidable-looking woman standing on Kay's doorstep.

'I'll bet this is a surprise an' all, ain't it, love?' chimed in the equally chipper-looking man beside her. 'Happy Christmas, love.' Kay's father, Bob Briggs, lowered the suitcase he was carrying and elbowed his way past his wife. 'Give us a kiss, Kay.'

'Dad! Mum!' Kay gasped as she was swamped by hugs.

'Blimey, you should see the look on your face,' chortled Lil Briggs in her smoke-roughened voice. 'You didn't expect to see us on Christmas Eve, now, did you?'

'Well – no, seeing as the weather's been so bad and there's snow forecast.' Kay stood back to allow her parents entry to the house with their armfuls of baggage.

'Well, how is everyone?' Lil demanded, looking around expectantly. 'Where's the little terror? We can't wait to see him, can we, Bob?' Lil Briggs pushed an assortment of raffia bags and parcels into Kay's arms. 'There's a few bits and pieces in there for Christmas and a cake and pudding I made meself.'

'Why didn't you let me know you were coming?' Kay juggled the parcels in her arms. 'I'd have got something in—'

'Decided to surprise you, so you wouldn't go to no expense on our behalf,' beamed Lil. 'Knowing you ain't got Alan at home this year and were on your own with the lad, we thought we'd come and keep you company for a few days.'

'A few days?' Kay repeated.

Bob and Lil nodded together. 'Don't worry, love, there's enough grub in them bags to see us all through a siege.' Lil turned her narrowed grey eyes on her daughter. 'The last time we saw our grandson was in March this year. Alfie was having a whale of a time at Len's. The boy was in seventh heaven in that lovely garden. Len had built him a swing an' all. What a lovely place to bring up a kid! Nice neighbours too. All very friendly, I must say . . .'

As Lil chatted, barely taking a breath, Kay was returned to the troubled years when she had lived at home after Norman's death. It had been a disaster from start to finish. Kay had recognized her mistake very swiftly as Lil had tried to find a replacement for Norman. An awkward suitor would turn up, one of her parents' friends' sons, or someone from the local LCC social club her bus-driver dad belonged to. Kay knew then she should have remained in her father-in-law's house where she had lived with Norman. But after Mr Williams Senior had died, the big house had seemed very empty. There had only been memories left in the silent corners. And it hadn't been long before Lil had persuaded her daughter to return the rent book to the landlord, and move out.

'It's cold enough to freeze the whatsits on a brass monkey,' barked her father, interrupting his wife's flow of speech as he rubbed the palms of his hands together. 'I hope you've got a nice fire going—'

'We had to change train's twice,' Lil continued, turning to the closed door of the front room. 'Me legs are like two lumps of ice. Now if I remember rightly this is the—'

'No, Mum!' Kay dumped the parcels on the floor. She caught Lil's arm. 'You can't go in there.'

'Why in heaven's name not?' Lil stared at her daughter in astonishment. The blush of colour on each of Lil's cheeks was as meticulously applied as the black mascara on her eyes. Contrasting with her short, silver-white hair and black astrakhan coat, Kay reflected that her mother still looked a daunting character.

'Because Vi's having forty winks,' Kay explained.

'Vi who?' frowned Lil, beginning to unbutton her coat.

'Vi Hill, my neighbour. I wrote and told you about her.'

'But why's she kipping in your front room?'

'Vi's lodging with us, Mum. I told you in my—'

'You've a lodger?' This time it was her father who looked surprised. He slipped the plaid cap from his head to reveal a handful of thin strands of dark hair combed over his bald pate. 'Do you need the money then, gel? Are you hard-up? You should have told us and we would have helped out.'

'No, Dad. It's nothing like that,' Kay assured him. 'Vi's been living here since the Blitz ended, when her house was bombed.'

Lil's left eyebrow swept up. 'So why didn't she evacuate? It would have been the sensible thing to do.'

'Vi's lived in Slater Street all her married life. She lost her husband and son before the war and her memories are all here. At her time of life she don't want to move anywhere else.'

'She might not want to,' protested Lil, 'and nor did we, but we had to leave all the same.'

'You had Aunty Pops to go to,' Kay reminded her mother. 'Vi has no one except us.'

Lil's face went a deeper shade of pink. But before she could speak, Bob nodded to the kitchen. 'Don't mind me saying, Kay, but I'd give me right arm for a nice, hot cuppa.'

'Course. Come along and I'll make a fresh pot.' Kay led the way to the kitchen.

'Hell's bells,' gasped her father as they entered the freezing room. 'I thought it was cold outside. But it's the ruddy North Pole in here.'

'Sorry,' said Kay, embarrassed. 'We wasn't expecting visitors.'

Lil shivered, shrinking down into the fur collar of her coat. 'It's a wonder you ain't got icicles on your washing-up.'

Quickly, Kay tried to clear the cluttered draining board. She was ashamed at the untidy state of her home. 'I was going to give the kitchen a once over but I didn't get round to it.'

'I know it's wartime and women are expected to pull their weight,' replied her mother as she watched Kay hurriedly return the crocs to the cupboards, 'but Alfie is your priority. Is it really necessary to work?'

'Most women manage a few hours, Mum. Like my neighbour, Babs. She cleans at the fire station. Her husband Eddie was called up in October. So we help each other out.'

'Babs?' repeated Lil with a frown.

'Babs, me best mate, and Eddie, her husband, and their two children, Gill and Tim. They used to live at the top of the street before they moved next door,' Kay replied. 'Remember I wrote to you about them losing their house in the bombing?'

Her mother waved her hand in the air. 'You may have mentioned it, love, but you know my memory for names. All I can say is, I'm shocked anyone with a family chooses to stay in such a dangerous area as the docks.'

Just then, there was a loud creak from the front-room door. Vi appeared, blinking her sleepy eyes. She was, as usual, wearing her knotted scarf and at least two jumpers under her crossover apron. 'Well, I never did,' Vi croaked, 'it's Kay's mum and dad, ain't it? I'm Vi Hill. You might not remember me but I met you once before. It was only in passing, when you called about a year after Kay and Alan moved here.'

Lil managed a smile. 'Yes, that would be right.'

'It's thanks to your daughter and son-in-law I still have a roof over me head,' Vi continued. 'Salt of the earth, they've been.'

'Rotten luck, about your house,' said Bob kindly. 'Must've been a shocker.'

Lil frowned at her husband, then made her way to the window. 'You've got a big hole in the fence, Kay. Your dad will soon have it boarded up, won't you, Bob?'

'Too right I will,' Bob agreed, rubbing his hands together again.

'No need, Dad,' said Kay, swiftly stowing away Alfie's dirty socks and vest in the laundry bag under the sink. 'I've given up trying to mend it as Alfie and Gill and Tim from next door use it as a shortcut. Saves going round the front.'

'And what's all that rubbish by the wall?'

'Alan didn't have time to put it anywhere else. It's been handy as I've used some of it for firewood.'

'If it was me, I'd put up a nice new fence and clear that yard completely.' Lil turned slowly and inspected the kitchen. 'You could do with a lick of paint in here too.'

'Yes, I've been meaning to get round to it.'

'You?' said Lil in surprise. 'Painting's a man's job.'

'It don't take a man to paint a wall, Mum.'

'You've enough on your hands as it is, what with your work and looking after Alfie.' Lil's eagle-eyed gaze travelled to the dresser. 'Where's that tea set I gave you?'

Kay felt her cheeks go crimson. 'I'm sad to say it got broken in the Blitz.'

'You should have packed it away, dear.'

'Yes, but it looked so nice.' Kay put on a bright smile. 'At least the house was still standing.'

Lil nodded slowly. 'Your father and I saw hundreds of houses missing in roads. Piles of bricks as high as mountains as far as the eye can see. Kay, your brother is still of the mind that you'd do far better to make a fresh start in Hertfordshire.'

'When did he say that?'

'We stayed with them in September.'

Vi reached for the kettle. 'Why don't you take yer mum and dad through to the front room, flower? The fire just needs a bit of coke and we'll soon be nice and cosy. Oh, it might need a bit of a tidy-up, but that won't take long. I'll do the honours and bring in the tea and a couple of sandwiches. Alfie should be back from next door in a minute. He's taken some of his toys in for later.'

'Later?' repeated Lil sharply.

'Yes, we're having a bit of a knees-up.' She added quickly, 'Anyway what about something to eat first?'

'Them sandwiches sound lovely, Vi,' said Bob, as he took his wife's arm and guided her out of the kitchen. 'Come on, Lil, let's stop gassing and find the fire.'

Kay followed, glancing over her shoulder to roll her eyes at Vi.

But in the front room, Lil recoiled; her nose lifted in the air, sniffing the cocktail of tobacco, camphor-rub and mothballs clinging to the warm air. Her gaze soon dropped from Alfie's homemade paper-chains strung across the ceiling to the assortment of Vi's clothes airing along with her undergarments over the open wardrobe door. Beside this was the dining-room table, invisible under the mountain of Alfie's toys, books, papers and pencils.

Kay glanced at Lil, whose bottom jaw hung open as she looked around her, trying unsuccessfully to hide her dismay.

Chapter Fourteen

'Well, this is very cosy I must say,' said Lil as she sat in Babs's front room, squeezed on a chair between Babs and Kay, with Vi seated at the end of the row. Kay was grateful to Babs who, when she heard that Bob and Lil had arrived, invited them to the afternoon's entertainment which was to be performed by the three children. Alice and Bert Tyler had called in earlier along with Jenny Edwards, but had left to join their families, leaving their empty chairs for Kay to arrange in a semi-circle in front of the window.

'Alfie don't know the words to the carols, Mum,' whispered Kay with a grin, 'but he sings along anyway.'

However, Lil's attention had strayed to Paul and Neville Butt seated with Bob on the couch.

'What does the younger man do? And how did he get hold of the food he brought with him?' Lil enquired as she narrowed her eyes in the men's direction.

'Paul works at the steel factory,' whispered Babs. 'His dad, Neville, worked there before him.'

'Paul has a friend, Rose, who works in the canteen,' Kay added. 'Sometimes she gives him the food that's left over, rather than it being wasted.'

'What does his wife think of that?'

'Paul's not married,' Kay informed her mother, smothering a smile as she glanced across at Babs. 'He seems to be a confirmed bachelor.'

Lil looked surprised. 'He's not in the services either?'

'No,' said Babs, just about managing to contain her amusement. 'He's in a reserved job.'

Just then, Gill stepped forward, pushing back her plaits. 'We're the three wise men,' she announced, elbowing her brother who nodded. Alfie grinned broadly under the yellowed net curtain that served as a cloak. Tim was wearing a curtain looped over his shoulders and secured by a safety pin. Gill had dressed in a long yellow frock of her mother's that was drawn together at the waist by Kay's leather factory belt. A passage from the Bible was read by Gill as Tim and Alfie stiffly pointed up at the star. When the stable and animals were mentioned, there were strange animal noises from the two boys. Dissolving into giggles, they began to fight.

Babs sprang to her feet and parted them. 'Now, for our last carol.' Babs began to hum the tune to 'Silent Night'.

Everyone joined in and when it was over, the applause was deafening. Kay and Babs handed round sandwiches, sliced sausages and pork pie. Added to this was the large, round, white-iced cake that Lil had brought. Cake was so scarce that Kay knew it would disappear in seconds.

When it was time to say goodbye, Paul bent to kiss her on the cheek. She knew Lil was watching and was relieved when Paul did the same with Babs, wishing them all a happy Christmas.

'Do you need any bedclothes?' Babs asked Kay as they all filed out into the cold winter's day.

'No, Mum and Dad can sleep in my bed. I've brought the mattress in from the Anderson for me. It's been airing beside the fire. I've got a couple of extra blankets in the cupboard.'

Babs's eyes twinkled. 'Well, shout if you need anything.'

Kay hugged Babs. 'Thanks for a lovely afternoon. Happy Christmas, love.'

'You too.'

As Kay was about to leave, Babs caught her arm. 'What do you think our men are doing this Christmas?'

'Thinking of us, I hope.'

'I wonder,' sighed her friend doubtfully. 'Eddie didn't seem upset in his last letter. He just said to have a good time. And gave me the weather report.'

'They can't say much else, can they?'

'No, s'pose not. Anyway, we got a Christmas kiss from Paul. That's as much romance as I'm likely to get this year.'

Kay thought it wasn't like Babs to sound so down in the dumps. But it was Christmas after all and she must be missing Eddie.

Kay shivered as she hurried in. A few flakes of snow drifted down. The pavement was icy beneath her feet. As she went indoors, even the cold passage felt warm. She could hear Alfie's laughter and her dad's teasing. Bob seemed to have mellowed. He had actually talked about Alan once or twice in a nice way. Perhaps Alfie's presence would ensure this would be a happy Christmas and, with luck, bridges could be built with her mother over the problems of the past.

'I never make me puddings without a drop of beer,' said Lil to Vi on Christmas morning. 'Gives a nip to the taste. And this pudding's no exception.'

Kay and Vi looked at the Christmas pudding in the white basin that had been stowed at the bottom of the raffia bag. It smelled delicious as it steamed on the stove.

'I'll give you a hand with the potatoes, Mrs B,' offered Vi, starting to tie on her apron.

'No need, dear,' said Lil firmly, shooing them from the kitchen. 'Too many cooks and all that. Leave the cooking to me. Though I ain't so sure I can make this canary go round for all five of us.'

Kay grinned. 'I queued a long time for that chicken, Mum.'

Lil cast her daughter a rueful glance. 'You don't have to skimp when you live in the country. The butcher down the road from us in Berkshire had some real heavyweights hanging in his window. I'd have brought a bird along if I'd known the state of your larder.'

'Your mum does have a point,' said Vi in a whisper as she and Kay walked into the passage. 'The thought of them big blighters hanging from the butcher's window has made me mouth water.'

Kay chuckled. 'There's enough meat on that canary to go round, don't worry.'

In the front room, Bob had pulled out the dining table and extended its sides. Alfie was already seated on one of the chairs, banging a fork on the table's surface. His granddad was playing the spoons beside him and after much laughter, the four of them began to sing 'Any Old Iron'. Soon Bob had enticed Vi into the small space beside the fire and linking arms, they danced around.

Kay found herself laughing so much that her eyes were watering. They hadn't had such a good time since Alan had come home on his brief twenty-four-hour November leave. Then they had celebrated Alfie's third birthday on the twelfth and done a lot of clowning around. As neither she nor Alan had known how long it would be before they saw one another again, they'd filled every minute with love and laughter.

As if Alfie had picked up her thoughts, he gave her the biggest of smiles – Alan's smile – as though Alan was saying that he was here in spirit with them on Christmas Day.

It was half past six on Christmas night and Bob was snoring in his chair. They were all recovering from Lil's mountainous dinner. Kay thought that if the canary had not seemed enough, then the vegetables and roast spuds had made up for it. The table's sides had been dropped again and the heavy lump of wood pushed back to the wall. The smell of Christmas cooking lingered in the air and Alfie was playing with his present from Lil and Bob: a train set that Bob had helped him piece together earlier.

'He's never had anything so special, Mum,' said Kay who sat beside Vi on the fireside chairs. Kay looked at the cheap toys she and Vi had bought. All second-hand from the market. Shabby but colourful building bricks, a hand-made soft toy in the shape of a giraffe and a dog-eared colouring book, together with some used crayons.

'We spare no expense when it comes to our family,' said Lil as she sat beside her sleeping husband on the couch. 'And as we ain't seen Alfie in a while it's nice to spoil him a bit.' Kay guessed what might be coming next and she was right. 'Your brother invited us for Christmas, but we said we was staying with you.'

'I hope he didn't mind.'

'It would have been better if all four of us had gone to Hertfordshire.'

'I couldn't have managed that, Mum.'

'I don't see why not. You wasn't doing anything else.' Lil bent to replace the toy carriage that had come off the tracks.

'Didn't know whether Alan was coming home,' Kay shrugged.

Lil sat forward. 'There's something else I want to talk to you about. We'd like you to visit us next year. After all, Aunty Pops ain't never seen Alfie. Last she saw of you was when her other half Tommy was alive, when they both came down to stay for Norman's funeral. She'd just got over her stroke then, remember? And was cussing the stick they gave her.'

'I'll have to see,' replied Kay, not wanting to make any rash decisions. 'Depends on Alan and his leaves.'

Lil threw her a hard stare. 'You could wait for ever, Kay, whilst it's you that needs a break from the East End. You've got to admit that London is a shambles. It's dirty and dangerous. We saw kids as young as Alfie running over the bombed sites as though they was animals.' When Kay tried to protest, Lil held her hand up. 'Agreed the city was a good place to live before the war. But it was different then. Respectable, like. Before the bloody Germans decided to invade.'

'They haven't yet,' Kay argued. 'And Alan don't believe we'll ever let them.'

'That's just his opinion, dear,' Lil said tartly. 'What's going to happen if the bombing starts again?'

Bob gave a loud snore and woke himself up. Blinking his sleepy eyes he asked, 'What was that? Did someone say something?'

'Yes,' answered Lil irritably, 'but you missed it. Kay, switch the wireless on. Let's catch up with the news.'

Reluctantly, Kay turned on the set. It was Christmas, the season of goodwill. It was miserable enough without Alan. She didn't want to hear all the tragic events told over yet again. But sure enough, the commentator was soon describing the sinking of Britain's formidable aircraft carrier, the HMS Ark Royal, back in November, and went on to give vivid descriptions of the Japanese attack on Pearl Harbour which had drawn America into the war. Kay glanced restlessly over at Vi who also seemed to be fidgeting in her seat.

'Time for supper!' Kay deliberately interrupted the voice. 'Who fancies cheese and pickled onions?'

'No thank you,' said Lil shortly. 'Me indigestion is playing up.'

'Well, mine ain't,' said Bob, giving Kay a smirk. 'I reckon I could do justice to a bite to eat. Now, Alfie, young man, where did we get to in our game?' Bob hauled himself from the couch and went down on all fours. 'Granddad will be the blue carriage and you can be the red.'

Kay grinned at Vi as they left the room together, eager to reach the safety of the kitchen.

'I'll go mad if I have to listen to one more miserable news broadcast,' said Kay as she and Vi stood in the kitchen about to prepare supper. 'Mum can't seem to get enough of them. Then, if she had her way, we'd be sitting there for hours after, picking the war to pieces.'

'Your mum ain't one to hold back,' agreed Vi as they began to spread the slim slices of stodgy wholemeal bread with the farm-made butter that Lil had brought. 'But as for your Aunty Pops, there's no harm in agreeing to go and visit her, is there? That'd put a smile on your mum's face.'

'Yes, but if I go without Alan, it will only turn into a battle of wits,' Kay answered as she placed the plates on a tray. 'On my own I'll be forced to fight my corner again. It was the same after Norman died when I made the mistake of moving back home.'

'How did your Norman get on with your folks?'

'He'd known them all his life. Like I had known Mr Williams and his wife when they were alive. When me and Norman got married we went to live with Bernard, his dad, just round the corner to Mum's. So Mum popped in most days and did a few jobs around the house whilst I was at work. She'd make a cup of tea and the occasional meal for my father-in-law and Norman appreciated that.'

'He must have been a good bloke.'

'He was. But when that bus knocked him down at the depot, I knew I should have felt sort of different. I mean, I was grieving, but it was like . . . as if me best friend had died.'

'That's no sin, flower.'

Kay looked into Vi's gaze. 'Norman was a trustworthy husband. I always knew where he'd be as he gave me his working timetable at the beginning of each week and I'd know the very second he was coming home for his dinner. He liked to do everything by the book. He was a stickler for routine. He never missed a day at work and when we were courting, if Norman said he'd call for me at five, he'd be there at three minutes to. I liked that then and was attracted to it.' Kay smiled. 'Norman was the kind of man Mum approved of and wanted me to find again.'

Vi chuckled. 'But Alan came along.'

Kay nodded. 'Yes, and it was then I forgot all about working to schedule. Everything I'd known before went out of the window. What counted was . . .' Kay felt herself blushing, '. . . just being with each other any moment we could get. Nothing mattered except . . .' She gave a little shiver at the thrill even the memory caused inside her, '. . . and that was how we got Alfie a bit earlier than we should have done.'

'Good on yer, ducks,' said Vi. 'I liked me moment of passion too.'

At this, they burst into laughter. As the sandwiches took shape, Vi said reflectively, 'If I was you, I'd be tempted to take the easy route this Christmas and just nod your head.'

'Yes, I'd come to that conclusion too.'

'Mind you,' said Vi with a cheeky grin as she turned the pickled onions into a dish, 'there'll be many a household in Britain that don't suffer in silence to keep the peace.' They both laughed again until, with difficulty, Vi lifted the overflowing plates. 'Your dad's got an appetite like a starved 'orse. Let's see if he can do justice to these.'

Kay followed with the tray of tea and a bottle of milk stout for her father. She was determined to remember Vi's advice and make sure that this was one household in the East End that didn't fall out over Christmas.

Chapter Fifteen

Unfortunately, Kay's resolve weakened on Boxing Day. Lil had risen early to cook breakfast and she summoned the adults downstairs. Kay had left Alfie sleeping after his exhausting day yesterday. Placing four generous portions of fried vegetables on the kitchen table together with accompanying rounds of fried bread, Lil turned the discussion to the subject she favoured most. One which Kay had been hoping and praying would not be aired again.

'You never met Kay's first husband, Norman Williams, did you, Vi?' Lil asked after a sip of tea.

Kay's heart sank. She knew what was coming next.

'No, Lil, I didn't,' Vi said politely.

'He was the perfect gentleman.'

'I'm glad to hear it,' replied Vi, 'as your girl is the perfect lady. And has luckily found herself a good match in Alan.'

Lil said nothing. Kay looked at her father whose eyes were glued to the bubble-and-squeak in front of him.

'Norman was a bus driver, and he loved his work,' continued Lil enthusiastically. 'He used to take Kay and me all over the city. He knew all the routes and the shortcuts and was a mine of information on London transport. You could always rely on Norman for advice on getting to wherever you wanted. He knew the timetables backwards. In fact, you could set your watch by Norman himself. He was a man of good habits and kept to them.'

Kay pushed away her half-eaten breakfast. 'Would you like some more tea, Mum?'

'No thanks, dear. You poured me a cup already.' Lil took another gulp. 'As you can imagine, it was handy having my daughter live just round the corner,' she continued. 'There wasn't much we didn't know about each other's lives.' Lil slid a long glance at Kay. 'Norman and Kay were childhood sweethearts, you know. Everyone used to say they were made for one another. When they got married me and Bob were the proudest—'

Kay stood up, scraping her chair noisily. Lil stopped in the middle of her sentence. 'What's the matter, Kay?'

'I think I can hear Alfie.'

'That's funny, I didn't hear nothing.'

Kay hurried into the freezing passage. Her heart was beating so fast that when she got to the top of the stairs, she could hardly breathe.

She hadn't heard Alfie at all. But it was the best excuse she could think of to leave the breakfast table. Kay sat on the top stair and pulled her cardigan round her. She leaned her head against the wooden banister and turned the slim golden band on the finger of her left hand. If only Alan was here now!

Her mother's voice drifted up from downstairs. Lil loved to live in her memories of the past. Sadly, they were very different to Kay's.

Lil and Bob decided they must get back to Berkshire in time for the new year. But Kay guessed that Lil wasn't keen to stay longer. The house was too cold for her.

'It's been very nice, but the weather's on the turn for the worse. We want to make sure we get home without being stranded,' said her mother politely as they prepared to take a taxi on Monday morning. Lil hesitated as she fitted her arms into the sleeves of the coat that Bob was holding up. 'And anyway, with you going to work tomorrow, Kay, and Vi taking care of Alfie, it don't seem we can be much use.'

'You don't have to go because I'm at work.'

Bob lifted the suitcase. 'Well, if we want to catch our taxi and not break our necks on the icy pavement, we'd better be off. Give us a kiss, Kay.'

Kay kissed her father and mother as Vi and Alfie appeared. Alfie gave them a picture he'd been colouring.

'Oh, ta, my love,' said Lil, giving her grandson a hug. 'Just look at how smart you look this morning in that nice coat Aunty Doris bought you. She said you'd fit into it by Christmas and she was right.'

'Now, watch your step out there, Lil, the pavements will be icy,' interrupted Bob, grabbing hold of Vi and plonking a kiss on her cheek. 'It's been nice seeing you again, love.'

As Kay opened the door a cold wind blew in. On it was the salt-tar smell of the docks and another wintry smell of bitter cold that overpowered everything else. The black taxi that her dad had ordered was pulling up in the road.

'I wouldn't like to be here next month,' called Lil over her shoulder as she stepped out cautiously, holding on to Bob's arm. 'It'll be like the frozen wastes of Sibera.'

Kay waved them off as Vi took Alfie back into the warm front room.

Kay exhaled a long, unbroken sigh; the holiday had ended without cross words, though at times Kay was certain that without Vi's help, she would have been perilously near to changing that state of affairs. She closed the door and went in, where even the freezing cold passage seemed welcoming.

Chapter Sixteen

As Lil predicted, 1942 had begun with snowstorms across the country. Kay listened to the wireless reports of Germany's aerial attacks on Britain and the exploits of small numbers of enemy aircraft that flew across the country. But the lull over London had continued.

'Listen to this,' said Vi one freezing January morning as they sat huddled round the fire. Vi had been given yesterday's newspaper by Jenny Edwards who always passed on Tom's reading; Saturday's headlines described the battles raging in other parts of the world. 'The German Panzers are racing forward to confront the English Eighth Army in the Western Desert, whilst the Russians are stopping the German invaders near Moscow,' read out Vi. 'The terrible weather is responsible for turning the pursuers into the pursued.' She looked up from the newspaper. 'Alan's mind will be put at rest that the enemy isn't having it all their own way. Though it don't sound too good for our boys in the desert.'

'I hope Alan's not there.' Kay sat with Alfie who had spread out his train set over the floor. The fire had been going since early, although they were getting low on coke. She would have to break into the twenty pounds soon. 'I thought Alan might give me a clue in that Christmas card that came late. But I should have known better. The army don't let their men give out any information.'

Alfie rolled a carriage along the track. 'Daddy an' Alfie go down the river.'

'When he comes home,' Kay agreed, smiling. Her mind went over the memories of them all together on Alan's leave. November seemed a long time ago now.

Alfie looked up at Kay with his big, brown eyes. He was such a handsome boy with all that dark hair and beautiful olive skin.

'Daddy comin' home?'

'He will one day.' Kay stroked his silky locks. 'And then we'll go down to the river like we used to.'

Alfie jumped to his feet. Kay and Vi laughed. 'We can't go yet, it's freezing.'

Alfie ran across the room to climb on a chair beside the window. He pointed out to the street. 'It's freezin'!'

Kay was still chuckling as she went to join him. He was putting short sentences together and for a three-year-old had a wide vocabulary. She knew playing with Gill and Tim next door had brought out the best in him.

But Kay's smile faded when she looked outside. The street was deserted. Except for one figure who stood quite still on the opposite side of the road. He was tall and wore a trilby hat and dark coat. 'Vi, come quickly!' Kay called, her breath lodged in her throat.

'What's the matter, flower?'

Kay swung round. 'Quickly, it's him! That man I told you about. The one I saw from the bus and again at market.'

But when Kay looked back at the street, it was empty. And by the time Vi reached the window, the snow had begun to fall on the deserted pavements in tiny white flakes.

'At ease.'

The Company Commander of Alan's unit, Major Campbell, didn't look up from his desk. He kept his sandy-coloured head bent and his back ramrod straight under his spotless uniform as he studied the documents before him. Alan relaxed enough to take in a breath and exit the salute he had just made.

After what seemed an eternity, the big man sat back and stared at Alan with an unwavering gaze. 'Your training is over, Lewis. And you've squared up to expectations. But now you are to begin a more specialized assignment,' the CC intoned in his Scottish burr, which was not surprising as it was in the heart of the Scottish Highlands that Alan had found himself, flown overnight by Special Operations from the base in Barnet.

'Yes, sir.' Alan didn't meet his superior's eyes, even though he was not standing to attention. Instead, he kept his gaze level with the window and the parade ground outside. In the freezing snow, he could see a sergeant giving two soldiers a dressing down. Alan recognized his mates who had been on jankers. The sergeant had singled them out as the laziest dogs he had ever come across. Now their weighted backpacks were to be carried around the camp at a fierce trot. Alan smothered a smile. The sergeant was right. They were lazy so-and-so's and deserved their punishment. But they were also damn good soldiers, and the army knew it.

'You've had experience of Spain?'

Alan swallowed and nodded. 'Yes, sir.'

'You're acquainted with the German raids on Guernica?'

Again Alan confirmed what his superior had said.

The CC paused before he said sharply, 'Which is why we're flying you back in.'

Alan made the mistake of catching the major's narrowed gaze. He saw in the man's eyes all he didn't want to see. From his youthful indiscretions in his teens to the moment when Alan had been stopped at the borders of Spain and France in his bid to escape for a new life. It was all there in the dossier before him, as thick as a loaf of bread. If Army Intelligence decided they needed you, then resistance was useless.

'Franco insists Spain is neutral, but we are convinced he is sympathetic to Nazi Germany and Fascist Italy. But then, Lewis, I believe you had full grasp of this situation in thirty-seven.'

Again Alan remained silent. He guessed an answer wasn't required. The army had got what they wanted – him. Major Campbell was reminding him of the power the army wielded; the odds were stacked heavily against a man escaping a second time from the might of the British government. And, just like the sergeant outside, he was attempting to extinguish any remaining resistance that Alan might secretly harbour.

Major Campbell expanded his barrel chest under his uniform. 'In approximately one month's time you will be flown to the borders of occupied France and Spain. There you will be joined by the French Resistance who will provide you with the false information that you are to plant in Spain. Is that understood?'

'Yes, sir.'

The officer studied him carefully. 'I cannot impress on you enough how vitally important this is to us, Lewis. I'm not at liberty to fully explain our tactics to you, but our Allied convoys are at risk to the U-boat patrols. At whatever cost, we must distract their submarine forces. Have I made that quite clear?'

As crystal, thought Alan, well aware of the officer's meaning.

'And Lewis?'

'Sir?'

'Until this war is over, your family will be told nothing of your past. Either of thirty-seven or the years before. But should you . . .' Again the big man's eyes flashed threateningly, '. . . should you give us one moment's cause for concern, the whole damn lot will come out. Whether you are alive or dead, it will be your wife and family who will live with the consequences.

Carry out your mission successfully and you will rejoin your family.'

Alan felt the sweat bead on his brow. His shirt clung to him. His uniform felt like the weight of the world on his shoulders.

'That's all.'

Alan saluted and swivelled on his heel. He marched out of the room and past the two guards. He had a vivid picture in his mind of what might happen in the future – Kay's face, her shock and disappointment – if the army exposed him for the man he had once been. If only he'd had the guts to tell her when they'd first met. But he'd wanted her more than anything he'd ever wanted in his life before and he hadn't been prepared to lose her.

When he reached the parade ground, the sergeant was still bawling his head off. His pals were running at speed, covered in the driving snow. The burden of their wet backpacks would soon be crippling.

Just like the secrets Alan carried inside him. Secrets the army used to manipulate men like him.

'Alan's letter arrived this morning,' said Kay. She was sitting with Vi and Babs in the kitchen one Saturday afternoon in the middle of March. The kids were playing in the yard for the first time in weeks. Like January, February had been a miserably cold month but now it felt that at last winter was on the wane.

'What does he have to say?' Babs squashed the butt of the cigarette she had been smoking into the stained glass ashtray. It wasn't long before Vi did the same, blowing the last lungful of cloudy air into the space above them.

'Not very much.'

'Same with Eddie,' said Babs with a shrug. 'It's censorship, ain't it? Eddie's favourite phrase is "loose lips sinks ships", – I dunno how many times he's written that. All I hope is he's not put on a merchant ship that's defenceless against the German subs.'

'The poor beggars,' sighed Vi, shaking her head. 'So you think Alan's in England still, Kay?'

'Yes, as he says he's training.'

'At least you know he's safe, then,' commented Babs.

'Not like our poor soldiers in Singapore,' Vi pointed out.

The three women nodded in silence. In February Kay and her friends had listened to the wireless reports as Winston Churchill had broken the news to the nation that the British troops had surrendered to the Japanese. He'd warned that the consequences of this for the Allies were grave. No one knew what was to be the fate of the British troops who had held out so defiantly in the Far East.

'Every time we get news like that,' complained Babs, 'it feels like it did last year in the Blitz. You start thinking of what you'd do if that door burst open and someone rushed in to attack you. Only this time, we ain't got our men with us to do the fighting.'

'Singapore is a defeat,' agreed Vi, beginning to roll another cigarette, 'but the Japs ain't won the war, nor has

Jerry. So don't go thinking along those lines. The enemy would like to put the wind up us in any way they can.' Vi grinned and stuck out her tongue to lick the thin paper. 'Like Kay here, thinking she's being watched all the time.'

Kay looked at Vi. 'Not all the time.'

'Have you seen him again?' Babs asked curiously.

'Not since January.' Kay had told Babs about the man. The trouble was, her two friends regarded the mystery with amusement as the stranger only appeared when no one else was looking.

'Perhaps he's undercover for the Food Office,' Babs suggested with a smile. 'Checking up on black-market coupons.'

Kay pulled back her shoulders. 'Well, in that case he's got a long wait.'

Leaving her two friends smiling, Kay got up from the table and went to the front room. She looked out of the window. There was no one there. Was it all the government propaganda that was getting to her and making her nervous? Only the other day she had been sitting on the bus and overheard a conversation behind her. One woman had remarked she'd seen her neighbour talking to a man who looked just like Hitler. This was impossible, Kay knew, but when she heard the woman's companion reply that it was best to report it to the police, Kay had been shocked. She didn't want to be part of this scaremongering. She would have to pull herself together before she too became part of the country's paranoia.

Chapter Seventeen

'I've made a couple of apple pies for Gill's birthday tomorrow,' Vi told Kay a few days later when Alfie had gone to sleep. It was Friday and a party had been planned for Gill's ninth birthday the following afternoon. 'And a jelly and blancmange, though the taste is never the same with dried milk. Me and Alfie made a few crackers from the newspaper but there's nothing in 'em. Still, they'll amuse the kids for a while.'

'How many children are coming?' asked Kay as she scraped the last of the nutty slack onto the fire in the lounge. The weather had been so bad, they had used more fuel than normal. The twenty pounds that Alan had left was now down to fifteen pounds and seventeen shillings. Twenty pounds had seemed a fortune when Alan had given it to her. She had kept it under the mattress for a long time, not wanting to break into it. But the winter bills had been heavy. Without Alan's wage coming in and only his army pay together with her reduced hours at the factory, there had been a big hole in the housekeeping.

'Two of Gill's friends and a mate of Tim's,' answered Vi. 'Plus Alfie, that makes five. But don't forget, Babs has asked the rest of Slater Street. Any excuse for a knees-up, eh?'

'Yes,' agreed Kay, yet feeling guilty about the two pounds that she had extravagantly given to Babs.

'I think I'll turn in, love.' Vi rubbed her eyes. 'Unless you want to come in and sit by the last of the fire?'

'No, I'm ready to hit the sack too.' Vi had looked tired when Kay had got home from work. The winter had been bad for her rheumatics. And Alfie was a live wire these days. As Gill's birthday was on a Saturday, Kay would be up early for work and Vi wouldn't sleep in either.

'Goodnight then, flower.' Vi pecked her cheek.

'I'll see to the lights.'

A few minutes later Kay flicked the light switch and the house was plunged into darkness. She was about to go upstairs when there was a knock at the front door. Kay stood still. It was almost ten o'clock. Late for someone to call. She wondered if Vi had heard the knock, but as Vi didn't poke her head out, Kay assumed she hadn't.

The knock came again, soft but insistent.

Kay put her cheek to the door. 'Who is it?'

'Kay? It's me. Paul Butt.'

Kay breathed out slowly and opened the door. 'Oh, Paul, it's you.'

'I hope it's not too late.'

Kay looked out on the dark street. Her eyes flicked through the shadows. 'No, but what is it, Paul? Is something wrong?'

'I thought you might be able to use a bag of nutty slack.' Paul Butt stood with his coat buttoned up to his chin and his fair hair blown over his face.

'Don't tell me it was left over from the canteen,' said Kay in surprise.

'I bumped into Babs yesterday on me way home from work. She said you'd both run out of coal. I've dropped a sack off next door and this one is for you. Me and Dad have plenty to keep us going. This don't come from our rations, if you see what I mean.'

Kay looked out to the street again, then beckoned Paul in.

'My mate is a coal merchant, you see,' continued Paul a little awkwardly. 'I came late as no one is about.' Paul hauled the sack over his shoulder. Kay quickly shut the door. She turned on the light by which time Paul had found the coal cupboard. He disappeared for a few minutes and then emerged, rubbing the dust from his hands. 'That should do you for a month or so.'

'Paul, how much do I owe you?'

'This one's on the house. Can't see the kids go cold. I hear it's Babs's girl's birthday tomorrow.'

'Yes, Gill's nine. They're all very excited about the party. How's your dad?' Kay asked politely.

'A few aches and pains. But he keeps going.'

'Will we see you both at the party tomorrow?'

'Hope so.' Paul paused, rolling the sack up and wedging it under his arm. 'And Alan? What's the news there?'

Kay shrugged. 'None, really. Only that he's finished his training.'

'He might get some leave before he's posted, then.'

'I hope so.' Kay didn't know what else to say. She felt a little embarrassed being alone with Paul at this time of night. He seemed to hesitate and she wondered if she should offer him a cup of tea in exchange for his generosity. But then she decided against it.

'Well, better be going,' he said at last.

Kay turned off the light then opened the door. 'Goodnight, and thanks, Paul.'

She watched him walk down the dark street towards his house at the end of the road. Once again she wondered why he had never settled down. He seemed to like kids and would make a good father. It was very generous of him to give her and Babs the coal. Kay wondered if he was still seeing the girl from his works.

Just then there was a movement in the shadows. Kay jumped, realizing the door was still open. She closed it quickly. Staying very still she listened for noises. There was only a loud snore from the front room. Treading up the stairs softly, she went into her bedroom.

She couldn't help herself. She had to look outside. The street was in darkness, the blackout well and truly enforced. There were just the shadows and the stars above. She pushed the thought of the stranger from her mind. If she went on like this, she would soon be getting on her own nerves. Let alone everyone else's!

The party was in full swing and Kay had no regrets about the two pounds she had provided for the celebration. The fun and excitement were worth every penny. The entire street had turned out for the occasion. The weather was fine and the children played both inside and outdoors. Jenny and Tom Edwards and their daughter Emily had brought the ale and port; Alice Tyler, the tea and dried milk from the factory where she worked as the tea lady. Bert Tyler had added his contribution, a tin of biscuits that had emerged from an unspecific source in the docks. The biscuits, as pure luxury, had been strictly rationed to two each for the children and one for an adult. The two spinster sisters, Hazel and Thelma, had made sausage rolls, though there was more pastry than meat.

Kay was surprised to see that nearly everyone had brought Gill a gift: a handmade peg-doll from the Tylers, a girl's annual from the Edwards, and from Paul and his father, a miniature set of carved drawers to hold all Gill's trinkets. Paul had made the gift and Neville had painted small red and yellow roses over it.

The tunes that Jenny Edwards was knocking out on the piano were all well-known favourites. 'By the Light of the Silvery Moon', 'If You Were the Only Girl in the World' and 'Hello, Who's Your Lady Friend', had been accompanied by the wartime favourites, 'Pack up Your Troubles in Your Old Kitbag' and 'Goodbye-ee', until the singing had finally drowned out Jenny's bad playing. Kay had called in the kids and the eating and drinking had started in earnest. Gill's birthday cake, a sponge consisting of more carrot than flour, had been sliced into minute portions and divided.

It was after they had sung 'Happy Birthday' and Kay and Babs had begun to clear the dirty dishes that Paul Butt joined them in the kitchen. He placed the plates he had carried on the draining board and, turning to Babs, nodded to the yard. 'I was able to get hold of the paint you wanted,' he said. 'I've put the tin in the Anderson, under the bunks out of harm's way. Brushes weren't so easy to find, but there's a decent sized one for the walls.' He gave his shy smile. 'Let me know when you want me to start. It'd have to be on a weekend or in the evening. But as the nights are drawing out, that won't be a problem.'

Kay saw her friend blush as she thanked Paul.

'What was that all about?' Kay asked curiously, when Paul had gone.

'Paul's offered to paint me front room,' she said, adding quickly, 'and before you say anything, I intend to pay him. The Tripps left the house in a terrible state, poor things. They was old and had no one to do it for them. Eddie was going to get round to the painting, but he never had time before his call-up. I was telling this to Neville the other day when we was queuing at the iron-monger's. I was hoping to get some cheap paint and do it meself. Of course, there wasn't any paint going and that was when Neville said he'd see what he could do.'

Kay smiled. 'That was kind of Neville.'

'I know. It's very good of the Butts.'

'You can't get paint even with coupons.'

Babs nodded. 'So when Paul offered, I jumped at it.' Babs narrowed her eyes softly. 'Tell you what, I could ask if there's any more going for your place.'

But Kay shook her head. 'No, Babs. I'd rather not.'

'Why?'

'I don't want any more favours.'

Babs grinned. 'You ain't like me, then. I'd grab anything going. After all, I need to take a pride in me place and give the kids a nice home. If I'm honest, Eddie could take years to do any jobs. In the meantime, the house will be falling down around our ears.'

'He is away fighting.'

'Might not be much different if he was here.'

Kay looked at her friend. She hadn't heard Babs talk like this before. Kay noticed that Babs looked very attractive today. She had grown her fair hair that she'd always kept short, and curled it carefully around her face. She wore lipstick too, something that she normally didn't bother with. And her smart two-piece suit enhanced her slim figure. She even wore high heels, a departure from the laced flats that she'd always worn before.

'Babs, have you heard from Eddie?'

'Yes, but he don't say nothing new. His letters are still all about the weather.' Babs laughed, shaking back her hair. 'Typical Eddie.'

Before any more could be said, Vi bustled in with a tray full of crocs. She was followed by Hazel and Thelma who carried the dirty glasses. The kitchen was soon full of chatter and Kay was despatched outside to Babs's Anderson to see what the children were up to.

But instead, Kay paused at the fence and looked across at her own house. Everything she saw reminded her of Alan. The windows with their borders of tough wood, the mended tiles on the roof, the yard that had once been covered in rubble and debris, now swept and tidy with a few timbers stacked across by the wall, depleted now as she'd used them for firewood. Her husband had left everything in good order. The interior of the house might need painting, as did Babs's house. But then it was a task that Alan would readily attend to. She knew she could rely on Alan as she had always done to keep house and home together. But Babs didn't seem to have the same confidence in Eddie. Kay tried to think back to their old house, the one that had been bombed. Had Eddie kept it ship-shape? Kay couldn't remember. What she could remember was that the house had always seemed homely and cosy, somewhere you could go and enjoy a chat with your best friend.

Kay looked back to Babs's house. Through the kitchen window, she could now see Babs at the sink. She was washing the dishes and smiling. She looked young and happy. The person beside her was Paul. He too looked happy. If she hadn't known better, she might have said that the pair only had eyes for each other.

* * *

It was gone seven when Kay, Vi and Alfie eventually left the party. As Kay drew the key up from the latch cord and opened the front door, her heart almost leaped out of her chest. She couldn't believe her eyes and for a moment she thought she was imagining the tall, dark-haired figure standing in the passage.

'Alan?' Kay gasped.

In three strides Alan reached them; Alfie was hauled up against his chest and Vi was flattened with Kay in his arms.

'Son, what are you doing here?' Vi said.

'I was given leave at the last minute.'

'Why didn't you come next door?' Kay wanted to know. 'You must have heard the racket.'

'Thought I'd make a cuppa first. What was the occasion?'

'Gill's birthday,' said Kay, 'but the whole street was there.'

'Any excuse for a knees-up, eh?' He laughed and hugged them all again.

'Daddy comin' down the river?' Alfie's inquisitive fingers went to the dark stubble on Alan's chin.

'In the morning, big man,' said Alan. 'You and me and your mum will take a stroll.'

'How long are you home for?' Kay asked.

Some of the light went out of Alan's eyes. 'I've got a twenty-four-hour pass.'

Kay said nothing. It was hard to keep her disappointment from showing.

'You'll want feeding, no doubt,' said Vi, heading towards the kitchen. 'Bet you ain't eaten today.'

'As a matter of fact, I haven't.'

Vi waved her hand. 'Sit by the fire then and I'll sort you out something tasty.'

'Thanks, Vi.'

Kay was bursting with questions as they crammed into the front room. She wanted to know everything: what Alan had done, where he'd been and most importantly where he was going to be posted. But, as they made space on the couch and sat down, Kay knew she had to be patient.

Alan plonked another kiss on Alfie's nose. 'You've grown, son. You'll be as tall as your dad soon.'

'I got a train set,' Alfie told his father, wriggling free of Alan's grasp. 'It's in the war'bode.'

Kay laughed. 'Mum and Dad bought him a train set for Christmas. Vi keeps it in the wardrobe. Go and get it, Alfie.'

'How did Christmas go?' Alan asked as Alfie scrambled away.

'It was all right. But I missed you.'

'What about Len and Doris?'

'We got a nice card and Doris wrote saying they're still hoping to adopt.' Kay kissed her husband quickly. 'But I want to talk about you, not them.'

Alfie returned holding a small red carriage. There was a big smile on his face and Alan hauled him up on his knee. 'We're gonna have some fun tonight, son.'

Very soon, they were all sitting on the floor in front of the fire. Kay watched her husband's big hands join the lengths of track. He looked so handsome in his soldier's uniform. It was the first time she had ever seen his black hair cut so short. His cheekbones were clearly defined under his beautiful tawny skin. She hoped the army was feeding him well. She couldn't stop looking at him. The old feeling slowly came over her. A pull of attraction from the pit of her stomach. When his eyes met hers, she knew he was feeling the same.

'I miss you,' she mouthed silently above Alfie's head.

'And I miss you,' he whispered back.

Kay burst into laughter as Alfie and Alan rolled on the floor, the train set forgotten. Alan's strong arms took hold of Alfie and lifted him into the air. There were screams of delight and deep chuckles.

Kay wished that every day could be like this. All that was important in life was holding the people you loved, being close to them and listening to their laughter.

Alan felt as though his whole body had been tranquillized with some wonder drug as he lay next to Kay that night. After making love, her body was warm and soft to his touch and he listened in contentment to her steady breathing. While away, he had hungered for her with such desperate need that he had dreamed of this moment a thousand times. Real dreams, daydreams, had removed him for a while from the reality of his life. They were good together; Alan knew that. After making love they seemed to slip into another world, far away from the one in which the war had trapped them. It was as though nothing had been before, not the long months of separation, nor the doubt that beset him of ever really having an honest life, an existence where there was nothing hidden. In the moments they came together, none of this mattered. It was just him and Kay . . .

'Alan?' She stirred, turning lazily to lay her hand on his chest. 'I was going to ask you so many questions. But now they don't seem important.'

'What sort of questions?' He looked at her in the darkness and wished he could read her eyes. He stroked her hair away from her face. 'You know I can't tell you much. But I will one day. When the conflict is over.'

'*If* it's ever over.'

'Listen, we're going to win this war. Until the day we do, I'll always be thinking of you and Alfie.'

'When will we see you again?'

'You know I don't know that either.' He kissed her full on the mouth. 'I was lucky to get this leave.'

'Does that mean you're saying goodbye for a long time?' There was a note of panic in her voice.

But Alan couldn't tell her anything. He couldn't tell a soul. He was frightened even to think of the mission himself. All war was dangerous, but the irony was he was not only at war with the Axis but with Military Intelligence too. Whichever way he looked at it, his Company Commander had brought the truth home to him. This time there was no escape. The day he had met Kay and fallen in love, he had forged his own shackles. Because he loved her so much, they were impossible to break. Kay had made him a better man, a faithful husband and loving father. The man he was, he had left behind. But the military had called him back to service and now he had to deal with the consequences of his past.

'Kay, do you trust me?'

For a moment she was silent. 'You know I do.'

He buried his face in her hair. 'I want you to remember that everything I've done since we got married has been for you – for us. For our family.'

'That's a funny thing to say.'

'You'll remember that, won't you?'

'Course, but—'

He didn't let her finish. Instead he kissed her, drawing his hands over her breasts and to her back, feeling the supple curve of her spine and instant reaction to his own arousal. Words, fortunately, were soon unnecessary and the passion that melted them together was all that mattered. All that counted. Tonight was what mattered.

To be in this moment, with Kay in his arms.

Chapter Eighteen

Over a week later, Vi turned on the wireless to hear of a new bombing campaign. This time it wasn't Russia, Singapore or El Alamein, but a place in the Baltic called Lübeck.

'Gawd almighty,' said Vi as they stood at the sink preparing vegetables for that evening's meal. 'Whatever next? The RAF has dropped 'undreds of high explosives and fire bombs on this little ship-building port I ain't even ever heard of before.'

They were silent as the news filtered through of the round-the-clock offensive aimed against arms factories built in the centre of this small town. 'I can't rejoice,' said Kay, putting down the potato she had half peeled. 'All those innocent men and women and kids going about their lives just like we were when the Blitz began.'

'And listen to the hoity-toity tone of that announcer,' huffed Vi, filling the pan with water. 'As if it's a personal victory. Reckon we are brainwashed to enjoy other people's suffering.'

Kay returned her attention to the vegetables, but soon she couldn't see. The tears had collected in her eyes as the BBC voice droned out all the statistics, reminding the nation of all the towns and cities in Britain that had been unrelentingly bombed in the past.

'Oh, stop it!' Kay turned the wireless off and put her hands over her ears.

'What's the matter, flower?'

'I don't want to hear any more.'

'Are you worried about Alan?'

Kay nodded. 'Course.'

'Come on, sit down a minute. I'll put the kettle on. The kids are all playing next door. We've got five minutes' peace whilst they're occupied.'

Kay slumped down on a chair. Was it right to kill others in retaliation, she wondered? Is this what the war was about? Tit-for-tat and so-called justice. Her head was spinning with the announcer's persistent claims.

As the kettle boiled, Vi sighed. 'No one said life is fair, ducks.'

'But when will this war stop?' Kay wiped her damp cheeks. 'How long do we go on hurting each other?'

'It's the human race. That's what we do best. Fight for our countries. If we didn't fight, the enemy would invade us.'

Once again they sat thinking. 'If only I knew where Alan was,' Kay said with a sigh. 'Not knowing is putting me on edge.'

'You'll get used to it, Kay.'

'Do you think so?'

'Nothing else worrying you, is there? Have you seen that stranger again?'

'No.'

'Did you tell Alan?'

'Didn't want to worry him.'

Vi craned her neck to look out of the window. 'Would you believe it, Paul's gone next door again. That's the third time this week he's called. Bit regular, this decorating lark, ain't it?'

Kay went to stand beside Vi. They watched the tall figure of Paul, dressed in overalls, disappear into the Anderson. He was gone for a minute then appeared with a tin. 'Must be for the decorating,' Kay said.

But Vi gave Kay a scowl. 'It don't take that long to paint four walls.'

'The house is in a bad state.'

'I hope that girl keeps a sensible head.'

'What do you mean?'

'Obvious, ain't it?'

Kay felt upset at this remark. 'Babs is only interested in her place looking nice.'

Vi didn't reply and instead made the tea. As Kay looked down at her half-peeled vegetables, she felt angry. The war distorted everything: people's lives and opinions. It was true, there was always temptation for lonely women. But Babs was different. She loved Eddie and her kids. Even so, Kay began to think about what Vi had said. At the factory, there were affairs going on all the time. Some of the women had taken boyfriends in their husbands' absence. Some even boasted of it. But Babs was a good mother and loyal wife. She had always put her family first. Kay began peeling the potato again. Babs was level-headed and would never stray.

She was sure of it.

On a sunny April morning, Kay received a letter from Len. He had written a page only and it was rather formal. He told her that Lil and Bob had asked him and Doris to Berkshire to stay for a week or two in spring. But he was too committed at work in the early months and only had time in late summer, August or September. He added that he thought it was a good idea if Kay brought Alfie along then too and they could all spend some time together.

Kay decided she would not hurry to reply as August and September were a long way off. It was nice that Len had written to her with the suggestion and it showed that Doris too felt agreeable to meeting up. However Kay didn't want to make an arrangement that she'd have to break if, by some miracle, Alan came home. Deciding that she might discuss this with Babs, she called on her friend the next morning.

'Kay, Alfie,' Babs said in surprise as she opened the front door to Kay's knock. 'Come in, both of you. I've been meaning to call round. Sorry about the smell of paint.'

'Is the decorating finished?'

'Not yet.'

In the front room, Kay was surprised to meet Paul, who was dressed in his overalls and splashing a green colour over the walls. 'Hello, Kay.'

'This looks nice.'

'Yes, it does,' agreed Babs. 'But Paul suggests hanging wallpaper in the passage to cover the holes.'

'Won't that be a bit expensive?' said Kay.

'No, I can get hold of some wallpaper at work,' Paul said with a shrug.

Just then, Gill and Tim came noisily down the stairs. 'Aunty Kay, can Alfie play with us in the street? The backyard's too small for rounders.'

'I don't know about that.' Kay hesitated. She was thinking of what Lil had said about kids roaming the streets of the East End.

'I'll watch out for them,' volunteered Paul, nodding to the window.

Kay saw Babs blush. 'I'm sure he'll be all right, Kay. Gill, you'll look after Alfie, won't you?'

'Yes, course.' Gill grabbed Alfie's hand.

'Off you go then.'

When the children had gone, Babs led the way to the kitchen. Kay thought that Babs looked exceptionally pretty in her summer frock and sandals, with her wavy blonde hair now styled at shoulder-length. Remembering she had intended to talk to Babs about Len's suggestion of meeting up, Kay realized that seeing Paul in the front room like that had quite put her off her stroke. Instead she said uncertainly, 'So, have you heard from Eddie yet, Babs?'

'Yes. He's due some leave soon,' Babs replied as she put the kettle on.

'Oh, that will be wonderful.'

'Yes.' Babs kept her back to Kay.

'You must be excited.'

'I am. It's just that I'm not holding out hope. You know what the services are like. They could cancel at a moment's notice.'

'I'll have the kids over when he's home. You and Eddie can enjoy a romantic evening.'

'Thanks.' Babs didn't smile. Instead she said quickly, 'And what about Alan?'

'Nothing since his last letter,' said Kay. 'Though I did have a letter from Len inviting me and Alfie up to Mum's in Berkshire later in the year. Said it would be nice for us all to spend some time together.'

'How do you feel about that?'

'I don't know yet.' Kay was on the point of giving the reason for her doubts when Babs spoke again.

'Kay, can I ask you something personal?'

'Course, what?'

'It's about Norman.'

'*My* Norman?' Kay was surprised.

'I suppose it's not exactly about Norman . . .' Babs looked uncomfortable as she hesitated. 'You've been married twice, Kay – you've loved two men. Do you ever think of Norman and your life together? In comparison with how you are now with Alan?'

Kay frowned. 'Is there some reason you're asking?'

'Yes, there is.'

'I loved Norman in my own way,' Kay said carefully. 'He was a good husband. We grew up together and neither of us went out with anyone else. It just seemed to be expected of us to get married.'

'But with Alan it was different?'

Kay smiled. 'Yes, very.'

Kay saw tears sliding down Babs's cheeks. 'Oh, Babs, whatever's wrong?'

'Nothing.' Babs sniffed and turned away.

'Is it Eddie? Are you just missing him?'

'No. It's not that.' Babs pushed her hair away from her damp face and once again gazed into Kay's eyes. 'You might not speak to me again if I tell you.'

'Don't be daft! You're me best friend.'

'You're the only one I can tell.'

'Is it to do with Paul?'

Babs nodded. 'Have you guessed?'

'I hope not.'

'It's not that I don't love Eddie, I do. He's a wonderful husband and father. We've been married ten years. But I can't help these other feelings.'

'What sort of feelings?'

It was a long time before the whispered reply came. 'I'm attracted to Paul and I can't think clearly – I can't get him out of my mind.'

Kay stared at her friend. It wasn't as though Babs was talking but someone else whom Kay didn't know. 'Babs, this isn't like you.'

'I know and I'm ashamed of meself. But it's the truth.'

'Is he – does Paul . . .'

'Yes, he feels the same too.'

'Has he told you so?'

'As he was leaving the other night and the kids were in bed, we were about to say goodnight. It was like something came over us. We knew it was wrong but neither of us could stop. We just couldn't help kissing.'

Kay felt as though she wanted to get hold of Babs and shake her. 'Babs, you're a married woman.'

'I know.'

'You've got to snap out of it. You're just missing Eddie. And what if the kids saw?'

Babs was silent, wiping her cheeks with her fingers. 'That's why I asked you about Norman and Alan. I wondered if you could love two men at the same time.'

'You're not in love with Paul. It's just an infatuation. Stop now before any harm is done.'

'Oh, Kay, I don't think I can.'

'Babs, you're risking your marriage. Think how hurt Eddie would be if he found out.'

'I don't know about that.'

Kay was shocked at this comment. 'Eddie adores you. You and the kids are his world.'

'All he writes about is the weather.'

'That's just Eddie. Listen, don't have Paul to work inside the house again. Put temptation out of the way.'

Suddenly there were voices from the passage. Babs quickly dried her eyes on the towel hanging from the nail driven into the side of the table. 'What's the matter, Gill, what's wrong?' Babs called, clearing her throat at the same time.

'It's a lady for Aunty Kay,' Gill shouted. 'She was knocking next door so I told her Aunty Kay was in here.'

Kay and Babs walked into the passage. Gill ran off leaving a woman with long blonde hair standing on the doorstep. Beside her was a young boy of about Tim's age.

'Can I help you?' asked Kay.

'I'm looking for Kay Lewis.'

'That's me.'

The woman raised one slim, black-pencilled eyebrow. 'My name's Dolores, but everyone calls me Dolly. And this,' she placed a hand on the boy's shoulder, 'is my son, Sean. Named after his Irish granddaddy.'

Once again there was silence.

'Have we met before?' asked Kay.

'No. But my surname is Lewis, just like yours.'

Kay frowned. 'So you're a relative?'

'You could say that, yes.' Dolly added with a tight smile, 'We're both married to the same man – that good-for-nothin' fly-by-night, Alan Lewis.'

Chapter Nineteen

'There must be some mistake,' Kay protested. 'You've got the wrong person.'

'I'm after Alan Lewis of Slater Street. Harry Sway told me he lives at number one hundred and three.'

'Harry? What's he got to do with it?'

'I met him in a pub recently. He described Alan down to a T. Seems your Alan and mine are one and the same.'

'That's impossible,' Kay insisted. 'I think you'd better leave before I call the police.'

Dolly Lewis laughed. 'Go ahead, love, call the Old Bill. You'll do me a favour as it's what I intend to do anyway when I leave here.'

Kay was so startled that she stood there open-mouthed.

'Kay, you don't have to listen to this nonsense,' Paul said as he strode in from the front room. 'Do you want me to see this lady out?'

'Stay right where you are, sonny boy,' snapped the woman, her eyes flashing. 'This is none of your business.'

Paul ignored her. 'Just say the word, Kay.'

In the silence that followed, Kay found herself considering his offer. But the woman's cold, bitter stare told Kay that she meant every word she said. 'You'd better come with me,' Kay answered, nodding to the front door.

'A bit of sense at last!' Dolly Lewis sneered.

'I don't seem to have much choice.' Kay pulled back her shoulders. 'I'll give you five minutes to say what you have to.'

'You'll be surprised at what I can tell you in half that time,' said the visitor, making Kay's heart sink.

'It's true, on me kid's life,' Dolly announced as she puffed heavily on a Woodbine and reclined on a chair in Kay's kitchen. 'You and me, love, have got ourselves hitched to a right scoundrel who left me and the lad here high and dry.' She nodded to the young boy at her side. 'Not satisfied with what he done to us, he pulled the wool over your eyes too.'

Vi's expression was one of pure disbelief as she stood at the sink, listening.

'You must be joking,' Kay gasped when Dolly paused to take a breath.

'No, love, I ain't. Why would I?'

'Appearances can be deceptive,' said Kay. 'Two men could be alike, but not the same.'

'And why should we believe you met Harry?' demanded Vi.

'It's the God's honest truth, ducks. I couldn't believe me ears neither when he told me Alan Lewis was alive and kicking in Slater Street.'

'We'll see what Harry Sway says about that.'

'Be my guest. He'll only tell you the same.' Dolly spilled ash from her cigarette into the ashtray. 'Mind, I don't blame you for being suspicious. It's no surprise to me that Alan had you fooled. He did the same to me when we first met.'

'And when exactly was that?' asked Kay.

'It was the summer of 1936. Me and my pals was having a laugh at some of them nutters up Hyde Park. Them blokes who think they've got all the answers to the world's troubles.'

'Speakers' Corner, you mean?'

'Yeah, soapbox corner, more like. Well, Alan had got himself quite an audience, some of 'em toffs an' all. See, he had this way with him, sort of looked at you with them dark eyes of his. Even if you didn't understand a word he said, you was impressed. So when he came up to me, we started chatting.' Dolly touched her hair. 'We made a good-looking couple, me and him. I liked walking out on his arm and being admired.' Dolly's smile faded. 'But my summer of love didn't last long. I fell with his kid and we tied the knot.'

'He married you?' Vi asked.

'And why shouldn't he?' Dolly Lewis looked insulted. 'With me slap on I wasn't a bad-looker.'

Kay's attention slipped to the little scrap who stood at his mother's side. Unlike Dolly who was dressed well, if tastelessly, in a figure-hugging two-piece suit and low-cut blouse, the boy's clothes were nearly falling off him. He was very thin. His arms and legs looked like sticks.

His shirt was frayed and grubby at the collar. His short trousers were not the right size, revealing the many cuts and grazes on his knees. The boots he wore were badly scuffed and down at heel.

'Have you a photograph?' asked Kay.

'Not now. What about you?'

Kay went to the front room. She was shaking and she had to calm herself before she returned to the kitchen. 'This is my husband,' she said, offering the photograph that was a copy of the one she had given to Doris. 'Now you'll see you've got the wrong man.'

Dolly stared at the photo in the wooden frame. 'This bloke's wearing a tin helmet.'

'It was taken the day Alan was given his Heavy Rescue uniform.'

Dolly peered closer. 'He's the right height and build.'

'But what about the face?' Vi insisted.

'I can only see half of it.'

'Surely you'd know your own husband!'

'Yes, course,' agreed Dolly quickly, changing her position on the chair. 'It's just that I didn't recognize him in all that clobber. Alan's a smart dresser usually. Likes the good things in life.' Dolly handed back the photograph. 'That's my Alan all right.'

'You wasn't sure at first,' protested Vi.

Dolly smirked. 'Listen, it's him. There's no mistake. Now, is there a cup of tea going and a drink for the kid? I was chucked out of me lodgings and I'm brassic. We've had nothing to eat all day.'

'Thought you was in a pub,' objected Vi. 'You had enough money to buy booze.'

'The drinks was bought for me. Ask Harry. Anyway, it's not for myself I'm asking. It's Sean I'm worried about. He ain't had a decent meal in days. If you ain't willing to do a nipper a small kindness, I suppose we'll have to go down the Sally Army.'

'Are you hungry, Sean?' Kay asked the boy.

He nodded silently, glancing at his mother. Kay noted how nervous he seemed, almost afraid to respond.

As Kay went to the larder, she didn't miss the satisfaction on Dolly Lewis's face. It was madness to think for a minute that Alan had ever known her, much less married her. If only there had been another photo that would have proved conclusively that Dolly Lewis had accused the wrong man!

At last, Kay and Vi found themselves alone. Kay cleared away the dishes from the small meal she had given to the boy and his mother. The thick slices of bread and dripping together with thin slices of Spam and cold mashed potato had vanished in minutes. Kay couldn't forget how painfully thin the youngster was. He looked as though he hadn't had a wash in weeks and Kay had seen something crawling in his hair. She had calculated the dates that his mother had given them; if Sean was born in April 1937, he was only nineteen months older than Alfie. Kay had met Alan in the autumn of 1937, on his return from Spain. She tried to think of how long Alan had said he'd spent fighting there. Was it six months or more? She couldn't remember.

'Kay, are you all right?' Vi asked as she helped her at the sink. 'You don't believe a word that woman says, I hope.'

'No. But it was a coincidence that her Alan's appearance was like my Alan's.'

'You've only got her word for that. There must be lots of Alan Lewises in London.'

'Why choose us?'

Vi shook her head. 'Dunno.'

'I'm worried about that boy. I think he was afraid of her.' Kay looked at the empty plates, remembering how he had pushed everything into his mouth as though he was starving. 'I don't know how she could see her son go hungry like that.'

'Chances are, all she was after was a hand-out.'

'She said she'd go to the police.'

'Just an idle threat, mark my words. She's not the type to have truck with the law.'

Kay's thoughts were spinning. She wanted to sort them all out and feel normal again. But she couldn't. She went back to the chair and sat down. Dolly's cigarette butts were in the ashtray, her red lipstick imprinted on them. Even the trace of her cheap perfume was still in the air. It was as if this woman had left her mark deliberately.

'What's up, flower?' said Vi, joining her at the table.

'She threatened to come back.'

'If she calls again, we'll fetch the rozzers ourselves. It's her word against yours. And I know who I would choose to believe.'

Kay nodded slowly. 'I'll go round to Harry's tomorrow. Find out if she really did speak to him.'

'Watch out for his wife, Glad. She won't like to think he's been drinking with a woman.'

Kay gave this some thought. 'I'll go to the ARP depot next week.'

Vi gave a long sigh. 'I was about to make some of Lenny's fudge. But that woman has put me off my stroke.'

'You can imagine how I felt when she walked into Babs's.'

'Did Babs overhear that nonsense?'

'Paul did too,' Kay admitted. 'He even offered to throw her out.'

'Why don't he keep his nose out of other people's business?' Vi said with annoyance. 'Sorry, but I don't trust that bloke.'

'Neither do I.' Kay looked away. She had let slip a remark she would have preferred not to make.

'Oh Gawd, Kay, do you mean—'

'I hope Babs will put an end to the decorating,' was the reply Kay chose to make.

'So that's what you call it!' Vi went over to the open back door. Folding her arms across her chest, she sighed deeply. 'This flamin' war. If it ain't one thing it's another. The men should be at home protecting their women and looking after their families. Didn't we learn anything from 1914?'

Kay had no answer to that.

Chapter Twenty

There was no sign of Harry Sway when Kay went to the depot the following week, and the month had ended before she finally managed to track him down.

'Did you hear the news on the wireless this morning?' Jenny Edwards said as she and Alice Tyler stopped to talk to Kay at the bus stop. Kay had left work early in order to catch Harry at the depot. 'The Luftwaffe's on the loose again.'

'Yes, I heard,' said Kay. All week at the factory there had been talk about the attacks on Britain's historic towns and cities. The renewed efforts of the Luftwaffe were making everyone nervous again.

'Jerry's threatened to bomb every building in Britain that's got three stars in this 'istoric tourist's guide,' said Alice. 'Well, that's bound to be us soon. London's got more 'istory than anyone.'

Jenny pushed back her headscarf. 'You wanna get your Anderson kitted out again, Kay. And watch out for your Alfie in the street. If we get some of them hit-and-run attacks, he could be shot down in the road.'

Kay felt a cold shiver run down her back. She was glad when the bus came along and put an end to the gloomy conversation.

'Bye, gel. Take care of yourself,' Jenny and Alice called as Kay jumped on the bus. She sat beside an elderly man who was reading from a newspaper. The headlines were all about the raids taking place. Kay looked out of the window on the other side of the bus. Members of the civil defence were unrolling barbed wire in the street and others were piling up sandbags. Was this a sign that they expected London to be bombed again too?

When the bus passed the Mudchute gun-site, Kay noticed the soldiers were inspecting the anti-aircraft machinery. She remembered when a high-explosive bomb had been dropped close by in December 1940. It had caused great devastation and the ack-ack gun had been put out of action. The activity going on there now was worrying. Were these more signs that London was next on the enemy's list?

The bus went very slowly because of the craters in the road. Kay held on to the seat in front of her as it swerved and bumped. Each time she looked from the window, she saw the ruins of buildings. They brought back the memories of that first night of the Blitz in September 1940 when Surrey Docks had exploded in a crimson ball of fire. The eerie red glow in the sky had soon become a common sight. Could all that happen again?

When Kay reached the depot ten minutes later, she was relieved to see Harry Sway standing outside. He was surrounded by a gathering of shoppers and workers, all of them talking about the same subject: the Baedeker raids, as they were now called.

'We're on red alert,' Harry was warning. 'But this time, if Jerry has marked our card then we'll be ready and waiting.'

Everyone was nodding and looking worried.

'Harry, have you got a minute?' Kay asked as she pushed her way through.

He ran his hand through his wiry, grey hair, replacing his helmet and pulling it down hard. 'You come about yer Anderson, love? Do you want me to take a look at it before it gets dark?'

'Why?'

'You wanna make sure it's up to scratch.'

'Yes, I know that, but—'

'There could be a rough time ahead,' Harry interrupted.

'So everyone says. But Harry, I've got something else to ask you.'

Harry gave her a frown. 'What's that?'

Kay didn't get a chance to ask as a big lorry with a canvas top pulled up next to them. One by one, members of the Home Guard climbed out.

'Here's me back-up,' said Harry. 'I'll have to go.'

She caught his arm. 'Harry, did you meet a blonde woman in a pub recently?'

He looked alarmed. 'Could've. Why?'

'I only want to know because someone named Dolly

called at our house. She said she'd spoken to you and you sent her round.'

'Matter of fact I remember her now,' the warden acknowledged, looking a little uncomfortable. 'I was drinking with me mates. She came up and asked a few questions. Said she was an old friend of yours and Alan's and wanted to look you up. Even bought her a Guinness as she said she was feeling poorly.' He put a hand on Kay's shoulder. 'Listen, love, don't want to put the wind up you, but if you hear the siren tonight, don't waste any time in getting the kid and Vi down the shelter. Now, I gotta go and get this sector manned.'

Kay watched him hurry off. Soon he was surrounded by the volunteers, some of them old enough to be granddads. Dressed in old and crumpled uniforms and without any weapons, they gathered around Harry, eager to do as he instructed. At least Dolly hadn't told Harry who she claimed to be, Kay thought with relief.

Kay decided to walk home as she pieced her thoughts together. Harry had only bought Dolly a drink because she said she was unwell. Dolly had made their meeting sound intimate. She'd also lied about being an old friend. So what other lies was she capable of telling?

'Anyfink for us, missis?' a voice called.

Kay stopped and looked at the cart in the road. Two young boys were pulling it along. They both reminded her of Sean with their neglected clothing and dirty faces. The notice on the side of the cart said, 'Salvage for the war effort'. The cart was piled up with newspapers, cardboard and rubbish.

'No, sorry,' Kay said with a smile. 'But if you come to Slater Street I'll have something for you.'

'Fanks, we'll do that.'

Kay continued her journey home. The sight of those poor children had made her angry. In dark times like these, when even the youngest were eager to help the country, Dolly Lewis – if that was really her name – was trying a fast one.

As Harry had suggested, that evening Kay made a flask of tea and sandwiches for the Anderson. She also placed the old tin pail inside with a piece of board across the top. No one wanted to go outside to the toilet in the middle of a raid. There was a general murmur of activity in the neighbourhood. Everyone had been thrown into a state of alarm again.

'Do you think Jerry will fly over tonight, Kay?' a familiar voice called as Kay was coming out of the shelter.

Kay joined Babs at the fence. 'I saw Harry Sway at the depot. He said it's best to be prepared.'

'Yes, I heard that too. When I put the kids to bed tonight, I told them the siren might go and if it did, to get dressed right away. I told them not to be frightened, but they only laughed and said it was exciting.'

'That's kids for you.'

Babs hesitated. 'Kay, has that woman bothered you again?'

'No, thank goodness.'

'Did she really see Harry Sway?'

'Yes. Dolly told Harry a different story altogether. Said that me and Alan were old friends and she wanted to look us up.'

Babs frowned. 'You should have let Paul throw her out.'

Kay looked at her friend. 'Is Paul still doing the decorating?'

'No. Eddie's coming home. I had a letter this morning. He writes he's really looking forward to seeing us. As it's a week's leave, he's going to take us up to Lyons.'

Kay studied her friend's face. What was she thinking?

'The kids will be pleased to see their dad,' Babs murmured.

Kay wanted Babs to be back to her old self; the Babs she knew, whose emotions weren't confused and made her sound like another person. And with Eddie home soon, perhaps everything was going to be all right again.

Though the East End wasn't seriously targeted, Kay woke up each morning to depressing news. There were many aerial assaults over Britain. Beautiful, historic towns like Exeter, Bath, Norwich, York and Canterbury had all been bombed. Other towns followed. The attacks continued well into May and every night Kay prepared a flask – just in case.

'Says here,' read Vi from the newspaper late one Friday afternoon as she sat on the wall, 'these hit-and-run missions of Germany's Focke-Wulf fighting planes is Hitler's latest tactics. There's just the pilot in the plane and he risks life and limb to swoop low and drop his bombs.'

Kay paused in her sweeping of the yard and let the warmth of the day wash over her as Vi continued to read the article. Eddie had been home on leave since the weekend and they all had a good chat earlier that morning. It had been good to see the family together once more. Eddie had asked about Alan but there wasn't much news to tell. Instead, Eddie had lifted Alfie into his arms and thrown him in the air, making him giggle, just like Alan used to. Alan would smile if he could see what Alfie was up to now. The yard was full of the kids' things, including an old wooden box that Tim and Alfie were making into a cart. She had loaned them the wheels from the pram, a length of rope and some other bits and pieces. Though without Tim, Alfie had no idea what to do with them and he was just sitting on the ground, winding the rope around the box.

Just then there was a distant rumble above, bringing Kay sharply out of her thoughts. The droning of planes was coming closer. 'Talk of the devil,' called Vi, closing the newspaper quickly and lowering herself from the wall. 'Is that the Luftwaffe or our boys?'

Kay scooped Alfie to his feet. They all went to stand at the Anderson's door, ready to dash inside.

'Whoever it is, it's someone in trouble,' said Vi, as they all stared upwards. 'Looks like Jerry's being chased by a couple of Spits.'

Kay shielded her eyes against the sun as the planes flew over at low altitude. It was clear the enemy plane was being chased by several British fighters. Before very long a dull groaning sounded and a plume of black smoke trailed in the sky.

The sickening whine of the Luftwaffe bomber going down caused Kay to look away. He might bail out in time or he might not. But everyone knew the chances of survival weren't good.

'Don't make sense, does it?' sighed Vi, blinking her eyes after looking into the sun. 'He might be the enemy but that don't help when you know it's his dying moments. Could've been one of ours. In the end, it's tit for tat, like these Baedeker raids. They're doing it 'cos we done it to them.'

'Let's go inside,' Kay suggested. On this lovely day she didn't want to think about the tragedies of war. 'Alfie, you'll have to make do with us for company this afternoon. Tim and Gill have gone to the park with their daddy.'

'Where's my daddy gone?' asked Alfie, pleating his small brow under his shock of dark hair.

'He's away fighting,' Kay answered. She bent down on one knee and wrapped her arms around him. 'But one day he'll be home. And we'll all walk down to the river again.'

Alfie gave a big grin. At three-and-a-half, he had strong pearly-white baby teeth and had lost his puppy fat. He looked so much like Alan that her heart skipped a beat. She was about to ask him if he would like some dinner when there was a knock at the front door. Vi went to answer it.

Expecting it to be the Chapmans back from their outing, Kay was disappointed to hear another voice.

Chapter Twenty-One

'Not you again!' Vi protested. 'You ain't welcome here.'

Kay took Alfie in her arms and hurried to the front door. Dolly Lewis and her son stood beside a man. Dressed in a garish, checked, oversized jacket and a wide-brimmed fedora hat, his narrowed eyes were fixed menacingly on Vi.

'What do you want?' Kay demanded. 'And who's this?'

'He's a pal of mine,' announced Dolly. 'Here to look after my interests.'

'What interests?'

'I want what's mine. What that blighter Alan stole from me.'

'Look, I've told you already,' Kay insisted, 'the man you're after isn't my husband.'

Dolly nodded at the man and he pushed his way in. Dolly quickly followed, dragging the boy with her.

'This ain't a bad gaff,' the man said as he strolled into the front room. 'It'd be a shame to mess it all up. You had better hand over the goods to Dolly or else.'

'Don't you try threatening us!' exclaimed Vi. 'Now, clear out, the pair of you.'

The man pushed Vi's shoulder. 'Shut up, you!'

'Leave her alone!' Kay stepped in front of Vi. 'Who do you think you are, forcing your way in like this? Get out before I call the police.'

'I told you, call 'em,' Dolly challenged again. 'When Alan ran out on me, he took some things that weren't his to take. When I reported the theft the coppers told me he was an ex-con and knew him of old.' Dolly drew in a quick breath. 'Now, if you've got me stuff tucked away somewhere, then you'd better own up before I get Sid on the job.'

'I don't know what you're talking about,' replied Kay. 'There's nothing in this house that belongs to you.'

'We'll see about that,' said the man, striding over to the sideboard. He peered in and knocked out the glasses. They crashed to the floor. One by one he went through the drawers, throwing everything out. Kay was terrified but she was angry too. She tried to stop him as he went to the wardrobe, but he pushed her roughly aside. 'There's only the old trout's tat in here and a train set,' he told Dolly as he tore down Vi's clothes.

'Who are you calling an old trout?' Vi yelled, but Kay caught her arm, shaking her head as the man strode up to her.

'Any more out of you and you'll get this.' He shook his fist in Vi's face.

'You'd better look upstairs,' said Dolly. 'And hurry. We ain't got all day.'

As he left the room Kay wondered if there was a policeman close by. If not, was it possible to run to the station with Alfie in her arms? But she didn't want to leave Vi alone with these two.

'Christ, Sean, what's the matter with you now?' snapped Dolly as Sean began to cry. 'You're a blessed nuisance, always moaning. Pull yourself together.' She walked to the door and looked up the stairs. 'Sid, what's keeping you?'

The little boy went very white. Kay went to him and, putting Alfie on the floor, she looked into Sean's ashen face. 'Are you all right, Sean?'

He shook his head. 'I'm gonna be sick.'

'I'm coming, I'm coming,' shouted the man as he ran down the stairs.

'What did you find?' Dolly demanded.

'Nothing. But then I ain't had time to turn the place over properly.'

Dolly turned to Kay and screwed up her face in anger. 'If you're so worried about my boy then you'd better see what you can do for him. He's your family after all, ain't he? Your kid and mine – they're the spit of one another.' She slid her hand through the man's arm. 'Come on, Sid, we'll leave Sean here while we go for a drink.'

'You can't do that!' gasped Vi.

'Who says?' sneered Dolly as she tossed back her head. 'If you decide not to cough up my things, it'll be the worse for you.' They walked out, slamming the door after them.

'The heartless hussy,' spluttered Vi. 'How could she leave her boy with strangers? And why does she think we're hiding her stuff?'

Kay didn't have time to reply as Sean leaned over and was sick.

Kay looked at the couch where Sean was lying. After she and Vi had cleared the mess, which had luckily gone over the tiles in the hearth and not on the square of carpet, Sean had fallen asleep.

'Poor little lamb,' sighed Vi as Kay swept the last of the broken glass into the dustpan and emptied it into the bin. 'What do you think's wrong with him?'

'Don't know, Vi. But he's dreadfully thin. How could she let him get like that?' Kay looked with pity at the little boy, his chin hidden under one of Vi's blankets. Alfie sat quietly at Sean's feet, holding the blue train that he had unsuccessfully tried to persuade Sean to play with.

'Is 'e gonna be sick again?' Alfie asked in concern.

'No, love. He'll be all right now.' Kay smiled.

'Will 'e play with me?'

'We'll have to see when he wakes up.'

'It's hard to believe she just walked off like that,' repeated Vi with a shake of her head. 'And that slimy spiv! Smashing our glasses and turning out all me clothes! I'll give him old trout!'

'What kind of things were they looking for?' wondered Kay.

'Did he do much damage upstairs?'

'No. Just looked through all me drawers. At least he didn't find the money that Alan left.'

'Where is it?'

Kay nodded outside. 'In the Anderson.'

Vi smiled, though she quickly returned to being angry as she gazed at Sean. 'All that about Alan being in prison and nicking her stuff. Do you reckon we should tell the law?'

'I'd have to go up to the local station. And they might come back while I'm gone.'

'I wouldn't let 'em in.'

Just then, Sean stirred, rubbing his eyes. 'Do you want to be sick again?' asked Kay.

'Where's me mum?'

'She'll be back soon.'

He stared at Alfie over the top of the blanket.

'Do you feel better?' Kay asked. 'Would you like something to eat?'

He nodded, wiping his dirty nose with the back of his hand.

'Me an' all,' said Alfie, grinning.

'You as well, tiger,' said Kay with a smile.

It was clear that Alfie had taken a shine to their young visitor.

'Look like little angels, don't they?' whispered Vi as they stood in Alfie's bedroom that night.

The two boys were asleep, both top-and-tailed and dressed in pyjamas. Though Sean was older he wasn't much taller than Alfie and the striped pyjamas, both sets old and darned, were a big improvement on his dirty clothes. Alfie slept in the bed while Sean occupied one of the Anderson mattresses placed on the floor. 'He was happy to play with Alfie,' Kay replied softly. 'And didn't seem to mind staying the night.'

'Not a murmur out of him,' agreed Vi, pulling her old cardigan across her chest. 'That woman should be put behind bars.'

'I won't go to work in the morning,' decided Kay. 'Dolly and her minder are certain to appear.'

'Your boss won't like that.'

'He'll have to lump it.' Kay switched off the light and they went downstairs.

'Don't fancy letting that flash package in again,' said Vi as they sat by the fire.

'We won't,' Kay said firmly. 'We'll keep both the front and back doors locked, like they are now. Then when they knock, I'll take Sean out through the yard and into the Cut, then go round to the front.'

'What if that idiot gets stroppy?'

'He won't, not where everyone can see him.'

'You could ask Eddie to help,' suggested Vi.

'It's his leave. I don't want to spoil it.'

With their plans made, they decided to go to bed. But Kay didn't sleep very well. She couldn't rest, thinking of what was going to happen tomorrow. To her surprise, both boys were sleeping soundly when she got up in the morning and it was only when Vi called them for breakfast that they appeared with yawns and sleepy faces.

'Is me mum coming?' Sean asked as he ate his porridge.

'I should think so,' said Kay, glancing at Vi. 'Do you live round here?'

But Sean only lifted his shoulders in a shrug.

After the boys were dressed, they played with the train set.

'It felt a sin to put them dirty clothes back on him,' said Vi as she and Kay kept watch at the window.

'I'd have rinsed them out if there was time,' agreed Kay.

'Still can't believe she just left him here.'

'Neither can I.'

All day they waited for the knock to come. But it never did.

After breakfast the next morning, Kay and Vi carried in the tin bath. 'Your mum and her pal will have to wait in the street if they come,' said Vi to Sean as she secured the back door again. 'A good scrub is long overdue. Now, drop your towel, love, and in you climb.'

'Don't want to.' Sean looked frightened of the water.

'Water ain't going to bite you, son,' coaxed Vi. 'And there's a niff in this kitchen that's making the place smell like a gorilla's armpit.'

'You'll like it, I promise,' Kay urged.

'Don't think he's ever seen a bath before,' frowned Vi, 'let alone sat in one. Tell you what, Alfie, you get in first.'

Kay nodded and Alfie enthusiastically stripped down and climbed into the water. 'See, it won't hurt you,' said Kay. 'It's lovely.'

'C'mon, Sean!' Alfie splashed the water. Sean jumped back but soon he was laughing. After a few minutes, Kay was relieved to see one foot go in and then the other.

'That's the ticket,' grinned Vi. 'Now have a good soak.'

It was painful for Kay to look at Sean's thin body. His bow legs, pronounced rib cage and stick-like arms were startling against Alfie's well-fed physique. But soon laughter was echoing in the kitchen as Vi attempted to wash them both with the Lifebuoy soap.

Kay found herself thinking again of what Dolly had said. With their wet hair slicked back and big brown eyes, the likeness between them was remarkable.

Monday 1 June dawned bright and clear. Once again, Dolly had not shown up. Leaving Vi briefly with the boys, Kay went to the factory very early. She had decided to ask for a few days off. She couldn't leave Vi to shoulder the responsibility of Sean. There was nothing else to be done but stay at home until Dolly put in an appearance.

'If everyone in this factory wanted to take their holiday on the spur of the moment, our planes wouldn't have no wings to fly with,' her supervisor complained. She felt guilty, but had her way in the end.

'What are we going to do, love?' asked Vi as they watched the two boys playing in the yard.

'I don't know,' said Kay with a shrug. 'What can have happened to Dolly?'

'P'raps she's done a bunk for good.'

'And abandoned her own son?'

'Could be what she wanted all along. P'raps she got the idea in the pub when she heard Harry talking.'

'So she made up this Alan, just to get rid of Sean?' Kay shook her head. 'No, I think she wanted something more. Or why else did she bring that man to look for her stuff?'

'So you think she'll be back?'

'Yes, I do.' Kay couldn't believe that a mother, even a mother like Dolly, would leave her son in such a way.

'Have you told Babs what happened?'

'Not yet. Eddie was due to go back yesterday.'

'Gill and Tim will call after school. You could give her the nod then.'

'Yes, I will.' Kay lowered her elbows to the draining board and rested her chin in the palms of her hands. 'I wonder if Sean has been to school.'

'Don't seem like it,' decided Vi.

'I'll get Alfie's crayons. See what he can do.'

But Vi tapped Kay on her shoulder. 'Don't go getting too interested. It's his mother's job to see to his education, not yours. You'll only get hurt when she takes him away.'

But Kay was wondering what kind of mother would neglect their child so badly. Did Dolly have a conscience?

Perhaps she was trying out her luck, believing Kay was a soft touch and would return only when it suited her.

'If he's not your child, then I haven't the authority to issue coupons,' said the woman at the food office a week later.

'I'm only asking for what a young boy needs,' Kay repeated. 'I took him to the doctor who said he's undernourished and must eat properly. He's got to have milk, orange juice and cod liver oil. He needs clothes and shoes too.'

'His mother should be here seeing to that, not you.'

'I told you, she's disappeared.'

'Have you reported her missing?'

'Yes. I was told lots of people go missing in wartime.' Kay had eventually decided to go to the police station. It had been a mistake. The sergeant at the desk asked some personal questions in front of other people. It was embarrassing to have to repeat what Dolly had said. Even after explaining it all, the policeman offered no help, saying it sounded like a domestic matter.

The woman removed her glasses and sighed. 'This is only the Food Office. You'll have to go to another department for missing persons.' The woman's tone softened as she saw Kay's distress. 'Look, I'm sorry, but rules are rules. Have you tried the Salvation Army?'

'I'm not asking for charity.' Kay picked up her shopping bag and left. What was she going to do? As she walked home, she decided she would use some of the fifteen pounds seventeen shillings in the Anderson to buy some clothes for Sean at the market. Somehow she would make ends meet. With her wages and Vi's small contribution, they could manage for a while.

Tomorrow she would revisit the town hall. This time she would take Sean with her and let them see how his health depended on the things the doctor had ordered.

Chapter Twenty-Two

It was the end of June and Dolly still hadn't shown up. Kay was beginning to think Vi was right. Even the woman at the council offices agreed that it looked as if Sean had been abandoned. 'I'll get someone to call and speak to you,' Kay was told at last.

To Kay's surprise, the next day a young woman arrived on the doorstep. 'I'm Miss Pearson from the Children's Welfare Department,' she explained. 'Is it convenient to speak to you?'

'Yes, come in.' Kay hadn't expected someone to turn up even though she had been promised.

Vi took Alfie into the yard and Kay sat with Sean in the front room. Miss Pearson asked Sean his name, how old he was and where he lived. Both Kay and Miss Pearson smiled when he said he lived at one hundred and three Slater Street.

'Thank you, Sean,' said Miss Pearson. 'I expect you'd like to join your friend now?'

After Sean had gone, Kay said quietly, 'He don't seem to know much about where he lived with his mother.'

'No, but I can see he's taken a shine to you.'

'He's never any trouble,' Kay agreed, going on to give an account of all that had happened since Dolly had appeared.

'So, Mrs Lewis, you have no idea where she is now?' Miss Pearson had short, curly brown hair and didn't smile much, but she seemed interested in what Kay had to say.

'No, I haven't,' Kay said.

'She left no forwarding address?'

'Like I told you, Dolly said she was going for a drink with her friend – the man who broke all me glasses and searched in the drawers for something that Dolly claimed was hers. We waited and waited but she didn't come back.'

'And you told the police?'

'Yes, I reported Dolly, not that it helped much.'

Miss Pearson frowned. 'I'm sorry to hear that.'

'If Sean had been found on the street I think they'd have taken more notice.'

'Yes, you may be right.' Miss Pearson frowned, her face clouding. 'Street children are taken into care by the authorities and put into orphanages.' She hesitated. 'Or some other kind of institution.'

'I don't like the sound of that.'

'In wartime, there are hundreds of displaced children. I'm afraid it's a growing problem. And one the authorities are failing to solve. In these unusual circumstances, you've been very kind to take Sean under your wing.'

'I don't mind looking after him,' Kay replied. 'He's no trouble and gets on well with Alfie and his friends. It's waiting for Dolly to appear that unsettles us all.'

Miss Pearson turned the page of her notebook. 'I can't do much to resolve that problem. But, you could make an application for temporary care of Sean. If granted, you would receive coupons and the things the doctor wanted him to have. There is a food and clothing allowance too.'

'What about school?' Kay asked.

'He would have to go, of course.' Miss Pearson wrote this down. She sat back then, pulling down the hem of her grey utility skirt over her crossed knees. 'You know it could be hard for you financially.'

'We'll manage somehow.'

'You could apply for a test of means.'

'No, thank you,' Kay answered at once. Undergoing a means test meant that every stick of furniture you had was evaluated, all your possessions such as they were put under a microscope. It felt like the very last resort and a disgrace.

Miss Pearson smiled. 'I've one more question. It's a rather delicate one. Is your husband aware of what's happened?'

Kay blushed. 'You can't write something like this in a letter.'

'No, I suppose not.' The young woman closed her notebook. 'Well, if you're sure about caring for Sean, I'll make the application?'

'Yes, please go ahead.'

Miss Pearson stood up. 'You'll be hearing from me soon, Mrs Lewis.'

Kay walked with her visitor to the front door. Kay glanced along the passage to the open door of the kitchen where the two boys were playing in the yard. 'You wouldn't take him away and put him in one of these institutions, would you?'

'We aren't known for dragging children off, Mrs Lewis,' Miss Pearson said with a rueful smile. 'In wartime our department has better things to do with its limited resources. However, this is rather an unusual case and I can't promise they will approve your application.'

'What about Dolly?' Kay asked. 'What if she comes round?'

'I would advise you to tell her we need to speak to her.'

With a nod Miss Pearson left. Kay wondered if she would ever see the young woman again. She was nice in her own way, but seemed more interested, just like the policeman, in writing everything down for her superiors, rather than solving the problem.

That night, after everyone was asleep, Kay was sitting in her dressing gown at the kitchen table, deep in thought. Jean Pearson had suggested a test of means, but the council representatives calling to inspect your home and everything inside it broadcast to the world that you were destitute. She couldn't have that, no matter how short money was. A family in Crane Street had been forced to give up their piano, she remembered, their only form of entertainment for the children, in order to receive help from the council. Alice Tyler had seen inside the house and said it was almost bare of furniture. A cold shiver at her neck made Kay quickly sip from the mug of cocoa she had made herself. Her pride would never allow her to be reduced to begging for help. If she was given the coupons for food and milk for Sean, it would solve half of the problem. But first and foremost, it was what the doctor had requested, that was most important—

Kay heard a slight movement behind her. Expecting to see Vi, she found instead a small figure watching her. Sean's dark eyes were almost fearful under his shock of ruffled hair. Alfie's striped pyjamas were ruckled around his thin calves, one leg up and one down. His pyjama jacket was unbuttoned, revealing his skinny chest.

'Sean?' Kay swivelled slowly on the chair. She felt she was looking at a frightened rabbit and one movement from her would send him scooting off. 'Can't you sleep?' she asked softly.

He lifted his hand and rubbed his knuckle in the corner of his eye. Kay slowly rose to her feet. Drawing her dressing gown round her, she looped the belt slowly at her waist. 'Would you like a drink of milk?' She pulled out the chair. 'Sit down and I'll pour you some.'

Sean, still looking alarmed, watched her go to the cupboard. While her back was turned, Kay heard him shuffle across the kitchen floor and the chair creak as he sat down.

When she'd poured a small amount of milk into an enamel mug, she placed it on the table in front of him. 'There you are. That will help you to sleep.'

Kay returned to her chair and watched him sip eagerly at the drink. She lifted her own enamel mug and finished her cocoa. For a few minutes afterwards Kay sat quietly with him. She could see his long lashes blinking, as though he was fighting off sleep. But she still had the feeling he'd be off if she made any sudden movement.

'Was it a dream?' she asked and smiled when he nodded. 'Alfie has them sometimes. But dreams aren't real, Sean. They go away. You mustn't be frightened.'

Sean gave a long yawn, revealing his gappy white teeth. His body seemed to relax but he showed no sign of leaving his chair. Very slowly, his eyes began to close.

Kay placed her hands on her lap. 'It's warmer over here,' she told him. 'Come and sit with me for a while before you go back to bed.'

Sean stared at her uncertainly, brought wide awake by this alarming suggestion. It was as though he'd never been asked to do such a thing in his life. Had he ever been cuddled or hugged, she wondered? Kay slowly held out her hand. 'Just for a few minutes. So we don't get cold in the kitchen.'

The little boy slipped warily from the chair. Moving towards her, he positioned himself at her knees, allowing her hand to gently slide around his waist and lift him onto her lap. At first he sat rigidly until Kay eased him against her, threading her fingers through his hair. She could smell the soap that she and Vi had used for the boys at bath time. She could also feel his stick-thin arms and bony ribs as she encircled him, laying her chin against the top of his head.

'You can always come down and talk to me if you should wake up,' Kay assured him. 'We can drink some milk and sit here like this. When you go back to bed, you'll fall fast asleep again.'

She felt him tremble slightly, then give in to her embrace and the warmth of her plaid dressing gown.

'Can I stay 'ere then?' she heard him mumble.

'Would you like to?'

In reply he nodded, allowing her to pull him closer and she too nodded in silent agreement.

Ten minutes later, he was snoring softly against her chest. She didn't want to disturb him as he seemed so content, his breathing matching her own.

Kay didn't know how long they sat there. But when she eventually woke him and hand in hand they ascended the stairs, she knew she had drawn closer to this orphan of the storm.

'Goodnight, God bless, sleep tight,' she told him, as she placed the blanket around him.

Kay guessed that Sean had never been shown affection, had not the least idea who God might be or understand the blessing that accompanied the kiss each night that he had slept here. Watching him slowly close his eyes, she was certain she saw a flickering smile on his lips and a soft sigh of contentment.

★ ★ ★

To Kay's great surprise, the very next week she received a letter from the Children's Welfare Department. Under supervision of the authorities, Kay had been granted temporary care of Sean as a war nanny. Furthermore, the doctor had confirmed her request for the concentrated orange juice, cod liver oil, priority milk and other vitamins. Kay was also allocated ten extra coupons to help with his food and clothing and fifteen shillings for his care for one month.

'That's a turn up for the books,' said Vi as Kay replaced the letter in the envelope. 'Thought we'd heard the last from that young lady.'

'She must have gone to the doctor,' said Kay, 'and checked on what I'd said.'

'I hope he told her just what a state Sean was in.'

'Must have done,' agreed Kay. 'Miss Pearson said she'd do all she could, but I didn't think she was listening.'

'I warn you, love,' Vi said firmly, 'don't go getting too fond of the boy.'

'Course not.' Kay tried to sound dismissive. But she knew she wasn't fooling anyone, least of all Vi. This little boy might be Alan's child although she was reluctant even to think about it. Sean's presence in her life could remind her of the pain that lies and deception might bring. But when she looked into Sean's eyes, she saw just a helpless little soul who had been deprived of the basic needs in his life: a mother's true love and understanding. Alfie had been given Kay's love from the start – for the nine months she had carried him in her womb then from the moment he had made an appearance on this earth. She believed it was a child's birthright to come into this world and be loved – at least, that was how Kay felt. She ached inside for any child who was robbed of it. Vi might give her all the warnings necessary about keeping her distance, but when it came to matters of the heart, Kay knew there were no bounds to her feelings.

The following day, two more letters dropped through the letter box. One was from Alan, the other from Lil. She opened Alan's first and was disappointed to read that his next letter might be a long time in coming. With all that was going on in his absence, she felt a moment's panic that any reassurance on his part that might relieve her of the worry of Dolly and Sean would be a long way off. She guessed he was being posted overseas. Where was he going? Was it to the desert? The wireless had reported that the Eighth Army was trying to beat back the German offensive at El Alamein. Or could it be somewhere in Europe or even further afield? Kay felt close to tears. Alan told her he loved her and missed her. He said his family gave him strength to fight for his country.

Kay didn't feel like opening Lil's letter. She thought she knew what Lil would want. And when Kay read it, as she suspected, Lil was making plans for Doris and Len's visit at the end of the summer. 'August is bound to be good weather,' wrote Lil. 'At the worst, it's wet but warm. Aunty Pops can't wait to see Alfie.'

With a deep sigh, Kay dropped the letter on the kitchen table. She looked out on the yard where Alfie and Sean were playing. Two little boys, one her own, the other whom she was caring for. What would her parents say if she wrote and told them about Sean, or worse, the accusations that Dolly had made against Alan? She would, of course, have to keep this to herself when she replied to Lil and regretfully suggest their visit was postponed.

Kay read Alan's letter again. 'I love you, sweetheart, and miss you.' She could hear his words in her ears, remembering with a sharp pang the last time he had made love to her.

'I wish you were here,' Kay murmured with a sigh and placed her lips on the lined paper filled with Alan's writing. She closed her eyes and tried to see his face. But all she felt was an ache inside that she knew would never ease, despite all that had happened, until he was safely in her arms again.

Chapter Twenty-Three

'It's me! Dolly. Open up!'

'Where have you been for the past four months?' Kay shouted through the locked front door. She was trembling.

'I've had things to do.'

'Things that were more important than Sean?'

Dolly pounded on the door again. 'I'm here now, ain't I? So let me in!'

Kay and Vi looked at one another. 'Has she got the spiv with her?' whispered Vi.

'Don't know.'

'What are we going to do?' Vi looked frightened.

After a silence, the front door burst open. Kay and Vi stumbled back as a splintering noise filled the air. The lock had come away from the wood. The rays of the low sun captured the outline of a giant of a man who stood beside Dolly. His head was hairless and shiny. He didn't seem to have a neck; it was lost in the muscle of his shoulders and arms bulging out from his dirty shirt.

'Who's this?' Kay demanded, trying not to look afraid. 'Where's your other pal?'

'Never you mind,' replied Dolly, walking in. 'Now, where's Sean?'

'Asleep of course, at this time of night.'

'Well, you can wake him up.'

'No,' Kay replied, folding her arms. 'Not at this time of night. Come back in the morning.'

Dolly looked up at her companion. 'I said she was a stubborn cow, didn't I?'

With a grunt, the man pushed past Kay.

'You can't go in there,' yelled Vi as with his shoulder he barged open the door of the front room. Vi put her hand to her head, swaying, as she grabbed hold of the banister.

'You're upsetting my friend,' Kay said, rushing to help Vi. 'Go away.'

'I want my stuff.' Dolly poked Kay in the shoulder.

'I thought you wanted your boy.'

'Don't worry, he's next on me list.'

There were bangs and thumps from the front room, then Dolly's accomplice appeared again. He shook his sweating head. 'If you can't find nothing, you'll have to give her a slap or two,' ordered Dolly.

Vi screamed as two big arms went around Kay and lifted her off her feet. Kay was thrown against the wall. A pain travelled down her arm as she tried to steady herself. The next moment a blow sent her reeling out on the pavement. Everything swirled in front of her as she realized she had stumbled out in the road, unable to regain her balance. She blinked her eyes fiercely to clear her vision but swaying, she felt her legs crumple beneath her.

Reaching out into thin air, she cried out softly as everything seemed to turn black around her.

'Kay, drink this.' It was Babs, holding a glass of water to her lips. Beside her was Paul. He was bending down, frowning as he looked into her face.

'You're safe now, Kay, they've gone.'

'Wh . . . what happened?'

'You fainted.'

Kay sipped the water. 'Where's Vi?'

'I'm over here, gel, in the chair,' said Vi. 'Don't worry, I'm all right. It's you we're worried about.'

Kay shuddered as the ugly memories returned. Dolly's accomplice had broken the door open and forced his way inside. The last thing she could remember was falling down on the road.

'That rotten Dolly,' muttered Babs. 'She and her cronies need sorting out.'

'Too right,' Vi murmured in a weak voice. 'The big lug clumped Kay round her head.'

Kay rubbed the tender bump by her ear. But it was her arm that hurt the worst.

'Paul drove up in his car just as you fainted,' Babs told her. 'The cowards ran off as soon as they saw him. Kay, I think we should get the doctor.'

'No. I'll be all right.' Kay gently moved her arm again. It was painful and tender, but it wasn't broken. 'Are Alfie and Sean safe?'

'They slept all through it.'

'Breaking and entering is against the law,' Paul said angrily. 'And so is assaulting you.'

'I've reported Dolly once,' Kay replied. 'I told them the whole story, but it didn't do any good.'

'But this time you were hurt, Kay. I'll take you to the station in my car if you're up to it.' Paul held out his hand.

Kay shook her head. 'No, I still feel light-headed.'

'In that case,' said Babs with a sigh as she got up, 'I'll make a cuppa and Paul'll see to the front door.'

When Kay was alone with Vi, she swung her legs down. 'Are you really all right, Vi?'

'Yes, love. But shouldn't you go to the law?'

'They won't believe me, and will just ask a lot of questions that'll only make me feel worse.'

'Well, if you say so.'

'Vi, I'm going to see Miss Pearson about Dolly.'

Vi nodded slowly. 'But will she know what to do?'

'I don't know. But it's worth a try.'

Babs came in with the tea and lowered the tray to the table. 'Are you sure I shouldn't call the doctor?'

'I feel much better now.'

'Paul's just mending the door.'

'That's kind of him. Babs, I don't know what would have happened if you and Paul hadn't arrived today.'

Babs put her hands on her hips. 'All the more reason to go to the law.'

Kay nodded. 'I'll think about it.'

Babs smiled. 'That means you won't.'

* * *

It wasn't till later in the week that Kay felt well enough to go to see Miss Pearson. Her arm still hurt, though the bruises had faded. The swelling behind her ear had gone down and at last she could walk without feeling dizzy.

'You must report this,' advised Miss Pearson. 'Of course, it's a little late now. But tell them everything that happened and if you can, bring a charge against Dolly and this man for what they did. And you do have a witness in Vi and your neighbour, although it would have been better if the doctor could have assessed your injuries.'

'I wasn't feeling well enough,' was all Kay could manage.

'I can't help you if you don't. Now, Kay, please do as I say.'

Kay finally gave in. Everyone seemed to think reporting Dolly and the man would do some good. But she suspected that she would be looked on with scorn as she had been the first time.

'I've a complaint to make,' she told the same policeman. After explaining what had happened, Kay lifted her arm and touched her head, trying to show where the damage had been done.

Sliding on his spectacles, the policeman frowned. 'Why didn't you call on us at the time?'

'I wasn't feeling well.'

He drummed his fingers on the desk. 'We get a lot of family upsets like this. It happens in wartime.'

'It's not a family upset,' Kay insisted, 'at least, not my family.'

He consulted the book on the desk. 'That's not what it says here. From our records it appears your first complaint was made against this person – named as Dolores, or Dolly, Lewis – back in May. This person visited you to say she was married to your husband and made a nuisance of herself whilst doing so.'

Kay nodded. 'That's right.'

'So what's that if it's not a domestic?'

'What I want to report today is that this woman came back again, with another friend,' Kay argued. 'The man assaulted me and my lodger, Vi Hill. Not to mention knocking down my front door.'

'Then why ain't this lodger here too?'

'Because she's at home, looking after the boys. One of them is my son, Alfie, the other is Dolly's son, Sean. The boy who she left with me the first time she came.'

The sergeant slid his pencil behind his ear. 'Look, whatever it is you've got to complain about, madam, you need evidence. You need witnesses. And if an assault has been committed, then it's fair to say we'd need to examine the victim or victims, which in this case is you and your friend. Well, one of you is standing right in front of me looking none the worse for wear and the other is at home with the kids. The alleged incident took place some days ago, and you don't know where the alleged attackers are now.' He heaved a big sigh. 'Have I got that much right?'

'Yes, but—'

'So where do you suggest we start?' asked the policeman, opening his arms. 'We're light on just about every aspect of this alleged happening. All we have is your version of a story that might or might not be true.'

'Why don't you believe me?'

'It's not up to me to believe anything. I only write down the facts.'

Kay was furious. As the people behind her made shuffling noises, she knew she was wasting her time again. She turned and, as she had before, tried to hold her head high as she left the police station, wishing she'd never done as Miss Pearson had advised.

Chapter Twenty-Four

It was almost a week later when Miss Pearson called round. 'Did you go to the police?' she asked as she sat on the couch in the front room.

'Yes.'

'What happened? I've been waiting to hear from you.'

Kay told her what the policeman had said and Miss Pearson looked very disappointed. 'Kay, I'm sorry, but you should have reported it at the time. Now there's little my department can do.'

'So I've just got to wait for her to call round again and break in?' Kay was still very angry. Every time she touched her stiff arm, she was reminded of that night.

'We can only take Dolly to task when we have evidence of negligence towards Sean or violence towards you.'

'Isn't abandoning him enough?'

'From what you've told me, I believe it could be. But first we've got to find her and that, at the moment, is our problem. There are so many displaced families in the East End, indeed all over London. Reaching them is almost impossible unless they register with the authorities. And I'm afraid to say, for one reason or another, many don't.'

Kay's anger slowly ebbed. She knew it was her fault that she hadn't agreed to let Paul take her to the police station to report the assault. Perhaps if she had, they would be out searching for Dolly.

'There is one thing I can do,' said Miss Pearson thoughtfully. 'I could write an official letter to Dolly saying she must present herself at our offices at once. I shall stress that failing to do so will result in the involvement of the police and welfare services. I'll request she brings all her current information, including her address and her identity papers. Coming from an official source, this might be enough to make her think twice before she or her accomplice acts violently or tries to take Sean again.'

'But you don't know her address.'

Miss Pearson took a breath, meeting Kay's eyes. 'You'll have to hand the letter to her in person.'

Kay didn't think Dolly would be put off by a letter, even if it was an official one. Would she even bother to read it? But, as Miss Pearson was trying so hard to help, Kay agreed.

'Meanwhile, I may be able to arrange a place for Sean at Quarry Street School.'

At this, Kay sat up, excited. 'The children next door go there!'

'I'll speak to the head teacher, Mr Barnet.'

Kay knew Sean would do well at school if given the chance. He could draw and colour very well and she read to him and Alfie each night. She also knew this young woman was doing everything she could to help and for that, Kay was very grateful. 'Thank you, Miss Pearson.'

'It's Jean, actually. May I call you Kay?'

Kay nodded, beginning to feel that at least there was someone who understood Sean's plight. Next time Dolly arrived, she would have a surprise. It was only a letter. But words, it was said, were mightier than the sword.

Kay, Babs and the four children, the three elders wearing their navy-blue and grey uniforms, were making their way to school in the gloomy light of a misty September morning; Jean Pearson had been true to her word and found a place for Sean. Kay watched the children run ahead, and every so often, Sean glanced round to catch her eye. She smiled as she always did, the brief reassurance that all was well now an understanding between them.

Kay hadn't had to buy much for Sean as Babs had given her all Tim's outgrown clothes. Even the satchel had cost next to nothing, bought second-hand from the market, she reflected with pride.

Both Kay and Babs wore headscarves and winter coats, and had shopping bags looped over their arms since they'd decided to call at the market afterwards.

'Just look at them,' said Babs, nodding to the four youngsters. 'You won't find better pals anywhere.'

Kay smiled. 'Alfie can't wait to join them in school.'

'It won't be long now. He's big for his age,' observed Babs. 'With all that lovely dark hair and wide smile, him and Sean could be mistaken for—' Babs stopped, going red. 'Oh, sorry! It just slipped out.'

But Kay was nodding. 'The thought's crossed my mind too. Though I know it can't be true they're half-brothers.'

'Course it can't.'

Kay shivered a little. Dolly had managed to plant a seed in her mind and it was very difficult to ignore, especially now that Sean was filling out and looking healthier by the day. The doctor had said that even the rickets was improving.

'Paul's painting the passage at the moment,' Babs slipped into the conversation. 'It's looking really nice.'

'Yes, I'm sure.'

'Kay, I can't stop seeing him.'

'Babs, it's up to you.'

'Do you blame me?' asked Babs sadly.

'No. But I'm afraid for you.'

'Paul is a good man, Kay, a really good man.'

'So is Eddie.'

'Yes, I know,' Babs admitted with a sigh.

Kay thought that Paul, for all his supposed goodness, wasn't averse to taking another man's wife. The policeman at the station's words rang in her ears. In wartime there were family upsets – domestics, he called them. Were Babs and Eddie to become one of these?

'What about Rose?' Kay asked.

'Who's Rose?'

'Paul's girlfriend, the one from the factory.'

'Oh, her. That was over long ago. And she wasn't really his girlfriend. Nothing serious, anyway.'

So Babs saw her relationship with Paul as something special, Kay thought in alarm. Kay loved her friend, wanted to support her as Babs had always done for her. But to watch Babs heading for disaster, which it could only prove to be if Eddie found out, was very upsetting.

'Paul slept over last night,' Babs said quietly, casting a sidelong glance at Kay. 'He had a day off work today and said he'd get stuck into the painting.'

Kay's heart sank. 'What did the kids say when they saw him?'

'He told them he'd called round early to start the decorating.'

Kay didn't know how to respond. What would happen when Eddie found out? It was the children who would suffer if their mum and dad quarrelled.

'Kay—' Babs began but stopped as Gill, Tim, Alfie and Sean came running towards them. They had their school caps on backwards and their coats over their shoulders like capes. Their laughter filled the air and echoed round the street.

Kay watched as they gathered round, laughing and talking all at once. They were so innocent and so happy; how sad it was that things in adults' lives came along to spoil all that.

Paul was walking down Slater Street towards them. Kay could understand why Babs was attracted to this man. Wearing his workmanlike paint-spattered overalls, he cut a handsome figure in his own way. The morning sun, which had now come out from the mist, shone down on his light-coloured hair and accentuated the blue of his eyes. Babs, who had taken in an audible breath at the sight of him, slowed her steps.

'Me insides go over when I see him,' Babs confided. 'I just can't help it.'

'Your insides probably did the same with Eddie, only you can't remember,' Kay whispered back. But Babs hadn't heard as she fixed her eyes on the approaching figure.

'Have you finished painting already?' she asked Paul as he met them.

'No, I've not got started, actually.' He looked at Kay. 'Just after you went, Dolly turned up.'

Kay's heart dropped. 'Where's Vi? What happened—'

'Vi's in Babs's place,' Paul replied calmly. 'I've made her a strong cup of tea and she's having a smoke.'

Kay gasped. 'Did Dolly come with her minder?'

'No, she was alone and started kicking up rough with Vi. The front door was open and I heard the ruckus, so I went out immediately.'

Kay was trying to walk towards the house at the same time as talking. But Paul grabbed her arm.

'Wait a mo, Kay. Calm down.'

'I knew I shouldn't have left her alone.'

'You wasn't to know Dolly was to turn up,' Babs told her, but Kay was full of guilt.

'It was probably a good thing as it happens,' Paul explained. 'Dolly was sounding off at the deep end. She stunk of booze, so obviously she'd needed Dutch courage to come round without muscle. Vi was keeping her on the doorstep, telling her that Sean was in school. That she was to go to Quarry Street and speak to the head teacher, Mr Barnet, if she wanted to know more about her son. When I pitched up, Dolly told me to shove off. I replied it was her who ought to do that and come back when she was sober. Then I saw Vi disappear indoors. When she came out again, she gave Dolly a letter. Told her it was from the authorities who knew all about her little games and were on the look-out for her. As drunk as Dolly was, she clocked this.'

'Did she read the letter?'

'Yes. And I won't repeat the language she used after.'

'Poor Vi,' Kay said in despair. 'It should have been me that faced Dolly.'

Paul shrugged lightly. 'For all her verbal, she did a bunk pretty quick.'

Kay managed to draw a deep breath. 'Thanks, Paul.'

'None are needed, Kay. I'm glad to be of help.'

'I'll go in and see Vi now.'

As Kay walked towards Babs's house, she was trying hard to compose herself. But at the sight of a grey-faced Vi sitting in Babs's kitchen, a roll-up trembling on her lips, Kay burst into tears.

'I'm sorry. I shouldn't have left you alone,' Kay blurted as she wrapped her arms around Vi.

'Don't be a silly moo,' replied Vi with a choked laugh as she took the cigarette from her lips and blew the smoke over

Kay's head. 'I give Dolly the letter, flower, and in company too – Paul was a witness, so she can't say she never got it. I reckon it was meant to be you wasn't here. And I can tell you this, as sozzled as she was, that letter worked like a charm. Miss Pearson done a good job and frightened the life out of her. I told Dolly we wanted her address so's we could give it to the welfare. She nearly collapsed on the spot.'

'I can vouch for that,' agreed Paul.

'And not a word about Sean, either,' continued Vi. 'Matter of fact, when I told her to go up the school, her reply didn't consist of no words to be found in the dictionary. Dolly don't care about Sean, not at all, except to use him when it suits her. The point is, she's convinced you have something of hers, or rather this Alan of hers has, though I reckon there's a lot more to that story than she lets on.'

'Well, it's a story I don't want to hear,' said Kay. 'I just wish she'd go away.'

'Don't we all,' agreed Babs.

'I don't think you'll see her anytime soon,' commented Paul. 'Vi's right, that letter gave her a nasty turn.'

Kay knew she had Jean Pearson to thank for this. But how long would Dolly's fear last? It was clear to everyone that Dolly was a neglectful mother, a liar and a bully. But, as wayward as Dolly was, it didn't mean to say all her story was untrue. As Kay reflected on this she shivered, her skin going cold and clammy; if this was the case then it could mean that her Alan and Dolly's might be one and the same.

Chapter Twenty-Five

Added to the fact that the two-seater Lysander plane was flying without any navigation other than the pilot's map and compass, Alan was seriously doubting that the six months of Special Operations training had been enough to prepare him for the ordeal ahead. Although he was kitted out with the latest gear – a camouflage canvas suit together with helmet and side ear extenders, goggles and a wealth of specialized equipment strapped to his body – the safety of the training grounds of Unit 105 in the UK felt light years away. The reality of the here and now was the pitch-black night, lightened only by the stars and his view of the land beneath, an ominous layered blanket illuminated only by an occasional twinkling. Somewhere in all that murk, the French Resistance were waiting for his arrival.

Alan lay his sweat-laden palm on the body-wrap beneath his clothes. He intended this as a reassuring action, his body and mind having undergone a harrowing year of preparation for this moment. But instead, fear filled him as he felt the holster of the 9mm pistol and silencer. He knew his life must depend upon the use of the weapon, the intent to kill another human being. By now, the lengthy SOE mock-interrogations and daily practice of guerrilla warfare that he had absorbed should have prepared him. But he was nevertheless too scared, almost, to breathe.

'You are fighting for your homeland, Lewis,' his instructors had repeated until it had become fixed in his head. He knew his future was at stake as well as that of the country. He had been told he must become ruthless. But was he? Many lives depended on the fact that the false information he was to plant in the military building would lead the enemy into British traps. But now, as the cold of the night slid its icy fingers into the folds of his flying jacket, Alan recoiled at what might be ahead of him. Could he really kill another man in cold blood? And if he was captured, would he have enough guts to end his own life?

As the noise of the plane's engine changed, he glimpsed five individual lights below. Five illuminations, just as planned. Torches set up by the Resistance.

The pilot raised his gloved hand to signal. The Lysander dipped and along with it, Alan's stomach. There was no time now for fear. He must work on the adrenaline. This was the border of occupied France and supposedly neutral Spain. He would not be able to think of Kay and Alfie again, with hope, until he had fulfilled his mission.

The plane levelled precariously and bumped down on the short stretch of flat that was used as a temporary runway. Alan silently listed the small weaponry packed in his haversack. Delayed action pencil fuses. Carefully prepared detonators to be used with the explosives the French would provide. Tinned steel tyre-bursters with mechanized triggers. Nitrated code-paper for swift destruction. One Sten gun, seven loaded magazines and four hand grenades. Pray God, only the detonators would be required on his perilous journey.

But should their plans fail, there was a final route. In the suede belt secured around his waist, lodged next to his armoury, lay the suicide pills.

Chapter Twenty-Six

Autumn was turning to winter and Kay still hadn't heard from Alan. She had hoped by Christmas she would receive a letter, even if it was only half a page to say he was all right. All through the days leading up to Christmas she had reminded herself she wasn't alone. Thousands of women were in the same position, perhaps worse, with sons, brothers, husbands and even fathers called up to fight at the fronts.

She received Christmas cards sent from her mother and father and Len and Doris. Her brother had written very little, with no mention of the subject of adoption, but at least he had replied to her own letter that she'd wrapped carefully inside a Christmas card. There was a note included in Lil's card to say that it had been a great disappointment not to meet up at Len and Doris's. The red-breasted robin and a church in the background covered in snow bore a resemblance to Monkton, Lil told her, and the church that she and Bob attended. Presents hadn't been exchanged in the post; it was far too costly in wartime. But there had been a one-pound note to be spent on Alfie. The other cards arranged on the mantle were from neighbours and friends: Jenny and Tom Edwards and their daughter Emily, Alice and Bert Tyler, the Press sisters, Stan and Elsie Tripp in Wales and Neville and Paul, whose card of the snowy Houses of Parliament was by far the most impressive.

This year Kay had agreed to the expense of a tree. Alan's emergency money was now down to three pounds, five shillings and a few pence. But Sean and Alfie had spent hours making decorations and the tree, standing by the wardrobe in the front room, made the house look festive.

All through Christmas Kay wondered if Dolly would turn up. But Jean's letter, Kay decided, must have kept her away. And before long, they were celebrating a new year. But in January, Vi's health broke down and Kay was very worried.

'Severe bronchitis,' pronounced the doctor. 'And a nasty bout too. I'll leave this syrup to help clear her lungs. And none of those for the moment.' He nodded to the tobacco pouch on the table.

'Life ain't worth living without me fags,' complained Vi later as she coughed and reached for her roll-ups.

'Take some of the syrup instead,' suggested Kay, levelling a spoon at Vi's dry lips.

Her friend swallowed the liquid under protest. 'Me fags won't kill me, but that might,' she exclaimed.

But the bronchitis persisted and Kay kept the boys in the kitchen for the next week. She didn't want Vi to be disturbed. But it was cold without the fire and the continual rain made the windows steam up and condensation pool on their ledges.

'You're going upstairs into a proper bedroom,' decided Kay one evening a few days later. She knew Vi wouldn't like what she was about to say. 'You can't stay down here like this, with the boys bursting in every five minutes. There's no privacy. You need to rest properly.'

'I ain't gonna take yer bed, love,' Vi spluttered.

'You don't have any choice,' Kay ordered. 'Now, put your arm around me and I'll help you upstairs.'

Vi protested but Kay knew she was too ill to argue. Step by breathless step, they managed to climb the stairs. They were both exhausted by the time they reached the bedroom. Vi was a ghostly white and wheezing noisily. Kay wondered if the effort had done more bad than good. But when Vi was tucked warmly into bed and the pillows propped behind her, she fell into a deep sleep.

Downstairs, Kay gazed into the embers of the fire. It was said that the smoky fumes of the coal worsened some illnesses and caused things like TB and pneumonia. If Vi wasn't any better in a few days, she would call the doctor again. By now, Vi didn't even want to smoke. And that was a very bad sign indeed.

'How's Vi?' Babs asked one afternoon the following week.

'She's resting better upstairs.'

'Do you want me to collect the kids from school? Or do you fancy a breath of air? It won't take us long to pop up the school and back.'

'All right. I'll come with you.'

Babs levelled her umbrella. 'You'll need your raincoat. It's cats and dogs out here.'

After a few minutes, Kay joined her, wearing her mac and boots. 'What a day! This damp don't help Vi's chest at all.'

Babs pulled her close under the brolly. 'Have you tried giving Vi peppermint and brandy in hot water? My mum used to give it to my dad when he had a cold.'

'I've tried everything,' Kay said with a sigh as she slipped her arm through Babs's. 'Lemon juice and onion, liquorice and even slippery elm. But they don't seem to be helping.' She glanced at Babs. 'Heard anything from Eddie?'

'Yes, I had a letter last week.' She paused. 'He seems to be his same old self, but did mention he would be pleased to get shot of the heat.'

'The heat? Does that mean he was posted to Africa?'

'Could be, as we won El Alamein in October and the wireless said recently that Monty's troops are leaving. What about Alan?'

'It's five months now since I've heard from him.'

'They say no news is good news, love.'

'I'm banking on that.'

As the rain dripped around them and they dodged the puddles, Babs's voice grew low. 'I've been doing a lot of thinking about Paul and me, Kay.'

'What brought that on?'

'I was in the grocer's and Alice and Jenny were there. Jenny asked me outright if I was having a fling.'

'What!'

'Yes, and I was with Tim too. It was lucky he was looking at the sweets. I told her it was none of her business.' Babs took a sharp breath. 'A pity because I've always got on all right with Jenny and Tom.'

'Jenny can be a bit blunt,' Kay said.

'It really upset me, Kay. I felt like a loose woman.'

Kay slowed her pace. 'Did you really think no one would notice what you and Paul were doing?'

Babs was silent for a moment, then shook her head. 'I don't know what I thought – all that was on me mind was Paul. I suppose I was fooling myself all along. But then Jenny's attitude brought the truth home. That's one of the reasons why—' Her voice broke, rough with emotion, 'Paul and me have decided to call it a day.'

Kay stopped, staring at her friend. There were tears in Babs's eyes. 'Oh, Babs, I knew it would end in heartbreak.'

'I suppose I did too. But I couldn't stop meself.'

'How did Paul take it?'

'He don't want us to separate. He says he loves me and wants me to write to Eddie and tell him the truth. But I couldn't do that. What if Eddie read it and was then—' Babs closed her eyes and shook her head. 'I said I had reasons for ending it with Paul and that was the other. How could I possibly write Eddie a "Dear John" letter when he's risking his life for us? That was the moment it all came clear. No, I'll just have to grit me teeth and bear it.'

'Are you in love with Paul?'

Babs nodded, her eyes full of pain. 'But I love Eddie too and I don't want to hurt him.'

After a while, they started walking again. The drip-drip of the wet from the brolly and the puddles that were now growing into small rivers gushing down the gutters seemed to echo the sadness and heartache that Kay's friend was suffering.

At last February arrived and Vi's bronchitis began to improve. Kay decided to keep the sleeping arrangements as they were. The benefits were that Vi had a space all of her own, and the boys could play in the front room on cold or rainy days. Kay slept on the put-u-up in the front room. She didn't mind. The warmth of the fire was cosy.

Kay was waiting at the grocer's one morning; she had decided to spend her coupons on a few rashers of bacon as she had saved her egg ration for the weekend.

Jenny Edwards and Alice Tyler joined the queue behind her and it was Jenny who spoke first. 'Haven't seen much of you lately, Kay.'

'No, it's not been the weather, has it?'

'Caught sight of you and Babs and the kids last Monday.'

Kay nodded. No one in the neighbourhood had actually mentioned Sean, though Kay was certain, after Dolly's visits, that word had got round.

'Nice little lad you've got staying with you,' remarked Alice.

Kay transferred her basket to her other arm in order to look at her neighbours. 'Yes, he is.'

Jenny and Alice nodded. 'Actually it was Neville who told us that you'd had an unwanted visitor. Fancy that woman dumping the boy on you. What a cheek!'

'Yes,' agreed Kay, without explaining more, 'but as you said he's a nice little chap. And I'm happy to look after him.'

'That's very good of you, I must say.' Jenny frowned curiously.

Kay knew she was expected to comment on Dolly, but instead she made her way forwards in the queue. There were two more customers waiting to be served. And two rashers left in the cabinet.

'Course, we don't want to speak out of turn,' continued Alice, tapping Kay on the shoulder, 'but we couldn't help noticing that Babs and Paul are getting friendly.'

Kay glanced sharply back. 'Paul's decorating her house.' She didn't hide the annoyance in her tone.

'Now, gel, don't take us the wrong way,' replied Alice tartly. 'Babs was our close neighbour once too. We just don't want to see her and Eddie split up. They're a lovely family.'

'There's no danger of that, Alice.'

Kay took her place at the counter and the grocer served her with the remaining rashers of bacon. When she had paid for her purchase and stored the wrapped bacon in her basket, she turned to Jenny and Alice. 'I hope, as Babs's friends, you both understand how much her family means to her.'

'We didn't mean to offend,' said Alice, looking contrite. 'You're right, Kay, we're her friends too.'

'I'm glad to hear it, Alice.'

Jenny gave a little sigh and nodded. 'Tell her I send me love, won't you? And if she wants a cup of Rosie one day, me and Alice's doors are always open. Same as they are to you, Kay.'

Kay smiled. 'Thanks.'

As Kay was walking home, she tried not to feel resentment at Jenny and Alice, whom she had always considered good friends. But this morning they had disappointed her. Wasn't it enough that they had all lived under the threat of bombing, without starting to gossip about their friends? However, Kay knew that they genuinely cared about Babs and Eddie. Indeed, it was Jenny's remark to Babs that had finally caused her to end the affair with Paul.

As Kay turned into Slater Street, she saw the top window of her house was open. A grey head poked out and slowly elbows emerged to lean on the windowsill. Vi turned slowly in Kay's direction and offered a shaky wave.

It didn't take long for Kay's spirits to lift as she waved back. Vi was on her feet again.

Chapter Twenty-Seven

'You sure you'll be all right if I call at the shop after school?' Kay asked Vi a week later. Vi was now sitting up in her chair in the bedroom, positioned strategically by the window to watch the world pass by. 'Babs can't fetch them today as she's at work,' continued Kay, still a little uncertain about leaving her friend alone. 'After that school was bombed in south London last month, I don't want the kids walking home without me or Babs.' There had been many casualties in January as a school had been targeted by the Luftwaffe and both teachers and pupils had perished. Since then, either Kay or Babs had been certain to collect the children from school. Once again, everyone was on the alert for daylight bombings.

'Don't fret over me, flower,' Vi assured her.

'I won't. But remember what the doctor said. Take the linctus instead of a smoke.' Vi was back to her regular smoking habits. The blanket Kay had draped over her knees was dotted with grey ash that had fallen from Vi's last roll-up.

'Righto, love, you can count on me.' After a good deal of coughing, Vi patted the turban that was once again tied around her head. She closed her eyes and let her head flop back.

Kay smiled as she left the bedroom and went downstairs to join Alfie. She knew the minute she left the house, Vi would be lighting up again. But despite this, Vi was regaining her energy and, on her good days, had even managed to get downstairs.

As the weeks and months had gone by, the fear of Dolly's unexpected arrival had lessened. Kay had convinced herself that Jean's letter had turned the tables on Dolly. And when and if Dolly showed up again, then at least they might discuss Sean's future in a sensible manner. With the authorities involved, Dolly would have to behave herself. And this could only bode well for Sean.

Hand-in-hand with Alfie, Kay made her way to school, reflecting on her hopes that she would soon receive a letter from Alan. What would he say when he knew about Dolly and Sean? As Jean Pearson had said, it would be a shock on his return to discover what had happened in his absence. But Kay always put this thought to the back of her mind. Instead, she dreamed of Alan's homecoming. She imagined the day he walked down Slater Street, his long legs striding towards the house, his lovely dark hair now cut into a short back and sides in line with his army uniform. And his dark eyes, waiting to glimpse her and Alfie. His strong arms sweeping them both up against his broad chest and his lips on her mouth . . .

'Gonna see Sean,' said Alfie, tugging at her hand.

Kay smiled as Alfie's excited voice drew her from her thoughts. 'Yes, and Gill and Tim too.'

'Gonna play 'opscotch.'

Kay laughed as Alfie broke away from her grasp and jumped the cracks in the pavement. Hopscotch was his favourite game and he never tired of playing it with Sean.

Soon they arrived at Quarry Street. The school's iron railings which had been removed for the war effort had been replaced by a flimsy wooden fence, which was now surrounded by women, prams and young children. The effect of the south London school bombing was still on everyone's mind. Mothers, their babies and toddlers all waited, ears alert for the warning siren, and eyes were trained on the blue patches of sky in between the barrage balloons. Kay joined them, acknowledging those women she knew and passing one or two comments as she wove her way to the gate.

Very soon she saw the tip of Gill's head, her plaits bouncing on her shoulders. Then Tim's sturdy figure became visible as he ran to Gill. Kay's eyes searched for Sean in the crush around them. He was always eager to see Alfie yet slightly slower than the more confident pupils to rush across the playground. But as she studied the bobbing heads, caps and satchels, her heart gave a thud. Sean was nowhere to be seen. The playground emptied and Gill and Tim walked slowly up to the gate.

'Where's Sean?' asked Kay.

'Don't know, Aunty Kay.' Gill looked anxious.

'Is he still in school?'

'Might be in the lav,' said Tim.

'Let's go and look.' Together with the three children Kay made her way into the deserted school. They searched the cloakrooms and classrooms and found them empty. Mr Barnet, the head teacher, was the only member of staff left. He joined them in another search. It was with a carefully concealed panic that Kay hurried into the empty toilets, cloakrooms and classrooms again. The lead weight in the pit of her stomach slowly expanded into her chest. The blood throbbed at her temples. It was a fear that Kay, over the past months, had convinced herself was no longer warranted but now became a terrifying certainty as Sean was nowhere to be found. A voice in her head wailed that Dolly had taken him.

It was Tuesday, the day after Sean had disappeared. Kay was at her wit's end. After ending the search with Mr Barnet, then trawling the streets with Babs until nightfall, she hadn't had a wink of sleep. Mr Barnet had made a report to his superiors and advised Kay that if Sean hadn't appeared by the morning, she was to inform the police.

Kay was the station's first visitor. The sergeant on duty turned out to be the policeman she knew. When she had come to a breathless pause in her story, he raised his eyebrows.

'Mrs Lewis, have you considered that this child might be with his mother?'

'Yes, course I have.'

'Well, then, I'd suggest you call on her first before making a fuss.'

'I'm not making a fuss,' Kay argued. 'I don't know where she lives. How many times do I have to tell you that?'

'Now, now, I'm only trying to help.'

'If she's taken him without telling the teachers she can't be called responsible, can she?'

'The boy must have agreed to go with her. She couldn't have carted him off screaming and kicking without someone noticing.'

'All right then, but what if it wasn't Dolly who took him?' Kay asked.

'And the kid is playing truant,' the policeman said, deliberately misunderstanding. 'Yes, now that's far more likely.'

'I didn't say that. And anyway, Sean likes school. He's never missed a day of term.'

'So what do you want me to do?' asked the sergeant with a frown. 'If we went looking for every kid that skipped school for a few days, we'd have no force left to deal with crime.'

'It's your job to help find missing people, isn't it?'

'He's only been missing one night.'

'One night is too long for a six-year-old. He needs to be searched for.'

The sergeant stroked his forehead with the back of his hand and heaved an irritated sigh. 'Look, I'll enter the details up and with the description you've given me, ask the bobby on the beat to keep his eyes open. If the boy doesn't turn up in another, say, twenty-four hours then come back and tell us.'

Kay stared angrily into the florid face of the burly man. 'What will you do then?' she demanded.

'Let's take one step at a time, shall we?'

Kay could hardly find her way home for the anger she felt. It wouldn't have taken much effort on the policeman's part to put out an alarm.

'There, there, flower, don't go upsetting yerself,' Vi said when Kay arrived back. 'You've done all you can.' Wearing her dressing gown and slippers, Vi was making tea. 'Those coppers ain't got no clue. They're all a load of big Henrys.'

There was a tap at the back door and Babs poked her head round. 'Any news at the police station?' she asked.

'No. What about at school?'

'I talked to everyone at the gate after I'd said goodbye to Gill and Tim. But nobody saw anything.'

'Did you see Mr Barnet?'

'He told me he was asking the children at assembly.'

'Someone must have clocked Sean leaving, surely?' said Vi, pouring hot water into the teapot.

Babs sat by Kay at the table. 'Where's Alfie?'

'He's playing with his train set.' Kay swallowed the lump in her throat. 'Didn't even want his breakfast. Keeps asking where Sean is. And I don't know what to tell him.'

'Last night Gill and Tim were very upset when they went to bed.'

Kay bit down on her lip. 'It must be Dolly. I know she's at the bottom of this.' It had to be Dolly. Sean wouldn't run away from school. He loved his lessons. He had done well at reading and writing, even arithmetic.

'You've got to tell Miss Pearson, Kay.' Babs patted her arm. 'She might be able to help.'

Kay nodded, forcing back the tears.

'Drink this,' said Vi, placing a mug in front of Kay. 'You've got to eat something, gel.'

'I'm not hungry.'

'Let's go out and search for him again,' suggested Babs. 'It's better than doing nothing.'

'I'll give an eye to Alfie,' said Vi.

'No, we'll take Alfie with us.' Kay didn't want to burden Vi. She was only just recovering and needed her rest.

'You won't get very far if you do,' pointed out Vi, folding her arms across her chest. 'Alfie's no trouble. We'll just sit in the front room with his train set. I won't be on me pins. It'll do me nose good as well and will stop me from staring out the bedroom window.'

Kay smiled. 'I don't know, Vi.'

'Well, I do. Now be off with you.'

Kay left the house to call for Babs. Now, added to her worries about Sean, she was anxious for Vi's health and strength. Vi was always willing to do more than her share. But Kay could see that the time had come when these efforts came at a cost to her recovery.

'Vi's got a big heart,' Babs said as they stood in the street. 'But she looks frail.'

'I was thinking the same,' agreed Kay. 'So I've decided to pack in me job at the factory.'

'Can you afford to?'

'I might be able to find work for just a few hours each week. It's a step I've been considering since Vi got ill.'

'I'll keep my ears open for something, if you like,' Babs offered.

'Thanks.' Kay smiled gratefully. 'Now, where shall we look for Sean?'

'Perhaps the park and then Island Gardens?'

'Sean loved the river as much as Alfie,' reasoned Kay. 'But Dolly wouldn't take him there. She might not even be living in the East End. Has Gill or Tim ever said that Sean has been bullied at school?'

Instantly Babs shook her head. 'They would have had Gill and Tim to deal with if that happened.'

Which brought Kay's thoughts back to Dolly again and her motives for snatching Sean.

Kay and Babs spent the day searching. Round and round they went, through the park and under the arches of the railway line. They sat on the bench in Island Gardens and watched the smaller children at play and, giving a description of Sean and a blonde woman who might be with him, made enquiries to anyone they came across. Many knew him at the market by now, especially Lenny at the tea stall who always kept fudge in his pocket to give to the boys. The traders promised to let Kay know if there was a sighting. Finally Kay and Babs searched the streets closer to home including Crane Street. However, since there were very few houses left standing here, their search took only a few minutes. Lastly they visited the demolished houses of

Slater Street, amongst them the Suttons' and Vi's and Amy Greenaway's, the teacher who had perished in the Blitz. But Kay was certain that Sean wouldn't go near these. He knew, like Alfie, that bombed sites were well out of bounds.

'The kids never go out of sight when they play in the street,' insisted Babs as they walked wearily to school to collect Gill and Tim. 'And if the boys ever tried to, Gill would keep them in line.'

'I'll ask again at the school gates,' said Kay, although after Babs's enquiries this morning, she knew it would be fruitless.

But it was news from Mr Barnet that finally put an end to speculation. He sent Gill out to ask Kay to join him in his room, whilst Babs waited outside with the children.

'This may not be of much comfort, Mrs Lewis, but when I called assembly this morning, I made mention of Sean and his "absenteeism".' The head teacher coughed. 'I had to choose my words carefully, not wanting to alarm the children.' He pleated his fingers as he sat behind his desk and paused, frowning over his spectacles. 'A child in Sean's class has offered information.'

'Who?' Kay asked anxiously.

'A girl called Ellen Kirby. She sits next to Sean in class. It was after the lunch break yesterday when the children were leaving the playground. A woman came to the fence. Ellen saw her call to Sean and he went to her.'

'What did she look like? Did Ellen say?'

Again Mr Barnet hesitated. 'A child of six or seven can't be specific, you understand.'

'No, course not but—'

'What was noted was the "yellow hair and red lipstick", Ellen's words exactly.'

'It's Dolly!' Kay expelled a sharp gasp. 'It has to be.'

'His mother? Mrs Dolores Lewis?' Mr Barnet nodded. 'Miss Pearson did explain the situation of course.'

'Did Sean go off with her?'

'Ellen didn't see any more. She was called inside.'

'And Sean was still at the fence?'

'We must conclude he was.'

Kay sat silently, her thoughts in turmoil. She had known in her heart it was Dolly who had taken him. Sean would have had no choice but to go with her. She was his mother after all. Dolly was afraid to come to the house because of Miss Pearson's letter. She had decided to take Sean from school instead.

'Are you all right, Mrs Lewis?' Mr Barnet was looking at Kay in concern. 'Is there anything I can do? Have you spoken to the police?'

Kay nodded. 'Yes, this morning.'

'And Miss Pearson?'

'Not yet.'

'Then perhaps . . .' He opened his arms in a gesture of defeat.

Kay stood up. 'Thank you.'

Mr Barnet stood too. 'Sean was a very good pupil. He showed promise and wanted to learn. In the short while he was with us, he made a remarkable journey.'

Kay didn't like Mr Barnet talking in the past tense, as if Sean was gone for ever. She said goodbye after the head teacher promised to let her know of any new developments. But Kay knew there wouldn't be. Dolly must have other plans for Sean.

Babs, Gill, Tim and Alfie were waiting at the gate. 'Well?' Babs asked, hope in her eyes.

'It was Dolly,' said Kay. 'A child called Ellen Kirby saw her at the fence and she called to Sean. But that was all she saw.'

'So we really don't know for certain what happened?'

'I'm certain it was Dolly. Ellen said she saw a woman with yellow hair and red lipstick.'

'But why did she take Sean,' puzzled Babs, 'after all this time?'

Kay couldn't answer that. She felt bereft. Against everyone's advice, she had grown to care so much for this little boy.

'That settles it,' Kay decided as they walked home. 'I'm giving in my notice to Mr Marsh tomorrow after I've spoken with Jean Pearson and told her about Sean.'

'Are you sure about leaving the factory?' Babs asked. 'Perhaps I could help out with Alfie a bit more?'

'Thanks, but you're a working woman with a family to look after. And I can't hope to see an improvement in Vi if she doesn't look after herself and get her rest.'

She and Babs fell silent as they made their way home. Kay was thinking about what she would say to Mr Marsh tomorrow. She knew he wouldn't want to let her go; the war effort needed all hands on deck. But her responsibilities at home were more important to her, by far.

Chapter Twenty-Eight

'Try not to worry,' Jean Pearson advised the next day as they sat in her small office with the desk piled high with correspondence and shelves overflowing with papers. 'At least we know Sean isn't roaming the streets.'

'He wouldn't have left the school grounds,' insisted Kay. 'That was why I was sure he was with Dolly.'

'And this girl, Ellen Kirby, didn't say more?'

'No, but it was Dolly by the description.'

Jean Pearson sighed, shaking her head slowly. 'Then we're still no closer to finding out where she lives.'

'What if she's with that big bruiser she was with before?' Kay felt in despair every time she thought of it. 'Or someone else just as violent?'

'We mustn't let our imaginations run away with us,' warned Jean carefully.

Kay smiled. 'You sound just like my Alan. He was always telling me that.'

'Good advice.' Jean nodded. 'Now, what can we do?'

'I don't know,' Kay said with a shrug. 'But there must something.'

'The facts are that Dolly has rights as his mother. It's very costly to pursue a legal challenge against parental care, even if we had more information. So how can we locate Dolly? She evades us every time.'

'That's why she went to the school. She was afraid to come to the house.'

'Yes,' agreed Jean, 'it seems that way.'

Kay and the young woman sat for a while discussing the situation, but soon there was a knock on the door and a clerk interrupted. Kay knew that Jean was a busy woman. There were others needing her attention and after a few parting words, Kay left.

When Kay arrived at the factory, she hurriedly changed into her overalls and turban. She was relieved to see Mr Marsh before he entered the entrance to the assembly line, and pulled him aside. As she expected, he received her news with clear disapproval.

'I'm sorry to hear you can't find your way to continuing with Drovers,' he said with a frown. 'Our troops abroad count on well-made armaments. What with Mrs Fellows having left us recently and Mrs Rigler being in the family way, we'll be three down on our most conscientious workers.'

'I'm sorry about that, Mr Marsh,' said Kay staunchly. 'But I've done all I can for the country. It's my family who need me now.'

'Is this to be a permanent state of affairs?'

'It is until I get meself sorted.'

'Well, it's a sad loss to the firm.' He managed a smile. 'When do you want to leave us?'

'Will a week's notice be all right?'

'So soon?' Once again Kay saw the disappointment written in his eyes, but there was nothing she could do about that.

Later that day as Kay was walking home, she knew she had come to the right decision. She wouldn't really miss the factory work now. Iris had left and her thoughts at work lately were always about what was going on in her absence from home. It would mean that she would have to be very thrifty, make the pennies stretch a lot further than she already made them stretch. But the peace of mind she would have was of greater value. Then her thoughts drifted to Dolly and all that had happened since Dolly's first appearance. She remembered how Dolly had kept demanding what this Alan of hers had stolen. How Dolly hadn't cared when Sean fell ill. Dolly had heartlessly ordered the man to attack Kay. She hadn't wanted Sean then or she would have taken him. Why had she taken Sean now? None of this made sense. Jean Pearson had proved by the letter that Dolly was afraid of the authorities. But the letter had also caused Dolly to snatch Sean from school rather than confront Kay. Again Kay wondered why it was that Dolly had taken a son she didn't want. A question to which there seemed to be no answer.

* * *

Kay couldn't go upstairs to the boys' bedroom without seeing Sean and Alfie playing there. Outside in the yard, where the Anderson stood with winter weeds clinging to its rusting sides, she remembered how they had made it into their den.

'No news from that Jean Pearson?' asked Babs as they made their way to school one chilly morning. Kay regularly walked with Babs and the children to Quarry Street, hoping that somewhere along the route, which Sean knew well, she might see him.

'No, nothing.'

'Thought about going to the police again?' Babs asked cautiously.

'Mr Barnet told me he notified them.'

'And they've done sod all. Don't seem right, does it?'

Kay gazed at the three children walking ahead. She pictured Sean with them, wearing his school uniform and jumping the cracks in the pavement. What clothes did Dolly have for him? Did she give him enough food? These worries kept going round in her head. She missed Alan so much. If only he was here now. He would know what to do.

'Can you stop for a cuppa?' Babs asked as, after seeing Gill and Tim into school, they made their way home.

'I'll tell Vi first, or she'll wonder where we've got to,' Kay said without much enthusiasm. After school she often walked down to the park or the river with Alfie in the hope that she might catch a glimpse of Dolly and Sean. But in her heart she knew this was a waste of time.

* * *

'I left Alfie to keep Vi company for a few minutes,' Kay said as she walked into Babs's kitchen. 'They're both down in the dumps. Vi got out the train set in the hope that Alfie would play with it. But since Sean's gone, he's lost interest in his favourite toy.'

'How is Vi's health now?'

'She still gets tired and I have to make her rest. At least being at home, I can put me foot down.'

Babs poured an almost colourless liquid from the teapot. 'Sorry, it's dishwater again, but I'm low on tea.'

'You should have said. I'd have brought some with me.'

'As a matter of fact, Paul said he might be able to get tea from the canteen.'

Kay blinked and stared at her friend. 'Paul?'

Babs blushed as she joined her at the kitchen table.

'Are you seeing him again?' Kay asked.

Babs looked out of the window and heaved a sigh. 'We met by accident the other day. He was driving his car and pulled in to the kerb. I was carrying my bags from the market. He jumped out and took them from me. Said he'd drive me home. The next thing I knew I was sitting in the car beside him.' She turned slowly and looked at Kay. 'But you don't want to hear all this. We're supposed to be talking about Sean.'

'Talking won't bring him back, Babs.'

'No, but it helps to share.'

Kay sipped the weak tea. 'I don't know what to do, Babs. Each day I go out looking. Wondering if Dolly might be in one of the houses I pass and Sean could be only a few yards away.' Tears filled Kay's eyes. 'I've got no rights at all where Sean is concerned. Everyone has made that clear from the start. From Jean Pearson to the police; even Mr Barnet and Vi told me not to get attached. But I can't stop caring about what happens to him.' Suddenly the floodgates opened. All the tears she'd kept at bay now slipped through her lashes.

'Oh, Kay, I know what you're going through. Love can be such a heartbreaker.'

Kay peered at her friend through her tears. 'This shouldn't happen to such a nice kid. Oh, if only Alan was here, he'd have put Dolly in her place straight away.'

Babs had a strange look on her face. 'You trust Alan, don't you?'

'Course.' Kay was shocked at her friend's question. 'Just like you trust Eddie.'

'I did once.' Babs looked down at her lap. 'But I don't think we ever truly know a person. Not really.'

'Babs, what do you mean?' Kay's tears dried quickly as she heard the doubt in Babs's voice.

Raising her eyes slowly, Babs said softly, 'Eddie had an affair after Gill was born.'

Kay gasped. 'Babs, why ain't you ever said?'

'We all have our secrets, Kay.'

'Who was it?'

'I was really low after Gill's birth. Dunno why. The doctor said I should buck up as the baby needed a healthy mother. I tried to, but I just got more and more depressed.

Eddie didn't understand – though he did his best. When he touched me I just seemed to freeze. It was awful for him. And I couldn't explain what was making me like it as I didn't know meself.' Babs pushed back her fair hair and looked into Kay's gaze. 'He found someone else. A woman who worked in the dock office.'

'Babs, that's awful.'

'I didn't blame him – couldn't, could I?'

'How did you find out?'

'Madge Sutton, God rest her soul, saw Eddie and this girl one night. They was arm-in-arm walking along the Commercial Road. Eddie had told me he was working late to bring in the overtime. He worked late a lot at the time although we never seemed to have much extra money. I realized why when Madge spilled the beans. When I confronted him about what Madge said, he admitted it straight off.'

'What did you do?' asked Kay, her tears forgotten.

'What could I do? I felt it was my fault that he'd strayed. I begged him not to leave me and Gill. That I'd change and we'd be just like we once were.'

'And he agreed?'

'Yes, but it wasn't easy for him or me. Eddie had fallen for this girl in a big way. It wasn't just a fling. I could see in his eyes I'd almost lost him. But we tried because of Gill and eventually things sorted themselves. We was lucky, there wasn't no gossip. Madge kept what she knew to herself like the good pal she was. And then I fell with Tim. But . . .' Babs hesitated, a frown clouding her pretty face. 'Our marriage wasn't the same again.'

'You never said or even hinted, Babs.'

'It was before you came to the island. Madge was the only one who knew. And when she and her family died in the bomb blast, I missed her. We'd known each other a long time.'

'Babs, do you think that's why you fell for Paul?'

Babs gave a humourless smile. 'What's good for the goose is good for the gander, you mean?'

'Well, it would have been understandable.'

Babs leaned her elbows on the table and turned the mug between her fingers. 'I don't really know why me and Paul hit it off. Why it even got started. There was just something between us, we were on the same wavelength. But we should have been older and wiser and not got involved. Now, it's almost as if neither of us care. We know it will end – has to. Like I said, Kay, love is a heartbreaker.'

'What are you going to do?'

'I don't know,' said Babs, sighing. 'I really don't know.'

It was with a deep affection for her friend that Kay reached out to slip her fingers over Babs's, tightening them until she could feel Babs's wedding ring digging into her own skin. A ring that was a symbol of the vows Babs had made with Eddie when they had once been young with the world at their feet.

Chapter Twenty-Nine

It was 2 March and nearly four weeks since Sean had disappeared. Occasionally, Kay considered the possibility that she may have been wrong about Dolly. What if Sean really had, for some reason, run away from school? Had he been unhappy? Had he wandered outside of the school gate? But Kay knew he wouldn't have done that, especially not when she reminded herself of Ellen Kirby's sighting.

'Come on, flower,' Vi said one morning when Kay returned from school, 'we'll go to market and cheer ourselves up.'

'Are you feeling up to it?'

'Course. I'm on the mend now.' Vi frowned at her thoughtfully. 'I don't need fussing over no more. Has Babs heard of a cleaning job going? I know she was looking out for you.'

'Not yet. But I'm sure something will come up.' Kay didn't like to admit that all of Alan's money was gone, but she knew that Vi was smart enough to guess, and she didn't want Vi to feel a burden. However, the time had arrived when there was only Alan's pay coming in addition to Vi's few pennies. Pennies that were growing shorter by the day. 'Best we make a plan though,' Kay added.

'You know I'll mind Alfie for you.'

'I'll ask Mr Barnet about a place for him in school in September. I don't want no extra work for you.'

'I told you he's no trouble, love.'

In the middle of their conversation, the letter box rattled. Kay hurried to look on the mat. Each day she hoped it would be a letter from Alan. But as usual, a forces envelope was not in evidence. This morning a grubby white envelope lay there.

Kay picked it up to frown at the large, untidy writing on the front. Like a child's, almost. She took it into the kitchen and opened it. After a few seconds, she gasped aloud.

'Vi, this is from Dolly.'

'Never! What does she say?'

'You'd better read it.'

The shopping forgotten, Vi squinted at the haphazard, badly spelled words. 'Your Alan that's also my Alan,' she read out, 'turned a blind eye to what I did, because he liked the money. He even married me, the bastard, to get hold of it. I told you, I was a good-looker once and successfully worked the West End. The rich punters had no complaints and paid well. It was easy enough to put a bit by. Or so I thought. Alan was a greedy sod and stole my Post Office book, one hundred pounds to the penny. Bring the book with you on Wednesday, or else you won't see Sean again. The Salmon and Ball pub, Bethnal Green, half seven Wednesday night.' Vi read the words again silently. Looking up at Kay, she blurted, 'The cow is blackmailing you.'

'This money is what Dolly's been after all this time,' Kay said quietly.

'Her ill-gotten gains,' Vi agreed, nodding slowly. 'Can't say as I'm surprised she was on the game. Probably still is. Are you going to show this to Jean Pearson?'

Kay shook her head. 'I'm going to sort it out myself.'

Vi was silent for a moment then frowned. 'The Salmon and Ball pub. That's near Victoria Park, ain't it?'

'Yes. I'll get the bus. There's one to Green Road.'

'You're really determined to go, then?' asked Vi in surprise.

'It's my only chance to find Sean.'

'She might have that big bruiser with her.'

Kay lifted her shoulders. 'I'll have to risk it.'

'I hope you realize she planned it all, the crafty bitch,' Vi argued. 'She took Sean to bargain with and made you sweat it out.'

'I still have to go.'

'She should be made to see her rotten threats don't work.'

'What would you do in my place?' Kay questioned. 'What if it was Pete Junior and you had a chance to get him back?'

Vi searched Kay's face. 'Point taken, ducks, even though Pete was me son and I have to point out that Sean ain't yours. But you love that little boy, don't you?'

'His mother don't seem to. And yes, I am very fond of him, Vi. I can't help myself.'

'In that case, you'll have to follow your heart.'

Kay sighed. 'I only wish I had the hundred pounds Dolly thinks I have. I'd give it over like a shot if it would bring Sean home.'

Vi didn't respond. Instead, she sat back and stiffened her spine against the back of the chair. Deep in thought, she sat in silence, then, placing her hands flat on the table, she expelled a long sigh. 'If you've made up your mind to meet Dolly then I think I'd better give you something.' Vi got up wearily from the chair saying she had to go upstairs.

'My darling Kay and Alfie,' Kay read aloud from one of the two letters Vi had given her. 'After all that has happened, I can't expect you to understand or forgive. But you must trust that our marriage is real and perfect. I could not have wished for a better second chance. It was you and Alfie that gave me an honest life. Before that, there was nothing. Nothing that ever needed to be told. But I suspect, if you are reading this, some of it already has. There may be many things said against me, but please trust me, although it might appear I have lived two lives, the day I met you was the day I felt reborn. Our life together is the one and only true record of the man who will love you for all eternity. So chin up, lovely, and God bless you both.'

'Ducks, are you all right?' Vi asked as she studied Kay's face.

'No, I don't think I am.'

'I don't know if I've done right,' Vi fretted, 'but Alan gave me the two letters and the Post Office book before he went away. Said I was to keep 'em safe. If he didn't come back then I should give them to you.'

'Did you know what was in the book?'

Vi nodded. 'Alan showed me. Said it was to set you and the boy up for the future.'

'Even so, didn't you think it was a lot of money?'

'Yes, but that was Alan's business.'

Kay felt her legs had been swept from under her. 'Why does he write, "there may be things said against me. I have lived two lives . . ."?' Kay shook her head in bewilderment. 'He can't mean Dolly!'

'Course not, love.'

'Then what does he mean?'

'Dunno. But it's the book that's important.'

'A hundred pounds,' Kay repeated as they studied the Post Office book again. 'But how did Alan get all this money? It's exactly the amount Dolly said was stolen.'

'The account is in your name, Kay. Not hers.'

'The date says the first deposit was in October 1941,' Kay said. 'Not 1936 when Dolly said she knew Alan.'

'There, you see, it's just a coincidence.'

'But where did Alan get a hundred pounds?' she asked again. 'He surprised me when he gave me twenty. But a *hundred*?'

Vi pointed to the other letter. 'Are you going to read that?'

'It's addressed to Len and Doris.'

'Might explain something.'

Kay opened the envelope to discover that, unlike the first letter, it was typical Alan. He was swallowing his pride to ensure his family's safety, a motive that Kay could understand under such circumstances. 'He asks Len to look out for me and Alfie if he don't come back from war. But there's no mention of the money.'

'Might not have wanted Len to know.' Vi raised her eyes. 'Look, whatever your worries about it, Alan loves you and you alone.'

'I want to believe he does.'

'Would it matter to you if Alan was married before?'

'It would if he was still married to her.'

'I can't believe it's in Alan's nature to do a thing like that.'

Kay put her head in her hands. What was Alan thinking of? Why was he writing in riddles? She wasn't sure now of what was real and what wasn't. Had she been wrong not to question Alan's past? But she had been so deeply in love with him, she hadn't cared. He had never insisted on knowing about her and Norman. Not that there was much to know. He'd just accepted what she'd told him. She had thought this was a fair compromise. They'd agreed to let go of the past and make a future for themselves. But the past that Alan had kept to himself was now, it appeared, coming back to haunt them. By his own written admission in the letter, Alan sounded as if he was not the man she thought he was.

Chapter Thirty

On Wednesday evening, Kay caught the bus from Poplar to Green Road. It was raining and she'd forgotten the umbrella. She found herself sitting in a damp coat and wet shoes thinking about what she would say to Dolly. Kay had the Post Office book in her handbag. She would promise Dolly that she would withdraw the money and hand it over and hope that Dolly would be satisfied. It was the closest Dolly would ever come to what she claimed was rightfully hers. Kay dearly hoped that Sean would be with her, though it was hard to believe that a mother would really agree to exchange her son for money.

It was still raining when Kay got off the bus and made her way to the Salmon and Ball pub. She knew the area well. As a child, Lil had brought her here to the Roman Road markets. Then it had been exciting, especially on summer days, when the heat and the smell of the horse-drawn brewery carts and bagel stalls filled the air. But tonight Bethnal Green was gloomy and depressing. The streets were crowded with people hurrying home from work. The heavy skies above added a threat to the blacked-out streets of London. Kay had heard a woman on the bus say that the warning alarm had been going off all day. Each time the siren wailed, everyone ran for shelter; Kay hoped and prayed the peace would not be disturbed this evening.

By the time Kay arrived at the pub her coat was wet through, her hair lank and dripping inside the collar making her shiver. The pub was crowded, the air full of smoke and chatter. There were mostly men drinking and a few women sitting at the tables. But there was no Dolly. Kay sat down just inside the door. She told herself that Dolly would soon arrive. Each time someone walked in, her heart raced. But it wasn't Dolly.

The minutes ticked slowly by. The clock on the wall said almost eight. What if Dolly didn't turn up?

When Dolly walked in at last, she was dressed in a light-coloured coat and black fur collar. Instead of joining Kay at the table, she went to the bar. Smiling at the landlord, she laughed and joked. Dolly swallowed the drink he poured her before walking over to Kay.

'Have you brought me money?' she asked, sitting down.

Kay nodded, still shocked by the fact that Dolly could carelessly down a drink and laugh and joke with the landlord as if this was an everyday occurrence.

Dolly grinned. 'I knew you had it all along.'

'Well, now I'm here,' Kay replied, 'where's Sean? Have you been looking after him?'

'Listen,' spluttered Dolly, leaning close, 'don't look down your nose at me, Miss Goody-Two-Shoes. Alan didn't ditch you and your kid. What would you have done if he did? I tried me best to bring up that boy. I could have done a better job if my thieving husband hadn't taken the bread from our mouths. But, seeing as you think you can do a better job of looking after the kid, I'm prepared to give you a chance. Just as long as I get what's rightfully mine.'

'You will,' Kay replied coldly. 'But I want to see Sean first.'

'All in good time,' Dolly dismissed. 'He's staying with a friend of mine.'

'Don't he live with you?'

'I'm not here to answer your questions,' Dolly snapped. 'It's the other way round. Now where's the money?'

Kay had told herself to keep cool, calm and collected. But Dolly always threw a spanner into the works. Her fingers were shaking as she opened her handbag and took out the Post Office book.

'Let me see that.' Dolly snatched it from her hand. Kay watched Dolly's reedy expression as she read the name inside. 'What's your name doing on it?' she demanded.

'I don't know,' Kay replied, trying to remain calm.

'The bugger must have changed it.'

'It doesn't matter,' said Kay, trying to play along. 'I'll draw it out and give it to you.'

Dolly looked at Kay with contempt. 'He was gonna make sure I never had it, the crafty good-for-nothing—'

'I told you, it's all yours,' Kay interrupted, tightening her fingers in her lap. She wanted to defend Alan, *her* Alan, who would never be capable of such deception. But she knew it was useless to argue with Dolly.

Dolly looked at her suspiciously. 'You want the boy that much?'

'Do you want your money back or not?' Kay asked again.

'I'm taking this.' Dolly slid the book into her pocket. 'Be here at ten tomorrow morning outside the pub. We'll go to the Post Office together. If you call in the rozzers, you'll never see Sean again.'

'You don't have to worry about that.'

Dolly stood up, looking around her. 'You'd better be on the level this time.'

Kay jumped to her feet. 'Before you leave, I want you to tell me something.'

'Now what?'

'You said you first met Alan in Hyde Park. That he was one of the speakers there.'

'So? What's it to you?'

'What was he talking about?'

Dolly laughed. 'Nonsense as usual. Trying to get blokes to join some army or other.'

'What army?' Kay grabbed her sleeve.

Dolly glared at her. 'Let go of me.'

'Please, Dolly!' Kay had to know.

'Dunno why you want to know that. It was somewhere foreign like Spain.'

Suddenly a high-pitched wail filled the air. Everyone got up and hurried to the door as the scream of the siren grew louder. Dolly rushed away to join the other customers hurrying from the pub. Kay stood there as if in a trance. Then someone pushed her forward. 'You'd better get going, love. There's a raid on its way.'

Kay nodded, still thinking of what Dolly had said about Spain. The man shoved her into the dark night and she stood on the pavement, not knowing which way to go. Then she saw Dolly's light-coloured coat. Kay elbowed her way towards Dolly as she went towards the entrance of Bethnal Green Tube Station.

Vi was worried. It was gone eleven and Kay wasn't home. She was to meet Dolly at half past seven. Kay should have been home by now.

Vi got up from her chair, turned out the light and for the hundredth time that evening went to the window. She peered from behind the blackout curtain. The street was in total darkness. It was silly to keep on looking, Vi scolded herself. Kay would soon be home, she was sure.

She sat down again. Alfie was fast asleep upstairs. The house was quiet and the ticking of the clock seemed very loud.

Vi's thoughts went over and over. That minx Dolly was two steps ahead of everyone on cunning. She was prepared to sell her own son. What mother would do such a thing? And what would Dolly say when she saw the account was in Kay's name? Kay had been certain she could talk Dolly round. But could she? And what if that big lug had been with Dolly and roughed Kay up again?

Vi went to the front door and opened it. She was really worried now. Kay could be lying in a dark alley somewhere, the rain pouring down on her. Vi knocked on Babs's door. She didn't want to wake the children. She didn't want to wake Babs either if she'd gone to sleep. But Kay might need their help.

The door opened. Babs and Paul stood there. 'Is she home yet?' asked Babs before Vi could speak.

'No.' Vi's voice was a croak as Babs pulled her inside out of the rain.

'I can't leave Alfie,' Vi mumbled. 'But I'm worried. She was supposed to meet Dolly at half seven.'

'I'll come back with you.' Babs reached for her coat to put on over her dressing gown. 'Paul will be here for the kids if they wake.'

'I don't want to trouble you.' There was a catch in Vi's voice.

'Try not to worry,' Paul told her. 'If she ain't back in an hour I'll get the car out of mothballs and drive up to Bethnal Green.'

Vi just nodded, swallowing her fear. She had never cared much for Paul, had never really given him the time of day after what he'd done behind Eddie's back. But as he patted her shoulder, she was glad he was on hand tonight.

* * *

At first, all seemed orderly if a little hurried as people made their way towards the narrow entrance of the Tube station. Dolly's light coat kept appearing in the darkness as Kay found herself shoulder to shoulder with strangers. Just then, there was a crash. More ear-splintering crashes followed and the sky above was lit briefly, revealing the terrified faces around her.

'The bombs are falling in the park!' a man yelled out. 'Hurry, or we'll never get down the Underground in time.'

'Jerry's overhead,' a woman cried out, pushing her way fiercely through the crowd.

'It's revenge for Berlin,' another man shouted. 'We flattened 'em good and proper the other night and now it's our turn.'

Kay felt everyone's panic. The surge of people was powerful as the fear of the bombs took over. As the station's entrance came into sight, Kay was almost lifted off her feet. She tried to turn back but the tide of bodies around her was too forceful. Inside the entrance there was hardly any light. She tried to grasp the handrail. If she could reach it, she might be able to prevent herself from falling. The rain had made the steps very slippery. But there was no handrail in the centre as she expected. A woman screamed at the top of staircase and Kay saw the baby in her arms. It was crying loudly. An elderly man fell behind the woman, causing congestion which only added to the panic of the surging throng. The woman and her child and the elderly man disappeared in seconds yet the crowd ignored them, pushing forward and plunging ahead. Men, women and children disappeared from sight in the well of darkness, with the noise of the screams and yelling rising to a terrifying pitch.

Kay screamed, her lungs feeling crushed as she tried to gulp air. The people behind her were forcing her on. Those in front were unable to move in the narrow neck of the darkened stairwell. Kay suddenly spotted Dolly who was screaming too, trying to fight her way back. Her face was white and filled with terror. Unable to save herself, her cries were lost in the nightmare sounds of all those who, like her, were being ignored and trodden down.

Kay's last memory of Dolly was of her hands clutching nothing but the air above her head. The movement was useless against the force of the crowd. Dolly was sucked under, as if in a vacuum, into the pit beneath. Kay was being driven forward. Like Dolly, she was succumbing to the force behind her. Desperate fingers, elbows, knees and feet thrust painfully into her back and legs. Unable to move, her chest was flattened, squeezing the last gasps of air from her lungs.

She found herself screaming, trying to turn back, her hands automatically going up, to claw at anything that might prevent her descent. But there was only the relentless motion of the crowd that swept her forward and down into the pitch-black darkness.

Chapter Thirty-One

The female ARP warden's face hovered above Kay. The woman's smile under her tin helmet made Kay realize that she wasn't dead.

'Wh . . . where am I?' Kay mumbled. 'What happened?'

'Lay back a minute, dear. You've had a nasty shock.'

Kay tried to look around her. Above her was a canvas roof.

'There's been an accident at the Tube,' the woman told her. 'You were one of the lucky ones. A man pulled you free from the crowd on the stairwell.'

'Dolly, is she all right?' Kay whispered.

'Who's Dolly?'

'Someone I know. I must get up and find her.'

'There, there, dear,' said the warden gently. 'Try to rest. You're safe now. You're in a temporary shelter erected close to the Tube. We're hoping to have the doctor here soon. Until then you must keep still. I have to go as we're very busy with casualties. But I'll be back shortly.'

The woman patted her shoulder and left. Kay realized she was lying on a blanket on the ground. As she moved her head to one side she saw there were others in the tent too. Some people were moaning and groaning, others calling for help. But there were also unmoving shapes covered by sheets.

Kay gazed up at the flimsy canvas. Many had perished in the Tube stairwell. She thought she had been about to die too. Who had rescued her?

She managed to sit up. Through the flap of the tent she could see lights twinkling despite the blackout. Her chest ached as though she had been stepped on. Her bag was miraculously beside her. Her wet shoes were still laced and on her feet. She shuddered at the memories of the terrified crowd that rushed back. Was Dolly dead?

'You should be resting.' The warden had returned and was bending over her again.

'Who was the man who brought me here?'

'I don't know. It's been too busy to keep track of everyone.'

Kay glanced at the rows of bodies. 'Are those people dead?'

'Don't upset yourself by looking at them. Now lay down. The doctor won't be long.'

When Kay was on her own again, she climbed to her feet. Was Dolly one of those bodies under the covers? She couldn't bring herself to look. Instead she picked up her handbag and walked unsteadily out.

On the ground, as far away as the pub in one direction and Victoria Park in the other, Kay could see rows of covered bodies. Ambulances were driving up and stretchers brought out to collect the dead and injured. Kay stumbled between the rows, staring at the terrible sights. A foot stuck out here, a leg and an arm there. The colour of people's skin was blue and purple, not pink. She found herself walking aimlessly amongst the dead.

A few drops of rain fell on Kay's face. She could hardly feel it. All she could think of was that stairwell and the crowd pushing forward as if it had a life of its own. And Dolly's arms and hands raised as she screamed for help. The look on Dolly's face was as if she knew what agony awaited her below. The screams still lingered in Kay's head: the wails and crying, the pitiful pleas from those around her who were caught up in the force of the crowd.

'Are you looking for someone?' an older man asked her. He wore an ARP uniform and was holding a file of crumpled papers. He looked tired and old, with his white hair untidily scuffed around his face.

'Yes.' Kay nodded shakily. 'I am.'

'What's the name? If they've been injured I can tell you what hospital they've gone to.'

'Dolly. Dolly Lewis. She was wearing a beige coat with a black fur collar. She has blonde hair and—'

'I've only got names, love. Not descriptions.' He ran his eyes over the papers. 'Name's not here, I'm afraid. But there's injured folk who haven't been able to say who they are yet and some without their identity papers.'

Kay knew Dolly wouldn't be carrying any identity. 'I'll keep looking,' she said weakly.

'You don't look so good yourself.'

Kay saw a red bus in front of her and was shocked when she found that even this was being used to transport bodies. There were carts and lorries, anything available to remove the dead and injured. A child was crying as she was put on a stretcher. She remembered the woman with the baby. They had both disappeared in the Tube entrance.

'There's more casualties in St John's,' she heard a policeman tell a crying woman. He pointed to the church opposite the Tube. 'The others have been taken to the Whitechapel mortuary.'

Kay stared at the place where she had almost lost her life. Now the entrance was crammed with rescuers. What had made the crowd panic? There had been the sound of something like rockets. Then, everyone had rushed into the stairwell. She felt sick at the memory.

Vi woke from her doze when she heard the car draw up. Unsteadily she got up from the chair. It was still dark when she opened the front door and saw Paul and Babs bringing Kay in from the car.

'She's lucky to be alive,' Paul said as he led Kay into the front room. The embers of the fire still held a little warmth as Vi helped Kay take off her dirty coat.

'What happened?' Vi asked as Kay sank down in the armchair.

'It was awful, Vi. So many people died.'

'Died!' Vi turned to Paul. 'What's she talking about?'

Paul thrust back his untidy hair. 'There's been some sort of accident at Bethnal Green Tube. But no one would tell me what happened. All I could see was bodies on stretchers. I found Kay wandering amongst them.'

'Was it a raid?' Babs asked.

'Don't know,' Kay whispered. 'I was in the pub with Dolly and the siren went. We went out and towards the Tube entrance for cover. There was a big crash nearby and everyone rushed forward. Dolly disappeared under the crowd.' She stopped, putting her hands over her face. 'I've never seen anything like it. Not even in the Blitz. There were children too, trodden under all them feet.'

They were all silent until Paul cleared his throat. 'How did you get clear, Kay?'

'I don't know. An ARP warden in the tent I was in told me a man pulled me out.'

'You said the siren went and there were crashes,' Paul murmured. 'Well, I had to leave the car on the other side of Victoria Park Square. The police had cordoned off the area. But I managed to slip through as the ambulances drove in. As far as I could see, there was no sign of a raid.'

Kay looked ahead with vacant eyes. 'People just started tripping. Then falling. And everyone kept on going down. It was like we was all being pushed, one on top of another.'

'Oh, Christ, gel, you were lucky to get out,' Vi said.

'You could have died.' Babs was wiping the tears from her cheeks.

'I was squeezed so tight I couldn't breathe,' said Kay.

They all remained silent again with only Babs sniffing until Vi touched Kay's shoulder. 'You need some rest, love.'

Babs nodded. 'We'll be next door if you want us.'

Vi saw them to the door. 'Thanks for your help, Paul.'

He smiled. 'Lucky I had a bit of petrol left in the car. I'd put it away for the duration, not thinking I'd need to use it again.'

As they left, Vi reflected that none of them had asked Kay about Sean. The terrible tragedy had put even him from their minds.

Chapter Thirty-Two

For the next few days Kay expected to hear an explanation of what had happened on the wireless. But there was only a brief reference to an accident at a Tube station.

'It's uncanny,' said Kay as she sat with Vi on the wall in the yard early on Saturday morning. 'It's like it never happened. As if I dreamed it all.' Wrapped up in their coats, they had been watching the three children play, while Babs made a visit to the grocer's. But the chill breeze and cloudy skies had caused Alfie, Gill and Tim to retreat to the Anderson.

'It happened all right,' said Vi, balancing a fresh roll-up between her lips. 'I ain't seen you in such as state as when Paul brought you home.'

'All those people were crushed,' said Kay, still haunted by the memories. 'But why? What was the reason? And Dolly, is she really dead?'

'Could be in hospital somewhere. But you can't traipse round every hospital to find out.' Vi sniffed.

'She wasn't on the ARP list that night.'

Vi took in a deep breath. 'Don't look good, does it?'

'If Dolly was killed, what's to become of Sean?'

'Search me,' said Vi with a sigh. With one hand she pulled up the collar of her coat and shivered. With the other she puffed fiercely on her roll-up, blowing the smoke into the cold morning air.

They sat quietly, each with their own thoughts, listening to the voices of the children playing in the Anderson. Above them the gulls were flapping and mewing. Kay looked around her at the familiar neighbourhood: the smoke-blackened buildings that bordered the Cut, the damaged roofs and taped-up windows of the houses, the hole in the fence that was the kids' path between hers and Babs's yards. All that was left of the fence was a few wooden stakes in the ground, supporting the saggy chicken wire. The roofs of the two Andersons were covered in winter moss. The only green in the yards were weeds which had even begun to grow over Alan's pile of wood wedged by the wall. Would he ever return to use it again? She hadn't heard from him for eleven months. Where was he? Was he thinking of her and Alfie?

Vi nudged her arm. 'Penny for your thoughts, ducks.'

'I was thinking about what Dolly said before the siren went that night.'

'What was that?'

'I asked her what this Alan of hers was speaking about when she first met him at Hyde Park.'

'What did she say?'

'She said he was trying to persuade men to join a foreign army. Somewhere like Spain, she said.'

Vi looked at Kay sharply. 'Spain, you say?'

'Yes. And Alan was in Spain.'

Vi gave a careless shrug. 'So it's a coincidence!'

'Like the hundred pounds?' Kay asked doubtfully.

'Knowing Dolly, she was lying through her teeth about Spain.'

'But why would she?' Kay questioned. 'She never knew Alan – *my* Alan – was there.'

Just then, Babs, dressed in her coat and scarf, with her shopping bag over her arm, hurried into the yard. Kay smiled a welcome, but it soon disappeared as Babs sped through the gap in the fence. 'Quickly, Kay, come and see – he's outside—'

'Who is?' Kay asked as Babs pulled her up.

'Quick! Quick!' was all Babs could splutter as they hurried through Babs's yard and into the house. The next moment they were standing on the pavement outside the front door. Babs looked up and down the street, an excited expression on her face. 'He was here a moment ago. I asked him to wait, but—' She stopped, shaking her head in confusion. 'He's gone now.'

'Who are you talking about, Babs?'

'A man was waiting on the opposite side of the road as I walked back from the grocer's. I was about to open me front door when he came across and said, "Mrs Chapman?" Just like that, as if he knew me. I said yes, it was and he said he had something for Mrs Kay Lewis, and would I pass it to you?' Babs drew a small package from her shopping bag.

Kay took it, and slowly drew out the contents. She gasped. 'It's my Post Office book!'

Vi came out to join them. 'What's going on?'

'Someone gave me this to give to Kay.' Babs nodded to the book.

Again Kay repeated her question. 'But who was he?'

'I don't know, as I ain't never seen him before. But he was tall and wearing a dark coat and a trilby hat with the brim pulled down over his face. Just like the bloke you described to us.'

Kay swallowed. 'The man who I thought was following me?'

Babs nodded. 'It must be him. He knew I was your neighbour. And he could only have known that if he'd been watching.'

Kay shuddered. 'You're putting the wind up me now.'

'But how did he get hold of your Post Office book?' asked Vi.

'It was in Dolly's pocket,' Kay said, breathing deeply, her thoughts returning to the Salmon and Ball pub. 'She took it from me, thinking I might try a fast one.'

'But why would she give it away?'

'She wouldn't,' Kay replied. 'The money meant everything to her.'

'He must have taken it, then,' whispered Babs. Then, giving a little gasp, she added, 'When Dolly couldn't put up a fight to keep it.'

All three nodded slowly. Dolly would never have let that book go. Not while she had breath in her body.

It was just before Easter when Kay had a visit from Jean Pearson. 'I haven't heard from you since February,' she said when Kay invited her in. It was a warm late April day and they sat together in the cool of the front room.

'Dolly wrote to me, saying she wanted to meet,' Kay told her, being careful of what she revealed. If she told Jean that Dolly had wanted money then Jean would only say that she should have gone to the police.

'Why didn't you come and tell me?'

Kay shrugged. 'Dolly insisted I go alone.'

'I see.' Jean sighed. 'I would have willingly come with you.'

'Thanks,' Kay said gratefully. 'But there was nothing you could have done. Did you read the article in the newspaper about the Tube accident?'

Jean looked alarmed. 'No, I didn't.'

Kay swallowed. She still found it difficult to talk about that night. 'We arranged to meet in Bethnal Green, but before we could say much, the siren went. Me and Dolly ran for shelter in the Tube entrance. Too many people poured into the stairwell at once and many were killed.'

Jean looked shocked. 'Kay, how dreadful!'

'Dolly just disappeared in front of me . . .' Kay shook her head, taking a deep breath. 'But I was pulled out.'

'Thank God,' Jean said. 'That must have been very frightening.'

'Yes.' Kay looked into Jean's puzzled face. 'Do you think you could find out the names of those who died?'

'Well, I could try,' Jean said thoughtfully. 'But without an official statement about the incident it might be difficult.'

'But why should such a tragedy be hushed-up?'

'It's wartime, Kay. We have to accept news is censored for the good of the general public.'

'But people died,' Kay insisted. 'Lots of them, children too.'

'I'm sure it's just a matter of time until the public is made aware of what happened at Bethnal Green. However, my main concern is for you. Are you sure you're feeling all right?'

Kay nodded. 'But what happened that night is hard to forget.'

'Is there anything else I can do?'

'Unless you can find out about Dolly or news of Sean, then no.'

As Kay saw her visitor off, she thought that there had to be families of the dead who were, like herself, waiting for answers. But perhaps Jean was right. It may be that the censors who had ultimate power over the publishing of information in wartime, and for reasons best known to themselves, really didn't want the public to know the whole truth.

Chapter Thirty-Three

It was close to the end of June when Kay decided to speak to Mr Barnet. Alfie was four and a half now and shooting up in size. He was tall and lean, like Alan, and had his father's dark eyes and shock of black hair. Each day he wanted to know when he could go to school with Tim.

'I'd like Alfie to start school as soon as possible,' Kay told Mr Barnet as she sat in the chair by the head teacher's desk. 'He's not five until November, but he's quite ready to come.'

Mr Barnet smiled at Alfie. 'Would you like to start school, young man?'

'I can say me times table,' Alfie announced confidently. 'And write me name.'

Mr Barnet smiled.

'My word, at your age, that's commendable.'

'Tim showed me and Sean how to do 'rithmetic.'

Mr Barnet looked over his glasses at Kay. 'Is there any news of Sean, by the way?'

Kay shook her head as she briefly thought of Jean, who had not been in contact. Kay knew her friend would have done everything in her power to discover any information about Dolly which might, as a result, have led to Sean.

'A pity,' said Mr Barnet. 'Sean was a bright pupil.'

'Is Sean comin' back?' Alfie asked hopefully.

'I'm afraid not, young man. But, if you are as eager as you sound to come to school, perhaps we can find you a place in September. Your teacher will be Miss Burns, who is in charge of Infants. I'm sure you'll like her.'

Alfie jumped to his feet. 'Can I go to school, Mum?'

Kay looked at Mr Barnet and he nodded. 'We'll see you on Wednesday 15 September. School starts later this year as some of the teachers are doing war work during the holidays. Now, I'll give you the relevant papers to sign, Mrs Lewis.'

Mr Barnet provided Kay with forms and lists to fill out but when they left the school, instead of jumping the cracks in the pavement as Alfie always did, he walked slowly beside Kay, his head bowed.

Kay stopped and brushed back his dark hair. 'What's the matter, love? I thought you'd be excited about going to school.'

'I am. But it ain't with Sean, is it?'

'We don't know where he lives now.'

'Don't he like me anymore?'

Kay pulled her son close and hugged him. She knew the bond between the two boys was close and that Alfie was missing Sean as much as she was. 'Course he likes you. You're best mates.'

'Will he come round again?'

Kay couldn't give an answer so she quickly asked Alfie if he'd like to stop at Lenny's stall for some of his favourite fudge. Alfie nodded, but Kay knew it was no fun eating sweets without your best pal to share them with.

It was a hot Saturday in July and Kay and Babs were shopping at market. They had left Alfie, Gill and Tim in Vi's care as they only intended to be away a short while. Vi was happy to sit on a chair at the front door and doze in the sunshine as the children played in the street.

'Alfie will be out of his sandals next,' said Kay as they sifted through the piles of second-hand clothes. 'I only bought them in spring. And I can't afford lace-ups just yet.'

'What about that Post Office book?' Babs said with a frown. 'It's what Alan left you.'

'Yes, but what if it isn't mine?'

Babs spluttered. 'Course it's yours! There's your name on it.'

'But where did it come from?'

'Do you think it was Dolly's? If you think that then it means you believe Alan was involved with her.'

Kay passed her hand over her wet forehead. 'Babs, I don't know what to think.'

'I know what I'd do if it was me. Sod whoever it belonged to and feed my family.' Babs lifted a pair of child's well-worn lace-up shoes. 'These are only a few pennies, but there are more Blakies than shoe.' She let them drop suddenly, blowing out a puff of air. 'Phew, it's too hot to go shopping. Let's have a glass of lemonade at Lenny's. He'll give us two for one if we smile nicely at him.'

Kay was feeling the heat too. There were wavy lines on the horizon, as the sun dazzled the eye. As they'd walked to market, the roads had been scattered with piles of horse dung that were baking in the high temperatures. Together with the salt-tar smell of the river, the mucky brown flotsam floating on its surface and the spillage of waste from the big ships, the day felt oppressive and humid.

Soon they found shelter under the shade of a tarpaulin that Lenny had erected over his wooden benches. As always, Lenny was obliging and only charged for one lemonade. Sipping her cool drink, Babs looked at Kay. 'I had a letter from Eddie yesterday.'

'Lucky you,' Kay said enviously.

'He said he's missing us.'

'That's nice.' Kay smiled. She knew her friend loved her husband, but Paul wasn't often out of her mind either.

'Did you tell Paul?' Kay asked.

Babs shook her head. 'Not yet.'

'Babs, this is all very risky. What if Eddie were to turn up out of the blue?'

'Why would he? I'd get a letter to say he was coming home on leave first.'

Kay sipped her drink. 'I haven't had a letter from Alan in nearly a year.'

'Now I feel even guiltier.' Babs blinked her blue eyes and pushed back her fair hair. 'There's you dying for news from Alan and me not knowing what to write back to Eddie.'

'I'm beginning to struggle with writing letters myself,' Kay was forced to admit. 'It's always a one-sided conversation.'

'Have you ever mentioned Dolly?'

'No. I wouldn't know what to say about her.'

'No, course not.'

'I feel confused, Babs. After what Dolly said about Spain and Alan's own words in the letter he wrote before he went away, I ask meself, why would he write what he did? And then there's the hundred pounds he put in the Post Office, the same amount that was stolen from Dolly.'

Babs leaned close and in a soft voice whispered, 'Kay, you told me before that you trust Alan. You still do, don't you?'

'He asked me that once, too.'

'Well, do you?'

Kay wanted to say she did. But lately she'd had many troubled thoughts. Thoughts that she tried not to think and yet they just bubbled to the surface. 'Some days I do,' she admitted. 'Other days I have my doubts. Like when I think back to the Suttons' funeral. Alan told me he was going back to the post. Instead he met someone else at the Pig and Whistle.'

'Yes, a relative of the Suttons'.'

'But was he?' Kay questioned. 'Could he, too, have been a part of Alan's past? The past that Dolly says she shared with him.'

'We all know what a good story-teller she was.'

'Yes, but Alan wrote about forgiveness and a second chance. Was Dolly once his wife, a mistake he realized he'd made and left her for reasons that are different to what Dolly said? Is Sean Alan's son, I ask myself? Alfie and Sean looked alike. You once said yourself, they could be taken for brothers.'

'Lots of kids look the same round here. All dirty faces and scruffy clothes.' Babs laughed.

'I wonder if Alan was trying to convince himself that Dolly and Sean didn't count? After all, Dolly said that her Alan hadn't even seen his son. It wasn't as if he held a baby in his arms, knowing he was a father. Or could Dolly be lying and Sean be another man's child?'

'Yes, that's possible I suppose,' Babs said with a nod.

'What did you think when you found out Eddie had had an affair?'

Babs was silent, until she gave a soft sigh. 'I couldn't believe he'd done it. I thought there was some mistake. My Eddie would never do such a thing! Then, as I struggled with the jealousy about another woman, I began to reason it out. I'd been in my own world after Gill's birth and it was a very lonely one. Eddie must have felt just as lonely.' Babs lowered her head. 'As for forgiveness? Well, you can forgive but you can't forget. Alan's never strayed whilst he's been married to you. He hasn't betrayed you, even if he was once married to Dolly before he met you. That was his past. There's a big difference in that, Kay.'

'Yes, but why didn't he tell me? Did he think he could always keep such an unhappy secret?'

'Perhaps he had good reason. And you have to accept you will only find it out when you see Alan again.'

Kay sat there, watching Babs hurriedly mop up a few spots of lemonade that had spilled on her dress. She wanted to answer Babs with the words, '*If* I ever see Alan again.'

But those words wouldn't come. Instead she thought of Alan's letter.

> After all that has happened, I can't expect you to understand or forgive. But you must trust that our marriage is real and perfect. I could not have wished for a better second chance. It was you and Alfie that gave me an honest life. Before that, there was nothing! Nothing that ever needed to be told. But I suspect, if you are reading this, some of it already has.

Kay was left wondering what all this could mean.

Kay sat up in bed, her eyes wide open. An answer had come to her in her sleep! How could that be? As she blinked her eyes and stared at the front-room windows covered in blackout and Alan's wooden frames, her mind searched frantically for the contents of the dream. She was back at the Salmon and Ball pub again. This time

Dolly wasn't sitting with her. She was joking and laughing with the landlord.

Kay's heart raced. Her mouth was dry as she tried to remember the clue. Even in her sleep she had known it was vital to remember. She strained to recall but the dream was illusive, sending a wave of panic through her. It was passing, drifting . . .

Then at that moment the pieces slipped into place. The pub's customers enjoying their drinks, the buzz of conversation, the haze of cigarette smoke hanging in the air. The landlord, his shirtsleeves rolled up as he leaned on the bar talking to Dolly. Kay felt like an invisible listener. She couldn't hear their words. But it didn't matter.

If anyone could shed light on Dolly, it was the landlord of the Salmon and Ball pub.

Chapter Thirty-Four

It was another hot July day and Kay's light summer dress was sticking to her skin. She had coiled her coppery hair up into a roll around her head, but damp wisps trailed around her ears and refused to stay in place. Before she'd left home, she'd made certain that Alfie was dressed in his cotton shirt and summer shorts. All Vi had to do was sit at the front door and doze as they played games in the street.

'You're certain you want to go back to Bethnal Green after all that happened?' asked Babs as they sat on the bus taking them to Green Road.

'Yes, I don't know why I didn't think of it before.'

Babs sighed, shrugging her shoulders. 'I hope this don't upset you all over again.'

Kay knew the Tube would be a reminder of the close call she'd had with death. The cries of those unfortunate people on the stairs had never left her. The sight of Dolly going under the crowd. But, over the months, she had kept the bad memories at bay. Now she must face them.

'I wish you'd let Paul bring us in the car.'

'No. I want to do this alone.'

Babs looked at Kay again. 'You do have me.'

Kay touched her friend's arm. 'I know that.'

When they got off the bus, a rush of heat poured over them. Mixed with this was the smell of the traffic and market stalls trading down the road.

Kay slipped her hand through Babs's arm. Babs looked at her and said again, 'It's not too late to get back on the bus.'

Kay smiled. 'Like you said, I've got you with me.'

They walked along the dusty, dry pavements. Even though it was a beautiful summer's day and people were strolling lazily along, Kay felt cold inside. It was as if she was entering the world she had left on the night of 3 March. When they reached the Salmon and Ball pub, Kay had to stop and take a deep breath. The doors were open and an old man was sweeping out the dirt into small piles.

'We ain't open yet,' he told them gruffly.

'Is the landlord here?' Kay and Babs peered inside.

'Who's asking?' The old man leaned on his broom, puffing and sweating.

'We are,' said Babs, sticking out her chin. 'Is he here or not?'

'No, but I'll get the barman.' He went inside and closed the door behind him.

'Do you think we should come back later?' asked Babs doubtfully.

But as she spoke the door opened and a younger man stood there. He had greasy dark hair and bushy eyebrows that grew low over his small, rather aggressive eyes. Kay recognized him at once. 'I thought you were the landlord,' she said.

'No, he ain't around. What do you want?'

'To speak to you for a minute,' Kay said quickly. 'I was here with a friend on the night of the accident at the Tube.'

His expression changed. 'I don't know nothing about that,' he rasped, and started to close the door.

Kay pushed it open again. 'You must do,' she insisted. 'Dolly and me were sitting together in your pub when the siren went. We both went to the Tube to take cover.'

'What Dolly do you mean?'

'Dolly Lewis. I watched you talking together. I know you know her, so don't say you don't.'

The man gave a grunt, wiped his big, hairy hands on his dirty apron and slowly opened the door. 'You'd better come in.'

Kay and Babs walked into the stale-smelling bar where the wooden chairs were turned upside down on the tables.

'You better be on the level,' the barman threatened. 'I'm not answering no trick questions.'

'Who's asked you trick questions?' said Babs, as they stood by the counter.

'You'd be surprised.'

'To do with what happened that night?' pressed Kay.

'It didn't happen, according to some.'

'Well, it did,' Kay told him firmly. 'I was here to see Dolly and we both left when the siren went. The crowd panicked when they heard something very loud, like bombs being dropped. Everyone surged forward down the slippery steps of the Tube.'

'I don't know about that. I went down in the cellar.'

'Well, you were lucky,' Kay said shortly. 'Dolly was in front of me and the crowd kept going forward. The last I saw of her was in the Tube stairwell.'

'Poor cow.'

'I've tried to find out about her, but there's no real news anywhere.'

The barman knitted his bushy eyebrows together. 'You're not wrong there, lady. But I tell you, there's some who's been snooping round here and asking questions.'

'The police, you mean?' Babs suggested.

'I dunno, do I? All I know is that I stayed here that night, took shelter down in the cellar. But there weren't no need. No bombs was dropped. And when I came up and went outside there was all those poor sods lying on stretchers as far as the eye could see.'

'You saw them too?'

'I'll never forget 'em.'

'So what was those noises then, the ones everyone thought was bombs?' Babs demanded.

'If you find the answer to that, love, I reckon you've found what caused the rush down the Tube.'

Kay's knees went weak. She gripped the bar. 'At least I've found someone who remembers the same as me.'

'Yeah, but when I started to tell these two blokes who came round, they said if I knew what was good for me, I wouldn't spread no rumours.'

'But it's not rumour, it's the truth.'

'You and me know that, love.'

'My name is Kay and this is my friend, Babs,' Kay told the barman. 'Who are you?'

'I'm Dave,' he said gruffly.

'And you know – or knew – Dolly?'

'What's it to you?'

Kay looked at Babs first, then said, 'Me and my friend are looking for her son, Sean. He stayed with us for a while, when Dolly first came to the Isle of Dogs. But Dolly took him away again. And if Dolly, well, if Dolly died that night, it means he'll be an orphan.'

'So that's the only reason you want her – for the kid?' Dave frowned suspiciously.

'What other reason could there be?'

He laughed. 'Plenty. Dol rubbed lots of people up the wrong way. Owed money right, left and centre. She was always skint, nicking from her punters even. The landlord told her to take her business elsewhere, but she still called in to see if there was any business about. So you can see, I don't want no trouble. I could lose me job.'

'We don't want trouble either,' said Babs. 'We just want to find Sean.'

'I felt sorry for the kid too, the way she dragged him from pillar to post.'

'You saw him?' Kay gasped.

'Once or twice she made him sit outside the pub as she sorted her punters. He had to stay there an' all while she found some place to do the business.'

Kay closed her eyes. Poor Sean!

'How long have you known Dolly?' asked Babs.

'Round about last Christmas. She fetched up here looking for trade,' he replied. 'But the kid only appeared on the scene a few months ago.'

'That must have been after she took him from school,' said Kay. Was she close to discovering something now? 'She said she had a friend that Sean was staying with. Do you know where this friend could be?'

Dave shrugged. 'Must be someone in the trade.'

Kate shuddered. 'Did she ever say anything about where she lived? Please try to remember.'

'No, Dolly was canny like that. Didn't let anyone know her business.'

Kay's heart sank.

'But I saw her once not far from here,' the barman remembered. 'I was on me way up to the Roman Road. I clocked her and the kid for a few minutes, then she disappeared down what's left of Stock's Lane.'

'What do you mean, what's left of it?' Kay asked.

'In forty-one, Jerry's planes knocked it out. It was a rotten slum anyway.'

'Does anyone live there now?' asked Babs.

'Might be one or two, I suppose.'

Kay looked at Babs. Their eyes met in hope. At least this was somewhere to go.

'If you're aiming to go there,' Dave warned them, 'Take a bit of heavy. Stock's Lane ain't no place for decent sorts like yerselves.'

Kay understood the warning. But she had no intention of stopping now. She had come too far to turn back.

Vi felt someone shake her. She was always slow to rouse from a nap lately, but this time, she had been woken from a deep slumber. She looked up and into the bright sunshine, the triangular newspaper hat she had made that morning falling down over her forehead.

'Hello, Vi.'

She screwed up her eyes, not recognizing the voice. The sun was still too bright to see properly. 'Hang on a minute, I'll get to me feet.' She stretched out a hand, but suddenly felt light-headed. A hand caught her arm and steadied her.

'Watch out there, love. Reckon you've had too much sun.'

Vi gazed at the familiar face. 'Why, if it isn't Kay's dad!'

'That's me, warts an' all.'

'Well, I never did.' Vi blinked, as she tried to shake off the dizziness that sometimes caught her off-guard. 'Oh, and it's you, Lil!'

'It's me, love,' said Lil. 'Where's our Kay?'

'She ain't home. She's gone—' Vi paused. She knew better than to blurt out that Kay was in Bethnal Green and following up on the events of 3 March in the hopes that she might discover Sean's whereabouts. For as far as Vi knew, Kay hadn't written to Lil about that night, nor did Lil know anything about Sean or Dolly.

Vi tried to gather herself, but then she saw Alfie playing up by the bombed site of her old house. Tim and Alfie had stripped to the waist and were throwing clumps of dried mud at each other. It was then Vi remembered that Babs had ordered a clean-up of the backyard and the Andersons. It was she, Vi, who had suggested the boys load their cart with the weeds and dirt that had grown over the tunnel roof and take it up the road to dump. The workmen had dug a hole for some reason and left it; a space that Vi had noted and thought could prove useful.

With a quick glance to the end of the street, Vi hoped she would see the familiar figures of Kay and Babs approaching. Unfortunately, the street was empty. 'What time is it?' asked Vi, completely forgetting Lil's question.

'Half one,' said Bob.

'Oh,' replied Vi vacantly. How long would it take Kay to get back on the bus from Bethnal Green?

'Where's she gone?' asked Lil, frowning. Her silver hair was styled smartly around her head and she was wearing a brown two-piece outfit. Bob wore his usual titfer and a big smile on his face. Vi wondered anxiously if, like last time, they'd come to stay.

'Is she out shopping?' asked Bob.

'No – well, yes,' Vi corrected herself. 'She's with Babs.'

'When did they go out?' asked Lil.

'Not long ago.'

'Well, we'll just have to wait.' Lil looked through the open door.

Vi suddenly remembered her manners. 'Come in and I'll make you a cuppa.'

'That'd be nice,' said Bob cheerfully. 'We're only down for the day,' he added, to Vi's relief. 'Jumped on the train and then got the bus to Poplar. Thought we'd see how our nipper is.'

'You mean Alfie?' said Vi, flummoxed, as she saw Alfie returning a fistful of dirt at Tim.

'Course we do.' Lil deepened the frown on her forehead. 'Vi, are you all right?'

Vi nodded. 'Just had a bit too much sun.' She took one last furtive glance at Alfie and the dirt fight and prayed Gill would have the sense to break up the fun and make the boys put on their shirts. Lil would have a fit if she saw her grandson looking like one of those street kids she so deplored.

Chapter Thirty-Five

'Kay, I don't like it round here,' said Babs anxiously as they made their way towards Stock's Lane. As Dave had informed them, the Luftwaffe had done their job well in this part of the East End. Though the markets and thoroughfares were busy and thriving on the hot summer's day, there was always a reminder of the bombing.

Kay and Babs stopped to stare down the winding alley in the heart of Bethnal Green. The area had once been the busy heart of London's rag trade. Kay remembered how her father had told her all about the capital's clothing sweatshops. But now only a faint reflection of the past remained: toppled walls that had once been the supports of the Huguenots' silk attics, finally polished off by Jerry's bombs; capsizing floors of a chapel that no longer contained an altar, just the frame of a glass-stained window and the fragments of tiles that might have once led to an altar. Beyond this the synagogue rose, untouched by the air raids, and there were still a few bagel-sellers, but even these traders, it seemed, were using the alley as a shortcut between the derelict buildings.

It was so dark and dreary here that even the sun seemed to prefer shining in the busier streets. One or two unsavoury characters passed them as they walked along. Babs stopped and pulled on Kay's arm.

'Even Dolly wouldn't live in a place like this.'

'It was where Dave said he saw her go.'

'Yes,' agreed Babs, 'but this ain't Dolly's style.'

'Let's look at that terrace of houses,' Kay suggested. 'There's a curtain in one window. Well, what's left of it.'

They approached the block of three terraced cottages. Two of the three doors were boarded up. The windows were also shut-off, a measure that must have been taken long ago, as the boards over the windows were as black and grimy as the crumbling red-brick and mortar.

Kay craned her neck upwards. There was no roof to be seen on the third house. It only seemed to be standing by the grace of the building beside it – a warehouse of some kind, whose large wooden doors were bolted and barred.

'Could there be someone living in there?' Kay pointed to the window with the ragged lace curtain. They walked closer, going as near as they dared. The broken pane of glass let out a strong smell of urine. Kay and Babs stepped quickly away.

'Lord almighty,' gasped Babs, covering her nose with her hand. 'It stinks to high heaven.'

Kay nodded, just managing not to gag. 'I'm going to knock at the door.'

'Don't,' begged Babs, clutching her arm. 'Nothing . . . nothing human can come out of there.'

'I've got to try.'

Kay walked cautiously up to the door and knocked. Seeing no movement at the window, she knocked again, calling out, 'Dolly! Dolly! It's me, Kay. I've got your money.'

Babs hurried beside her. 'What did you say that for?'

'If Dolly's in there, she'd come out at the mention of money.'

They waited. Kay thought she heard something, but then decided it could be a rat. She'd seen one or two scampering across the road. Then there was a creak and a shuffling noise.

Babs clutched her arm as they waited. Kay felt her knees knock as the door slowly opened.

'Whatdywant?' The hiss came from inside the dark hovel. Kay and Babs stepped back again. 'I . . . I'm looking for Dolly, Dolly Lewis,' Kay spluttered.

'Yer out of luck. She ain't here.' The woman's face was old and haggard. Too old for Kay to put an age to. A long nose and shifty eyes took in their presence and a filthy, bony hand came round the rotten wood of the door. 'Anythin' else yer want to know, yer'll 'ave ter pay for.' The hand opened to reveal a dirty palm, encrusted with what looked like oil and grease. The smell was so overpowering that Kay tried to hold her breath. Forcing down her heaving stomach, she took a shilling from her bag. It wasn't much, but it was all she had. Slowly she stepped forward and placed the money on the woman's palm. It disappeared in a second.

'Don't! Don't shut the door!' Kay stuck her foot in the gap. The smell made her eyes water. 'Have you a boy in there, a young boy of about six? His name is Sean.'

'Get away or I'll 'ave the dogs on yer!'

'And I'll come back with the bobbies,' replied Kay in desperation. 'Just tell me if he's there.'

'Course he ain't, yer silly moo,' came the reply. 'A kid can't pay me the rent. Nor would that mean sod wot gave an eye to 'im. I booted 'em both out.'

'Where did they go?'

'How should I know?' spat the woman. 'Now bugger off.' She pressed the door hard against Kay's foot. Kay yelped with pain and fell back. The door slammed.

Babs put her arm around Kay. 'The old witch. Did she hurt you?'

'No, but what if she's lying and Sean's in there?' Kay bent and rubbed her foot.

'Why would she lie?'

'To get rid of us.'

'Dolly can't be there. Sean was her way of getting her money.'

Kay nodded. 'I think Dolly died that night.' Kay looked up at the building. She turned to Babs. 'I'm going to get help.'

'Who?' Babs asked in surprise.

'Jean Pearson.'

Babs looked around and shuddered. 'Can't see Jean coming to a dump like this.'

'She will if I ask her.'

Babs looked at Kay and grinned. 'We'd better get going then.'

As they hurried out of the slum Kay glanced behind her. Was Sean inside that terrible place? Or were they too late?

Alfie burst in the back door, Tim beside him, their faces so filthy the rims of their eyes stood out in gleaming white circles. Vi took in a sharp breath. Neither boys wore their shirts. As for sandals, they were barefoot, pushing out their dirty chests and beating them as they ran in the kitchen.

Vi looked at Lil, who was seated on one of the kitchen chairs drinking her tea. Lil's tea splashed into the saucer. 'Alfie, is that you?' demanded Lil. 'Where have you been?'

''ello, Gran.' Alfie smiled widely. His teeth shone white under the dirt.

'Young man,' said Bob, getting up from his chair, 'what do you think you're playing at?'

'We live in the zoo,' said Alfie, proudly beating his chest again. 'Me an' Tim are monkeys.'

'You look like ones an' all,' laughed Bob. 'But you can't bring all that dirt in your mother's kitchen.'

'Me mum won't mind.'

Tim nodded. 'We can sound like monkeys too.' They both beat their chests and howled.

Was it not for the fact that Lil was speechless, staring at the small heaps of dried mud falling on the floor as they yelled and began to prance around, Vi would have joined in their laughter. They were little monkeys indeed.

Lil's head snapped round. 'Has Alfie been running the streets?'

Vi was about to declare they hadn't, but Alfie answered first.

'We been in a 'ole the men dug.'

Lil clattered her cup in the saucer. 'Have you been playing on bomb sites?'

'We're not allowed on them,' Vi was relieved to hear them say.

'Well, at least you're not likely to get blown to bits,' Lil said, scowling at Bob. 'Bob, bring in the tin bath. We'll soon have these two sorted out.'

'But we're playin' a good game, Gran.'

'You were, love, and it was nice while it lasted, but now you've got us to talk to. We're only down for the day and half of it has gone already.' Lil rolled up the sleeves of her cardigan. 'Now, take off them dirty shorts, both of you.' She marched them out into the yard, calling over her shoulder, 'Start boiling some water, will you, Vi?'

Bob glanced at Vi. 'Lil ain't one for messes.'

'It's only a bit of fun,' said Vi, rising to her feet. She felt giddy again and Bob reached out.

'Leave this to me, darlin'. Go and have forty winks.'

Vi nodded. 'Don't mind if I do.'

He grinned. 'We've got a nice surprise for Kay. A train ticket for her and the boy to come up to us in September.

Should be nice weather then. And it will give her a break from the Smoke.'

Vi nodded. 'Very nice an' all. Well, I'll leave you to it.'

Vi made her way upstairs and, after closing the door to the bedroom, hurried over to the window.

'Hurry up, Kay,' she whispered to the empty street. 'There'll be trouble in paradise if you don't arrive home and explain to your mum that Alfie ain't a street urchin.'

Sitting on the bus to Slater Street, Kay and Babs were discussing their visit to Jean Pearson. Hampered by the traffic from Bethnal Green to Poplar, they hadn't arrived at the council offices until late that afternoon. Then they'd had to wait until Jean arrived back from business elsewhere.

'Do you think Jean will go to Stock's Lane as she promised?' asked Babs reflectively.

'She said she would put it to her superior.'

'Don't think she'd want to go there on her own.'

Kay frowned. 'Nor would I if I was her.'

Babs sighed, pushing her damp hair away from her face. 'Let's hope this time, they'll get their act together.'

By the time they arrived at Slater Street it was almost half past six. There were no children in the street and Vi's chair, positioned by the front door, was empty.

'Bit quiet round here,' said Babs, frowning.

'P'raps they're in the Anderson,' said Kay. 'Let's go round to the Cut and surprise them.' But when Kay and Babs arrived in the lane and looked across the wall, both yards were empty.

'Look, the boys cleared all them weeds,' said Babs, delighted. 'And all the dirt too.'

Kay smiled at the sight of the scraped-clean Anderson roofs. Just then the back door of Kay's house opened and the two boys ran out. They were dressed in clean clothes with their hair parted on the side and shiny fresh faces to go with their smiles.

'Gran's been here,' shouted Alfie as he ran towards them. 'She says we're goin' to stay with her for an 'oliday. What's an 'oliday?'

Kay caught Alfie as he clambered up the wall and jumped into her arms. She smelled Lifebuoy in big wafts as she hugged him against her. Then Gill ran out of the house, eager to see Babs.

'Alfie's gran washed the boys in the bath,' she giggled. 'Everyone saw their willies.'

Tim spun round and pushed his sister over. Soon the children were shouting and laughing, returning the yard to its normal mayhem. Above the racket, Vi appeared at the kitchen door, rolling her eyes heavenward.

Chapter Thirty-Six

'Sorry, love,' Vi apologized that evening, as she sat with Kay in the front room after Alfie was in bed. 'I'm afraid your mum didn't take kindly to the fact Alfie was playing in the street and in a bit of a state. I think you're gonna get it in the ear when you see her next.'

'It can't be helped,' Kay replied as she placed a mug of hot tea beside Vi. 'Just the day I needed to be here and I wasn't.'

'At least you spoke to Jean Pearson about that dump.'

Kay nodded. 'She tried to be helpful.'

'When's she going to this Stock's Lane?'

'She has to get permission first.'

'Do you reckon they'll find the lad?'

Kay had been convinced the old woman was hiding something or someone. 'I can't be sure,' she admitted. 'I can't bear to think of him living in a slum like that. But at the same time, if the chips were down, I'd rather him be there, where they'll find him, instead of disappearing again.' Kay looked at Vi and smiled. 'Thanks for what you did today, Vi.'

'I didn't do nothing.'

'You didn't land me in it with Mum.'

Vi laughed. 'Alfie did that all by himself.'

'Mum will have to take us as she finds us. Anyway, she might have forgotten all about it by the time we go to Berkshire.'

'You're going, then?'

'It's not on the top of me "to-do" list, but I can't disappoint them again. Especially as they paid the fare. And anyway, Alfie was excited when I explained what a holiday was. He hasn't had one before.'

'Like your dad, I think a change of scenery will do you both good,' Vi agreed.

'We'll have to be back for the fifteenth when Alfie starts school.'

'September will be a busy month.'

Kay smiled ruefully. 'Would you like to come with us? I know Mum would make you welcome.'

But Vi began to shake her head even before Kay had finished speaking. 'No, flower, not me! As nice as the country sounds, I'd prefer to be here where I can wander down to the shops if I want. Or go to the market. Or just sit outside the front door and watch the world go by.'

'I don't like leaving you on your own.'

'Babs is next door.'

'Vi, if a letter from Alan arrives—'

'I could post it on to you.'

'Thanks.'

'Leave it ter me.'

'I hope I hear from Jean soon,' Kay murmured, her thoughts on Sean. 'Because if she doesn't go to Stock's Lane, then I'll have to.'

'But the old lady won't let you in.'

'She will if I give her some money.' Kay was thinking of the Post Office account.

It was early in August when Jean appeared at the door again. Kay could tell by the look on her face that it was not good news.

'We were too late,' Jean told Kay regretfully as they went into the kitchen and sat down. 'The place had been abandoned.'

Kay swallowed down her bitter disappointment. She had been telling herself that by some miracle, Sean would be found. Tears filled her eyes. She seemed destined never to find Sean, no matter how hard she tried.

'I'm so sorry, Kay.'

'You didn't find anything – anything at all – to prove Sean had been there?'

'Only this. Can you identify it?' Jean took an envelope from her bag and drew out a scrap of dirty paper. Under the muck smeared over it there was a child's drawing. Kay recognized the shape: a blue train carriage.

'Yes,' Kay gasped. 'It's the carriage from Alfie's train set.'

'Are you sure it's Sean's drawing?'

'Without a doubt. He would have had his drawing book and crayons in his satchel.'

'We didn't find any of those.'

Kay fingered the piece of paper. 'Can I keep this?'

'If you like.'

Kay looked at the drawing. 'So what happens now?'

'We've given our findings to the police and asked them to list Sean as a missing person.'

'Is that what Sean is – missing?'

'His description will be circulated to all the constabularies.'

'That's something, I suppose.'

'I did try to find out about Dolly,' Jean said with a sigh, 'but with no success.'

Kay nodded. 'I guessed that might be the case.'

'Don't give up hope, Kay.'

Kay tried to smile, but after her friend had left, Kay went into the front room and took the train set from the wardrobe drawer. She placed the drawing beside it. Sean had memorized the blue train perfectly. He must have been scared and lonely when Dolly took him to that awful place. She hoped and prayed that he knew she would try to find him.

Kay held the carriage close, together with the scrap of paper. She wouldn't lose hope, yet she knew it would be almost impossible to find Sean amidst the numbers of missing and displaced children that were a result of this terrible war.

Chapter Thirty-Seven

It was early September. Kay and Alfie arrived at Monkton Station to find Bob waiting on the platform to greet them. He shouldered his way through the crowds, eager to relieve her of her bags.

'Good to see you at last,' he said as he kissed them on their cheeks and ruffled Alfie's neatly combed hair. 'My word, son, you've scrubbed up well since last I saw you.'

Kay went red. 'Sorry I wasn't there that day, Dad.'

'Couldn't be helped. Now, Alfie, are you ready to have the time of your life?' Bob grabbed Alfie's hand and marched them through the people leaving the small station. Kay noticed the many different uniforms about, not just English, but American too.

'We've got a lot of activity here,' shouted Bob over his shoulder. 'There's an air force base a couple of miles away and Monkton is the closest shopping centre. So we get to see a lot of those chaps.'

Kay blushed when she received smiles from the handsome servicemen dressed in their sleek uniforms and tilted caps. Compared to the elegant women who accompanied some of them, she felt dowdy in her cheap and cheerful floral dress and market-bought sandals. Even her hair was untidy from the panic they'd had leaving early this morning in order to catch the bus. They'd made it to the station with only a few minutes to spare. She hadn't been able to pile her hair on top of her head in attractive curls. Instead, her coppery locks were flying across her shoulders and over her forehead, straying into the long lashes that fringed her grey eyes. They passed other women too, all smiling and giving the eye to the troops. Some were from the Women's Royal Air Force, others looked like Land Army girls in their shirts and trousers. The station was very busy for a small place like Monkton, and Kay said as much to her dad as they emerged into the sunshine outside.

'You might have a surprise,' continued Bob, 'when you see how lively we country bumpkins can be. Now come on, here's our coach. The council lays it on at midday for people who want to go straight to the town centre.'

Kay sat by the window on the coach and Alfie on his granddad's knee. Like Hertfordshire, the farms, lanes, hundreds of trees, cows, cottages and tractors whizzed by. Kay wondered if Alfie remembered living in the country with Len and Doris. She always reminded him of his Uncle Len and Nanty in Hertfordshire; though it was years since he'd seen them, they were part of his family and she wanted him to know that. Studying his face, she was surprised to see his attention was on a young girl sitting on the opposite side of the coach. She was eating sweets from a brown paper bag and making them look very delicious.

'Can I 'ave a big bag of sweets, Granddad?' Alfie asked, unable to take his eyes off the sight of the sweets slowly being popped into the girl's mouth. Kay noticed she was very well dressed with nice shoes, and her mother also looked very smart in a red two-piece suit and saucer-shaped hat to match.

'We'll see what we can sort out,' said Bob, grinning and patting Alfie's arm. 'That's Flora Cuthbert,' whispered Bob to Kay. 'She's on the town council. Very well-to-do. Goes up to the city a lot and rubs shoulders with the top brass. Flora Junior goes to a posh boarding school. Must be the last of the wee mite's holiday and she's making the most of it. Your mum plays whist with Flora at the church hall.'

'Mum's taken a shine to whist,' agreed Kay. 'Goes on about it in her letters.'

'Keeps her busy,' said Bob with a rueful smile.

'So what's Aunty Pops's place like, Dad?' Kay asked as the coach trundled along.

'Too big for her to manage really, since Tommy died,' said Bob. 'And even when Tommy was alive he didn't do much. He was a travelling salesman before the war and away a lot.'

'Do you and Mum intend to stay with Aunty Pops?'

'You'll have to ask your mother about that.'

'Would you like to come back to the East End one day?' Kay persisted.

Bob gave a gentle shrug. 'I've got used to country life now. Your mum and Aunty Pops rub along all right. And me, well, I've got the bowls club; all me mates are there.'

'Are they like your pals from Poplar?'

'Not really,' her dad admitted. 'When you've worked for London Transport for three decades you're part of a clan. Just like your Norman was. A damn good bus driver who'd have drawn his pension if it wasn't for that damn accident.'

Kay's smile faded. She knew how close her mum and dad were to Norman. Which was one of the reasons why they hadn't taken to Alan. Her first husband was a hard act to follow and Alan hadn't tried, anyway. He was his own man.

As if reading her thoughts, her dad nudged her arm. 'Didn't mean to bring back painful memories, love.'

Kay resisted the urge to say that memories concerning Norman were no longer painful. Falling in love with Alan had given her a new life to lead. She had long ago come to terms with the shock of Norman's premature death and the abrupt end to her first marriage. She had hoped that this holiday would prove different; that she could talk to her parents about the life she planned with Alan together on the island after the war. They had talked about buying their own house on the island, of doing it up and, with Alan's skills, making it a home to be proud of. It was a pipe dream, Kay knew, but it was theirs.

'Won't be long now. Monkton's just down the road,' said Bob. 'Your Mum and Aunty Pops are on the edge of their seats waiting to see you. Now just look at that! You can't beat a nice little English cafe, even in wartime, perhaps especially in wartime, where you can enjoy a poached egg on toast!'

Kay looked out of the window following her father's glance. The sun was shining above a black-beamed thatch-cottage tea-room with a notice outside advertising the use of fresh farm eggs. The last time she had seen a sign like that was when Alan was beside her as they had travelled to Len and Doris's.

Aunty Pops's house was big indeed. Kay had imagined a kind of cottage like Len and Doris's Albion. But it was, so her dad explained, a house built only thirty or forty years ago. Under the strong-looking slate roof were pale coloured bricks and workmanlike windows that were nothing like the lattice ones she had been expecting. There weren't many trees or flowers around. Instead an allotment spread out on either side of the front path.

'This is my veggie patch,' said Bob. 'I'm out here a lot as we grow all our own veg.' He laughed. 'In the Smoke I wouldn't have known what to do with a spade. But here, we're all encouraged to dig for Britain. Big part of the war effort, see.'

'D'you grow any sweets, Granddad?' asked Alfie.

Bob chuckled. 'I ain't managed sweets yet, son. But give me time. One day I might be able to turn a broad bean into a gobstopper.'

The front door flew open and Kay saw her mother appear. Wearing a belted navy-blue dress and red scarf, she looked as smart as ever. Her short, silvery hair gleamed in the sunshine and a brooch sparkled on the lapel of her jacket. Behind her was an older woman, also with silvery grey hair cut short, who Kay vaguely remembered as Aunty Pops, Lil's older sister. She was shorter than Lil, wore trousers and a cardigan and walked with the aid of a stick.

The two women hugged Kay and made a great fuss of Alfie. 'Nice to see you after all these years, love,' said Aunty Pops, her wrinkled face as brown as the grubby old cardigan she wore. 'Me and Tommy came to stay with your mum for your poor Norman's funeral.'

Kay hoped Aunty Pops wasn't going to provide more discussion on Norman. 'Yes, a long time ago now, Aunty Pops.'

'The lad don't smile much, does he?' said Aunty Pops, thankfully moving on to another subject. She too ruffled his hair and received one of his long stares. 'Never mind, we'll soon get to know one another. Come on in and make yourselves at home.'

'Well, you're here at last, my girl,' said Lil, sliding her arm through Kay's while Aunty Pops and Bob walked behind them with Alfie. 'Better late than never, I say. I'm sure you'll enjoy yourselves so much you'll be wanting to stay on a few weeks more.' She stood still. 'Nice for the lad not to have to find his fun in the streets.'

Kay knew her mother was hinting at the day they came to visit. 'Alfie's got to be back for the fifteenth,' she said. 'It's the start of the school term.'

Lil waved this aside. 'He ain't gonna be expelled for being a week or two late, I'm sure!'

Kay didn't argue the point. She knew that if Vi was here she'd be rolling her eyes and giving a mischievous grin to the back of Lil's neatly combed head.

It was early on Friday morning and Vi looked out of the window onto the street which hadn't yet filled with kids. It was a nice time of the morning, just the gulls screeching and the river traffic beginning its hustle and bustle. Lifting the sash she breathed in the morning air and enjoyed its freshness as it circulated the bedroom. Then, as she was about to turn away, she saw a figure in uniform come marching down the road, arms swinging.

Vi took in a sharp breath. It was Eddie!

'Oh, my Gawd,' she gasped, hiding behind the lace curtain. 'Now the cat's really among the pigeons.'

She stood back, her heart thumping wildly. She'd only been speaking to Babs yesterday in the corner shop. Babs hadn't said a word about Eddie. She couldn't know he was coming home.

Vi listened for the knock on Babs's front door, or would Eddie pull up the key, she wondered. But she heard the knocker go, a succession of loud raps that was Eddie's signature tune. Minutes later there were screams of delight. Vi could hear Gill and Tim, and Eddie's deep voice in reply.

Vi couldn't remember if Paul had stayed overnight. He was such a regular visitor now that she'd accepted his presence whenever she saw him. She listened, wondering if she'd hear raised male voices. Angry yells? But there was nothing more than the children's happy cries and the bang of the door.

'It had to happen,' Vi murmured to herself, shaking her head miserably. 'Babs is gonna have her work cut out on this one!'

It was early evening on Saturday and Kay was getting Alfie ready for an evening out. They were all going to a dance at the church hall. Lil had bought tickets at her whist club; included in the price was a buffet, a raffle and a glass of punch.

Kay smiled at Alfie's long face. He didn't like his new clothes. And although they had cost an absolute fortune, Lil had insisted she make the purchases. The shop had sold children's clothes for years and much of their stock was pre-war. With Lil's coupons added to Kay's, Alfie had been kitted out with new short trousers, a smart white shirt, a sleeveless V-neck jumper patterned with wavy rainbow-coloured lines and, of course, a brand new pair of lace-up shoes just right for school.

'Why ain't me shoes got Blakies?' Alfie complained as Kay urged him to put them on his feet and pull up the long grey woollen socks that were another of Lil's purchases.

'Because new shoes don't need Blakies.'

'I like Blakies,' objected Alfie. 'They make a loud noise.' Alfie frowned down at his feet. 'And these are too tight.'

'No, they're not. The man measured you.'

'I ain't ever been measured before.'

'Well, now you have.' Kay climbed to her feet, trying to decide what she would wear for tonight's entertainment.

'I don't like me collar done up.' Alfie wrestled with his shirt button. 'I'm gonna get hot in this.' He pulled at his jumper.

'Alfie, your gran bought you all these nice clothes. She wants to see you wearing them tonight.'

'Do I have to wear 'em when I get home?'

Kay resisted the urge to laugh as Alfie pulled a face.

'Come on now, Alfie, cheer up.'

But Alfie's shoulders slumped. 'I'm gonna see Aunty Pops.'

'All right. But don't get dirty.'

Kay watched Alfie slope off, still pulling at his shirt. Over the past few days, he had bonded with Aunty Pops, whose idea of having fun was the same as Alfie's. She would join him in the back garden where she would sit on a chair and watch the noisy planes fly over. Alfie would sit beside her on an upturned pail and, with her encouragement, hurry off to tinker with the broken water-pump or the wheel-less bicycle that leaned against the tumbledown shed. He had spent many hours with Pops, as together they investigated the mechanical wrecks hidden under long grass in the yard.

Meanwhile, Kay had shopped in Monkton with Lil. She had been introduced to Lil's whist friends and even invited to join in their club. But Kay was no whist player and had preferred to enjoy the town with its rows of small shops and quaint cottages.

Kay studied her limited choice of two dresses hanging in the big wardrobe in hers and Alfie's bedroom. 'It's either the flowery one,' Kay pondered, 'or the blue and white dress from out of the arc.'

Kay settled for the blue and white dress and spent time on her hair, rolling each finger-bang to the top of her head. When all was in place, she added tiny imitation pearl earrings that Alan had given her before Alfie was born.

She sat down on the bed with a long sigh as she thought of the evening ahead. What was the point in dressing-up if Alan wasn't with her? If he was a prisoner somewhere, or injured or starving, he might never come home again. And what of Dolly and Sean? Alan had once told her that in leaving behind their pasts, they could start afresh and make every day count. It upset her to think that he might have been talking about Dolly when he said that.

'You ready, love?' Lil called from the bottom of the stairs.

'Coming, Mum.' Kay stood up quickly, pushing all her troubled thoughts away. She was determined to enjoy the evening with Alfie. She wanted him to have happy memories of his first holiday and she was sure Alan would want that too.

Chapter Thirty-Eight

'Jeez, you can dance, li'l lady,' grinned the young American who had asked Kay to be his partner. He'd introduced himself simply as Gene and had told her he came from America. He was stationed at the local air force base.

The band had played some very lively music. The last tune had been a version of Glen Miller's 'Chattanooga Choo Choo'. Kay hadn't had time to catch her breath. Yet she seemed to have been able to keep up with the steps and not show how out of practice she felt.

'I think I'd better sit down for a minute,' Kay said as the music stopped and everyone applauded the band.

'I'll give you five minutes.' The handsome serviceman grinned. 'Then I'm coming back for more.'

Kay made her way to the table at which Lil and Bob were seated. Alfie and Aunty Pops were missing, but there were remnants of cake crumbs surrounding Alfie's half-filled glass of lemonade.

'Just look at our Alfie,' Bob told her proudly. 'Up on the stage, see? Pops has taken him to get the band's autographs.'

Kay laughed. 'He'll be showing them off at school, no doubt.' She sat down on the hard wooden chair and peered through the thick cigarette smoke that hung like a blanket over the cavernous wooden-floored room with its long glass windows criss-crossed by sticky tape. As there now appeared to be an interval, the bass and trumpet players and pianist were all enjoying a drink. The drummer handed one of his drumsticks to Alfie and soon there was a loud crash and bang. Everyone looked up to the stage. There were cheers and laughter as Alfie enjoyed himself playing on the instrument.

'Reckon we've got a budding musician in the family,' said Bob, taking a gulp of his beer and tucking into the remains of a sandwich. 'He was enjoying the music so much he couldn't sit still.'

'Takes after his mother,' said Lil, nodding at Kay. 'You're still pretty fast on your pins.'

'Oh, I was never that good at dancing.'

'You did all right with Norman at the social club.'

Kay glanced at Lil and took a deep breath. Norman's name had come up frequently that night. Bob had said how nice it was to be all together again, just like it used to be in the old days. Lil had agreed and said the church hall reminded her of the social club they had all supported in Poplar. So when Alfie disappeared with Aunty Pops to the basement games room, Kay had accepted Gene's offer to dance. He had whisked her round the dance floor to music from Glenn Miller and Jimmy Dorsey's big bands, and even showed her the Jitterbug which he told her was all the rage back home.

'Course, your Norman wasn't into all this modern stuff. He liked a good old-fashioned waltz or quickstep,' continued Lil.

'Alan and me liked stepping out,' Kay answered, determined not to be drawn on Norman. 'Though we didn't get much chance before Alfie came along.'

Lil gave a frown. 'That's what comes of rushing into a family, love. You don't get the opportunity to let down your hair. Then before you know it you've got responsibilities.'

'I wouldn't have had it any other way, Mum.'

'Obviously not,' returned Lil with a sniff. 'As a matter of fact, I said the very same thing to Len and Doris when they last visited.'

'You did?'

'I was shocked when Len said they wanted to adopt.'

'Why were you shocked?' asked Kay in surprise. 'Doris and Len would make wonderful parents.'

'Yes, but to their own child, not a stranger's.'

'How do you know that?'

Lil's heavily powdered cheeks blushed red. 'It stands to reason. What if the child comes from – well, a common sort of person, not a decent type? It could follow in its parents' footsteps. After all, blood is thicker than water, so they say.'

Kay could hardly believe she'd just heard her mother express such an opinion. 'I hope you didn't tell Len and

Doris that!' she exclaimed. 'Doris would have been very upset.'

Lil folded her arms. 'It's not up to me to tell them their business.'

'No, it certainly isn't, Mum.' Kay fought to smother her indignation as the pianist tapped the microphone, indicating the music was about to start. With a clench of her tummy muscles, Kay realized her feelings of outrage at Lil's remark ran deep. Having had Sean in her life clearly disproved Lil's theory. Sean couldn't be blamed for having Dolly as his mother and was a loving, innocent little boy. It was true, when Doris had told her that she and Len were considering adoption, Kay had decided that such a measure didn't appeal to her. But only because she doubted her ability to love another child as much as Alfie, not realizing love could be formed in many different ways.

'For our second half,' the pianist announced, bringing Kay quickly back to the present, 'we're playing a firm favourite, "The Lambeth Walk". So grab your partners and let's set the floor alight.'

Kay saw her dad nudge Lil's arm. 'Come on, love, we know this one. None of your acrobatic stuff, just a good old shoe-shuffle.'

As her parents left to dance, Aunty Pops returned, looping the handle of her walking stick over the chair. 'Phew, I had to elbow me way back through the crowd. Left your Alfie with the other kids. He's palled up with a few of the boys and enjoying himself.'

Kay was glad of her company. 'Oh, he'd like that. I think he misses his friends.'

'Would they be Gill and Tim and the other lad, Sean?'

Kay looked quickly at Aunty Pops. 'Yes, did Alfie tell you about them?'

'That's all he goes on about,' said Aunty Pops with a smile. 'They sound good kids. 'specially that Sean. Said he stayed at your place for a while.'

Kay nodded, feeling the tears sentimentally spring to her eyes. 'Yes, he did.' She didn't add more, trying to swallow her emotion as the lost little boy filled her thoughts.

Aunty Pops leaned close. Kay got a whiff of the fertilizer she'd been using on the garden that afternoon. 'Don't mind me saying, but you wanna take no notice of your mother. She harps on a lot about the old days when I know your heart isn't in them.'

Kay smiled, clearing her throat. 'So you noticed?'

'Oh, yes, love. But she'll come round. You have to be careful you don't live too much in the past as you get older.'

'Mum was very fond of Norman.'

'Yes, but the world's moved on now.' Aunty Pops leaned back in her chair. 'I'd like to meet your Alan one day.'

'I hope you will, Aunty Pops.'

Kay felt a tap on her shoulder. She looked up at the tall young man standing at her side. 'Join me in the next one, Miss Kay?' he asked.

Kay saw that Lil and Bob were coming off the floor. She nodded to Gene and stood up. Even though she had no idea of how to dance the Lindy Hop, it was better than dwelling on the past. Common sense told her there was no way she would ever see Sean again, yet he would always be there in her thoughts and her heart too.

At the evening drew to a close, Kay had enjoyed herself despite the crush on the dance floor. Gene had twirled her around so fast she'd literally been swept off her feet. Now, the evening was almost over and Alfie was still enjoying himself with the other children in the games room.

'Last waltz coming up,' Lil said just as Gene walked up to the table.

'May I have the honour?' he asked Kay with a grin.

'Yes, go on, Kay,' Lil urged. 'Enjoy yourself.'

'You've got some real nice folks,' the young man told her as he led her onto the floor. 'And that youngster of yours is a cute kid.'

She nodded proudly as they stood waiting for the music to play. 'Alfie's never stayed up so late before.'

'That's a swell name.'

'My husband and I think so.'

'Is your husband in the services?'

'Yes, but I don't know where Alan's fighting.'

'It must be tough for you.'

As the band struck up a soft refrain, Gene held her close. Kay listened to him humming the tune and she recognized it as one that she and Alan had always loved. 'When I Grow Too Old to Dream' had beautiful words and as they danced, she heard Alan singing them as he used to. Suddenly her throat filled with a painful ache. Salty tears stung on her lids. She thought of the passion they had shared, a passion that had never died and only become stronger through the years. Despite Dolly entering her life and claiming to be married to the man Kay loved, Kay still refused to believe that Alan would ever do anything to jeopardize their happiness.

'Kay?' Gene's voice broke into her thoughts.

'Oh, sorry, what did you say?'

'I was wondering if you and Alfie would like a ride out in the jeep sometime.'

Kay didn't want to hurt his feelings but she knew that these young servicemen could get very lonely away from home. 'Thanks, Gene, but I'm afraid the answer must be no.'

'Are you sure?'

She nodded, laughing. 'You should have danced the night away with a pretty unattached young female.'

He laughed too. 'Don't worry I've got – how do you English say it – strong skin?'

'Thick skin, you mean.'

'Jeez, I gotta lot to learn!' He looked down at her with twinkling blue eyes and held her close. 'It sure would be nice to have you teach me.'

When the dance was over, Gene took her back to the table. 'There's still time to change your mind,' he whispered as he held up her coat.

Kay looked at him, amused. 'You certainly don't stop trying.'

'For the prettiest girl in this room, it's not difficult at all.'

As Kay took Alfie's hand, she blushed. It was a long, long time since she had been flattered like this. And though Gene's compliments had made her remember what it was like to be viewed as a real woman again, the only whispered words she wanted to hear were from Alan. The only arms she longed to be dancing in were his.

Chapter Thirty-Nine

Vi woke up on Saturday morning with a deep sense of unease. What was she worried about? This was the question she asked herself each morning as she roused from sleep. Ever since her house had been bombed she'd not felt her old confident self. But this morning, as she climbed out of bed, she remembered Eddie coming home. Since then the kids had played in the street as usual, but there was no Babs mooching about in the yard. And certainly no Eddie.

Vi began to dress, wondering if Kay and Alfie were enjoying themselves. Vi missed them. She didn't like rattling around in the house on her own. But she knew Kay needed a holiday even if she wouldn't admit it.

When Vi had knotted her scarf on the top of her head and put on her apron, she went downstairs. She opened the back door and peered cautiously into Babs's yard. Not a peep from anyone.

After deciding all must be well, she made herself a cup of tea. Perhaps nothing had been said about Paul. If that was the case then, depending on how long Eddie's leave was, trouble might be avoided.

Vi tried to concentrate on what she had planned for the day. A visit to Jenny and Alice, that was it! It was a long time since she'd seen them for a chat. She'd take her basket as well and continue to the market. It was a bit of a haul these days, but the weather was nice. And if she stopped at Jenny and Alice's for a gas, she'd break up the journey.

Five minutes later, with her basket over her arm, she was closing the front door behind her when she heard Babs's voice. Then Eddie's. Soft at first, but growing louder. The window was open, with Babs's lace curtain blowing out on the breeze.

Vi paused. She couldn't help but overhear. Eddie's voice rose, clearly filled with anger. Vi knew the Chapmans were quarrelling. Not an ordinary quarrel, but the other kind, where people started to belt it out, careless of their neighbours or anyone who might be in the vicinity.

Vi took a breath and began to walk away. When love, betrayal and jealousy were on the cards, the very worst always came out in human nature. As it was with Babs and Eddie today.

'Howdy, Kay.' Said Gene when Kay opened the door early the next morning. She had only just finished dressing in her summer skirt and short-sleeved blouse. Her hair was unbrushed and spilled untidily over her shoulders. Alfie was still asleep from his late night. And the rest of the family didn't seem to be about. It took Kay a few minutes to realize who the caller was. She was surprised to find the young uniformed American of last night, her dancing partner. Stroking a tanned hand over his blond crew cut he smiled broadly.

'What are you doing here?' she asked, startled.

'Your ma invited me round for English tea. Something to do with – ah – eleven, is it?'

'Oh, I expect you mean elevenses.'

'That's it!' Gene looked apologetic. 'Am I too early?'

'Not at all, young man,' a voice said behind Kay. Lil joined Kay, beckoning their visitor inside.

'If you're sure,' Gene said, waiting for Kay to step back so that he could enter.

'Course I'm sure, my love,' said Lil, nudging Kay's arm sharply. 'As I said last night, we British are grateful to you American boys for standing with us against the enemy. You deserve a warm welcome in this country. And you'll certainly find one in this household. Now come in and we'll have a nice cuppa, as I promised you, outside in the sunshine. Bob and Pops are putting out some decent chairs out for us to sit on.'

Lil bustled off, leaving Kay with Gene who gave Kay a guilty frown. 'I guess my visit comes as a surprise to you?' he asked.

'Yes, it has.'

'Mrs Briggs spoke to me last night when you guys were boarding the coach home.'

'Oh,' said Kay again, trying unsuccessfully to hide her disappointment. Her morning would now be taken up with entertaining, when she'd promised Alfie they would pack a picnic to eat in Alfie's favourite spot, the wooded hill close by.

'Gee, now I feel kinda bad,' Gene said with a sigh. 'I'm making a darn nuisance of myself.'

Kay pushed back a stray lock of her hair from her face. 'No, that's all right,' she replied. 'Follow Mum along to the garden. I'll just run a comb through my hair.'

'Your hair looks just dandy to me.' His eyes roamed over her, studying her with mischievous blue eyes. 'Reminds me of the forests back home at this time of the year. Kinda glowing, like they were lit up from the inside somehow.'

Kay felt herself blush. She pointed the way to the garden again, then hurried upstairs. She stood in the bedroom, gazing down at Alfie who was still asleep in bed. She hadn't expected to see Gene again. Why had Lil invited him round?

'Time to get up, sleepyhead.' Kay pulled back Alfie's covers.

Alfie woke, rubbing his eyes. 'Are we goin' for a picnic.'

'Yes, but first we're having breakfast.'

'Do I have to dress in me new clothes?'

Kay laughed. 'No, just your shorts and shirt.'

'That's all right then.' Alfie was soon out of bed and when he was washed and dressed they went downstairs. The back door was open and Kay saw the garden table was set with the best china tea set. A large fruit cake had been carved into slices and Gene, Lil, Aunty Pops and Bob were all gathered round.

'Come along, you two.' Lil waved to the empty chairs next to Gene's. Kay sat down and Alfie climbed on her lap. He rubbed his sleepy eyes and yawned.

'We sure had a ball last night,' drawled Gene, grinning at Alfie, then at Kay.

'Yes, indeed,' said Lil as she poured the tea. 'Just what Kay needed to lift her spirits.'

Kay glanced quickly at Gene. She hoped Lil wasn't giving him fresh hope.

'Now, tell us about yourself,' continued Lil, handing round the cake. 'What part of America do you come from?'

'I live with my folks in Texas,' Gene said as he ate. 'Dad works in construction. Mom works in a local store.'

'Do you follow in your father's footsteps and work in the building trade?' asked Bob.

'No, sir,' Gene replied firmly. 'I work in aircraft engineering. I kinda got a bug for airplanes real early on. Liked to know how they worked from a real young kid.' He nodded to Alfie. 'Not much older than this little guy.'

'Oh, Alfie loves 'em too,' said Aunty Pops. 'We sit here watching them go over every day.'

'We're hoping to persuade our daughter to leave the Smoke and come and live here,' said Lil. 'It would be safer for Alfie.'

'Mum, you know that me and Alan haven't any plans to leave the island,' Kay said quietly.

'The Smoke?' interrupted Gene. 'What's that?'

'The Smoke is another name for London,' Bob told him. 'We're from the East End originally. Kay still lives there. But East Enders have had a rough time of it and we worry about her.'

'Yeah, we heard all about the Blitz,' Gene said, looking at Kay. 'It must be rough on you.'

'It was,' said Kay. 'But the raids aren't so bad now.'

'Even so,' said Lil, folding her hands tightly in her lap.

'My dad's a soldier,' said Alfie, grinning at Gene. ''e's fighting the en'my and when he's bashed 'em all to bits, 'e's comin' home to take me down the river again.'

Gene laughed, ruffling Alfie's hair. 'Your dad sure must want to get home quick, son.'

'He's gonna build me a boat an' all.' Alfie was all smiles.

'Is it wise, Kay, to encourage Alfie to think that?' Lil said shortly. 'You don't know for sure about the future. Things could turn very dark indeed.'

'Hey, Alfie, you gonna walk me out and show me some of them big carrots your grandpa is growing?' Gene rose and smoothed down his uniform. 'Thanks a bunch, Mrs Briggs, for a great English cuppa and cake.'

'You're not going yet?' Lil asked in surprise.

'I gotta get back to base.'

'Well, feel free to call again.'

Kay stood up. 'I'll see you out too.'

Farewells were said and Gene accompanied them through the house to the allotment at the front. In the bright sunshine, Gene lifted Alfie into his arms. 'You look after your ma, now.'

Alfie nodded, grinning.

'Thank you, Gene,' Kay said quietly.

'What for?'

'You don't really have to rush off to base, do you?'

'Not really. Kinda felt in the way a bit.'

'I'm sorry about that.'

'Guess I'm feeling homesick. The way you and Alfie talk about your Alan – well, I sure as heck hope my folks are missin' me that much.'

'I'm sure they are.'

'Take care of yourself, honey.'

Kay watched as Gene lowered Alfie to the ground. The big American bunched his knuckle and gently touched Alfie's cheek. 'You take care now. Your pa's gonna be real proud of you when he comes home. And you can tell him from me, his American brother, that I think he's a lucky guy. A very lucky guy indeed.'

Kay smiled. 'You take care of yourself too.'

He gave her a cheeky salute, swinging his broad shoulders as he swaggered away.

Alfie tugged at Kay's skirt. 'Is 'e really Dad's bruvver?'

'Not blood brothers. But brothers in spirit.'

'What's that mean?'

'Well, it's like being a close relative because you admire each other a lot.'

Alfie's dark eyes widened. 'You mean like me an' Sean?'

Kay's heart squeezed. She knew Alfie loved Sean as much as she did. 'Yes, like you and Sean.'

'Is Sean gonna come back one day, like me dad?'

'I don't know the answer to that, Alfie. But I do know that wherever Dad and Sean are, they're thinking of us, just like we're thinking of them.'

'Can we go 'ome?' Alfie asked, wriggling free from her grasp and kicking the dirt.

'Are you missing your pals?'

'An' Vi-Vi.'

'Me too.' Kay gave him a big grin. 'Can you wait a few more days?'

'If we 'ave a picnic, I can.'

'Come on then.' She held out her hand and in the warm September morning, heavy with the scents of the countryside, they strolled lazily into the house.

Chapter Forty

It was Monday 13 September and they were, at last, going home. Lil and Aunty Pops had bid them a fond farewell and Bob stood waving on the platform as the train pulled out of the station.

Once again, the countryside rushed by, the never-ending fields, trees, hedgerows and small towns and villages. But it wasn't until they had boarded the bus from London city centre to Poplar that Kay allowed herself to be really excited. As bad as the bombing had been and as wounded and blighted by ruins as London was, it was home. Kay knew Alfie was excited too. He couldn't stop talking about Tim and Gill. He wanted to show Tim the screwdriver that Aunty Pops had allowed him to keep as a souvenir of his first holiday. It was stowed safely away in the brown case along with a few souvenirs: a quarter of a pound of boiled sweets for Tim and Gill, a knitted tea cosy from the whist stall for Babs, and for Vi, a new flowered headscarf. Lil had been very disappointed to see them leave. But in the end, she had accepted defeat. Kay smiled to herself.

Twelve days spent in the countryside was quite a feat. But, to her surprise, she and Alfie had enjoyed a good time.

At last the bus arrived at Slater Street and Kay and Alfie stood on the pavement looking around them.

'Home sweet home,' Kay murmured appreciatively. Nothing had changed in their absence. The tall black chimneys of the factories were still belching out smoke. Jenny and Alice's houses still boasted whiter than white front doorsteps. Slater Street snaked ahead: the untidy, weed-covered remains of the bombed houses, the kids' chalk markings on the pavements, the sound of the river traffic, dozens of noisy hooters and the clanking of cranes and machinery. It was all as Kay remembered and oh, so very welcome.

'Can I call for me mates?' Alfie couldn't wait to run down the street.

'We'll have something to eat first.'

'I ain't hungry.'

'Yes, you are,' Kay told him, happy to see the cheeky smile on his face again.

From the front room window, Vi spotted Kay and Alfie. She'd had a card from Kay to say that they'd be arriving back on Monday afternoon. And sure enough, here they were, right on time!

Vi had cooked a nourishing mutton stew, with split peas, pearl barley and two large onions. The smell was drifting out into the road as she opened the front door.

'Oh, Vi, it's so good to see you.' Vi was smothered in hugs.

'You an' all, love.'

'Are you all right?'

'Course I am.'

'Something smells good.' Kay sniffed the air.

'Thought you'd need a good square meal after all that gallivanting.'

Kay laughed, dropping her case inside the door. 'I don't think we did much of that!'

'Well, now,' said Vi as Alfie slid his hand over hers and pulled her into the house. 'What's all the rush for?'

'I wanna see Gill and Tim.'

'Ain't I good enough for you?' Vi held his face between the palms of her hands. 'It's all right, son, I'm not about to slobber over yer. Just pleased to see you again, that's all.'

'So are we,' said Kay with a grin.

Vi glanced quickly at Kay. 'Plenty of time for Alfie to see his mates. I want both of you to tell me about your holiday.' She crooked her finger and led the way to the front room.

Reluctantly, Alfie sat on the couch and dutifully relayed his news. 'I got a lot of posh clothes. And Aunty Pops gave me a screwdriver. I'm gonna show it to Tim. Can I go now?'

'No, not yet.'

'It was a lovely holiday.' Kay sighed and kicked off her shoes. 'But it's wonderful to be home.'

'Can I play with me train set?' asked Alfie restlessly.

'Good idea,' said Vi. 'You occupy yourself for a bit whilst me and your mum get dinner.'

'Can I go out after?' Alfie said with a pout.

'We'll see.' Vi raked her hand through his hair. 'You've got ants in your pants, young man.'

'I ain't. Me pants are new. Me gran bought 'em.'

Everyone laughed and Vi made the most of the moment; after all that had happened to poor Babs and the kids in Kay's absence, there hadn't been much, lately, to laugh at.

'Poor Babs,' said Kay with a gasp as she stood at the sink with Vi, listening to the story of Eddie's return.

Vi nodded. 'Eddie only stayed the night.'

'Have you seen Babs and the kids since?'

'I spoke to Babs over the fence. She told me the kids kept talking about Uncle Paul and Eddie confronted her. Asked if there was anything going on. Babs told him and then the balloon went up. As for the kids, I've seen Tim picking fights with his pals in the street and young Gill's not had a word to say for herself.'

'Oh, Vi, how awful.'

Vi turned down the gas. 'The kids must have heard everything. The row went on all day. I heard 'em at it when I left in the morning and they was still at it when I came back.'

'Did you see Eddie again?'

Vi shook her head. 'Babs told me he left in the early hours threatening to go round Paul's and knock his block off.'

'Did he?' Kay gasped.

'Dunno. Reckon Babs will tell you when she sees you.'

'I'll call round tonight after Alfie's in bed.'

'Reckon it's best Alfie don't go round there today,' said Vi. 'And you have a word with Babs first.'

'Has Paul called?'

'I ain't seen him, no.'

Kay shook her head sadly. 'What a mess!'

'Come on now, tell me all about your holiday.' Vi stirred the delicious-smelling stew. 'Did your mum behave herself?'

Kay rolled her eyes. 'No, but then, it was no surprise. She kept dropping hints and especially in front of Gene.'

Vi stopped stirring. 'Jean? Do you mean Jean Pearson?'

'No. It's Gene with a G.' Kay told Vi all about the young serviceman and Vi's eyebrows rose until they almost touched her scarf.

'Was he handsome?'

'Very.'

'Did he ask you out?'

'Me and Alfie together, in his truck.'

They both burst into laughter. Vi was shaking her head as she picked up the spoon again. 'Go on with you, what did you say?'

'No, of course.'

'I knew that'd be your answer.'

'Why did you ask me, then?'

Vi cackled. 'Just for a laugh. Gawd only knows you can do with 'em round here these days. Now, let me see to this, make sure that meat is falling off the bone.'

Kay smiled as Vi turned her attention back to the big pot steaming on the stove. Leaning her elbows on the draining board, Kay stared dreamily into the yard. Alfie's cart and frayed rope stood by the Anderson. Fresh weeds had quickly replaced the old ones and the fence was sagging so much it would only take a breath of wind to bring it down. Babs's yard was much the same: an upturned wooden chair with a broken leg propped in the corner, a few scatterings of toys. Overhead, the skies were blue, though there were dark clouds threatening to the north. A September breeze blew coolly through the window as if to say that summer was almost over.

How was Babs feeling? Kay wondered. What had gone on with Eddie and Paul? She would find out this evening when she called round.

'It's only me. Are the kids asleep?' Kay whispered when Babs opened the door to her soft knock.

Babs nodded and Kay stepped inside. The house felt chilly, with the only light coming from the kitchen. It was as if the life and soul had gone out of it.

'Oh, Kay!' Babs threw her arms around Kay. 'I've missed you.'

'And I missed you.' They hugged and while Babs was in Kay's arms, her friend gave a soft sob.

Kay patted her back gently. 'It's all right, it's all right,' Kay whispered as Babs continued to sob, sucking in deep breaths that shook every part of her. 'Come along, love. I'll make us a cuppa.'

With her arm around Babs's waist, they made their way to the kitchen. Babs sank down on a chair, blowing her nose on her hanky as Kay put the kettle on to boil. Kay sat down too, holding Babs's hand on the table and squeezing it a little as Babs tried to compose herself. When at last her friend had stopped weeping, Kay thought how washed out she looked. Her eyes were puffy and red, her hair lank and hanging around her shoulders. Her face was so grey and gaunt that her skin looked like paper had been stretched over it.

'Oh, Babs, you look terrible.'

'I feel terrible.'

'Vi told me a little about what happened.'

Babs nodded, her stare full of pain. 'It was awful.'

'Did you tell him about Paul?'

'No, the kids did. Tim talked about Mummy's friend, Uncle Paul. Eddie soon cottoned on. After that, I couldn't lie to him.' The tears began trickling down her cheeks. 'I told him everything.'

'What did he say?'

Babs shook her head, unable to speak for a moment. 'At first, he couldn't seem to believe it, just kept asking me why. Was it because of the affair he'd had when Gill was born? I told him no, it wasn't. And then he got angry. He knocked the chairs over and broke me vase. I've never seen him so angry before. I told the kids to go outside and play. But neither of them wanted to. They were frightened. Oh, Kay, what have I gone and done to us?' Babs folded her arms on the table and lay her head on them, sobbing once more. They were loud, desperate sobs that had the tears springing to Kay's eyes.

After Kay had made the tea, she tried to get Babs to drink it. But she wasn't interested.

'Have you eaten today?' Kay asked.

'I ain't hungry.'

'You've got to have something.'

Babs slowly raised her head. Kay was shocked at the sight of her friend's deep distress. Kay pushed the mug closer and Babs's thin fingers grasped it.

'What happened then?' Kay asked softly.

'Eddie told me he'd never let me and Paul have the kids.'

'What did he mean by that?'

'He said that no other man was ever gonna be father to Gill and Tim. I tried to tell him no man ever would, that Paul wasn't like that and it only made him more furious. He got hold of the carving knife, said he was going round Paul's. The army had trained him to kill and that was what he was going to do.' Babs closed her eyes and the choked breaths came afresh, shaking her body.

'Babs, he didn't—'

Babs shook her head and opened her tear-filled eyes. 'I screamed at him, implored him, begged him on me knees not to do it. I thought he meant what he said. He had this look in his eyes, a mad look, like he was ready to do what he threatened. Then he put the knife to me throat—'

'He what!' Kay gasped, her hand going up to her mouth.

'I think he'd have done it, Kay, but Gill came downstairs. She threw herself at me and him and . . . and—' Babs paused, her lips trembling. 'Eddie dropped the knife and held her and Tim tight. They was crying, both of 'em. We was all crying, all of us. It was terrible. Terrible.'

Kay tried to comfort her, but Babs was in no state to listen. She was in a world of her own, a nightmare world that she had never expected, had never imagined could happen. Kay held her friend close again. 'Have you managed to get any sleep?'

'No, I can't shut me eyes without thinking of it.'

'I'll stay with you tonight.' Kay went into the front room and shivered. It was freezing. The scuttle had some coke in it and pieces of wood and balls of newspaper. She put them all into the grate and made a fire, waving a paper fan and slowly encouraging the flames to catch to the wood. Very soon the heat of the fire was warming the room and Kay went back to the kitchen. Babs hadn't moved. But she was silent, her head resting on her arms, her lank hair falling across her face.

'Babs, come into the front room.' Kay helped her to stand up and slowly they walked through the passage to the flickering shadows in the hearth. Babs stood there, looking into the fire. Kay took her shoulders and guided her to the couch. 'Lay down here, I'm going to fetch a pillow and blanket and you can sleep in the warmth by the fire. Then I'll tell Vi I'm staying.'

Kay hurried upstairs and looked into the children's bedroom. Gill was asleep in her bed and Tim in his. Kay thought what a terrifying experience it must have been for them to see Eddie holding a knife at Babs's throat. What had happened after? Had Eddie carried out his threat and gone to Paul's?

Kay took a blanket and pillow from the big double bed in Babs and Eddie's room. She gave a shiver as she gazed around. The Tripps's house had been a refuge for Babs and Eddie after their own had been bombed. But now it felt cold and unloved. Why did all this have to happen when they had been such a happy family?

Kay made her friend comfortable on the couch and decided to wait till Babs was asleep until she told Vi what was happening.

To Kay's surprise, Babs soon closed her eyes and drifted off. Kay guessed she hadn't slept properly in days. Returning to the kitchen, Kay looked in the table drawer. The carving knife was in its place by the wooden spoon and ladle. If Eddie had used it on Paul, it wouldn't be there now.

Chapter Forty-One

That night, Kay slept in the big fireside chair keeping watch over Babs.

'It's all right, everything's all right now,' soothed Kay, going to her friend's side when she woke up in the early hours.

Babs's head sank back to the pillow. She looked at Kay with a haunted gaze. 'Kay, what's going to happen to us?'

'Life will sort itself out.'

'How do you know that?'

'Because it always does. You and Eddie have gone through too much to let this come between you.'

After Babs had fallen asleep, Kay couldn't get a wink. So she went into the kitchen and cleaned the dirty sink and swept the floor. She put out the bowls and spoons for breakfast and when dawn broke, she sat down on the chair and began to doze. It would be a while yet before Babs and the children woke.

'Is Mum all right?' Gill asked when she came downstairs in her nightdress, followed by Tim still dressed in his pyjamas.

'Yes, but she's having a lie-in. Come and sit down and I'll make you your porridge.'

The two children did as they were told. Kay knew that whatever she said couldn't take away the memory of what had happened to their once happy family. She tried to go on as normal and made the porridge, then sat down with them as they ate.

'Your mum told me your dad came home,' she said, trying to clear the lump in her throat. They looked so young and innocent to be caught up in such turmoil. Gill's hair fell loose around her shoulders and Tim's pale face still had a sprinkling of freckles.

'Did she tell you what our dad did?' asked Gill.

'Yes. But sometimes people do silly things when they're angry.'

'Why did our dad get out the knife?' asked Tim gruffly.

Kay looked into their unhappy faces. What was she to say? The truth would hurt so very much and it certainly mustn't come from her.

'He didn't mean any harm, Tim.'

'Was he going to kill Mum?'

'No, your dad would never do that. He loves you both very much.'

'It ain't our fault then?' asked Gill in a faint voice.

'Course it's not, love.' Kay smiled. 'Things happen in families sometimes that upset everyone. None of us are our normal selves when we quarrel. If you can be patient, I'm sure Mum and Dad will soon be themselves again.'

'Is Mum gonna be all right?' Gill asked, holding back her tears.

'Yes, but she needs to rest. Now, eat up your porridge and get dressed as Alfie's waiting to see you.'

The children nodded and slowly picked up their spoons.

While Babs slept late that morning, Kay took the children to see Alfie. They were soon playing together in the yard and happy to get back to their old routine. Vi cooked a big dinner of corned beef and mash for everyone and after that, Kay called round to see how her friend was. To her relief, the rest seemed to have done her good. Babs had brushed her hair and changed into a clean skirt and jumper.

'Thank you for staying with me last night,' she said to Kay as they sat by the fire. 'Dunno what I'd have done if I hadn't had you to talk to.'

'That's what friends are for.'

'Kay, what have I been thinking? I had to face Eddie sometime. Just didn't think it would turn out like that.'

'Did Eddie go round to Paul's?'

Babs shook her head. She pulled her hanky from her sleeve. Her eyes filled with tears but she kept them back. 'No, he must have had second thoughts, thank God. But Paul came round here and I told him . . .' she paused as tears filled her eyes, 'that it's all over between us.'

'Did he accept that?'

'I told him about Eddie and how upset the kids had been. He said he would do whatever I wanted.'

Kay watched Babs trying to hide her pain. 'Do you still love him, Babs?'

'I don't think we could ever be happy after this,' Babs murmured. 'I nearly died of guilt when Eddie cracked up. It wasn't his fault. I drove him to it. Eddie is a good man. He was just desperate. I know how he feels as, after his affair, I felt as though things would never be the same. Still, we managed to put the past behind us and got back to being a family. I only hope that Eddie will forgive me and we can try again.'

'Perhaps you should tell Eddie that.'

'I've written to him and asked him to have me back. Told him I'd never be unfaithful again. That I loved him and am sorry for hurting him.'

'Is that what you want?'

'It's not just me, it's the kids. And I'd never stop blaming meself if something happened to Eddie.'

'But you have to go back to Eddie for all the right reasons.'

'Aren't the kids enough?'

Kay sighed. 'It's only you that can answer that, Babs.'

Babs looked down at her skirt, playing with an invisible speck of dirt. 'I've got to put Paul out of my thoughts.'

'But can you do that?'

Babs glanced up, her gaze resigned. 'I remember my kids' faces when they saw what was going on with me and Eddie. As if they hadn't had enough with the bombing and their dad being sent away to war, they had to see their mum and dad fighting so violently.' Babs shook her head. 'No, it's the end for me and Paul.'

'Will Paul leave you alone?'

'When he came round after Eddie had gone, it was a relief to know that Eddie hadn't gone round there and carried out his threat. But I asked Paul to stop calling and said I meant it this time.' Babs gave a little sob. 'He just walked away.'

Kay sat quietly, watching Babs, her best friend, as close to her as a sister. There was nothing more she could say to help. Babs had to bear this heartache all on her own.

'Things always get better in time.'

Babs nodded tearfully. 'I've got plenty of that.'

'Tomorrow I'll take the kids to school if you like.'

But Babs gave a shaky smile. 'No, we'll all go together. It's your Alfie's first day of term and I want to be there when you wave him off.'

They sat a while longer in the warmth and quiet, the two friends each with their own thoughts.

Kay knew it would be a sad time ahead for Babs. The decision she had made was a hard one. She had sacrificed Paul for the sake of her kids and her marriage to Eddie. But whether Eddie would return to pick up the pieces was another matter.

As Babs had said, *if* Eddie returned at all.

That night, Kay and Vi were talking about Babs and Eddie as they washed the dishes after supper. 'I hope

Eddie will be able to forgive and forget,' Kay said pensively.

'He ain't gone AWOL has he?'

'Babs thinks he must have gone back to barracks as the military police would have called round if he hadn't.'

'Poor blighter. Fancy coming home to that.'

'Babs has written, asking him to forgive her.'

'What does Paul have to say about all this?'

'He's accepted it. He has to.'

'I'm not so sure.' Vi frowned thoughtfully. 'He persuaded her back to him once before.'

'I don't think he will this time.' Kay placed the china back in the cupboard. 'Babs is suffering too much and Paul must see that. He's a decent enough sort, after all.'

'Yes, but he needs to make his own family.'

'Yes, I suppose so.' Kay rubbed her eyes. 'I think I'll have an early night.'

'Course.' Vi folded the tea towel onto its peg. 'I wish you'd have yer own bed back again.'

Kay smiled. 'I've got a nice warm fire to kip by.'

'What about Babs?'

'I told her I'd take the kids to school in the morning. But she said she wanted to come with me to see Alfie off.'

Vi nodded. 'That's a good sign. School will set us all back to normal.'

Kay hesitated. 'Oh, I'll just run an iron over Alfie's new shirt before I turn in.'

Vi grinned. 'No need. I done it all today.'

'Oh, Vi, what would I do without you?'

'Goodnight, flower, get plenty of rest ternight.'

'I don't suppose there was a letter from Alan while I was away?'

'I'd have posted it to yer, love, if there had been.'

'Yes, course.'

'You'll get one soon. Don't give up hope.' Vi winked as she began to climb the stairs, groaning a little as she held her hand to her chest.

Chapter Forty-Two

The letter came one late October morning while Kay and Babs were walking to school. Vi stood there on Kay's return, the envelope heavy in her hand.

'It's perishing,' Kay began, peeling off her woollen scarf and gloves. 'We'll have to think about ordering some coal—'

Vi held out the telegram. A blue envelope sent by the War Office and marked Priority was what every woman dreaded. Vi had felt sick at the sight of the telegram boy who had delivered it.

Kay's busy smile faded. She stood there, staring at it.

'You'd better come and sit down.'

'You're sure it's for me?'

'I'm afraid so, love.' Vi's heart felt so heavy it could have been a lump of lead in her chest. 'Let's go by the fire.' Vi sat on the couch with Kay.

'I don't want it,' Kay said. 'Throw it away.'

'Come on, love, you have to read it.' Vi took hold of Kay's wrist and gave it a shake. 'Sooner or later, you must.'

Kay turned her head away, staring vacantly at the wall.

'Listen, Kay, there ain't another choice here. This is news of Alan. And it might not be so bad.' Vi knew that neither of them believed this. There was no reason for a telegram to be sent from the War Office unless it was bad news. Vi placed the blue envelope in Kay's hands. 'Go on, open it.'

Kay sat there, the blush on her cheeks from the cold weather fading. The lock of auburn hair that fell over her face trembled as did her fingers as she slowly opened the envelope.

Vi watched her as she read it, Kay's long eyelashes fanning her cheeks as a muscle moved in her jaw. Vi knew that the shock was setting in.

'It's from a Major Campbell,' Kay whispered. 'Alan has been reported missing in action. He says, "At this very sad time, I cannot offer you more information. If further details come to light then you will be promptly notified".' Kay turned to Vi, her voice soft and trembling. 'What does that mean? Has Alan been killed? Is he dead and they're just not saying it?'

Vi shook her head quickly. She had no idea what the telegram truly meant. But she was going to cling to the hope that it meant that Alan was still alive. 'No, Kay. The major ain't saying Alan's dead. He's writing what he knows and that ain't much. Missing in action is what he says. The word "dead" don't come into it.'

Kay's eyes were wide with fear. 'I can't think straight.'

'Then I'll do the thinking for you,' Vi said firmly, hiding the deep fear inside her. 'Alan's missing, right? Just missing. Could be anywhere, couldn't he? Think about it, Kay. He could be hiding from the enemy. There's lots of blokes who've done that, like the accounts you read about in the papers. The fact is, they ain't got a body. Sorry to say that, love, but Alan would want you look at it that way.'

'But missing in action!' insisted Kay, not listening as she choked back her tears. 'I don't know where my husband is! He could be dying in a foreign land or he could be—'

'Kay!' Vi shook her again. 'You must stop this. You're not a widow yet.'

'Ain't this as good as?'

'No, it isn't! What good is it you cracking up? You know what Alan would say if he heard you right this moment. He'd be a bloody wreck, that's what. After all, he was always telling you not to let your imagination run riot. And now that's just what you're doing.'

Kay turned her head slowly. 'Vi, I can't help it.'

'Yes, you can. You've got Alfie to think of.'

Kay nodded, her expression still terrified. 'Yes, but I – I just—'

'Turn your mind to all them rescues Alan did,' Vi urged as she saw Kay swallow back her breath. 'Look at how many people he saved in the Blitz. If anyone can look after himself, it's Alan.'

'Oh, God, I hope so.'

'That's it. Keep hoping. And praying. And you'll see him again.'

Kay lowered her chin, her lips trembling.

Just then, the back door slammed and they jumped. Babs hurried into the room, dressed in her coat and scarf. She stared at the telegram. 'Oh Kay!'

'Alan's missing in action,' Vi said quickly.

'I'm so sorry.'

Vi looked at the two young women who had had their fair share of problems – yet had overcome so many of them. But how was Kay going to get through this?

'Kay,' whispered Babs softly as she sat by her, 'I'll remind you what you said to me after Eddie had gone. Be strong for the kids' sake, you said. Alfie can't see you go to pieces.'

'I know.'

'Alan would say chin-up, wouldn't he?'

Kay silently pressed the hanky that Babs gave her over her damp eyes.

'That's the stuff, Babs,' agreed Vi, trying to ignore the pain in her chest that was becoming a regular visitor lately. This news had done nothing to help it. 'Your Eddie will make it. So will Alan. Them two boys have got too much to live for to let Jerry take it away.' She picked up the telegram that had fallen on the floor and folded it into her apron pocket. 'I'm going to make a cuppa and when I come back I want to see a smile on your faces. Let's have no more tears now.'

Vi rushed out to the kitchen and leaned against the table. She wiped the sweat from her brow and waited for the pain to pass. The telegram had scared the life out of her. That Major Whatshisname could've said more, couldn't he? That was the army for you. No bedside manner, not even in death, the sods.

Vi winced as the pain tightened. What was she thinking! Alan wasn't dead. He couldn't be! If there was a favour in life she owed to anyone it was Alan Lewis. He'd always been like a son to her. Doing all her odd jobs and looking out for her. He'd taken her in when her house was bombed and given her a home. He'd always been there, ready to make her life easier. Someone like him couldn't be dead. Not Alan.

December had rushed up like a steam train, Kay thought, as she and Babs shopped in the market for small presents for the children. Neither of them was going to have a tree this year; they couldn't justify the expense. Though Kay still had the money in the Post Office account, she was determined not to spend it. The answer to its origin would have to come from Alan himself. As she had done every day since that telegram, she sent out her love to him and a quick prayer. It was the way she coped now, reminding herself daily, as Vi had insisted, that while there was no news it was good news.

Kay glanced at the stalls in the market; there was plenty to tempt her, but she was determined to be thrifty. Now that Alfie was settled at school she would get through

Christmas and find a job in the new year. Vi wouldn't have the responsibility of looking after him then, and the problem of money would be solved.

'What do you think of this?' Babs's question brought her out of her thoughts, as Babs turned over the tattered pages of a book. 'Tim would like this annual but the front page is missing. Still, it's not in bad condition for sixpence.'

'Yes, it looks all right,' agreed Kay. She sometimes found her mind wandering, her resolution to stay strong about Alan weakening. And it was Christmas. A special time of the year that she and Alan had loved. Thinking about presents and festivities didn't hold any appeal.

Babs paid for the book and slipped it into her shopping bag. Glancing at Kay, she frowned. 'We don't seem to be in the mood for shopping. Let's have a coffee at Lenny's to warm us up.'

Kay nodded, barely noticing the decorations that were strung around the stalls. There were not very many but the traders had done their best in what were increasingly tough times. The greengrocery stalls were busy with shoppers, though the supplies of fruit were limited. No one had seen a banana in years.

In the late morning, the handmade red, yellow and blue paper chains around Lenny's stall fluttered in the breeze. Kay and Babs drank their coffees in a subdued mood. 'Do you and Vi and Alfie want to eat with us on Christmas Day?' Babs asked. 'We could share the expense like we did last Christmas.'

'That'd be nice,' Kay said. 'On Christmas Day we could have something different for a change. Bubble and squeak always goes down well with thick slices of bread.'

'Then, after, instead of being stuck indoors, if it's not raining we could walk down to the river,' Babs agreed excitedly.

'You know, Babs, I can't believe it's the end of 1943 and almost a new year. So much has happened since war was announced in 1939.'

'Yes, our lives have certainly changed in four years,' said Babs, nodding. 'Have you heard from Jean Pearson recently?'

Kay shook her head. 'I know she's very busy with lots of other cases to see to. Perhaps she's given up hope of ever finding Sean.'

'Dare I ask – have you?'

Kay shrugged. 'Sometimes I want to return to that house in Stock's Lane. Just to satisfy myself he's not there.'

'You wouldn't go on your own?'

'No, I'd ask you to come with me.'

Babs smiled. 'So you have been thinking about him?'

'He's always in me thoughts.' As they were talking, an elderly man with a walking stick approached.

'My God, it's Neville Butt, Paul's dad,' gasped Babs. 'I haven't seen him in months. Since before Eddie came home and me and Paul—' Babs stopped, her face clouding. 'He's coming over to talk to us.'

Kay saw that Neville's appearance had changed dramatically. He was bent over and shivering in the cold, despite his warm coat, hat and scarf, all of which seemed to swamp his frail figure.

'How are you, Neville?' Babs asked.

'Missing me boy.'

'Paul?' said Babs in surprise.

'Yes, didn't you know? He enlisted.'

Babs put down her coffee. 'He's left his job?' she asked in a shocked voice.

'He chucked it in, saying there was no pleasure in it. I told him he was daft, but he wouldn't listen. If it wasn't for you, Paul would still be safe at home.'

'Wh . . . what do you mean?' Babs stammered.

'He couldn't forget you. Had to go away. You should have put a stop to it long ago. You had a good husband in Eddie.'

'I don't think you should say that,' said Kay. She saw that Babs had turned white.

'Somebody has to,' Neville muttered. 'It's the truth. Not that the women round here will admit it openly. They just talk about it behind yer back.'

Kay stood up. 'Neville, that's an unkind thing to say.'

'No, it's not. It's the truth.' Without looking at them again, he turned away, slowly disappearing in the crowd.

Babs gave out a shaky sigh. 'Oh Kay, I didn't think I could feel much more guilty. But now I do. I haven't said anything to you but Neville's right. Jenny and Alice go out of their way to avoid me now. I saw Jenny's daughter, Emily, at the corner shop last week and she seemed embarrassed about saying hello.'

'You never said,' Kay said.

'You have your own problems.'

'But we're best mates. I'll speak to Jenny and Alice when I see them.'

'I'd rather you didn't, Kay.'

'Why's that?'

'They've got a right to be the way they are. I was carrying on with Paul behind Eddie's back.'

'That's nobody's business but yours.'

'I found out Gill had been insulted at school. And Tim was in fights because of the names he was called.'

'Is that what made you decide to end it with Paul?'

Babs nodded. 'I saw what I was doing to the kids and Eddie. Neville's right, I should have been stronger. If I had been serious about stopping it, I could've prevented Paul from getting in so deeply.' She brushed the hair from her face. 'He wouldn't be at war now, Eddie would be none the wiser and the kids wouldn't have had to see their dad put a knife to me throat.' She stared at Kay. 'I didn't know that loving someone could hurt so many people.'

Kay saw the grief on her friend's face that had aged her so much over the past few months. Babs was paying dearly for the happiness she had tried so hard to grasp with Paul.

Christmas Eve was spent at Babs's house. There were wafer-thin slices of chicken to celebrate and baked potatoes and vegetables to smother the plates. The children performed their play once again and Kay was amused to see how Alfie's confidence had grown since he had started at school. Gill gave him the parts of all three wise men to play, while Gill was Mary and Tim was Joseph and the shepherds. But the tableau soon erupted into laughter when the baby's head fell off. The doll was returned to Gill's bedroom and the evening spent playing charades.

On Christmas Day, after opening their few presents and enjoying a fry-up, Kay and Babs took the children to the river and then the park.

'Any news from the War Office?' Babs asked, hugging herself in her heavy winter coat, well-darned at the collar and cuffs.

'No,' replied Kay, equally muffled by the thick wool collar attached to her herringbone coat. 'I don't turn on the wireless these days as it's all bad news, although Vi listens to the BBC reports as she sits in her chair.'

'Berlin was bombed by the RAF and thousands perished. Dreadful,' said Babs, her warmth breath filling the air as they took their places on the bench, while the children ran wildly on the green. 'They're German families and are only the same as us. It's the madmen who run their country that should take the punishment.'

'Don't let's think about war,' said Kay, listening to the joyful laughter of the children as they ran on the frosty grass.

'There's been good things that's happened,' said Babs nodding. 'Like your Alfie going to school. And Vi getting better. Any regrets about leaving Drovers?'

Kay threaded her hand through the crook of her friend's arm and grinned. 'No, but being a lady of leisure is hard work.'

Soon they could hardly speak for laughter, causing the children to hurry over and stare at them.

'What's wrong?' asked Gill in concern.

'Nothing, but laughter is the best medicine,' Babs spluttered. 'And it's free.'

Tim and Alfie had crimson cheeks and drips on their noses. Kay handed them a hanky, giggles erupting once more as she and Babs saw the funny side of nothing in particular; a brighter end, she decided, to the long and lonely year without Alan.

Chapter Forty-Three

Kay had known that the early months of 1944 would be cold and lean, but keeping the house warm was almost impossible. Added to the work of chopping up the firewood and eking out the coal, the Luftwaffe flew over again in January.

'Thought that would happen,' said Vi one bitterly cold day as the British planes droned overhead, chasing off the enemy. 'Wasn't going to let us get off scot-free.' Kay was busy making up the fire as Vi's poor circulation made her legs swell and she was often unable to do much other than sit with her feet up listening to the radio. They were both dressed in coats, scarves and boots. Even the bombs that dropped on London were not as important as survival in the cold.

'Well, it's nothing like as bad as the Blitz. But all the same, it's frightening when they fly over this way.'

'Did you hear on the wireless that Jerry is supposed to have dropped two hundred and sixty-eight tons of high explosives and thousands of incendiaries on south-east England? It's a wonder we ain't been blown sky-high,' Vi pronounced from her chair. Kay knew the constant reports from the BBC only added to Vi's irritability.

'Well, there's always the Anderson,' commented Kay lightly, her fingers filthy and cold as she arranged the wood in the grate. 'But it's like a freeze-box in there, as you know.'

'You won't get me back in there for love nor money,' agreed Vi with a contemptuous snort. 'Dunno how we managed it before. No wonder Londoners call this the Little Blitz. Makes you wonder what's coming next.'

Though Kay agreed with Vi, she tried not to let her fear get the better of her – or the cold. Vi had never really got back to her old self and in the dark days of winter her cough had returned leaving her breathless at the slightest movement.

'Let me give you some help, flower,' tutted Vi, trying to get up.

'Move and I'll clock you,' threatened Kay with a grin.

Vi gave an unexpected chuckle. 'You know what?' she asked dryly.

'What?'

'I'm fed up listening to meself.'

Kay was on her knees and turned round slowly and giggled. Careful not to place her dirty hands on the chair or Vi's clothes, she leaned across and plonked a kiss on Vi's cheek.

'What's that for?' asked Vi in surprise.

'Reminding me how lonely I'd be without you moaning.' Kay saw Vi blush, waving her hand dismissively and blowing out derisively with her lips.

Just then, another wave of bombers flew over. Kay rushed to the window. 'Don't panic. They're ours, I think. P'raps the bombing won't last long,' she said hopefully, returning to tend to the fire.

But in February, she was proven wrong.

'Whitehall, Horse Guards Parade, St James's and Chelsea have all been attacked,' Vi read from the paper one afternoon just before Kay left to collect Alfie from school. 'Watch out as you go,' Vi added warningly as she did every day. Kay closed the front door and before knocking on Babs's door, glanced up at the sky. It was dull and grey still with a trace of the snow that had fallen all over the country.

Babs did the same when she emerged, swathed in a thick, woolly scarf over the collar of her coat. As they did every day, they talked about the noise of the British guns in the night, seeing-off the bombers, which kept them both awake. 'Lucky to have such good defences, I suppose,' said Babs as they went. 'Glad it wasn't us, though. Did you hear Whitehall got it again in the early hours?'

'Yes, so Vi said.'

'Harry Sway called by and told me to tell you in the event of the docks being targeted, we're to evacuate immediately to the Underground where everyone seems to be going these days.'

Kay grinned. 'I'll get him to tell Vi that.'

'Legs still bad, are they?'

Kay shrugged as they turned the corner towards Quarry Street. 'It'd be like getting the Queen to move from Buckingham Palace.'

'No chance of that,' said Babs, smiling.

But just a month later Kay read of the close shave that central London had taken. 'The buggers dropped them phosphorous incendiaries followed by high explosives near the palace,' shouted Vi angrily from the front room as Kay was cleaning the kitchen, as once again there seemed to be dust everywhere.

Kay didn't answer, but sank down on a chair, looking out at the grey spring day. She was fed up with all the bad news, the cold and the shortages. Then a reluctant smile lifted her lips. Conditions weren't half as bad as they could be. During the real Blitz she remembered returning to the house to discover there was dust covering even the Spam!

Chapter Forty-Four

It was a warm and sunny day when Kay looked out on the yard from the kitchen window to see Alfie and his friends playing near the Anderson. Neither she nor Babs allowed the children to venture into the street now because of the danger of Germany's new weapons of mass destruction, the Doodlebugs, as everyone called them. Kay had taught Alfie to stay alert, listening out for the pilotless aeroplanes packed with explosives that could be heard from some distance by the menacing drone of their engines. It was when the flying bombs stopped making the terrifying sound and fell to the earth that tragedy struck.

Kay sighed heavily as she reflected on the long campaign of air raids that had once again forced Londoners to take shelter. No sooner had the Little Blitz ended in April, than the Doodlebugs began in June. Even the success of the D-Day invasion, when people assumed the war was almost won, had been forgotten in the onslaught of Hitler's vengeful new weapons.

Kay opened the back door and saw Vi sitting on the wall. As usual, she was darning, a thread and needle in one hand, Alfie's grey school sock in the other. Every now and then, she would take a puff of her roll-up, then balance it back on the bricks and give a hacking cough.

'Everything all right?' Kay called.

Vi looked up at the sky. 'I ain't heard none of them blighters yet.'

'Come on in for a cuppa.'

'Don't like leaving the kids out here with no one to watch.'

'I'll leave the door open. If there's a Doodlebug coming our way, we'll hear it.' Kay knew there was little they could do to protect themselves anyway. If one of these 'buzz-bombs', as they were also known, fell to earth then there was little chance of escape for the people below it. Every Londoner prayed the eerie rattling noise of their engines didn't stop overhead. Kay always felt guilty for wanting it to drop elsewhere. But she had felt sick at the sight of the pictures in the newspapers. After a Doodlebug strike, there was nothing much left of the buildings it exploded on, and even the Andersons were of little protection.

'Harry Sway reckons our ack-ack boys are intercepting a few of the stray ones,' Vi sighed as she entered the kitchen. 'Some of 'em hit the cables of the barrage balloons. But those that do arrive on target do worse damage than any of the Luftwaffe's bombs.'

'And we thought the air raids were bad enough,' said Kay as she poured the tea. In the cool of the kitchen it just seemed like another beautiful summer's day. But below the surface, everyone was living on their nerves.

'I was reading about the Lewisham bombings,' Vi complained glumly. 'Fifty-one killed in the blink of an eye and at the Aldwych, almost as many. Then there was the Guards Barracks, over sixty soldiers perished it was reported, and more.'

'Come on, take the weight off your feet,' Kay urged, filling Vi's mug to the brim. She could see that although Vi had weathered the long years of the war and been an inspiration to them all, since the Doodlebugs had started she looked at the end of her tether. 'Is it your chest troubling you?' Kay enquired gently. 'You're not going down with bronchitis again?'

'Just getting old, love.'

'You're only as old as you feel,' said Kay, smiling.

'Blimey, that's gorn and done it. I should be six feet under by now if that's true.' They both laughed.

Kay sat forward, folding her arms on the table. 'Do you fancy a nice port and lemon tonight?'

'I ain't had port since before the war.'

'All the more reason to enjoy one now.'

'No, ducks, port don't appeal when there's no celebration to be had. Anyway, we can't afford those kind of luxuries.'

Kay's cheeks flushed with guilt. 'Yes, we can. I've a confession to make. I broke into that hundred pounds.'

'Don't surprise me, flower,' Vi said dismissively. 'After all was said and done, you couldn't get that job you was after, not with what Jerry had in store.'

'Nevertheless, I feel ashamed. I dropped me principles.'

'Principles don't put food in yer mouth, ducks.'

'I don't suppose I'll ever know where that hundred pounds came from. Alan was the only one who knew.'

'*Was*!' Vi exclaimed loudly. 'You ain't given up on him, have you?'

'I'll always have hope, Vi.' Suddenly there was a loud knock at the front door. They both gave a start.

Kay rolled her eyes. 'Those blasted Doodlebugs make me jump at any old noise.'

'Me too. Wonder who it is.' Vi was about to get up, when Kay pushed her gently back. 'Sit down and finish your tea.'

When Kay opened the front door she took a sharp breath. The last person she expected to see was Jean Pearson.

Both Kay and Vi looked shocked as they sat in the front room with their visitor. 'You say you may have found Sean?' Kay repeated Jean's words in bewilderment. 'Why can't you be certain?'

'Remember Kay, it's almost two years since I've seen him.'

'Where is he?' Kay held her breath. Had Sean been found in some slum like Stock's Lane or on the streets begging? These thoughts had often troubled her.

'This boy is a patient in a North London children's sanatorium,' came Jean's startling reply. 'He was admitted with tuberculosis just over a year ago. He was very sick but has shown signs of improvement.'

'TB?' Vi gasped.

Jean nodded. 'I'm afraid so.'

Kay felt her stomach sinking. Tears filled her eyes as she swallowed on the lump in her throat.

'The sanatorium recently received a letter,' continued Jean. 'It was written anonymously, giving the date of the boy's admission to hospital a year ago and naming the Isle of Dogs as his former home. Naturally, the hospital authorities were baffled. So they contacted my department and last week, I went there. I had no idea then who I was to find. But when I saw this child, although being very thin and pale and with his hair shaven, I thought I could see a resemblance to Sean.'

'But who would write a letter about Sean?' Kay questioned. 'Who would know he lived on the island?' She gave a soft gasp. 'Could it be Dolly? Is she still alive?'

Jean frowned thoughtfully. 'I've considered that, Kay. But if it was Dolly, what motive could she have for leading us to Sean? Why not go to the sanatorium herself? She is his mother, after all. And yet, if she has no interest in him, why write to the sanatorium?'

'So if it wasn't Dolly,' asked Vi, 'could it be that friend, the one Dolly said she left him with?'

'Unfortunately, it's only the boy who can shed light on the mystery.' Jean paused.

'So have you asked him?' Kay said bewilderedly.

'This child has no memory of what took place before he was admitted. Not even his name. So the nursing staff call him David, a name to which he now responds.'

Kay put her hand over her mouth to hide her distress.

'I'm sorry,' said Jean quietly. 'But remember, he may not be Sean.'

'It doesn't matter,' whispered Kay hoarsely, 'whoever he is, he must have suffered.'

'In my professional capacity I have to ask you if you would be prepared to help me identify him,' Jean murmured. 'But speaking as a friend, I must remind you that you're under no obligation at all to do so. There is no guarantee he'll recover from the TB. And even if he does, he certainly won't be fit to leave the sanatorium for some while.'

'Jean's giving you the plain truth,' said Vi with a nod. 'Sean ain't your blood, although I know you felt like he was family. But as much as your heart may go out to any child in trouble, you've put time between you and the past. This lad is ill. He's in a world of his own. Who's to say it's the right thing to do, to make him come out of it? P'raps it'd be better to leave the past behind, once and for all.'

At Vi's warning, Kay was filled with doubt. This boy, whether it was Sean or not, was beyond her help. Was it time, as Vi said, to leave the past behind?

'All I can suggest,' Jean said in a quiet voice, 'is that you take time to decide. If you agree to see him, I'll take you to the sanatorium. But if your answer is no then I quite understand.'

Kay was steeling herself; either way, it would be a painful step she was taking. Her heart was telling her one thing and the voice of reason another. Sean, as much as Kay cared for him, was Dolly's son. Dolly had caused him unbearable suffering. Even if he recovered, how could she help him?

It took Kay only a few moments to make her decision.

Chapter Forty-Five

'We're close now,' said Jean one late August morning as she drove Kay through the tree-lined streets of North London in her small car.

'This must be a very expensive place to live,' remarked Kay as she noted a few late office workers travelling to the city. Despite the threat of the flying bombs, they were smartly dressed in suits and many wore bowler hats. The housewives, too, looked smart and elegant in their tailored coats and hats. 'There's not a turban or raffia shopping bag in sight!'

'Yes,' said Jean, smiling. 'It is very pleasant. We could stop for tea on our way back if you like.'

'As much as I'd like to, I'd better get back.' Kay sighed softly. 'Babs has taken Alfie, Gill and Tim to the school open day and I'd like to be there when they get home to hear all their news. Mr Barnet's showing the parents and children the reinforced cellars of the school that will be used, if necessary, in an attack.'

Jean nodded and turned the car into a narrow lane bordered by tall, leafy trees and green bushes. The track seemed to go on for ever as they travelled into the heart of the wood. As they passed through an open gate, a large notice greeted them. 'Visitors without passes are forbidden to go beyond this point.' Another notice attached to the gate read, 'Trespassers will be prosecuted'.

'The sanatorium is hidden in its own grounds,' Jean informed her, 'for the safety of the patients inside and also for those in the wider environment. All visitors must have passes, as we have. Special clothes are provided to wear in some parts of the hospital. This is to prevent further spread of the disease.'

'Is that where Sean – I mean – this boy is?'

'No. Not now.' Jean smiled quickly. 'He's currently a patient in Primrose Ward. The children are transferred to this ward when the doctors feel they are out of immediate danger. Fresh air, cleanliness and healthy food are vital to their recovery. Not easy, of course, in wartime. And, as always, we must remember there are no guarantees of success.'

'So he is getting better?' Kay asked, a little bewildered.

'We would hope so.'

Kay felt anxious at Jean's vague reply. What if this boy was Sean and he fell very ill again? She had been forced to accept that, as time went on, it was unlikely Alan would return. As the months had passed, she'd had time to try to adjust but there was continual fear inside her. A feeling each morning that the very worst had happened yet she was still trying to have hope. Now she was having to face the fact that Sean also might die. Was she strong enough to endure all this?

Suddenly a big house appeared in front of them. Kay stared at its forbidding exterior. There were three storeys and many long, gabled windows, all crossed with tape. The central doorway had no window at all and was made solidly of wood. She thought it looked like a door that might be barred on the inside with a lock and chain. Kay couldn't help a little shiver.

Jean took the path to the left. It was signposted 'Primrose Ward' and continued round the side of the building. Smooth green grass flowed down to the trees and nurses in light-blue uniforms accompanied children of all ages, shapes and sizes. Some children sat in wheelchairs, some at tables and on chairs. The morning sunshine lit up the gardens, casting shadows across the lawns.

'Well, what do you think?' Jean asked as she parked the car outside a blue-painted door that directed them again to 'Primrose Ward'.

'It's better than I imagined.' As the engine of the car faded, stillness seemed to enfold them. Kay could even hear the birds singing. 'In fact it is quite pleasant.'

'I thought that too. Shall we go in?'

Kay hesitated. She was frightened now.

'Are you worried it won't be Sean?' Jean asked.

'Yes,' Kay admitted. 'But I'm also worried it will be and I'll see how sick he is.'

'TB is a cruel disease and as I told you, there's no

guarantees.' She paused. 'But I do hope this works out well for you, Kay.'

Kay knew Jean was doing her best to put her at ease. But now the time had come, she felt very unsettled indeed.

The matron, dressed in dark blue with a white cap and gleaming silver buckle at her waist, showed Kay and Jean into a spacious, light-filled room. The wooden floors were swept very clean, without rugs or carpets. The doors led out to the balconies and lawns. There were many open windows and fresh air washed in, smelling of newly mown grass.

'You can go through to the gardens from here,' Matron told them. 'The children are allowed to sit or wander around, but they mustn't exert themselves. Many are still struggling to regain the full function of their lungs. There are visitors too, but I must ask you not to address David when you see him. If you are certain you have found the boy you think is Sean then please come to me at once. For the child's sake we must tread carefully and not alarm him. Now, is there anything you would like to ask, Mrs Lewis?'

Kay nodded. 'Has David ever spoken about his past?'

'No, I'm afraid not.'

'Has he lost his memory?'

'The doctors think he has an amnesia caused by shock,' the matron explained, 'since when he was found wandering in the streets of the East End, he was dirty and clearly neglected, unable to answer any questions about where he'd been living.'

'Can they cure this amnesia?'

The matron gave a slight shrug. 'Over time he might regain his memory. At the moment, our concern is the TB. He was undernourished and extremely sick when he first came to us. His recovery has been slow and, for the child, quite enough to contend with.' She looked at Kay curiously. 'Do you know anything about tuberculosis, Mrs Lewis?'

'Only that my mum was terrified at the mention of it,' Kay had to admit. 'If someone in the neighbourhood caught it, the men came from the council with masks to take them away and disinfect the houses. It frightened a lot of people, especially when those neighbours never returned.'

'Sadly TB has a stigma,' agreed the matron. 'It was claimed to be a disease of the poor that started in the slums, caught under impoverished circumstances. But I can assure you that TB has touched every kind of family. The children admitted to this sanatorium come from all walks of life. But from our observations, David must have been subject to a great deal of neglect. Had he arrived here a week or two later, I don't think he would be here today. His lungs were in terrible shape. And, as you have been warned, there is still some way to go before we are out of the woods.'

Kay's heart went out to the child, no matter who he was. No wonder he had tried to forget his past!

'Just to warn you that the bell for the children's lunch is not long off,' the matron told her firmly.

Kay nodded. 'Thank you.'

When the matron had gone, Jean touched Kay's shoulder. 'I'll wait here.'

Kay walked nervously into the sunshine to join the other visitors. Some were strolling, others sitting peacefully. Some children sat in wheelchairs or on garden seats and benches. Others read books, or walked slowly over the grass. They all had the same look: white faces with bluish or brownish rings around their eyes. Unlike healthy children, their movements were slow and the bent posture of some made them look old before their time.

Kay studied each child as she passed. With every face, she wondered if the next one would be Sean.

Vi, Babs and the three children were making their way towards Slater Street. 'As if it ain't enough with the real Doodlebugs flying over,' Vi complained, 'we had to take part in an imaginary evacuation to the cellars! I ask you, what use was all that?'

'Mr Barnet wanted to time how long it would take to get his pupils to safety,' Babs pointed out reasonably. 'It's a big responsibility for him. Most schools have closed and it's in some doubt as to whether ours will keep open.'

Vi stopped and took in a breath. She was sounding like a miserable old cow lately. What was wrong with her? 'You're right, gel. Shut me up if I'm getting to be an old nag.'

'Vi, you're never that. This war going on for so long is getting to us all. And you must be worried for Kay.'

'That I am, love,' Vi admitted as they began to walk on. 'She's had enough to cope with Alan—' she glanced at Babs who nodded. Vi knew neither of them wanted to put into words what they were thinking. That Alan had been gone too long now to hold out any hope of his survival. It was almost a year now since they'd heard from the War Office, which in itself was very bad news. Not that she'd say so to Kay, who still put up a pretence of hope, as did they all. Vi often wondered about her dear Alan's fate. She prayed that it had been swift and not painful. There were some terrible things on the wireless and in the papers. Pictures of atrocities and tortured prisoners of war. Together with the bombing, poor Kay had had a very rough time. But hadn't she let herself in for more heartache with seeing this boy today? Either way, the knowledge of who he was, either Sean or another sick and unfortunate child, could only lead to a very distressing encounter.

'Frankly, Vi, I think it's a long shot that it might be Sean,' Babs said. 'If it is and he's got TB, that disease ain't something you can take lightly. What can Kay hope to do about it?'

'Who would write a letter to the sanatorium and get all the past raked up again?' muttered Vi. 'That's what I'd like to know!'

'It's got to be Dolly, up to her old tricks again.'

'I reckon you're right. Just trying to stir up trouble. And Kay fell for it.'

As they came to a grass mound, covered mostly with weeds and with the notices that had once been erected by the ARP, now dislodged and fallen over, Babs sighed. 'Every time I come past here and see what's left of the Suttons' and our places, I wonder how any of us have got through this war.'

Vi was thinking the same thing. She remembered with fondness Howard and Madge and old Mrs Sutton, and young Robert and Kevin, as if it was yesterday. As if she almost expected to see them walking out of that mound, Madge with her shopping basket over her arm, hurrying to find sausages for the boys' dinner. Robert and Kevin on their bikes, cycling off up the street no-handlebars, yelling out noisily like the mischiefs they were . . . yes, it was as if they were just there, a breath away!

'It seems like yesterday me and Eddie was bombed out,' Babs said as she gazed sightlessly at the dwindling pile of bricks a few yards up the road where the Chapmans' house had once stood.

'Have you heard from him?' Vi asked.

'No, and I can't say as I blame him. So I just keep writing the same old letter, about Gill and Tim and how much they miss him.' She paused, her breath caught in her throat. 'I always put a PS and ask him to forgive me.'

'You can't do no more,' Vi acknowledged, wishing she could help and knowing she couldn't. It wasn't Babs she blamed for having an affair, or for Eddie taking it the way he had when once he'd had a bit on the side too. Or even Paul for taking another man's wife, when he knew darned well that Babs wasn't his to take. It was the war she blamed, making people do things they never would, putting them in unnatural situations. And she knew without a doubt she'd go on blaming the human thirst for blood under the guise of a word called war, until she took her last breath.

'I saw Neville last week,' Babs murmured, still looking into space. 'He told me Paul was wounded in France and brought back to a hospital at Portsmouth.'

'Gawd, gel, is it serious?'

'Neville didn't think so. He's going to visit him in a day or two. But at his age, he don't fancy a long journey by train. If it wasn't for me, Paul would still be at the steelyard.'

Vi looked hard at Babs. There seemed to be no expression on her face, as if she was drained of emotion. Vi didn't like the way Babs had been looking lately. It wasn't just that she had let herself go, didn't bother about her hair or clothes or looking scruffy and washed-out. It was something on the inside of her that had died. The everyday mask she wore was for the kids' benefit alone and it was sad to see. 'Listen, Babs, don't start blaming yourself,' Vi said gently.

'Who else is there to blame? We all know why Paul enlisted. Neville said it himself.'

'Neville didn't care for being left to fend for himself,' Vi corrected. 'The truth is Paul's no coward, Babs, and joined the conflict to fight for his country. You'd do well to remember that, rather than listening to a bitter old man.'

Babs blinked her pale blue eyes and smiled. Vi noted yet again how there was no energy or life behind it. That was just part of how she coped these days, smiling without any real joy.

Suddenly the noise of the children's shouts stopped abruptly. Both Vi and Babs turned to look at them. Gill, Tim and Alfie were all staring up at the sky.

Gill was the first to shout. 'Mum, I can hear one of them bombs flying over!'

Vi listened for the distant drone; it was a dreadful, ominous sound. One that everyone knew and feared; a kind of mechanical rattling that grew in intensity as it came closer.

'Come here, kids,' Babs yelled in a high and frightened voice. She opened her arms.

Vi felt sick with fright as she saw Gill grab Alfie's hand and pull him along. What were they all to do, out in the open like this? As the children crowded round, the noise grew louder. 'Oh, Gawd, it would have to happen now,' Vi wheezed. She put her hand on her heart. It was thumping wildly. She was filled with panic. What if the Doodlebug stopped overhead?

Just then, a door of one of the houses flew open. Vi saw it was Jenny Edwards. She had her hair in curlers and was wearing her apron and carpet slippers. 'Come on inside, everyone, quickly!'

'Oh, thank God,' cried Babs as Jenny ran out and

herded the children together, pushing them all in front of her. 'My Jack and Emily are at work. There's only me at home, so we can all squeeze in the cupboard under the stairs.'

But Vi wasn't paying attention. She was looking upwards. The noise seemed to be coming right over them. Her heart went into overdrive as she waited for the deadly weapon to appear.

Kay walked slowly through the beautiful garden, feeling the soft, spongy lawn beneath her sandaled feet. The air smelled clean and fresh and scented with grass. The children here read from books on their laps or played board games. Some just sat quietly as the nurses wandered between them. Kay thought how strange it was to be amongst children who didn't shout and scream. Every now and then, there would be a cough, a rasping clearing of the lungs and a nurse would hurry to the child's side. Kay saw how this terrible sickness had transformed their lives. They had given themselves up to an unnaturally calm existence. The serenity in the garden felt powerful, healing. Even the nurses spoke softly, and moved carefully amongst their charges. The wheelchairs they pushed seemed to glide noiselessly.

Kay came to a small group of children. They were sitting on wooden benches with blankets tucked over their knees. One girl was drawing in a book. The boy next to her had a shaven head. Was this boy Sean?

Kay walked closer. The boy was sitting with his back

to her. He could be seven, close to Sean's age. Without trying to draw his attention, she moved around the group. The girl stopped drawing and looked up. She had dark hair pulled back from her face and very sad eyes that seemed almost indistinguishable from the bluish patches beneath. Kay smiled and received a smile in return. The boy with the shaven head looked up. Her hopes were instantly dashed. He had pale eyes, though the skin beneath them was shadowed. His broad forehead and bone structure were nothing like Sean's.

Kay walked on. Soon she had come to the end of the garden, bordered by a high stone wall covered in a vine of pretty purple flowers. A mossy stone cherub stood in the centre of a small concrete pond. There were five or six children sitting around it on chairs. No water came from the cherub, but it didn't seem to matter. Kay thought how tranquil the picture looked.

She walked towards the waterless fountain. The scene before her could have come from one of Alfie's picture books. A typical English summer's day, except all the children were wearing warm clothes and had pale, ghostly faces.

Kay stood still, her knees weakening at the sight of one boy. He stood with his back to her: small-boned, with slender shoulders and a thin neck under his close-cropped dark hair. Dressed in a thick jumper and trousers, he moved slowly away from the others. Kay caught her breath. His bowed legs seemed too thin to support his body. Just like Sean's had been when Dolly had first left him.

It was all Kay could do to stop herself from hurrying forward. But then she remembered the matron's warning. Kay waited patiently by the wall, hoping the small figure would turn. When eventually he did, a pair of large, dark eyes gazed back at her and Kay knew her search for Sean had finally ended.

'Sean?' she called softly, then remembered he was now accustomed to hearing another name. 'I mean – David?'

There was a moment when Kay thought he recognized her. She knew if he did, she would ignore the matron's orders and gather him in her arms. But she realized quickly that she had been mistaken as he stared at her unknowingly.

'Do you remember me?' she still found herself asking. 'It's Kay. Kay Lewis.'

No answer came, of course, and Kay stood uncertainly. All her hopes of a joyful reunion dissolved, leaving her feeling powerless and suddenly tearful. She had been so close to this child once.

Kay cleared her throat and blinked away the tears. She couldn't let him down now. He had suffered so much and lost even the mother who had not wanted him.

Forcing her weak legs to move, Kay sat down on the curve of the fountain. She wanted to take him in her arms, but knew it would only confuse him.

'Would you like to sit here too?' she asked, patting the warm stonework beside her. 'It's a nice sunny spot, don't you think?'

The memory of the night in her kitchen when he'd

woken from a bad dream suddenly sprang back to her mind. Then, as now, he'd had no experience of true affection. It was only through time and perseverance that they had forged the bond between them. Perhaps this bond wasn't forgotten, she found herself hoping. Perhaps it could be found again.

'That's it, sit here.'

Placing his small bottom beside her, he looked up, a frown across his forehead. Kay thought how white his skin seemed, almost glowing in contrast to the dark circles around his eyes. But his hair was beginning to grow back and though his jumper was buttoned up to his chin, she could hear no terrible wheezes from his chest.

'Perhaps you don't remember me,' she said softly, 'but that doesn't matter. Because I remember you.'

Sean continued to stare at her, watching her face curiously.

'You once stayed with me and my son, Alfie. You even went to school.'

There was just the slightest tremble on his long lashes, the twitch of his dry lips. Kay said very gently, 'Would you like to hear some more?'

As the sun warmed them and the birds sang in the lofty trees, Sean squirmed his thin body around, kicking the stonework with his heels. After what felt like a very long moment, he nodded.

Kay smiled again, daring to place her hand close to his on the mossy green patches of the fountain. 'Your other friends were Gill and Tim who lived next door. The four of you played in the yard. Sometimes in the Anderson shelter and sometimes in the street.' Kay added very quietly, 'Slater Street.'

At this she saw him stiffen and she was afraid that he was about to stand up. 'Don't worry if you can't remember,' she added swiftly, 'it was a long time ago. But there is something you might like to see.' She brought the folded picture out of her pocket and placed it beside his hand. 'You drew this lovely train with Alfie. It's a very good drawing. The train set was yours and Alfie's favourite toy.'

She watched him pick up the paper and unfold it. Kay remembered the day he had drawn the train with Alfie in the front room. It was the same image that he'd drawn later at Stock's Lane.

As he studied it, Kay watched carefully. At first there was nothing, but then she saw something – a tiny widening of his eyes, a breath held in his thin chest.

Then, as the matron had warned, a bell rang. All the children began to move, but Sean continued to stare at the drawing.

'You can keep it,' Kay said and took the paper, folding it carefully into his trouser pocket. 'When you look at it, you can think of me and Alfie.'

The bell rang again and Kay stood up. She didn't want to leave. 'I don't know how soon I'll be able to visit you again,' she told him, her voice filled with emotion. 'But I promise to write. Would you like that?'

To Kay's bitter disappointment he turned away,

beginning to follow the other children across the lawn. Kay watched him go, trying to keep her tears in check and ignore the desperate ache inside her.

Just before he reached the terrace he stopped and turned very slowly. Kay lifted her hand to wave. When she saw him smile, she waved even harder. It was only a smile, but it meant more to her than any action or words could say.

Vi, Babs, Jenny Edwards and the children were huddled together in the darkness of the under-stairs cupboard. Even in here, they could hear the dreadful sound: a tinny rattling, growing steadily louder. They linked arms, each one of them shaking with fear. Vi knew that hiding in a cupboard would make no difference if the bomb fell on them. But it was something to do, to make the terrifying moments go quicker. To reassure the youngsters. They were all praying the bomb would fly over. But this too was a terrifying thought, as others would die, if not them.

'Will it drop on us, Vi-Vi?' Alfie squeezed himself closer. Vi hugged him tighter.

'We'll be all right, son.' Vi stroked his hair, feeling its familiar thick texture. Despite what she said, she didn't really believe they were going to survive. This time the Doodlebug was close. As if it was in the cupboard with them, echoing around the confined space. She had never felt like this before. It was true terror, the gut-wrenching certainty inside that you and your loved ones were about to die. If Babs hadn't pulled her into Jenny's house, she'd be out there right now, looking up at it, waiting for it to drop.

'Mum, I'm scared,' sobbed Gill.

'Don't worry, love, we're all together,' whispered Babs in a strangely calm voice.

'Yes, Gill, love, your mum's right,' Jenny added. 'We've been living in Slater Street too long to get blown out of it now.'

Because of the dark, Vi couldn't see the others' faces. But what Babs and Jenny had just said impressed her. There might have been ups and down between them all in the past, but when it came down to it, they were friends and neighbours, solid as a rock. It had taken a Doodlebug to show them that friendship and neighbourliness could survive the effects of this miserable war. Old Adolf would be right put out if he thought he had done them all a favour!

Vi smiled in the darkness, ready to accept whatever fate befell them. She felt at peace; the fear had receded. Her brave friends and neighbours were around her and so were these lovely kids. Pressing Alfie's face into her coat, her gnarled fingers lovingly caressed his hair again. As the noise overhead drowned out all her thoughts, she was barely conscious of the sudden silence; the silence to end all silences as the flying bomb's engine cut out and the weapon fell to earth.

Chapter Forty-Six

Kay listened to the rumble of the car's engine. She was purposely fixing her attention on the noise, keeping her thoughts at bay. She gazed out at the many bushes and the tall trees of the sanatorium's green wood. It looked different now; familiar and non-threatening. Even the rolls of hidden barbed wire didn't seem intimidating. She had found Sean.

When they came to the gate and drove through it, Kay sighed deeply. She had never expected to travel here today and find Sean. Not in her heart of hearts.

'Kay, shall we stop for tea as I suggested earlier?' Jean glanced anxiously in her direction.

Kay shook her head. 'No, I'd like to get home now.'

'Will you tell Alfie?'

'No, not until Sean's better. And that could take a long time.'

'I think that's very sensible.'

Kay didn't refer to the drawing or the brief moments she'd shared with Sean. She thought Jean might not approve of disobeying the matron's orders.

Jean nodded her agreement as she turned the steering wheel. 'Matron said that as you've confirmed it's Sean, on your next visit you can spend more time together.'

'I'd like that.'

'Meanwhile, she feels confident to tell him that you visited for his benefit today.'

'I don't know when I'll be able to visit again, Jean. But I'd like to write to him. Would that be allowed?'

'I should think so.'

'What will happen when he's better?'

The young woman hesitated. '*If* he gets better, remember.'

Kay looked at her friend. 'That little boy deserves a new start. I'd like to be able to help him somehow.'

'I admire your resolve, Kay.' Jean quickly drew her attention back to the road.

Kay folded her hands in her lap. She knew Jean, as usual, was the voice of reason. For the rest of the journey Kay sat quietly, thinking about her next visit to Sean. She would come while Alfie was at school and be back in time to collect him. But with the Doodlebugs raining down, it might be some while before she could feel confident enough to leave her son again. For the time being however, she would write to Sean, telling him that his friends from Slater Street would one day be with him again.

Harry Sway coughed, trying to clear the filth from his lungs, while making his way through the ruins of Crane

Street. The path ahead was hidden under a thick, sulphurous cloud of smoke and fumes from the fractured drain. Amidst all the debris and chaos there were shadowy figures moving slowly about. Fire engines and ambulances were trying to weave through the mayhem. Shattered glass, bricks and roof tiles were strewn along a haphazard path. A block of four terraced houses had disappeared with one flying bomb strike.

Harry had never thought that tragedy could strike again in this area. Many roads had taken hits of some kind or another in the Blitz, but rarely had a whole neighbourhood been brought to its knees as it had been in Crane Street and Slater Street.

'How many dead?' he asked the rescue crew, as he wiped the dirt from his face under his tin hat.

'Five in Crane Street – so far,' replied the man brusquely. He was covered in sweat and dirt, his helmet askew on his head as he wrestled with the stretcher and the motionless blanket-covered body beneath it. 'Thank God most of the houses left in this road were empty. It was the blast of air that caught Slater Street, as if the bomb gave a bloody great fart where it fell. All the houses have been damaged, and the two gaffs over there closest to the terrace also took the impact.'

'Struth,' Harry mumbled. 'Have you got any names?'

'An old boy, Neville Butt, and the two biddies next door, Hazel and Thelma Press.'

Harry groaned in distress.

'You knew 'em?'

'I've known Hazel and Thelma for years. A nice couple too, never married, salt of the earth. And Neville, well, he lived with his son Paul until the lad enlisted. But Paul took a bullet in France after the landings. I was going to organize some transport for the old geezer to visit him in hospital.'

'He won't need it now.' The man grasped his shoulder. 'You'd better not go any further, chum.'

'But I need to get down to the other end of Slater Street. See if there's anyone there that needs help.'

'Too dangerous. Leave it to us.'

'But I—'

'Sorry, I can't let you through.' The man held out his filthy hands. 'Go back to the post and get yerself a cup of Rosie.'

Harry nodded resignedly. It was probably best in the long run. But people he cared about, his friends and neighbours and his wartime charges, lived down there. It was his sector in the Blitz. He regarded Slater Street as his patch, his turf and he'd always tried to look out for those who lived there. Like old Vi and Kay and Babs and their kids and the Edwards and Tylers too. Now it was the end of the line. He couldn't bear to think what had become of them. Instead, he concentrated on picking his way back to the post over the bricks, mortar, wood and masonry of Crane Street. Coughing with the dust that stubbornly filtered back into his lungs, he acknowledged the blackened faces of the fire engine crews that were dousing the flames of the many small fires. The search in the demolished buildings would continue till nightfall, any casualties sent to hospital, the dead to the morgue. Harry forced his shaking hands over his cheeks, suppressing a sob that welled up from deep inside of him.

'It's just so bloody unfair,' he muttered to himself. 'As if the East End ain't suffered enough. Someone needs to give that ruddy Hitler his comeuppance.'

Another cloud of dust enveloped him as he stood still listening to the clanking, shunting and grinding of the rescue vehicles and fire engines. He should by now be accustomed to devastation and loss of life. But these flying bombs were equal to no other.

'Harry Sway, is it?'

The voice came from a few yards away. A police officer stepped towards him, his boots covered in dust and his uniform unrecognizable as navy blue. The cone-like helmet on his head was the only clue to his profession.

'How can I help you, chum?' Harry cleared his throat and braced his shoulders, hoping the tears in his eyes were masked by the grime. He had a job to do and looking as sick as a parrot was going to help no one.

'I've got someone asking for you at the post. A young woman by the name of Jean Pearson.'

'Dunno her, pal. Is she from Crane Street?'

'No, she don't live round here.'

'What's she want then?'

The policeman took off his helmet and swiped his hand through his dark hair. With a compassionate tug of his heart, Harry noted the white patch where his helmet had been. Like him, the copper had seen sights today that no mortal should be made to witness. 'She's with someone else, a Mrs Lewis would it be?'

'You mean Kay?' Harry gasped. 'Thank God for that! Is she with her kid?'

'No, she was out for the day. She's pretty shook up, Harry. You gonna have a word with her?'

'I'll come right away.' He shook his head sadly. 'Her old man was in the Rescue Squad before he was called up. The poor sod went missing in action in forty-three.'

The policeman heaved a sympathetic sigh. 'Some folks seem to have all the bad luck. Listen, I'll get one of the lads to drive 'em up to the hospital. We've got two of our blokes up there, with all the latest information as it comes in.'

Harry experienced a moment of panic as he felt the bile of fear rise in his throat. 'Christ,' he complained loudly, 'this is a rotten job.'

The two men turned round and made their way through the ripped and mangled remains of Crane Street towards the post.

Kay found herself standing in one of the long Victorian-embellished corridors of the Poplar hospital. The combination of disinfectant and ether that pervaded the air was sickening, added to the pitiful sights of the shocked, weak and wounded being ferried in. The waiting area was full of the relatives of the missing. Like her, they wanted to find their loved ones. The Doodlebug that had fallen on Crane Street was not the only one to fly over East London that day.

Kay was thankful that Jean had stayed with her. Harry Sway had been relieved to see them but didn't know anything about Alfie, Vi, Babs and the kids. Slater Street was a no-go area. Kay didn't remember much of the journey in the truck. What was she to discover at the hospital?

'Kay, are you listening?' Jean was shaking her arm as they stood in the busy stream of people. 'The doctor's here.'

Kay stared into the gaze of an older man in a white coat. He had grey, dishevelled hair and looked at her over the top of his half-moon spectacles.

'Mrs Lewis? Mrs Kay Lewis?'

Kay felt faint as she nodded. What was he going to tell her?

'Your son is safe, also Mrs Chapman and her children, who I believe are your neighbours. A few bruises and scratches but nothing untoward. They took shelter with another neighbour and were brought to safety by the rescue teams.'

Kay felt the life drain from her legs as tears of relief slipped down her cheeks.

'Come, come, my dear. It's very good news for you.'

'When can I see them?' she managed to croak.

'All in good time. There is however . . .' the doctor paused, '. . . a set-back for Mrs Hill.'

'Vi?' Kay's heart jumped in alarm. 'Wasn't she with the others?'

'Yes, but we think she suffered a stroke. I can't tell you very much just yet. We shall of course be doing tests.'

Kay gasped. 'But – but is she going to be all right?'

'We certainly hope so. Is Mrs Hill normally in good health?'

'I – I thought she was getting over the bronchitis she had last year. But she was worried sick about these flying bombs.'

'Well, I suggest you see her now, just for a few moments. Then the nurse will take you to your son and friends.' The doctor hesitated. 'I understand from the police authorities that you are on their list for accommodation. Arrangements are being made for you all to be taken to a shelter.'

'A shelter?' Kay repeated. 'Why can't we go home?'

'The impact of the Doodlebug has rendered all the properties in Slater Street unsafe. I thought you'd been made aware of that.'

Kay quickly wiped away a tear. She couldn't believe this was happening. Why hadn't Harry told her?

Jean touched her arm. 'Is there anything I can do?' Her voice was full of pity.

Kay stared at the white coat of the doctor who was now talking to someone else. She shook her head. No one could help. The Doodlebug had seen to that.

* * *

Vi knew she was somewhere familiar because of the smell – the disinfectant and ether – just like when they'd rushed young Pete to hospital and he'd been lying in that room, separated from the other patients because of the infection that diphtheria spread. But the doctors and nurses needn't have worried that her boy would become a problem. No, he'd not resisted the disease for long. Even though he'd been young, on the brink of manhood and expecting to live a long and full life, he had passed quickly with the fever. The doctors had said that if anyone had a chance against the diphtheria it was Pete Junior. But nevertheless, he'd drifted and within a few hours he was taken from them.

Vi thought of young Pete now, where she preferred to think of him. A tall, handsome young man with his dad standing by his side, enjoying the bright lights of heaven together. Two beautiful souls who she believed would continue for all eternity. She'd like more than anything to be with them. She wasn't afraid. She wasn't in pain. If only they would they come for her . . .

'Vi?'

Someone was calling. Was it young Pete? No, he would have called her 'Mum'. Vi struggled to open her eyes.

'Vi, it's me, Kay.'

Vi peeled open her eyes and looked around. The ceiling was a white blur and the walls a very pale green. She tried to move her head but she couldn't. She felt a trickle of spit at her chin. Strangely she couldn't seem to wipe it away.

'Vi, can you hear me?'

Vi wanted to answer but she couldn't quite get her mouth to work properly. Not that it mattered very much. She would like to go back to where she was, waiting for her two Petes. She knew sooner or later they'd be along and she didn't want to miss them. And she had plenty of patience to wait. At this thought, she wanted to laugh. Big Pete had always assured her she must have patience to have married a mug like him.

'Don't try to talk, Vi. You've had . . . had a rough time, but you're going to be all right. And everyone's safe: Alfie and Babs and the kids. Everyone.'

Vi felt Kay's hand around hers. The hospital walls became clearer, the windows and then a nurse in blue uniform. So she was in hospital, after all, not at heaven's gate!

'Oh, Vi, I should have made you rest more.'

Vi heard Kay's voice drifting in and out of her head. Her words were soft and trembling, muffled by tears. But the poor cow needn't be sad! Quite the opposite. Vi wanted to explain she was happy just waiting here, she wasn't ill in the least.

A picture of Jenny Edwards, Babs and the kids lit up in Vi's mind. They were huddled together, waiting for the bomb to fly over. She'd been stroking Alfie's hair, when the noise above had stopped and then there was only the silence.

Vi tried to move her lips. She couldn't. But again, it was of no real concern. It was like she was as free as a bird inside her head, flying and soaring all over the place. It was a lovely feeling. If only she could tell Kay that.

'I'm not allowed to stay for much longer,' Kay was whispering. 'I – I just wanted you to know that I'll see you soon and – and that we're all rooting for you.' Kay squeezed her hand tightly.

Vi tried to tell her that she needn't worry, needn't worry at all. That now she was feeling sleepy, very sleepy. Once again the floating feeling filled her. A freedom from the worries that had put her in chains for so long. Vi wanted to laugh. She couldn't even remember what those worries were now!

'Bricks and mortar don't matter,' Kay was saying softly, tearfully. 'It's people who do. Remember the Blitz when we never really knew for certain if we'd see the light of day? I was always glad to see me house and knew somehow we'd manage as long as it was still standing. But today, knowing that you and Alfie and Babs and the kids are safe . . . it's all that matters.'

Vi nodded as best she could. Though that movement too was probably all in her head.

'You're going to get better, Vi.'

At the risk of seeming ungrateful, Vi was hard put to say whether she cared much about being part of *this* world again. Just thinking about her boy and her other half waiting to meet her was a revelation. She knew now that death wasn't to be feared but to be welcomed. She also knew – though she didn't know how – that it hadn't been her time to go in Jenny's under-stairs cupboard. She knew the good Lord would take her when he was ready and not before.

'I've got to leave you now,' Kay was telling her. 'I don't want to. But the doctor said not to tire you.'

Vi tried to squeeze Kay's hand. The mumbling that came from her lips didn't sound like 'Cheerio, flower'. But perhaps that bloody bomb had deafened her after all! She wanted to crack that joke to Kay, but she was drifting fast . . .

Then, as the wave of peace claimed her, she found herself floating out into the sky. As though she was really no weight at all on the surface of the cloud.

Chapter Forty-Seven

Kay was so tired, she didn't care about the snoring, coughing, wheezing and releasing of wind that would in normal times be met with a joke and crude sense of cockney humour. She knew, as did Babs, who was also trying to fall asleep on the mattress beside her, that they were now refugees, their temporary shelter an old Aldgate warehouse. They had been told they would never go back to Slater Street. That they were the lucky ones. Neville, Hazel and Thelma had perished. Kay couldn't stop thinking about them. They had been friends and neighbours all through the Blitz yet one single bomb had brought their lives to an end.

Kay sat up, pushing the blanket back. She felt hot and sticky. Thank God it was summer and not winter and at least they were provided with the basics of life: a soup kitchen and temporary latrines, a wash house, straw mattresses and one blanket and a pillow apiece. They had been made as comfortable as possible under the circumstances. The result of the latest wave of Doodlebugs to drop on London had swollen every shelter beyond its normal capacity.

Kay looked over at her friend. 'Babs, are you awake?'

'Yes.' Babs sat up too. 'Are the kids asleep?'

'There ain't been a whisper from them.'

'You know, Kay, I was so proud of them today,' Babs said softly as they glanced at the three motionless forms under the thin blankets. 'When the rescue crew prized opened the door of Jenny's cupboard, they didn't shed a tear between them. We'd been stuck in there for a good hour before the rescue crew was able to let us out. But the kids were more concerned for Vi when she was laid on a stretcher and put in the ambulance.'

'Babs, it was awful seeing her in hospital like that. She couldn't speak properly. I think she was trying to tell me something.'

'Kay, don't be upset. She's alive, ain't she? After all, she would have been in the house if you hadn't gone to the sanatorium. It was going to the school that saved all our lives.'

'Yes, I know I should be grateful. And I truly am. I'll never forget waiting at that hospital, not knowing—' Kay stopped. She had to pull herself together. She looked at the children again. They were all well and safe. And as she'd told Vi, that was what mattered.

'I can't stop thinking about Neville,' Babs whispered. 'Paul's never going to see his dad again. And Thelma and Hazel – they was never any trouble.'

'Yes, they were all good neighbours.' Kay and Babs were silent, lost in thought once again.

'Do you think our houses are still standing?' Kay eventually asked.

'The bobby that drove us here said the houses in Slater Street were now designated as unsafe. I thought the ceiling was coming down on us in that cupboard. And you should have seen Jenny's place when they dug us out. The front door had fallen in and the passage wall had a great big hole in it where the bricks had come loose. And the dust – it was everywhere!'

'Poor Jenny. Where will they go?'

'Last I heard they was being taken over to East Ham to a refuge centre there.'

Once again they fell silent. They had been told by the police that their possessions, if recovered, would be sent on to them. But what that meant, she didn't know. Meanwhile, the Sally Army would give them what was needed tomorrow.

'At least you found Sean,' Babs said, trying to sound brighter. 'Tell me again what happened.'

'He looked so small, Babs. Not even as tall as Alfie. All his lovely dark hair had been shaved and only grown a little. I wanted to fling me arms around him. But the matron warned me not to as she didn't want him upset. Even so, I talked to him.'

'You wouldn't upset him,' Babs said indignantly. 'He was happy with you and Alfie. When will you see him again?'

Kay sighed. 'That Doodlebug has changed everything. But I told him I'd write.'

'What did he say?'

'Nothing,' Kay said reflectively. 'But he smiled. And that was enough for me.'

'The bomb did more than take away our homes. It changed all our future.'

'What will you do, Babs? Where will you go?'

'To Essex, most likely. At least we've got relatives there. Though I dunno if they'll be too pleased to see us again after having Gill and Tim all that time before.' Babs looked at Kay. 'What about you?'

'Alan wrote in that letter he wanted me and Alfie to go to Len and Doris's. But I can't see meself doing that. Poor Doris was upset enough before when we took Alfie away.'

'So you'll go to your mum and dad's?'

'Like you, I don't have much choice, Babs.'

Babs gave a sudden chuckle. 'Your mum will say she told you so. That the East End was too dangerous to live in.'

Kay smiled. 'We gave Hitler a run for his money, though.'

Babs leaned her elbows on her knees. 'You know, I never realized there were so many kinds of farting. Little ones and whistly ones and whopping great bangers. Trying to sleep here tonight has been an education.'

At this, they burst into soft laughter. Kay knew it was laughter that could have easily been tears. But for her and Babs, their sense of cockney humour was a release and they welcomed it. They sat together, talking of the old days, of Eddie and Alan and their lives with their neighbours and close friends in Slater Street; a time they knew had now drawn to a close. They'd shared many ups and probably more downs together, but they'd always been there for each other. Now even that was set to change.

'Whatever happens, we'll write, won't we?' Babs insisted. 'We'll keep in touch.'

'Course we will.'

Later, as Babs lay asleep, Kay found herself wide awake. What would have happened if Alan had been here today? She knew he would have moved heaven and earth to see that she and Alfie were safe. He would have scooped them up and protected them and, in that very special way of his, taken all their worries away. She felt the loss of him deeply and she knew Babs missed Eddie too. And that part of her would always remember Paul. Although their life in the East End had ended, they had been blessed with survival. As she drifted into sleep, she thought she could hear Alan's voice softly whispering in her ear. His words always gave her courage. 'Chin up, lovely, tomorrow's a new day.'

And it was.

Chapter Forty-Eight

Nine months later

'At 2.41 this morning, 7 May 1945, peace came to a battered Europe,' the commentator intoned, his voice sombre as it came through the kitchen wireless, causing Kay, who was seated on the bench outside the back door, to jump to her feet and wave fiercely at Pops in the garden.

'Pops! Pops! Come quickly, it's over!'

Wearing her boots and leaning heavily on her stick, Pops's journey down the path was slow. 'You mean it?' she asked breathlessly as she neared. 'Is the war really over?'

'As good as. Come on, we'll just catch the last of the news.'

Kay and Pops eagerly pulled up their chairs to listen to the rest of the broadcast. But as they sat there, the joy of the unconditional surrender by a devastated German army to the Allies was tempered with sadness. So much devastation was left in the wake of this second world war that had come only twenty years after the first, Kay reflected. London had been pulverized by an even more lethal weapon: the new killing machines, the V2s. These had caused even greater destruction than their predecessors. Londoners had been blasted out of their homes once again and Kay had thanked God for the safety of Monkton. But even here, they hadn't been shielded from the terrible atrocities that were printed every day in the newspapers. Unimagined horrors had been discovered in the Nazi death camps. For millions of Jews, Poles and other victims, the victory had come too late. There had been disbelief at the report that on 30 April 1945, Hitler and his wife Eva Braun had committed suicide in Berlin.

'Well, at last the world's come to its senses,' said Pops, mirroring Kay's thoughts as she tipped the cloth cap back from her wrinkled brown forehead. 'Perhaps now we'll have that long-awaited peace.'

'Yes,' agreed Kay, smiling. 'Though it's hard to believe.'

'The news will take a while to sink in,' Pops said. 'But as soon as Winnie gives the people the go-ahead, there'll be no stopping the celebrations.'

Kay nodded. 'Mum and Dad took Alfie up to the church hall this morning. Her whist club is planning a party.'

'Didn't you want to go too, love?' Aunty Pops's eyes twinkled. 'There's no Yanks about now. You'd be safe.'

Kay laughed as Aunty Pops teased her. 'I wonder where Gene is now and if he survived the war?'

'Let's hope so. He was a nice young man.'

'I thought I'd write to Babs,' Kay said as she turned off the wireless. 'In her last letter she said she'd heard from Eddie. He's waiting to be demobbed and wanted to know if he could see the kids.'

'Do you reckon they'll patch up their differences?'

'They're both changed people now, Aunty Pops. The war saw to that. But they love their kids. And perhaps there's a chance for them as a family.'

Aunty Pops got stiffly up from her seat. 'Any more news from Vi?'

'No, I've heard nothing since January. She wrote then that she'd been transferred from the convalescence home to somewhere in Woking. Her writing was none too clear but she said she was trying to get used to walking with a stick.'

'It's not twelve months yet, love, since her stroke,' Aunty Pops reminded Kay. 'It took me a good couple of years to get used to this.' She waved her stick in the air. 'I didn't lose me speech like Vi did, but me legs went for a burton. So I know what she's going through. When you write next, tell her from me that it just takes time and patience. Though, of course, I must admit I can't do the things I did when my Tommy was alive.'

'Do you still miss him, Aunty Pops?'

'As much as I did on the day he died, ducks. Just as you do your Alan. But my Tommy went of natural causes, whilst the war took Alan, and that seems cruel. 'specially with the nipper so young.'

Kay felt the sting of carefully suppressed tears. Since leaving the East End she had forced them away daily and it was just as difficult now as it had been nine months ago to accept that Alan must be dead.

'You're not alone, love,' Aunty Pops said tenderly. 'There's many bereaved young women like you – not that that's much consolation. Now, if it's the future you're worrying about, you needn't. You're welcome to stay here. There's plenty of room in this big house as you well know.'

'Thanks, Aunty Pops.' Kay didn't like to say that although she had grown used to Monkton, and had even come to like it, her heart was still aching for Slater Street. Even in the ruined state it must be in, the island was in her blood and it would take a long while before that fact changed. The docks, the dirt, the tarry, salty smells, the markets, the smoke-covered houses and busy factories, long rows of whitewashed front steps, the constant noise and the faces of her friends and neighbours. But what was the use of pining for a place she couldn't have? The cockney community she knew and loved had all but disappeared. It was reported in the newspapers that even the air that East Enders breathed was still tainted with the sulphurous gases of war. How could she think of returning?

Aunty Pops patted her hand. 'The offer's there if you want it. Just thought I'd say. Now, I'm going out to dig up a few more dandelions before they take over the paths.'

Kay watched her aunt shuffle her way out of the house and bend, with the help of her stick, to take up her small trowel and poke at the weeds. Her dad was still not the best at gardening, and like Uncle Tommy turned a blind eye to nature's rampage, as her mum called it. He now disappeared daily with Alfie, taking him to school in the town centre and collecting him again at four. Kay smiled. Between her dad and Aunty Pops, Alfie was well and truly spoiled and had even made new friends. But, like Kay, he still missed his old home. He remembered everything clearly, as she did. He never tired of talking about Gill and Tim and, to her amazement, still spoke of Sean. Kay had kept in touch with Jean Pearson explaining that, although she couldn't visit Sean, she had written to him, and she knew from Jean's reply that Sean was finally on the road to recovery.

Kay got up from the table. She had long ago learned to do as Alan advised her: turn off her imagination when it came to matters she could do nothing to resolve. Instead she would write to Babs about the end of the conflict and her hopes that Eddie would soon be demobbed. The letter would take some while to arrive in Essex. Perhaps as it did, Eddie would be making his way home to the family he missed so much.

Kay wandered round the kitchen and into the front room. Sunshine streamed through the clear glass of the windows, now free of tape. The scent of the fields and the cattle grazing in the pastures, the fragrance of the roses that Aunty Pops had planted outside the front door told her it was too beautiful a day to stay inside.

Ten minutes later, she had put on her floppy sun hat and was making her way towards town. A soft breeze lifted her long coppery waves from her shoulders and cooled her hot skin. Now that the conflict was over, what was she to do? Aunty Pops's offer was generous and very kind. But Kay missed having her own home. She couldn't have Slater Street but what if, like Babs who had put her name down on a list with the council in Essex, she decided to stay in Berkshire?

Kay thought of the remaining thirty pounds in her Post Office account. The money was dwindling. She had given Aunty Pops a small amount each week to put towards hers and Alfie's keep. Would it be possible to place what was left with a landlord as rent on some kind of accommodation? Berkshire was a far cry from Slater Street, but it was clear her dreams of returning to the city were to remain just dreams.

She had seen a notice in the window of the cafe in town. A part-time waitress was needed. The shifts, she had noted, would fit in with Alfie's school and she was sure she could learn the trade quickly.

Perhaps the radio broadcast this morning was the wake-up call she had needed.

'I'm sorry, love, I really am.' The elderly shopkeeper sighed. 'I took on someone a short while ago. And I never even advertised the position. I had two young women like yourself come in this morning, one after the other. It was the news on the wireless that did it. Really looks like the war is over.'

'I was told the same at the cafe,' Kay said disappointedly. 'The lady who owns it sent me here.'

'And I'd've took you on like shot, my dear, if I hadn't been suited,' the grocer agreed. 'You're young and look strong enough to help me with all the greengrocery, which I've had to manage on my own since war broke out. There's lots of young women like you who've done grand at filling in for the men but now that our boys are coming home they'll want their old jobs back again.'

'Do you know of anywhere else I might try?' Kay asked hopefully. She had even made enquiries at the Post Office which had a board in the window with all sorts of notices pinned on it. Mostly there had been items for sale, but one or two were for rooms to let. She'd already tried two of them. The first, a set of rooms over a garage, had no garden and were reached by a rather dangerous set of spiral stairs. The next had been a small terraced cottage close to the shops. The woman had refused her as the rent, she said, would be beyond the means of an unemployed mother.

'Can't say as I do,' answered the shopkeeper. 'But you could look in the Post Office window.'

'I already have.'

'Well then, try the next village. Or perhaps the farms, though after having had the Land Girls for the duration, the farmers are bound to want cheap labour. Your best bet is to try the bigger towns.'

Kay nodded. 'Thanks, anyway.'

She stepped out into the bright sunshine, replacing her hat. All her enthusiasm had faded as it became clear that renting rooms without the security of a job was impossible. What was she going to do?

The sight of the baker's opposite, with a sign announcing 'Freshly baked scones and tea' made Kay pause. She had told Aunty Pops she was going to spend a couple of hours in town and now she didn't feel like going home. She wanted to sit quietly with her thoughts and, after buying a newspaper, she returned to the baker's.

Kay sipped at the tea the assistant brought her, but with little enjoyment. It was clear the grocer was right. Ex-servicemen were, so the paper reported, returning to take up their old jobs. The women who had filled them since the outbreak of war were also refusing to give up their positions; for the duration of the conflict they had proved to be as skilled and as hard working as the men who had left them. Many of them wanted to keep their independence, like Kay. Finding work, whether full- or part-time was going to be difficult, especially in a small town like Monkton.

Kay placed her elbows on the table and gazed down at the open newspaper. While walking down the lane she had been planning on providing for herself and Alfie in their new home. But it was just a pipe dream. Alfie was seven in November. He was growing up fast. Kay's thoughts went to her son's future. What lay ahead for him? Without Alan as part of their lives, what would they do?

'Is this seat taken?'

Kay lifted her head slowly, staring up at the outline of a tall man. With the sun behind him, flowing in through the bakery windows, he reminded her of someone.

The voice, the broad shoulders – she narrowed her eyes to see who it was.

Suddenly she was being swept to her feet, the breath leaving her body as Alan hugged her in his arms. She mumbled choked words. The husband she thought was dead placed his lips on hers and kissed her, making her realize this was no dream. He was holding her tightly in his arms, as though it had only been yesterday that she'd left them.

Chapter Forty-Nine

He was dressed in civilian clothes, a pair of casual trousers and a dark jacket. Kay noticed that her husband still had his lovely, thick, dark hair, but it was cut so short that it accentuated his prominent cheekbones which protruded from a gaunt and hollowed face. The bones of his shoulders were sharp under his jacket, causing it to hang loosely on a frame that had visibly lost weight. Alan was the same man, she knew, but he was frighteningly unfamiliar.

'I've been watching you,' he told her, taking her hand. 'Through the window. Just drinking you in from a distance.' His voice was rough and hard, as though he was controlling his emotions with difficulty. 'I didn't want to shock or upset you.' His dark but weary eyes held hers. 'My God, Kay, you're so beautiful. More beautiful even than the picture I had of you in my mind.'

Kay opened her mouth to speak but she couldn't.

'I wanted to write and warn you,' he continued. 'But my CO suggested I wait until after I was debriefed and had adjusted to being back. Kay, I've missed you and Alfie so much.'

'Alan? Alan, is it really you?' She held his face in her hands.

'It is, darling.'

'But I thought – I was told—'

'I know. I know all about it.'

Kay swallowed. 'Do you know why me and Alfie are here – that our house was bombed?'

He nodded. 'Yes, I know everything.'

'Who told you?'

'My CO, Major Campbell.'

'But Alan, he sent me a telegram saying you were missing in action. After that, I heard nothing. I – I thought you were dead.'

'And so I should have been.' He drew her close and for a few silent moments they clung to each other. 'Can we talk privately? Is there somewhere we could be alone?' he asked huskily.

Kay nodded, still unable to believe that Alan was here in the flesh. But he was and his eyes told her how much he wanted her and she knew there was only one place she wanted to be with her husband. Linking her hand through his, they walked slowly out into the sunshine.

They lay together on a bed of bracken under the newly budding leaves of the oak tree. Kay felt at peace, at rest. Their need had been too urgent to deny. Arm in arm they had climbed the hill and at the top, Alan had spread his jacket over the warm wooded floor. In the seclusion of the copse, they had once again become lovers. The sun warmed them, shining down through the branches, dappling their entwined bodies with soft light.

This was the secret place, she told him, where she and Alfie liked to come. It was a secluded spot hidden in tangled thickets and filled with birdsong. They would bring a picnic here and enjoy a game of hide and seek. Kay looked up gratefully to the canopy of nature above them that had provided such a welcome homecoming for Alan.

'This is a beautiful spot, Kay,' he whispered as she traced her fingers over his bare chest and he in turn touched the straps of her petticoat with trembling fingers. 'Thank you for bringing me here.' He kissed her tenderly, wrapping her against him and holding her tightly.

Kay knew it was enough to have him beside her. But as she looked at his thin body, she ached for him. She could now see the sharp jut of his ribs and the hollows under his collarbone. She knew he had endured hunger and pain. But how much?

'Alan, where have you been and how did you survive?'

He stared ahead, his eyes far away. 'I was captured on the French border after completing my mission. I spent over a year under Nazi lock and key, but with help from the Resistance eventually managed to escape and was given sanctuary in a safe house until Paris was liberated.'

'Oh, Alan, it must have been awful.'

'Not as bad as it might have been,' he said quietly. 'After all, I survived.' After a few seconds he continued. 'When I was first called up, I was sent for training with

Military Intelligence associated with my rescue work here at home.'

'Are you saying you were a spy?'

Alan looked into her eyes. 'Kay, I was recruited long before the war started.'

'But Alan, how could you get involved in something like that?'

He looked away again as though collecting his thoughts and when he eventually spoke, his voice was a rough whisper. 'Me and my two brothers were taught to thieve by our father. We became little experts at helping Dad in his life of crime. Although we knew it was wrong, we were afraid to disobey him and the only peace we had as a family was when he was in prison. When Mum died and I ran away to sea, I thought I'd escaped him and the life I so hated. But one day, years after, I returned home to look for my brothers. But they had long gone and I found Dad very sick. I should have left him – but he begged me not to leave.' Alan's face hardened. 'He deserved nothing from me, I knew. Yet I stayed with him until he died.'

'Alan, that was a kind thing to do.'

'Perhaps. But that decision cost me my future. The law arrived and fitted me up for one of Dad's crimes. I was arrested, tried and found guilty.'

Kay gasped. 'But you were innocent!'

'Who was to believe me, the son of a professional thief? I was sent to prison, where a man visited me. If I agreed to join in the battle against fascism, I would be pardoned. The truth of it was, a second war with Germany was imminent and Military Intelligence needed its spies. With my experience, skills that could only have been gained through learning about crime and subterfuge from an early age, I was a perfect candidate.'

'But you'd left that life behind when you went to sea,' Kay insisted.

'So I thought. And if I'd never gone back that day, perhaps I would have led an entirely different existence.'

Kay felt the tears smart. 'But then you would never have met me.' She leaned towards him and whispered, 'None of this changes us, Alan.'

He shook his head sadly. 'You'd better know the whole story, Kay, before you decide on that. You see, I didn't go to Spain to fight for freedom, but on a mission to steal Franco's gold. Britain was afraid Franco's wealth would empower the Axis. That couldn't be allowed to happen. Whilst there I witnessed a beautiful and historic town being ripped apart, just as the East End was during the Blitz. A soldier beside me died.' He paused, slowly meeting her gaze. 'This soldier's name was Alan Lewis.'

Chapter Fifty

'But how could that be?' Kay was struggling to understand.

'The dead man was Alan Lewis. But *I* was Jack Harper.'

Long seconds passed as she stared at her husband. 'Your name is Jack – Jack Harper and not Alan Lewis?'

'Alan Lewis, the man who died, told me he was a member of the International Brigade. He claimed to be an idealist, fighting for freedom and justice. He had no family, apparently, and no ties back home. So when the bullet obliterated his face, I saw an opportunity. I would take his identity, become him, and Jack Harper, the thief and puppet of the military, would die. He even looked like me. His death seemed the answer to a new life. But, as I made my way back to Britain, Military Intelligence arrested me.' His face darkened as he laughed without mirth. 'All I had done was to fall deeper into their power. They allowed me to keep the identity, which served well for espionage purposes. I was told that if, or rather when, a second war broke out, I would be recalled to service. That was the price of freedom once again.'

'So your name is Jack, not Alan?' Kay said, staring at the man she thought she knew and loved.

Alan nodded. 'But I left Jack behind a long time ago.'

'Alan – Jack – I don't know what to call you.' For the first time, Kay felt afraid. What did this all mean?

He took her in his arms. 'I'm Alan, I've always been Alan with you,' he insisted. 'Neither Alan Lewis nor Jack Harper, but the Alan you know. Now you know everything, Kay. Does it change things between us?'

'But why didn't you tell me when we first met?' There was so much to understand.

'Because I was afraid of losing you.'

'You would never have done that.'

'Oh, Kay. Can you forgive me?'

'For not telling me who you were?' Kay shook her head slowly. 'The name doesn't matter, but secrets do.'

'I know that now.'

The tears slid from her eyes as she looked at the man she had always loved. The man who said he loved her. Did she really believe a name mattered? Did the past count at all if you truly loved someone? If you knew them to be good and kind, a wonderful husband and father, a man who would always be there for you. 'The dead soldier lied to you,' she told him. 'Dolly, his wife, came to our house and claimed to be your wife. She brought a young boy who she said was your son. It was a very unhappy time.'

Alan groaned softly. 'My commanding officer told me in my debriefing.'

'But how did he know about Dolly?'

'MI knows everything about its agents, Kay. We are under constant scrutiny. Dolly was considered a threat from the moment she knocked on the door. Every letter you wrote, every one of our friends and neighbours were vetted. Even Eddie and Babs's move to next door was approved by ministry officials.'

Kay took a sharp breath as her thoughts whirled. 'There was a man in a coat and hat – I kept seeing him—'

Alan nodded. 'He was the one who pulled you out of the Tube stairwell.'

'Alan, he saved my life.'

'Yes, thank God.'

'But what about the hundred pounds in the Post Office account? I thought it could have been Dolly's,' Kay protested. 'And Sean – he looked so much like you—'

'Both unfortunate coincidences, Kay. The money was legitimately yours to use and Sean was Alan Lewis's son with Dolly. Sean's father's appearance was not unlike mine, which was one of the reasons I took his identity. And, in defence of my superiors, after the death of his mother, they were responsible for his safe recovery and later, the letter sent to the sanatorium.'

'So Dolly is dead – really dead?'

He nodded.

Kay stared into her husband's dark and soulful eyes. Tears of relief and love filled her own. How could she have ever doubted him? But Dolly had tried to convince her and the things she had said had seemed very real.

Alan, her Alan, was a good man who would never have done the things that Dolly had accused him of. Yet, as guilty as Alan was of keeping his past a secret, she was as guilty for ever doubting his love and allegiance to her and Alfie.

He brought her to him, kissing the tear-splashed skin of her cheeks. 'Please don't cry, Kay. It breaks my heart to think I've hurt you.' Lying beside her on the soft ground he whispered words of love in her ears. There were so many more things she wanted to know, but were any of them really important now? She and Alfie had survived and so had Alan. The complicated paths they had led were a result of their love for each other and in her heart she accepted this. Very soon, she lost herself in the desire that filled every part of her body, knowing that living for the moment was the only thing that mattered now.

Later, when the sun was a scarlet orb in the sky and tiny white clouds scudded across its surface, they made their way down the hill, arm in arm. Kay knew that whatever had happened in Alan's past, his love and loyalty had given her happiness from the moment she had met him. She knew too that like many men caught up in war, Alan's part in the conflict had been orchestrated by a force greater than she could imagine. He had told her that every country had its most secret weapon in the men they manipulated to fight wars on their behalf, and she believed him.

But Kay also understood that she and Alan shared a love so deep and true that now they could survive anything that life had in store for them.

'Are you ready to meet my parents?' Kay asked with a smile as they retraced their steps through the green fields that led towards Monkton.

Alan stopped and, taking her into his arms, kissed her tenderly. 'I've endured three years without you, Kay. Imprisonment and its privations were nothing to the fear of thinking I might never see you or Alfie again. I shall never be able to thank your parents and Aunty Pops enough for taking care of you. We must build bridges with Len and Doris too. They're good people and were right when they felt they couldn't trust me.'

'But they didn't know the man I knew,' Kay whispered. 'The man who I fell in love with.'

Alan held her closer. 'There's one more thing I've to tell you before we meet them.'

Kay looked anxiously at him. 'Is it good or bad?'

'I'll leave you to decide that. Kay, I've been back to Slater Street.'

She gasped in a breath. 'Have you seen our house?'

He nodded. 'It was the first thing I did after my debriefing.' Alan gently brushed a lock of coppery hair from her face. 'Darling, there will be no return to number one hundred and three, I'm afraid.'

Kay held back the tears. She had always held a small hope that the house could be lived in again.

'That doesn't mean we can't go back to the East End,' Alan said quietly.

'We can't, with no home.'

'There are new kinds of temporary houses being built on the island. Some even with a little garden and a patch of grass. It would tide us over while we got on our feet.'

'Alan, don't tease!'

'I'm not. My CO pulled strings to get me a job in the docks.'

'Your CO!' Kay gasped. 'Does that mean you're still a spy?'

Alan threw back his head and laughed. Soon Kay was laughing too, and he wrapped her tightly in his arms. 'No, that's all over now. I'm a free man. I've earned my liberty and intend to make the most of it. And that means making you and Alfie happy. Do you really want to go back?'

Kay wiped away the tears from her face. 'More than anything.'

'We'll need a house with three bedrooms of course.'

'Three?' Kay stared at her husband.

'I spoke to your friend, Jean Pearson, too.'

'You know about Jean?'

'I told you, my CO knows—'

'Everything!' Kay interrupted ruefully.

He nodded, smiling. 'You'll be pleased to know she told me that Sean will soon be well enough to leave the sanatorium.'

'Alan, there's something I have to ask you. Something very important to me.'

'If it's important to you, Kay, then it is to me too.'

'It's Sean. Could you ever think of adopting him? I know it's a big step to take. But he means a great deal to me.'

Alan looked deeply into her eyes and pressing his thumbs gently on her arms, he whispered, 'I took a man's name and identity. It's only fair that in return I do something for him. I'd like to give his son the chance of being part of a family – *our* family. And if adoption is what will make you happy, I'll move heaven and earth to achieve it.'

'Oh, Alan,' Kay cried, 'having Sean back again is something I never thought would come true.'

His dark eyes twinkled. 'You've not asked me about the third bedroom yet.'

'I can't take no more surprises!'

He grinned. 'It'd be going spare for the occasional visitor, right? And I've been told there's a certain someone needing a holiday, lives over Woking way.'

Kay's eyes widened. 'You know about Vi too?' She laughed and before Alan could speak, she added, 'But of course, your CO knows everything!'

'One thing I'll say for my former profession, they were thorough.'

'Alan, I've missed Vi so much.'

'So what do you say?'

'What do you think?' She flung her arms around him. 'Alan, I'm frightened this will all go away. That somehow the war won't let go of us.'

He held her tight. 'Don't be afraid. It's our time now, sweetheart. Every second we've got is precious. It's time to make the world a better place for our children.'

Kay felt happiness and hope bubbling inside her. Alan was right. The war *was* over, it had finally happened. Their new lives were about to start, but with each other, appreciating each moment as it came.

She couldn't wait to write to Babs and Vi and to Len and Doris and most of all, she couldn't wait to see the island again. It wouldn't be Slater Street, she accepted that. But one day very soon, she and Alan and Alfie and Sean were going to wake up to the familiar smell of the docks, the sight of fires belching out smoke from the hundreds of bomb-damaged chimneys and the calls of white-winged gulls mewing and sweeping low over the curves of the river.

THE END

Carol Rivers

A Sister's Shame

They'd give up everything to dance on stage, but could they lose each other?

London's East End, 1934. Eighteen-year-old twins Marie and Vesta Haskins work at the local shoe factory to bring in a few pennies for the family, but they've never given up on their dream of treading the boards in the West End. When a brand new East End club opens its doors, the girls audition for the show and are over the moon to land two nights a week with their cabaret act. But little do they realise that the villainous Scoresby brothers are using the club as a front for a very different line of business.

Seeing what is going on behind the smoke and lights of the stage, sensible Marie vows to leave her job at the club before it is too late, but headstrong Vesta has fallen for the Scoresby's handsome right-hand man, Teddy, and unwittingly leads her whole family into the Scoresby's clutches. Will Marie be able to save her family from disaster? Or will Vesta's determination to become a star tear the Haskins family apart?

Paperback ISBN 978-0-85720-830-9
Ebook ISBN 978-0-85720-831-6